SMALL TOWN GIRL

SMALL TOWN
girl

M...be proud of who you are and where you come from. Your roots are deep.

PROLOGUE

THE CAPTAIN OF THE FOOTBALL TEAM PINNED ME WITH AN arrogant stare, narrowed his gaze, and silently dared me to challenge him. "Lee, I see now why you've never bothered to nail Masyn." Alex snickered and high-fived Mark Holloway, the guy sitting next to him. "You'd be better off with a warm apple pie. There'd be more participation from the filling."

He wasn't really talking to me so much as running his mouth about my best friend. Alex had started dating Masyn at the end of our freshman year. They'd been hot and heavy all summer, and I'd listened to his shit in the locker room more times than I cared to admit, too afraid to speak up in her defense. Masyn Porter wasn't the girl he made her out to be to his buddies...or anyone else who'd listen to the filth he shared after practice. But just like everyone else who heard his pornographic tales, I didn't have the guts to call him out on any of it, even though I knew none of it had happened.

Everything about high school was a popularity contest none of us wanted to enter, yet we all longed to win. Making the varsity football team my sophomore year had taken me one step closer to the coveted spots at the top of that totem pole. Unfortunately, it also put me in a position to hear things I previously hadn't noticed.

I was one of two underclassmen who practiced and played varsity, and the pressure to fit in and be a part of the team was worse than any temptation I'd had to try drugs, alcohol, or cigarettes. I'd spent the better part of two months biting my tongue and forcing my mouth shut, just to stay on the good side of people I didn't really give a shit about but who could make or break me in the social hierarchy at Harden High. Something I had never thought I'd care about until I stood the chance of losing my footing on the popularity ladder.

Alex Hartford ran the football team and the school. The star quarterback and All-American senior held the keys to everything good in high school. The teachers loved him, the girls all lusted after him, and every guy wanted to be him.

Except me.

I continued pushing food around on my cafeteria tray, hoping he'd shut up or move on to another topic. What I should have done was shove my fist into his mouth and then hand him his teeth and make him choke on them.

"You couldn't warm her up?" Mark hung onto Alex's side and tried to lick his face while the rest of the table laughed at the show the two put on.

I'd never prayed for lunch to end, but hearing that bell would put a cork in his mouth. I could have gotten up, I could have walked away, yet knowing how that would play into the drama already unfolding, I kept my head down and remained silent. Being on the receiving end of Alex's hatred wasn't a place any kid in this school hoped to land. We all kissed his ass so he'd keep from kicking ours—literally or metaphorically.

"Dude, hell couldn't warm that frigid pussy. It was like fucking an ice cube. I'm surprised my dick didn't get hypothermia." Alex's voice carried through the double doors and up the empty hallway with each crass word he uttered. It wouldn't surprise me if people in the next county overheard him. "She just laid there stiff as a board. If it weren't for all the hair on her head, I might not have been able to tell the difference between the two. The girl doesn't have a curve on her body."

"Maybe she hasn't hit puberty, yet." Someone farther down the table joined in with a chuckle. "At least you wouldn't have to worry about knockin' her up."

"I'm starting to wonder if she wasn't one of those babies whose parents had to decide whether she was a boy or a girl, and they made the wrong choice. What are they called? Hermaphrophobes?"

"Hermaphrodites, dumbass." Chad Connor had no problem correcting the term, but he didn't do anything more than I did to stop the conversation.

Alex pointed at Chad like a lightbulb had gone off in his head just hearing the two words Chad had said. "That would explain how she ended up with a name like Masyn. Her parents thought she was a boy, and the doctors said they got to pick. Since they already had three sons, they decided on a daughter."

"You slept with a chick who has a penis and a vagina?" Mark put his fist in front of his mouth like he'd just burned the varsity QB at his own game. Fist bumps and high fives flew around the table.

My jaw clenched, and I feared I might break a tooth.

"Nah, dude. Other than her not having any hair between her legs and looking like she's twelve, everything down there was normal. But most of you would fill out a bra better than she does."

"She must suck a mean dick for you to have spent six months chasing her around."

I no longer had a clue who said what, and I didn't know why I still sat in this seat not defending Masyn. I could call Alex out. I could tell every guy on the team sitting at this table that he'd never gotten past feeling her up. She'd never laid eyes on his dick, and he'd certainly never spent any time between her legs. In fact, her refusal to do any of it was the sole cause of their breakup, followed by his retaliation. The big man on campus had been dumped by a tomboy in the tenth grade, and now he was trying to save face.

"I'll give her that. She took me and my cousin Tim right before school started." Alex didn't even have a cousin named Tim. His mother and father were the only children on both sides. "My parents weren't home, and we rode the train all the way into town. She squealed like a pig. I'm surprised the neighbors didn't call the cops the way she screamed our names." They might have if it had actually happened.

The laughter and jokes at our table got increasingly louder as the rest of the cafeteria quieted down. Alex wasn't aware he had everyone's attention when he jumped on Mark's back and acted like he was fucking him from behind with his hand around the guy's neck and the other pulling his hair. He called out Masyn's name in the throes of his performance, and Mark took on her role in their acting duo, spouting every profanity he'd ever seen written on a bathroom stall.

If Alex hadn't been so caught up in making his teammates jealous by trying to make himself look good, he might have realized he had a captive audience. Every student with fifth-period lunch witnessed the act and knew who he mocked.

"You should have brought her to practice and let us all take a turn." The voices blended together with the hoots and hollers from the rest of the team.

"Shit, when I found out how many dudes she'd been with, I cut that whore loose."

"She can suck my dick any day."

"Wrap it before you tap it."

"I'm sure if you want some action, she'd be happy to dish it out. Just be prepared to do all the work. And you might want to fuck her from behind."

"I don't give a shit how flat-chested she is. If she wants some of Daddy, I'll let her bounce on my pogo stick."

"Mr. Hartford!" Principal O'Malley hollered from across the room, and everyone at our table went silent until Alex faced the administrator.

"Eww." There was a chorus of hushed murmurs, the other students acting scared for Alex.

"Yes, sir?" Alex returned with the voice he used to suck up to every adult in this school.

"My office. *Now.*"

He grabbed his backpack and threw his lunch in the trash, and the rest of the table watched him go. The other students in the room resumed their conversations, and I took the opportunity to escape. But the second I stood and turned around, I met the decimated stare of Masyn Porter.

There, at a table that normally bustled with her friends, she sat with her hands in her lap, her shoulders rounded and her back curved in defeat, staring at me. Her eyes glittered with tears, and her cheeks were flushed with embarrassment. Masyn's chin quivered as she fought against my betrayal.

The moment I saw her expression I knew, right then and there, that I'd sealed my fate with my best friend. I loved her, and I hadn't bothered to save her.

ONE

"I just walked out." I answered my best friend's call as I punched the clock, finishing another week at the grind. "I have to go home and shower. Try to get the grease off my hands and look presentable."

I couldn't stop the laugh that rang through the phone. Beau didn't give a shit if I had black outlines around my nails, but I knew his fiancée sure as hell did.

"Are you going to make it to the church on time?" Beau's apprehension could've been nerves or Felicity riding his ass.

I'd never let him down and I wasn't going to start today. "I'll be there."

"Sounds good. See you in a couple of hours."

I ended the call as I continued through the parking lot of the machine shop I'd worked at since graduating from high school. Beau had gone off to college—where he'd met Felicity— but most of our graduating class had stayed in this one-horse town our parents brought us into.

"Lee!" Masyn hollered from her car.

I turned toward her and kept walking backward.

"My car won't start. Can you take me home and then pick me up for Beau's rehearsal thing?"

Masyn was like one of the guys, and she had been since we were kids. Her hands matched my own, and so did her work ethic—she hung with the toughest of men with grace. I didn't have time to drop her off across town and then pick her up later. "I'll take you home to grab your shit. You can shower and get ready at my house. I don't have time to make two trips. Come on."

She huffed, resigned to my solution. "Fine." Her head disappeared from sight when she ducked into her car and then quickly reappeared and shut the door.

I turned toward my truck when I saw her jogging in my direction with her Dickie work shirt tied around her waist. Regardless of whether she was one of the guys, she was still a chick and deserved to be treated like a lady, so I opened her door and helped her into the truck, trying not to take notice of her ass in the process. She situated herself on the bench seat, and I paused, captivated by how small her hands looked while she buckled her seatbelt, and how dainty they appeared covered in grease. She was oblivious to my interest. It wasn't until I realized she was staring at me the way I was staring at her fingers that I snapped out of my trance and closed her door. The instant I cranked the engine, Masyn had her hand on the dashboard, finger-fucking the radio.

"Just because we live in Podunk, USA, doesn't mean we have to listen to the same type of music." Her smile melted hearts, even though she wouldn't let anyone have hers.

"There's nothing wrong with country."

"There's nothing right about it, either." She slid her fingers into her hair and unwound the tie that had held it in a knot all day. When she let it down, an urge to reach over and grab hold of it swept through me, and damn, was that impulse ever a force to be reckoned with. I wanted nothing more than to sink my hands into those heavy strands and take control. It was the color of motor oil—black when you looked at it straight on—and streaked with golds and browns when the sun hit it, and when she let it down, it was my wet dream come true—long, thick, and perfect to grab on to.

It was easier to let her have her way than to fight with her. She'd win regardless. Masyn Porter didn't know it, but she'd owned me since tenth grade. Right about the same time that Alex Hartford had demolished her in front of the entire student body—that day, that very event, had cut her off to the male population. It hadn't opened her up to female relationships, it just shut her out of relationships entirely.

Six years hadn't dulled that memory; I could recite every word that bastard spouted in the lunchroom about her body, and what he had claimed he'd done to it. She probably could, too. Every word had been lies. I knew it. Yet I hadn't stood up for her. I sat there silently while Alex, the quarterback for our high school team—King Shit on Turd Hill—took her down because she'd refused him. When she'd put the brakes on, the rejection sent him to the top of his mountain to reclaim his manhood and destroy her in the process. Alex was a dick.

Masyn forgave me, but she hadn't dated since—not really. There'd been a handful of nights out here and there, just nothing that stuck. One bad apple had ruined her for the rest of us. And to my knowledge, she was still just as pure as the day he'd painted a scarlet *A* on her chest. She would have had to be super secretive to hook up with anyone for me not to know about it.

After Beau left for school, the two of us remained and took jobs at Farley's Machine Shop right after graduation. I think Old Man Farley gave her a job as a joke...turned out, the joke was on him. Masyn had three brothers who all tinkered with cars, and she had a mechanical mind. She took to machining like a fish to water. I'd give my left nut to be able to do what she could with a lathe or mill. I refused to admit the kind of hard-on I got watching her write programs for CNCs or turning a piece of metal.

"Is that AC/DC?" I grimaced when we stopped at a light—one of four in town.

She squinted and gave me a shit-eating grin. "I'm surprised you recognize it. You know, since it's not Willy, Waylon, or Garth." Her smug look only enticed me more.

"Whatever makes you happy, sweetheart."

She punched me in the arm with brute force. Her pint size was deceiving. At five-foot-nothing and a crisp hundred-dollar bill soaking wet, she could still take me down even though I was a solid foot taller and had every bit of a hundred pounds on her. With one hand on the steering wheel, I used the other to rub the spot she'd nailed.

"What the hell was that for?"

She arched one brow with a curt stare. "Sweetheart?"

I rolled my eyes. Masyn believed I called every female sweetheart, and it drove her insane to think she was one of the masses. But that wasn't the case; I called every female darlin' or hon—sweetheart was reserved solely for her.

Thankfully, she didn't live more than about five minutes from the shop—just in the opposite direction of the five minutes I lived. I hated the crap part of town she rented a house in—mill hill. When we were younger and the textile mills were still in full swing, this was a solid, working-class neighborhood. Those industries died out and the mills shut down; the people moved out and found work in other cities. Now they're low rent and not terribly safe—I didn't even want to speculate about the illegal activity that took place on the streets when the sun went down.

I acted like Harden, Georgia, was a hotbed of drug smuggling and gun running. The reality was, the biggest scandal to take place in this town was the mayor's wife being caught on the sidewalk with an open container...in broad daylight. Nothing bad happened in this nook of the world, mainly because no one knew it existed. Truth be told, I was overprotective and the idea of something happening to Masyn drove me batty.

"Give me ten minutes." She hopped out of the truck before it even stopped moving in her driveway.

The moment the door closed, I changed the radio station back to something that didn't make my ears bleed. I closed my eyes and leaned my head back on the seat to wait for her. Neither of us were terribly excited about the wedding of the year, much less participating in it.

Beau Chastain came from old money, and he was marrying new money in Felicity Holstein. The difference was Beau didn't give a shit about the number of dollars in a bank account —probably because he didn't know what it was like not to have them.

Those same dollars defined Felicity. This was where old money and new money differed. Old money had always been; for generations, these families were rooted in wealth, so no one alive knew what it was like not to have it. Whereas, new money typically came about with the dot-com era, and they flashed it as often as they did their business cards. And Felicity was definitely a flasher.

Felicity Holstein was one of those girls who went to college to find a husband. And once they were married, she had their lives planned out. Not one minute of it would be spent in Harden, Georgia, either.

Masyn and I begged Beau not to propose at Christmas, but the fool did it anyhow. They graduated from college two weeks ago, and she couldn't wait to add her name to his trust fund. I swear, if their parents wouldn't have gone ballistic, Felicity would have tried to get him to elope.

Eight minutes after she had disappeared inside, the front door reopened, and Masyn threw her crap in the back. Wrapping her fingers around the oh-shit handle, she then used the running board to hoist herself up. No sooner had she settled in the seat than she reached out to poke button three on the stereo at the same time she buckled her seatbelt. "Let's go."

"You got everything? We won't have time to come back."

"Yep."

"Dress?"

"Got it."

"Shoes?"

"Check."

"Makeup? Jewelry?"

"Unfortunately, yes to both."

She didn't need either. Her skin was like porcelain—even when it was marked with streaks of black from a machine, it was perfect and smooth.

"Pantyhose?" I had no idea where that question came from.

Masyn didn't respond. Instead, she stuck her hand in her pocket under the seatbelt and pulled on a wad of what I assumed were hose. They stretched but finally broke free, and the leg snapped across the cab of the truck and popped me in the face.

"Got it." She laughed, and her eyes glittered with humor.

The melodic sound brought a grin to my lips. "What about clothes to stay at my house tonight?"

"I'm not staying with you, Lee. You can bring me home."

"What if I drink too much?" This was an ongoing battle. She didn't really drink. I did. Masyn felt it was her duty to get me home safely after every field party, night at a bar, or... rehearsal dinner. Since she usually drove her car, that made dropping me off easy. Tonight, not so much. She was no stranger in my home, so I didn't know why it mattered where she slept.

"I'll take your truck home after I drop you off."

"Like hell. Go get clothes." It wasn't like she didn't have her own room at my house. Other than Beau, Masyn was my best friend in every aspect. We'd never hooked up. Never shared a bed. Hadn't so much as kissed.

"Can't I borrow a pair of boxers and a T-shirt?"

Music to my ears. "Have it your way." I put my hand behind her headrest, turned to look over my shoulder, and backed out.

"Do you think this is going to be as bad as we're anticipating?"

"Stick with me, sweetheart. I've always got your back."

Her little fist landed on my exposed ribs.

"Ugh. Damn, that hurt. What the hell, Masyn?"

"Stop calling me sweetheart. I'm not one of your minions."

I'd never stop calling her sweetheart. I didn't care how
many times she hit me. Each bruise was a reminder of me
ruffling her feathers, which I loved to do. "I'm sure it won't be
as bad as either of us are expecting."

When Beau came home last summer and announced to his
family he wanted to propose at Christmas, they were thrilled.
We were not. In the land of the Chastains, the Holstein name
was as prestigious as their own, just in a different circle. The
girl could have been an absolute hag and they still would have
encouraged the union in order to expand their realm. Although
I'd hoped they had seen redeeming qualities in Felicity that
Masyn and I had yet to become acquainted with. I didn't want
to believe Beau's parents would encourage a marriage for social
status.

But I guess I was wrong back then.

Masyn shook her head slowly as she spoke. "I don't know,
Lee. She didn't even try to get to know us when Beau brought
her home over Christmas. And anytime I tried to talk to her,
she snubbed me. I thought that crap only happened in movies.
It was clear she thought we were beneath her."

"If that were true, she wouldn't have asked us to be in her
wedding party." It was a lie, and we both knew it.

Beau asked me to be his best man, and I had no doubt he
forced Felicity to include Masyn on her side, or he would have

put her in a tux on his. Beau came from class, and at the heart of it, he was as Southern as the two of us. The three of us met in kindergarten, and if it hadn't been for us, Beau would have had his ass beaten on more than one occasion. He didn't come into his own until high school.

The glare I received in retort told me Masyn thought the same thing I did. "Not even you are that oblivious."

"Who cares why we were asked? Would you really want to miss being a part of Beau's wedding?" I already knew the answer. I'd asked myself the same question countless times.

"He's making a mistake." She was adamant.

"Agreed." There was no point in trying to dissuade him.

I'd yet to see what Beau was attracted to. Outwardly, Felicity was a knockout. Unfortunately, the moment she opened her mouth, she lost all her appeal. Catty. Shallow. Pretentious. Those were a few of my favorite adjectives to describe her. The only thing I could figure out was that this girl had some magic pussy and gave it up freely. Even that wouldn't be enough to make me listen to her wail like a banshee for the rest of my life. I'd rather be alone and get a dog.

"Promise me you won't leave me by myself with her harem?" Masyn was tough as nails.

I had no doubt she could hold her own with Felicity and company, but if she needed my reassurance, I'd always give it. "Isn't a harem some kind of sexual group? Like one man, a gaggle of women?"

"You know what I mean. I don't fit in, and she'll make sure I know it." Her arms were folded across her chest, and her bottom lip poked out slightly.

"Maybe we're being unfair. Felicity was only here a few

days over the holidays. It was the first time she'd met Beau's family and his two best friends. That's a lot of pressure."

Masyn cocked her head and looked at me like I'd sprouted a third arm. Without another word, she turned the radio up so loud, even my thoughts plugged their ears and shut down. Angry-girl music would only serve to rile her up. Thankfully, my house was only a couple of blocks farther.

Watching her while keeping my eyes focused on the road was difficult. I knew these streets like the back of my hand, but I couldn't account for oncoming traffic. As much as I'd like to get lost in the sight of her, ending up in the hospital because I'd totaled the truck wouldn't be good for anyone. I opted for quick glances from the corner of my eye, and I took a second to admire her when I searched for other cars at a stop sign.

I parked in front of the garage and grabbed her bag and dress from the back seat. She hopped down to the cement, and I got lost in the bounce of her thick hair. The light hit it at just the right angle, bringing all the different colors out like a kaleidoscope.

"You coming?" She shut the door without waiting for me to answer.

When I came up beside her, she snatched the keys from my palm and opened the front door. She moved so quickly, I caught a hint of her in the air, and it lingered in my nose. Most guys enjoyed soft smells on women—lilac, vanilla, roses. Not me. There was nothing sexier than the scent of burnt oil on Masyn's hair. She did a man's job every day, yet there wasn't a hard edge to her other than that scent. It contradicted everything about her. Her voice was as feminine as they come, soft like an angel. Stylists would envy her hair. Dermatologists would praise her skin. And models would covet her perfectly proportioned and dainty body.

I followed her inside and kicked the door closed with my foot. She tossed my keys on the counter as she passed the kitchen and beelined for her bathroom. Technically, it was the guest bathroom, but Masyn was the only guest I ever had, so by default, it was hers. I dumped her bag on the floor next to the sink and then leaned in to hang her dress on the back of the guest room door—also hers.

"You've got an hour before we need to leave," I reminded her.

"I'll be done before you are."

"Is that a challenge?"

"Depends. Is it a cash bar tonight?"

"Seriously doubt it. It's the Chastains' tab."

"Hmm." Masyn tapped her finger on her chin. "If I'm done first, then I get to go home tonight, regardless of how much you drink."

"And if I win?"

She shrugged as though the answer were obvious. "Then I stay here."

"I'm getting the short end of this stick. You already agreed to stay here."

"Then what do you want?" Her brows dipped in the center and created a crease above her nose. She turned the shower on, waiting for me to answer. Cheating was clearly part of her plan.

"For you to dance with me at the wedding tomorrow." Not a clue where that request came from. I can't dance for shit.

"You can't dance. Pick something else." She unlaced her

work boots, pulled each one off her feet, and dropped them with a thud on the tiles, gaining further ground in this race.

"Nope. That's what I want." I was being set up. She'd be in the shower before I reached my bedroom. My only saving grace would be her mounds of hair that she'd have to wash and dry... since it smelled like grease and likely had a good bit in it.

"Fine." She pushed me out, slammed the door, and I took off.

I didn't wait for the water to heat up. After I stripped my clothes off, I jumped under the spray and hissed with the chill that prickled my skin. It took the hot water longer to reach the back of the house, but I couldn't waste time.

Beau had made a point—more than once—to tell me how much it meant to Felicity for my hands not to look like I'd worked on cars in the parking lot of the church, so I needed extra time to scrub them. It was a hopeless cause. The cuticles were stained from years of manual labor in a machine shop, but I tried all the same. And then I washed my hair three times in an attempt to remove the stench I knew lingered there, and I scrubbed my skin as if peeling off the top layer might make me more presentable.

I wasn't a bad-looking guy. In fact, most girls seemed to think I was fairly attractive. Picking women up hadn't ever taken much effort; I just never wanted to hold on to them. They simply weren't what kept my interest. Working out kept me in solid shape, running kept me lean, and I was blessed with a nice physique. I ate like a horse and played as hard as I worked. Beer flowed like sweet tea on the weekends, and I didn't have anyone to answer to.

Other than Masyn.

The mere thought of her woke parts of me that needed to go back to sleep—if I had any hope of winning this bet. I didn't have time to rub one out while thinking of the little spitfire in my other bathroom. Images of her naked body danced through my mind, and my dick twitched. I'd never seen her completely bare, but she'd worn some swimsuits that didn't leave much to the imagination. That was the beauty of an in-ground pool in my backyard. She loved the sun and the water...she also loved the privacy my fence provided.

Stop. Stop. Stop. I chastised myself and forced my thoughts toward lizards and nuns.

When I turned off the water, I listened closely and couldn't hear anything...including the sound of the shower down the hall. Quickly wiping away the water, I then wrapped myself in a towel and peeked my head out of my bedroom door. The hair dryer down the hall came to life, and I grinned knowing I had this in the bag. I still had to shave and put on church clothes, but Masyn would spend a minimum of thirty minutes drying that mess of hair. If she straightened it, I could add another fifteen minutes to that. And if she planned to curl it, we'd be late.

I stepped back into my room and left the door open so I could keep track of her progress. The towel still hung loosely on my hips when I saw my reflection in the mirror. I'd gotten a little more hair on my chest over the last couple of years, and the trail from my belly button to my dick was now clearly defined. It had taken nearly two years out of high school for me to fill out, but I wasn't the boy I remembered seeing for so long. The roughness of my jaw against my palm dictated shaving. I'd hoped the five o'clock shadow hadn't emerged and I could skip this step. I'd never had a hard time growing out a beard in a day or two, so bypassing the razor was not an option, or else I risked unleashing the wrath of Felicity.

There was something about the sound of a blade on coarse hair that was almost hypnotic. With each swipe, my eyes focused on the skin to avoid cutting myself. In no time, my face was baby smooth. And I stared into my own green eyes wondering what Masyn saw when she looked at me. Since she never dated, I didn't have a clue what she looked for. She may hate blonds, which would eliminate me. Or it was possible that she liked thin intellectuals—although, not likely—which would put me at the back of the pack entirely. The only thing I had to base her taste on was her relationship with Alex, and he certainly wasn't the gold standard by which to assess her preference.

The blow dryer stopped. There was no way she'd finished with her hair unless I'd been staring at myself for the better part of twenty minutes. Without further hesitation, I slapped after-shave on, spritzed some cologne and walked through it, and crossed to my closet to find something suitable to wear. I no sooner had on a white dress shirt and grey slacks—unbuttoned, untucked, and unzipped—than a knock came at my open door.

Holy mother of God. She was breathtaking. Not to mention totally uninterested. Her breath didn't hitch. Her pupils didn't dilate. Her nostrils didn't even so much as flare at the sight of my bare chest. Nevertheless, my body let loose with all three of those embarrassing actions while I gawked at her.

"Can you zip me up?" Masyn grabbed her hair with one hand, held the front of her dress with the other, and turned her back to me.

I rarely saw her in anything other than Dickies at work or jeans on the weekends. Occasionally, she blessed me with shorts or a swimsuit, just never a dress. It took everything I had in me not to run my fingers down her exposed spine and kiss her bare neck. Instead, I did as she asked and raised the zipper, praying I didn't pitch a tent standing there. I held my breath until she turned, uttered a quiet "thank you," and walked out the door.

If I were more of a gentleman, I'd let her win and allow her to drive my truck home tonight. However, I was far too competitive, and I enjoyed waking up with Masyn Porter in my house too much to concede without a fight. Three minutes later, I leaned against her bathroom door and watched her finish dabbing and brushing on her makeup.

"I hate you," she groaned.

"You love me."

"There's a fine line between the two."

"You ready?"

She glared at me in response, acknowledging my win. After she slathered shiny crap on her lips, she turned toward me. "How do I look?"

"Like a girl," I chided just to get her goat. Then I pressed my lips to her forehead and grabbed her hand to tug her out the door.

WEDDING OF THE YEAR WAS AN UNDERSTATEMENT. Felicity was going for largest ever. I'd never seen so many people at a rehearsal in all my life, and weddings in the South were a big deal. I'd lost sight of Masyn within five minutes of walking through the doors to the sanctuary. Beau's brothers were the only people in the processional I knew, but that was two more than Masyn had on the bride's side.

I stood at the front of the church waiting for instructions when Felicity found Beau to air her complaints in a stage whisper.

"We should have had the wedding in Atlanta. This place is too small and pictures are going to look awful. There isn't enough space for the wedding party on the stairs, Beau."

It was impossible to tune her whining out, and the mention of hicks and the backwoods didn't endear her to any of the locals within earshot, either. Yes, Harden was a small town filled with hardworking residents, but Beau's family and friends didn't lack for class or clout. She'd insisted on inviting everyone this side of the Mason-Dixon Line, and in the process, she'd ended up with his friends he'd grown up with. Simple didn't mean ignorant. And blue collar didn't equate to less important.

"Felicity, there's nothing we can do about it now. Getting married in a church wasn't optional, and you're not a member of one." This had been the one thing I knew they'd argued about since he had proposed. Her family was agnostic, which might as well have meant they worshipped the devil in small-town Georgia. And his were devout Southern Baptists. Even if Beau hadn't insisted on a church wedding, his parents would have.

I reminded him of being unequally yoked as often as possible without flat out telling him not to marry her, but he'd glare at me and ask me to name the last time I had sat through a sermon. It wasn't me that was marrying someone outside of my faith, and my time in a pew had nothing to do with the hag he was about to give his last name.

She finally stomped away to bark at her attendants. All I could do was shake my head.

"Don't start, Lee." My best friend was on the verge of blowing his top. I could see it written all over his face. The splotchy-red cheeks and pink-rimmed eyes gave him away every time.

He had the fairest skin of any dude I'd ever come into contact with, and any time he got pissed off, he looked like he'd rolled around in poison ivy. He closely resembled an albino, or at least he did in my mind. Masyn always said albinos didn't have reddish-blond hair or hickory-colored eyes, but since neither of us had ever seen one in person, I didn't think she could be too sure.

I held my hands up in surrender. "I didn't say a word." Even though we both knew I would. "You give me the signal, and I'll get you out of here faster than you can hogtie a calf."

"One semester of 4-H and you'll never let me live that shit down."

"You are in the house of the Lord. Watch your language." I kept my expression blank, waiting for him to hit me, and half hoping he'd get the humor in my reference to *Steel Magnolias*.

He did neither, and instead, he rolled his eyes. "Jesus. You're a lost cause."

I pulled him aside—as much to the side as I could with a thousand people packed in here like trash in an overflowing can no one wanted to empty. "Dude, seriously. Why are you doing this? You're twenty-two. You do *not* have to get married just because you graduated from college."

Our conversation was interrupted by hollering in the distance. "Oh my God, can you *please* stay put. You don't have to be well bred to stand still." Felicity's voice carried across the altar and to the opposite side of the church. I was shocked she hadn't burst into flames yet.

I stared at my best friend and took a deep breath. "Please tell me that wasn't directed at anyone we know."

"Based on the way Masyn is chewing on her bottom lip and glaring at Felicity, I'd say it's a safe bet that it was."

"You're going to stand for that shit?" A year ago, Beau would have trampled anyone for talking to Masyn that way. Funny what love does to a person. "She's one of your best friends."

He ran his hands through his hair, and the red on his face only got more prominent. "What do you want me to do, Lee? Cuss my fiancée out? Make a bigger scene?"

"You can, or I will." I didn't give a shit who Felicity Holstein thought she was. In Harden, Georgia, she was a nobody without Beau by her side, and even then, I wasn't impressed.

"Just stay put. I'll be back."

Beau's younger brother, Braden, sidled up beside me. "He's going to have his hands full with that one." He wasn't really talking *to* me so much as *next* to me. Braden and Bodie were twins, and both cared for Felicity as much as I did. "I'd rather die alone." He shook his head and sauntered off to talk to one of the other groomsmen.

I couldn't agree with his sentiment more. Even so, I'd been

left with either alienating my best friend or shutting my mouth until this was over. At the end of the weekend, Beau and Felicity would leave for their honeymoon in Paris and then move into their newly purchased house outside of Atlanta. We'd go back to seeing him on the occasional weekend and major holidays. All I could hope for was that he'd come home alone from time to time. Otherwise, I'd have to find a way to kidnap him from his parents' house and force him to slum it without his wife.

Felicity didn't single Masyn out. Still, she had nothing nice to say to any one of her bridesmaids. They walked too fast, they stood too close, they weren't holding their ribbon bouquets in the right place, yadda, yadda, yadda. She barked at those girls like a ferocious dog hellbent on ripping a posse of intruders to shreds. On the second run-through, she made one of the girls cry, another one yelled back, and a third stomped out. It didn't appear her friends were any more enthused about this union than Beau's, and most of them didn't really even seem to like her.

"That girl who left is Felicity's sister," Bodie commented from my right. "Her name's Peyton."

I already liked Peyton.

Beau glared over his shoulder at his brother in an attempt to silence him. Either Bodie didn't care, or he didn't see him. Either way, he kept talking. "She thinks Felicity is a gold digger. Felicity says Peyton's an old maid."

With Beau's back to me, I chanced questioning Bodie. "How old is she?" I hadn't gotten a good look at the girl, but she couldn't be much older than Felicity, and she definitely wasn't out of her prime.

"Twenty-four. She's in grad school. Felicity says women only go to grad school when they couldn't land a husband in undergrad."

"Does anybody really believe that crap anymore?"

"The Holsteins do. They're part of the group who marry so they don't have to work."

Bodie was about to say something else when Beau turned not so nonchalantly and snarled under his breath, "Would you two *shut up*?"

"Dude's going to have a heart attack before his twenty-third birthday married to that shrew." Bodie hadn't tried to lower his voice; half the people here turned to gawk at him, and a handful snickered.

"Seriously, Bodie?" At least Beau wasn't sticking up for Felicity, either. He only tried to silence his brother to keep the peace.

Bodie simply shrugged, as if what he'd said hadn't been ugly, just true.

"Please tell me this is almost over." Masyn came out of nowhere to stand by my side.

I extended my arm to escort her out of the door and to my truck. "Just getting started, sweetheart."

Smack.

I winced and ignored the playful slap to my stomach. "Did she really yell at you?"

"No more than she did everyone else. It's not a secret she doesn't want me in the wedding, Lee."

"She probably doesn't want you to look better standing next to her." Masyn could have worn a potato sack and flip-flops and outshined Felicity on her best day. Because no matter how pretty you are on the outside, ugly shines through.

"Well, since she has everyone in the free world standing as an attendant, I'll be in the next county over at the end of the second line. She's safe if that's what she's worried about."

We'd reached the doors to exit the building when Felicity stopped us. "Marilyn. You need to be in limo four."

"Masyn," I corrected her.

"Whatever. Limo four." She flipped her hair dismissively and went after her next victim, but I grabbed Felicity's forearm.

"Masyn's riding with me."

"Beau..." Felicity called out in a whine that would get an alcoholic drunk. "Why can't they cooperate?"

I waved, leaving Beau to deal with his girl. "You okay?" I curled my fingers on top of hers, now clinging to my bicep.

"Fine." That word was a lie, regardless of when it came out of a woman's mouth. She was anything other than fine.

"You want to talk about it?" I helped her into the truck and stared at her rich-brown eyes.

She quickly refused, and I let it go. We had less than forty-eight hours until Beau and Felicity were heading to the airport. Surely, we could make it through one weekend without one of us committing a felony like attempted murder.

Masyn studied something out the window and didn't even reach for the radio. I changed it to her station, hoping to drag her out of her melancholy mood in the few blocks we had to drive. When I cranked it up, she finally turned her head and leaned over the center console to kiss my cheek.

"Thank you."

I didn't need to ask what for. I already knew. Masyn was

well aware I had her back, even against Beau. After that shit with Alex in tenth grade, I'd promised her I'd never stay silent again. I'd always give her the chance to fend for herself first—she wasn't helpless—but then I'd go in for the kill. Whether it was getting her out of the limo from hell or turning the music up loud enough for it to vibrate her teeth, it didn't matter because she knew both were for her. One day, she might realize everything I did was.

TWO

By the time we reached the country club, Masyn had calmed down with the death metal music that rattled the windows. Good thing she'd worn her hair down, otherwise, an updo would be a complete mess with all the head banging she'd done in a handful of blocks. She took my arm again, and we walked inside. The scene was completely different, and so was Felicity.

She and Beau greeted each person at the door and thanked them for coming. His parents were next in the welcome wagon, and I thought the whole thing was strange. This girl had more personalities than Sybil. I could only guess what her mother had said to her, or better yet, Beau's mother. Mrs. Chastain reigned supreme in these parts. She was head of every women's committee in the county, did countless hours of volunteering, led the church bizarre, and put on the town's fall festival every year. She was as Southern as apple pie and moonshine, right down to the accent and the debutante balls.

"Masyn, dear, you look lovely tonight. Hopefully, I'll be

attending *your* wedding in the near future." Mrs. Chastain turned her attention to me. "Don't wait too long, Lee. Someone might sweep her out from under you."

Dear God, this woman had been hitting the sauce already. "We're not dating, Mrs. Chastain," I reminded her for about the hundredth time in six years.

Masyn had been trapped in a welcoming hug from Mr. Chastain, while my conversation continued with his wife.

"Fiddlesticks. Just because you don't label it, doesn't mean it doesn't exist." She waved her hand at me and grinned. "Seriously, Lee. Your mother would roll over in her grave to know you hadn't made an honest woman out of Masyn."

I wouldn't know. My mother had died when I was three, and I remembered very little about her. My father had struggled to raise me after she'd passed away. Not because he couldn't support us financially, he'd never stopped grieving her loss. To this day, it controlled him. I'd finally convinced him, after graduation, to move to the city and get out of this town, where memories bogged him down like quicksand. He seemed a bit happier now that he didn't live in the past, but I could only attest to what he told me since I didn't see him much.

"I'll take that into consideration, Mrs. Chastain." I loved Beau's mom. She'd been meddling in my life since we were kids; I didn't expect her to stop now. Luckily, she'd done the same to Masyn. Oddly, she'd never pushed Masyn toward Beau. Even as little kids, she'd coupled the two of us.

She leaned in and kissed my cheek. "Don't drink too much tonight. You hear me?"

"Yes, ma'am." I stopped myself from striking a rigid pose and saluting her. I'd been smacked enough for one day.

A tug on my hand finally pulled me through the line of greetings. If it had been anyone else, I might have bitched about them being rude. That tiny hand was as familiar as the smell of motor oil. Masyn could drag me anywhere she wanted to go, and I'd follow willingly.

Masyn held my hand and clutched her side with the other. "I'm starving. Please tell me this is a buffet and we don't have to wait for a seated dinner."

I raised my eyebrows and let her form her own opinion. A buffet—that was laughable. *I* would have a buffet, or hell, maybe even a barbeque. Beau Chastain would not. And I doubted Felicity even knew what one was. "How about a drink instead?"

"You shouldn't drink on an empty stomach."

She was right; I shouldn't. But we both knew I would. This wasn't my social scene, regardless of the fact I'd grown up in it. I had spent more time with Beau's family than I had my own. When my dad had flaked out, the Chastains had picked up the slack. And somehow, Masyn fit into the majority of my child-hood memories. Her family was good as gold, and they welcomed me the same way the Chastains had. In some ways, when my mother died, it left me with two moms and three fathers. I picked up Masyn and her three brothers, and Beau, Bodie, and Braden, as well.

Outsiders wouldn't have a clue the Porters and Chastains came from different social standings—and in my opinion, *that* was the sign of true class. On the other hand, despite her high-class upbringing, I suspected that Felicity wouldn't stand a chance of fitting in with the likes of Beverly Chastain.

"You're going to anyhow, aren't you?" The pout that

formed on Masyn's lips almost had me giving in. Almost. If she would press those plump lips to mine, I would become an active leader in a movement toward prohibition.

"Come on. What kind of froufrou-umbrella drink do you want?" We found the nearest bar while she contemplated her choices. It didn't matter what she ordered; she'd swirl it around with the straw until the ice melted and likely never take more than a sip or two.

Even with heels on, she still barely reached my shoulders. The music made it difficult to hear her, although, I didn't mind leaning down to have her speak into my ear. The heat from her breath drove me insane in the best possible ways. I was a glutton for punishment.

I ordered her a mai tai and a Bud Light for myself. "Do you mind waiting for this while I find the head?"

"Can't you just say bathroom? You haven't spent a single day in the military."

No, but it sounded a hell of a lot better than "take a piss" or "find a urinal." I gave a curt nod. "Fine. I need to use the bathroom."

She lifted her chin and crinkled her nose. "I'll wait right here." Her tone edged with a mixture of humor and smugness.

I'd been here enough times that I could find the men's room with my eyes closed. The trip there was uneventful. Getting stopped on my way out was unexpected.

"Excuse me." After nearly knocking Peyton over, I stepped to the side, and allowed her to pass.

However, she moved with me and placed her hand on my chest. She had to think I was one of the Chastains. "I was hoping to run into you."

"You did. Literally."

Peyton giggled at the sight of my awkward grin. "You're Lee, right?" So much for my theory that she believed I was related to the Chastains.

"I am." There was no point in acknowledging I knew who she was. That would imply I cared.

"I'm Peyton Holstein." She extended her hand, which I shook briefly.

"Nice to meet you."

I couldn't deny Peyton was an attractive girl. It was easy to see that she and Felicity were related, and they both favored their mother. They all had the same strawberry-blonde hair and blue eyes, an angular nose, and high cheekbones. Peyton, however, had a softer appearance—friendlier maybe.

"I've heard a lot about you from Beau. He speaks very highly of you."

Here's where I became the asshole. "Yeah? So he told you all about my job at the local machine shop? And the fact that I barely graduated from high school because I was more inter-ested in ditching school and hanging out on the lake than learn-ing?" I wasn't interested in any woman related to Felicity Holstein. If their family believed college was for finding a spouse, she needed to enroll somewhere other than the school of hard knocks.

"He mentioned you were rather worldly, and, uh"—she cleared her throat—"good with your hands..." That was one way to spin things. She trailed her manicured finger down the buttons on my shirt before gently tugging it just above my waist. "I prefer real men."

Aah. Peyton was one of those chicks who wanted a bad boy

to take home to piss off her parents. I'd bet money she didn't get her trust fund until she married, and bringing someone like me to meet the family would virtually ensure that got changed to prevent her from breaking the social-class boundaries.

Her shoulders dropped, as did her hand from my shirt. "Look, Beau said you were a nice guy. I'm only in town for the weekend and wanted someone to hang out with. I don't want to be here any more than you appear to, and I thought it might make things more fun." Honest Peyton was much more likable than flirtatious Peyton.

"You're welcome to hang out with Masyn and me."

"Where's he sitting?"

"She."

Confusion marred her prim expression. "Excuse me?"

"Masyn is a she."

"What an odd name for a girl." She didn't say it with contempt, rather with bewilderment.

"She has three older brothers. Her mother gave up hope for a girl by the time she arrived. She planned on Mason, so when she got pink instead of blue, she switched the *O* to a *Y*." I pointed over to the woman in question. "That's her."

"The mechanic girl?"

I wasn't able to read her tone. Mine beamed with pride. "That's her. You'd be amazed at what she can do with a piece of metal."

"I don't follow."

"I'm sure you don't." It was short and slightly rude, neither of which she deserved, but I wasn't interested in leading her on.

"Are you two...*dating*?" She said the word as though it might bite her.

"Nope. She and Beau are my best friends. We've been a threesome since kindergarten." I didn't care if she thought I meant in a ménage. I'd love to see her sister's twisted face when she repeated that line.

"Guess you're a foursome now."

"Hardly."

"You don't like Felicity, do you?" That was a loaded question, and one I didn't think was in my best interest to answer.

"Do you want to meet Masyn? She's waiting for me." Again, I pointed in her direction. This time, Masyn saw me and gave me that look to ask what the hell I was doing with the sister of the shrew.

"I'll catch up with you guys later. Maybe we can have a drink after dinner."

"Yeah, sure."

Peyton continued into the ladies' room, and I grabbed my beer from Masyn.

Masyn's eyes followed something over my shoulder, which I presumed was Peyton's exit. "What was that about?"

"I'm not sure if she tried to pick me up or use me against her parents, or possibly to piss her sister off."

Masyn nearly spat her drink on me when she laughed. "What?"

"She's into *real* men...you know, those of us who work with our hands and get *dirty*."

"She did *not* say that to you!"

I shrugged one shoulder. "Truth."

Masyn turned her nose up and her lips followed in disgust. "Gross."

"What the hell? I'm not gross."

"No, she is. Can you imagine if she's anything like her horrid sister?"

Before I could warn Masyn of Beau's impending arrival, she'd stuck her foot solidly in her mouth.

"Really, guys? This is what you do behind my back?" His hurt was evident. The brown of his eyes darkened to the black of betrayal.

Leave it to me to keep things real. "Technically, we've said it all to your face, man."

"I'm sorry you can't see what I do." There wasn't a stitch of truth in a word that came out of his mouth. His flippant tone gave him away, as did those red splotches taking over his neck. Beau would need to speak with far more enthusiasm to convince me he loved this girl.

"Beau, she's a bitch. Even her family thinks so. Why are you doing this?" I couldn't help but wonder what she had on him. It was clear he was miserable and doing his best to keep his cool. Beau had never been into high-maintenance women. He had always dated women more like Masyn. The only difference was they all came from families more like his than ours.

"Because it's the right thing to do." Beau's canned response only further proved how disconnected he was from Felicity.

"What?" I wasn't sure if it was Masyn or me who said it first.

"Can you guys try to play nice until we leave Sunday, please? It means a lot to me." Beau was never one to beg. He was also never one to put Masyn and me in a box and try to cover us with a lid.

Masyn looked at me for approval. I studied Beau. Something was going on, even if he wouldn't tell me what. "You sure you don't have something you want to share? We could grab a couple of beers, head out to the patio, and kick back and shoot the shit. No one will miss us."

Beau stared at the exit that led to the golf course. Longingly. Then he clapped me on the shoulder, plastered the Chastain smile across his face, and faked happiness. "Nope. I'm good. You guys take a seat. They'll be serving dinner soon."

The instant he was out of earshot, Masyn pulled on my hand to get my attention. "What was that about?"

"Not a clue."

I WAS GRATEFUL THERE WEREN'T ASSIGNED SEATS FOR THIS shindig. I couldn't handle being paired with Felicity's friends for a four-course meal. Luckily, Masyn and I ended up at a table for ten with seven other people we'd known for years—even if we weren't close to them—leaving one remaining seat next to me. I'd hoped it would stay vacant, yet just as I was about to release the breath I didn't realize I'd been holding, Peyton's hand landed on my shoulder.

"Is anyone sitting here?" Peyton directed her question to me, but others answered, and she pulled out the chair.

It didn't escape my attention that she wasn't assigned to a seat with her sister or anyone else in the wedding party; I just chose not to address it. I might not be from her side of the tracks, but I wasn't raised in a barn, either. I introduced everyone at the table to Peyton, and in a few minutes, I was surprised by how readily she engaged the people sitting with us. Even Masyn talked to her with ease. By the second course, I had to admit, she wasn't nearly the wench her sibling was, nor did she seem to be cut from the same designer cloth.

Peyton was in the middle of a story that had the entire table laughing, including me, when Masyn tapped me on the forearm and pointed over to the corner of the large room. Beau and Felicity had pulled away from the crowd, and Beau appeared to have a severe case of hives again—he'd better stock up on Benadryl before he left the country. His chest heaved, and the red splotches were turning more of a purplish-blue than crimson. If they continued to grow, the patches would become one, and someone might think he wasn't getting oxygen—Felicity metaphorically strangling the life out of him.

Peyton hit a lull in the conversation, so I leaned over to whisper in her ear, "Any idea what's going on between the two of them?"

She was startled by my closeness and turned toward me. When I pointed back to her sister, she looked at them and took a deep breath.

"Not a clue. But whatever it is, it has my mother in as big an uproar as it does Felicity." Peyton didn't take her eyes off the couple as she spoke. "Every time I come into the room, they stop talking or change the subject with zero finesse. It's like they think I'm daft and don't know they're hiding something." Her fingers rolled the stem of her wineglass while she stared at her sister.

"I take it you two aren't close?" I didn't mean to sound as incensed as it came off, and the sharp huff at the end didn't help.

Peyton sipped her wine, still staring at Beau and Felicity.

Her throat moved gracefully when she swallowed, and then she scoffed, "Hardly." A chink in the Holstein armor.

"Somehow, I got the impression you were."

Her attention finally drifted back to me, and she angled herself slightly in the chair, turning her knees toward me. "I'm sure. Any version of a story Felicity tells will spin her in a positive light. She'd never admit to anyone that we don't even remotely like each other, even with her hand still holding the knife she'd just stabbed in my back." She crossed her legs, took another sip of her wine, and rolled her eyes in an unladylike fashion that had me grinning. "But if you find out what it is that's going on over there, I hope you'll let me in on the secret."

Masyn peeked her head around my shoulder to talk to Peyton. "You think there's something wrong, too? See, Lee? It's not just us."

Peyton shrugged and finished her wine before setting the glass down on the table. "All I know is Beau tried to call off the wedding several weeks ago when I was home from school. I kept waiting for someone to tell me they'd broken up or, at the very least, postponed this illustrious event"—she shifted her gaze and indicated the spread of lavish waste around us—"but it never happened. There've been a lot of closed-door conversations between Felicity and my parents, though. That much I can confirm, although that's all I can tell you. I've been in New York at school."

"Wait, don't your parents live in New Jersey? How has Felicity been home when she goes to school in Atlanta?" Masyn's interest in Felicity's whereabouts only detracted from the issue that actually mattered—Beau tried to call off the wedding.

"My dad flies her back any time she wants to come. Company jet." Again, Peyton flitted her eyes in irritation, as if Felicity jet-setting was a joke, and we'd missed the punchline.

I didn't have a clue that Beau had tried to stop the nuptials. Masyn didn't either—that was evident from the little gasp that had escaped her mouth when Peyton shared that tidbit.

"Why don't you just ask your mom?" Masyn thought all families were like hers—close-knit without secrets.

"Are you kidding? My mom would help Felicity bury a body, and then send the police on a manhunt for some schmuck who didn't exist. And even if she answered, I couldn't trust that anything she told me was truthful." Peyton's tone was indifferent, though I could tell she spoke from experience.

My dad and I certainly didn't have a perfect relationship, and my definition of family was a tad dysfunctional; even so, I knew beyond a shadow of a doubt, none of them would lie to me. It wasn't until Beau got caught up with Felicity that I'd ever believed he'd even hidden anything from me, and that hadn't happened until this past Christmas.

"Surely, between the three of us, we can get an answer before the wedding tomorrow." Masyn was on a mission to save our friend from a fate worse than death—divorce. "I can't bear the thought of Beau marrying someone he doesn't want to because she's holding something over his head."

Suddenly, Masyn and Peyton were fast friends, and I wondered if Peyton would be coming home with us. That might be hot. When they got up to go to the bathroom together, I was done. They'd bonded over secrets, a dislike for Felicity, and merely having nothing better to do than meddle. Masyn didn't have female friends, and I'd never witnessed her gossip.

I'd tuned out of the conversations around me to eavesdrop on one taking place not so far away between Mrs. Chastain and Beau's aunt Bonny when Masyn smacked me for no apparent reason and out of thin air. The music was too loud for me to hear anything beyond our table anyhow.

"That's brilliant. Lee, you should see what information you can get out of Mrs. Chastain. She loves you. I bet she'd give you the key to her deposit box at the bank and combo to her safe if you asked for it."

"I am *not* asking Beau's mom for gossip. Forget it." I used this as my opportunity to get up. "I'm going to take a piss." I'd spoken a little louder than intended, and several people at the table laughed—hence the reason I usually said I was "going to the head."

Masyn feigned annoyance with fluttered lids and muttered something to Peyton, who giggled. I ignored them both, headed down the hall, and took my time relieving myself in the swanky bathroom. It had an attendant who handed out terrycloth towels instead of there being a paper towel dispenser on the wall. Just as I tucked my junk back in my pants and raised the zipper, Beau happened to make an appearance.

I'd had more than my fair share of alcohol. I also knew this wasn't the time or place to have a conversation. Still, I wasn't able to let my friend piss in peace. "Nice party."

"Thanks. I'll tell my mom you enjoyed it."

I couldn't say for certain—probably because of the alcohol running rampant in my veins—but I'd bet money that he'd emphasized the word "you" to indicate he was glad at least one of us had.

I leaned against the wall and stared at the side of his head.

An odd thing to do when a man was taking a leak. Yet even recognizing that it was weird, I didn't stop. Go figure. "What the hell is going on, Beau?"

"It doesn't matter. I just need to get through this weekend."

"Why won't you talk to me?" I doubted I had any viable solutions to his problems other than to tell Felicity to go fly a kite, or to drop her off in the middle of Lake Martin with weights tied to her ankles and tell her to swim to shore. I wanted Beau to recognize he wasn't alone in whatever this was.

"I'll tell you about it when we get back from Paris. Now isn't the time."

"Yeah, and then it will be too late."

THREE

ONE BEER TURNED INTO MORE THAN I COULD COUNT, AND by the time Masyn dragged me out of the rehearsal dinner, I was a hair away from telling Felicity where to shove it. She had Beau by the balls; I just didn't know what with. I'd picked at dinner in favor of scoping her out, watching her interact with him and his family, trying to gauge her end game. Mrs. Chastain wasn't buying her act, either. The way she pursed her lips anytime Felicity spoke to her—or near her—was a dead giveaway. Had I not consumed so much alcohol, I might be able to figure out why she was going along with the marriage of her son to a wretched witch. She didn't care *that* much about name and clout even if she *did* want her kids to marry well.

"Give me your keys." Masyn held her hand out, waiting for me to hand them over. The parking lot was nearly deserted, and only the hum of the streetlights broke the silence.

The keys were in my pocket. And my slacks were made of thin material. If she stuck her hand in there to reach for them,

I'd get a cheap feel. It was wrong, but I'd done it so many times, Masyn didn't think anything about it. I turned around—my back to her front—to make it easier for her to access.

Oddly, she hugged me from behind before diving her hands into my pockets. Her cheek was warm on my spine, and I wanted her in my arms. Yet turning to face her broke the spell, and she grabbed the keys quickly, without so much as a brush up. The warmth of her hand pressing against my chest quickened my pulse. If she just tilted her head, I'd have an invitation to taste her lips. Instead, she used me for balance to reach down and remove her heels one at a time. The girly shoes dangled from her fingertips when she rounded the front of the truck to take the wheel.

"You're staying at my place tonight, right?" It was the deal, but I wouldn't make her if she didn't want to.

"A bet's a bet."

"I don't want you to stay because you lost a bet. Not to mention, you have to dance with me to pay that debt off—staying here had nothing to do with it."

She moved the seat up, buckled her belt, and adjusted the rearview mirror to account for our height difference. Then she turned the radio down, although not off, and positioned herself to cup my jaw with her soft, cool hand. "You're making omelets in the morning. That's your penance for poor behavior and intoxication. Now put your seatbelt on."

I hadn't done anything I shouldn't have other than consume a few too many bottles of beer. "That's all you want?" I asked, fumbling around until I found the belt and got it clicked into place.

She nodded, turned the key, and took off out of the parking lot.

"You're a cheap date."

"And you'd be an easy lay. But we don't all get what we want." She shrugged indifferently and giggled.

The sound of the engine tried to cut off my thoughts as we merged onto the main road. Even drunk, I hadn't missed that insinuation. "Wait, what?" The two words slurred a bit when I spoke, and the world around me might have shifted.

Now she decided to turn the radio up. To a deafening level. "I can't hear you." She mouthed the words and pointed to her ear.

To keep from getting sick, I needed to watch the road, but I was too lost in being an easy lay. "You want to lay me?"

An unsightly grimace drew her features in, and she gawked at me while we sat at a stoplight.

No. Wrong. I amended my crude words. "Sleep with me?" Still not right. "Sex. You want to have sex with me?"

Masyn winked and did a piss-poor job of concealing a giggle. "I can't hear you."

Now she was just fucking with me. "Are you mad because I'm a little inebriated?" I held up two fingers to indicate the tiny space that existed between me and sobriety. This was punishment for all the times she'd begged me not to get drunk and I'd done it anyhow.

She turned the stereo down a few decibels. "Yes, you are drunk. And no. Why would you think I'm mad?"

"Why would you say 'we don't all get what we want'?"

Masyn could have me anytime—she just had to say the

word. Hell, she didn't even have to say it. She could take her clothes off, and I'd get the hint.

"I didn't say that."

"You did!"

"Stop yelling. We'll be home soon."

"Why?"

"Because you don't live far from here."

"No, why did you say that?"

"Say what?"

I swear to God, this woman would be the death of me.

"I'm just messing with you. I know it's not like that between us. You said I was a cheap date. Everyone in town knows you're an easy lay."

She was wrong. I might play the field, but I didn't sleep with random women—or any at all. Not to say I didn't get my dick wet; it just wasn't in anything other than some chick's mouth. I wasn't a virgin, but it had been several years since I'd had actual sex—oral didn't count—I'd learned that from Sissy Starnick in eighth grade Sunday school. I'd never tell Masyn that. The last thing I wanted her to know was that I was as inexperienced as she was...or close.

Before Alex made his proclamation in the cafeteria in tenth grade, he'd laid claim to Masyn's virginity with vivid details in the locker room. He was a senior, and we were sophomores. It made me mad as hell that Masyn dated him to begin with. Then, to hear him talk about the things they'd done sent me into orbit. In retaliation, I'd slept with Cynthia Green, the head cheerleader and Alex's ex—two birds, one stone kind of thing. Although technically, it was just the one bird—Cynthia.

It went on for several weeks—Alex shit talking and me boning Cynthia—before Beau got pissed and confronted Masyn. She vehemently denied having done anything other than let Alex feel her up. According to her, she'd never even seen a dick in person, much less felt one. Seeing her expression in the lunchroom, it was clear she'd told us the truth and still held fast to her virginity. I never touched Cynthia again, but by that point, my reputation was established, and Masyn never believed anything different. Truth be told, I hadn't tried to set the record straight.

Although, if she actually thought about it, she was with me most waking hours of every day, whether at work or outside of it. I had no idea who I could be fucking or when I'd be doing it without Masyn present to witness it. Bathrooms were great for a quick blowjob; they were *not* the place to take a girl against the wall...especially not the dives I drank at.

"I'm not an easy lay." I sounded like a petulant child on the verge of tattling or throwing a temper tantrum.

She giggled and patted my head. "Oh? Do you make them work for it?"

"Who? Make *who* work for it?"

"I don't know. Your entourage. The girls you call darling and sweetheart."

I shook my head, trying to explain. "There's only one."

"Why didn't you tell me you're dating someone?" Her giddy mood turned south real quick.

"I'm not. Jesus, Masyn. When the hell would I have time to date and you not be aware of it?" My tongue was thick and the words rolled into each other.

She pulled into the driveway and I hopped out. I stomped all the way to the door before I realized she had my keys and I couldn't get in. When she caught up to me, she didn't put the key in the deadbolt. Instead, her hands found my hips and turned me toward her.

"I'm sorry, Lee. I didn't mean to upset you." She stared up through the height distance, waiting for my forgiveness.

If I weren't drunk, this would be the time to tell her she had it all wrong. The girls she'd seen on my arm or in my truck were nothing more than something to pass the time. Since I was inebriated, my confession would be seen as alcohol-induced rambling. And other than the comment she'd made five minutes ago about not getting what she wanted, there had never even been a hint that she felt the same way about me that I did her. So, I held on to my pride.

"No worries."

She came in for a quick hug, and I inhaled the fresh scent of her shampoo. I still preferred the smell of oil on her to flowers any day. Her tiny frame pressed against my side warmed me from the core and spread throughout my body. I'd sell my truck to buy her affection if it were for sale. Once she opened the door, I stumbled over the threshold, nearly busting my ass in the entryway. The same way she'd done a hundred times before, she reached out to keep me from falling and helped me back to my room.

I closed my eyes to pray for the room to stop spinning, and I tried to pull my shirt over my head.

Her laughter reminded me I wasn't alone. She took her hand away from her mouth to point to my chest. "You have to unbutton it first."

When I lifted my lids, she was there in front of me. Her tiny fingers plied the buttons from their holes and then tugged on the hem. My arms felt like deadweight at my sides, and I swayed with her touch. Stopping her when she went for my belt buckle took a monumental effort. This dance would turn erotic, and I wouldn't be able to stop. My mental function might be impaired, but my physical wasn't. I concentrated on anything repulsive that came to mind to will my dick to lay low.

She held her hands up in surrender. "I was just trying to help."

"I got it. You need to get some sleep. Festivities start at ten."

"I'll set the alarm on my phone. What time do you want me to get you up?"

I didn't intend to ignore her question; I just couldn't stand any longer when my bed was so close by. Quickly stripping down to my boxers, I tossed my clothes into the corner and crawled onto the mattress without considering I was nearly naked with her two feet away.

As I dozed off, a soft, moist pair of lips brushed against my forehead, and then the blankets shifted when she pulled them over me.

"Night, sleepyhead."

The mattress bounced under the weight of an object. It didn't take me long to realize who did the jumping. I covered my head with the pillow and tried to block out the light of day and Masyn's exuberance. Nothing could quiet the pep in Masyn's voice. She was a morning person. I was not, especially not after drinking.

"You have omelets to make. Hop up."

"If you don't stop that shit, you're going to break the bed. Then I'll have to sleep in the guest room with you."

She stopped bouncing and grabbed the edge of my shield. "I can't understand you with that pillow over your head."

I held on, and the tighter I squeezed, the more she tugged and leaned backward, trying to use her weight as leverage. Then I let go. A smile spread across my lips when she stifled a squeal and then harrumphed when her ass hit the bed. Even though I knew she watched me, I couldn't help it. I skimmed my gaze up her bare legs until my eyes reached the hem of my boxers, high on her thigh. She always had to roll the waistband down to keep them from falling off, which made them more like booty shorts. I let my gaze crawl higher and my breath caught in my windpipe. My shirt she wore had ridden up, exposing her flat stomach. The amount of restraint it took not to tear my clothes off her proved unreal. Something about seeing her in anything that belonged to me made my dick twitch and my mouth salivate.

She sat up, crossed her legs, and covered her lap with the pillow she'd stolen. "We have two hours before we have to leave."

I snatched the pillow back and stuffed it under my head. "Good. That means I have another hour and a half to sleep."

"Nope, nope, nope. You promised me eggs. And you definitely need to shower. The stench is oozing from your pores. *No bueno.*"

I lifted my forearm to my nose. When I smelled nothing, I raised my wrist a little higher. The stout aroma wafting out of my armpits would make even a mother cringe and doubt her love. "Fine," I conceded. "But I'm showering before cooking."

Masyn rolled off the end of my bed and then sprang up like a jack-in-the-box. Naturally, she felt better than I did this morning. Of course, she hadn't consumed the amount of alcohol I had last night, either. I would never admit that she might have been right. I'd pay for it all day today, and likely into tomorrow. There was an open bar at the reception, and I'd need to visit it frequently to keep from killing Felicity.

"Sounds good. I'm going to jump in and rinse off, too. I'll meet you in the kitchen."

Fifteen minutes later, we were both barefoot in front of the fridge. Masyn had put my boxers and T-shirt back on, and I had donned a pair of sweatpants minus a shirt. There was no point in getting anything out when I was going to have to change again in an hour. The two of us moved around each other like we cooked together daily. Everything about being with Masyn was natural. Other than hiding how I felt about her, things between us were always perfect.

"You should ask Peyton out while she's in town."

I turned from the eggs I was cracking into a bowl to stare at her.

She looked up from the veggies she was chopping and lifted her eyebrows. "What? She's completely into you. And you wouldn't have to worry about her wanting a relationship. It totally works for your lifestyle."

"So what, you're playing matchmaker now?" I didn't like it. Not one bit. And I bit my tongue to keep from arguing with her about what she believed my history was like.

She shrugged. "The two of you had chemistry."

"What? The fumes from the machine shop have affected your brain."

"You were nice to her."

"I'm nice to you, too. Should I ask you out?" It slipped from my tongue before I could stop it.

"Pfft. As if I'd ever date you, Lee Carter."

Dagger. To. The. Heart.

"So you want me to date Peyton Holstein? That's just mean."

Masyn grabbed the vegetables she'd chopped and tossed them into the frying pan in front of me. "Oh, please. She's gorgeous. Comes from money. Has a degree. Would it be so horrible to end up with someone like her?"

"Masyn, girls like Peyton don't date guys like me. Ever." And I had zero interest.

"You should ask. I bet she wouldn't turn you down."

Masyn had never pressured me, or even encouraged me, to ask out another girl.

"She's leaving Sunday." Not that I cared. "And we have wedding crap planned for every minute until her plane takes off."

"Maybe she'd change her flight."

"Or not."

"You won't know until you ask. How cool would it be if you ended up related to Beau because you two married sisters?"

It would be fantastic if Masyn had a sibling that didn't have a dick that Beau could suddenly betroth, but since she didn't, it would never happen.

"He's making a mistake."

"So are you."

"By not asking out someone I don't know who doesn't live here? Have *you* been drinking this morning?"

"Nope. Just want to see you happy."

"I am."

"Okay. Then do what you want."

There was something off between the two of us. A tension that never existed before. We ate in silence and then did the dishes the same way. She excused herself to change, and I watched her walk down the hall and disappear into her room.

FOUR

I didn't have a clue what we were doing at the church at ten in the morning when the wedding didn't start until four this afternoon. The guys had been separated from the girls, so with no ability to talk to Masyn, I was left wondering what she was doing—not that this was the place to try to have a conversation. I wasn't the only one who'd consumed too much last night. Everyone in this room looked rough, except Beau—because he wasn't here. And I wasn't the only one grumbling about the arrival time and wondering where the groom was.

Braden and Bodie were both present, and Beau was staying at his parents' house. "Braden, where's Beau?"

"Probably getting drunk. He and Felicity kept the neighbors up half the night."

The other guys in the room hooted like the couple had had an orgy with the Chastains down the hall.

I, however, got the message loud and clear. "Any idea what they fought about?"

"Hell no. Bodie and I went down to Sadler's after the rehearsal dinner. They were still bickering on the porch when we got home." Figured they went to the only place open and still serving alcohol that late at night. Any other time, I would have been with them.

"Where was your mom?"

"In the living room listening to it."

I'd had enough. I wasn't in the best of moods as it was, but I'd be damned if I was going to sit here with a dozen jackasses I didn't know while Beau cried in his cornflakes at his parents' kitchen table. I left my tuxedo jacket on the back of the chair I'd been sitting in and pushed through the other groomsmen to get out the door.

I finally found Mrs. Chastain near the sanctuary quietly talking to the wedding coordinator, but they stopped whispering once I got close enough to hear their conversation. Just before I reached Beau's mom, she patted the girl on the arm and gave her a smile I'd seen countless times in my youth. It was the one that assured you everything would be okay—it was plastic, and I knew from experience it meant shit was about to get real.

She drew me in for a hug and kissed my cheek before stepping back. "Good morning, Lee."

"Hey." I wasn't sure how to start this conversation. "Can we talk for a minute?" It was a step in the right direction. Hopefully the words would come.

"Certainly, dear. What's on your mind?" She clasped her hands in front of her and tilted her head to wait.

I guided her into the sanctuary, thinking we wouldn't be disturbed, only to find people milling about, arranging flowers and rolling out a satin carpet down the center aisle. There was nowhere the two of us could go where we wouldn't be overheard. At this point, I no longer cared.

"What's going on with Beau?" I attempted to keep my voice low, so we didn't draw attention.

Her lips flattened into a thin line before lifting into a prim smile. "I'm not sure what you mean."

I ran my fingers through my hair, stopping at the crown to grip handfuls and hoping it would release a little of the tension running through me. "There's something wrong. We both know it. Why is he marrying this girl?" My voice carried, and heads turned in my direction.

Mrs. Chastain straightened her spine and pulled her shoulders back. She'd gone stiff as a board and didn't even attempt to maintain a happy expression. "He's made a commitment that he intends to see through." She swallowed hard as though the words nearly choked her.

"I don't mean to be disrespectful, Mrs. Chastain, but if he has doubts before he makes a legal commitment, shouldn't he reconsider?"

"Sometimes our actions prevent us from walking away from our obligations, Lee."

I couldn't stand when people talked in riddles. "What could he possibly have done that would sentence him to a life of unhappiness?"

"Now, now. Don't be melodramatic. Weddings are stressful. I'm sure everything will be fine tomorrow."

"And if it's not?"

Her eyes filled with tears she fought not to let fall. "I don't know." She tried to hide her anguish, and finally gave in like she was confessing a holy secret. "I wish he'd talk to you."

"You can tell me what happened. I'll do what I can to fix it. But without information, he's a sitting duck and Felicity's got the rifle."

She pursed her lips and shook her head. "It's not for me to tell. I tried to get him to come home earlier...alone." Her delicate fingers swiped at the stream now trailing her cheeks. "At this point, I doubt anyone can change his mind."

I could sure as hell try. "Where is he?"

"Still at the house."

"And Felicity?"

"I'm not sure, dear. She wasn't there when I left, but I haven't seen her here, either. Maybe you could ask her sister. She's down the hall with the other girls."

"Any details you can give me would help a lot. If I don't know what I'm arguing for or against, I'm fighting a lost cause."

"Go talk to him, Lee. If anyone can get through to him, it would be you." So that's how we were going to play this. She was going to let me take the rap for unraveling whatever he'd gotten himself into. "If I hadn't promised to keep his secret, you'd be the first person I would tell."

My head was pounding, and grinding my teeth didn't help. I couldn't yell at her or shake her until she gave up the dirt. "I'll see what I can do."

"You're a good boy. He's lucky to have you."

"We'll see if he thinks so."

I didn't waste any more time trying to pry information from Beau's mother and took off in the direction of the dressing room the girls occupied. When I reached the door, I jerked it open, not realizing there might be women changing six hours before the actual event.

"Close the door!" someone shouted.

"Shit." I spun around so my back was to the room. "Where's Peyton?" I called out. I couldn't make out the voices of anyone behind me. I only knew two of these girls, and neither of them spoke. I almost turned around until I remembered I wasn't supposed to be in here anyhow.

"Want to step into the hall?" Peyton's voice came over my shoulder.

I cracked the door and slipped through to keep from exposing anyone else to passersby, and Peyton followed. Once I heard the click of the latch behind me, I faced her. She really was beautiful in a high-society sort of way. I hadn't noticed how full her lips were or how the color of her eyes glowed a deep blue. Now I had a hard time diverting my attention away from her to focus on why I was here. Peyton waited for me to speak, and my heart calmed and my anxiety ebbed with her patience.

"Do you know where your sister is?" I finally formed words, but I wasn't able to hide the bite behind them. "I'm sorry. I don't mean to snap." This wasn't Peyton's fault any more than it was mine.

"She's at the hotel. My mom said she stayed out with Beau and was sleeping later than planned." Her proper façade slipped, and she struggled to keep from rolling her eyes. In the process, her lids fluttered, and her upper lip tipped slightly.

"Any idea what they were talking about?"

"We talked about this last night."

I vaguely remembered that. "Refresh my memory."

"No one has let me in on whatever happened. I quit asking

because all I was doing was making Felicity and my mother angry. Whatever it is, it's not good."

At least I knew the bride wouldn't be at the Chastains' when I got there. One less person to deal with.

Peyton grabbed my hand when I attempted to leave. "Where are you going?"

"To try to save my best friend from making the worst mistake of his life."

"Take me with you." Her eyes begged me to give in.

"I can't. There's no way he'll talk if you're there."

She appeared disappointed, although she nodded her head in agreement. "I understand." She held out her hand. "Give me your phone."

"What?"

"Let me put my cell number in it. Then if you need reinforcement, you'll be able to reach me." Her fingers wiggled and waited, palm up.

I pulled the phone from my pocket and handed it to her. She quickly entered her information and then opened the camera app and took a selfie. I wasn't sure why she felt the need to attach a picture of her face to her contact card—it wasn't like I'd forget who she was. I watched as she sent herself a text, taking my number without having to ask for it. Then she handed my cellphone to me and sashayed back into the room we'd just left.

———

"BEAU?" I CALLED OUT FROM THE FOYER AFTER LETTING

myself in. Without a reply, I started toward the stairs, hollering his name louder this time. "Beau!"

"I'm upstairs. Stop yelling." He sounded as hungover as I felt.

As I took the steps two at a time, I heard him pad down the hall toward his old bedroom. By the time I reached the landing, he'd disappeared. I'd spent so much time in this house, I could navigate it blindfolded. And I knew exactly where he'd be. On his back on the bed with a forearm covering his eyes and his knees hanging over the side—just as I suspected.

I took a seat in the lounge chair in the corner. His bedroom was the size of my living room and kitchen combined.

"You want to tell me what's going on?"

"Not particularly."

"Do it anyhow."

He groaned and sat up, dropping his arm to his side and his hands into his lap. "There's nothing to tell."

"The hell there's not. You've done nothing other than fight with Felicity since both of you pulled into town. Your mother's in tears. You're pissy. The neighbors apparently know more about what's going on than your best friends. So don't tell me there's nothing to share, or I'll walk next door and ask the Corkles."

By the time Beau finally met my stare, the color had drained from his face...including the splotchy red he was notorious for. His eyes were puffy, although I doubted he'd been crying—likely just hadn't slept. Overall, the dude looked like shit. Not even a penguin suit and an expensive pair of shoes were going to pretty up this pig.

"Have you ever made a mistake so big there was no coming back from it?"

I'd made tons of mistakes that defined my life—Masyn and tenth grade ranking high on the list—but it was the life I was destined to lead. I didn't believe in regrets. No one expected the kinds of things from me that they did from Beau. "I don't guess so. But I don't think there's anything you could have done that your parents can't fix."

He stood and started pacing. "Yeah, well...they can't fix this one." He dragged his hands through his hair and scrubbed his face like he might find an answer if he were able to molt.

"Still don't have a clue what we're talking about here, man."

"You and Masyn were right. I never should have proposed."

I didn't need that confession to know it was the truth. "Okay...so you made a mistake. You haven't said, 'I do,' so don't." It seemed a rather simple solution to me. "Divorce will be far harder than telling a bunch of people that you don't give a shit about anyhow that you're not getting married."

"It's not that easy."

"The fuck it's not. If it's that hard, just don't show up. I'll tell them you aren't coming." I had no qualms about taking one for the team.

"My trust fund is at stake."

Back to riddles. "And?" Jesus, join the real world who have to work for a living and put that college education to good use.

"I signed a prenup."

If he wanted to play puzzle games, he should have started talking the moment he arrived in town, not hours before he was set to walk down the aisle. "English, Beau. We don't have all day." God, I needed aspirin.

"She's pregnant."

I couldn't have heard that right because if I had, that would mean Beau was a moron who hadn't wrapped his pecker. I leaned forward in the chair and put my elbows on my knees. "Come again?"

"You heard me."

"Why the fuck would you get her pregnant if you had doubts about marrying her? That's what condoms are for."

"We used them. Every time."

I was missing large pieces to be able to complete this picture. "Okay, so you knocked her up. That doesn't mean you have to marry her."

"You don't get it."

Well, duh!

My patience was wearing thin. "Spell it out for me."

"I realized a couple of months ago I'd made a mistake. I tried to be mature about it and talk to her. Needless to say, it wasn't well received."

"Yeah, chicks don't dig being dumped."

"I wasn't trying to break up with her. Just postpone the wedding for a while."

"So why was that a problem?"

"It wasn't as monumental then as it is now."

At this rate, he'd be married with kids by the time I figured out the heart of the matter. "Beau, could you tell me what you're up against so we can figure out how to get you out of it?"

"I lose my trust fund if I get a girl pregnant that I'm not married to." Well, shit, that complicated things. "I could deal with that part, even though it would suck. But when we started planning the wedding, her parents insisted on a prenup." He let out a heavy sigh and sat on the edge of the bed. "In that contract—and it's definitely a legally binding contract—I agreed to pay for any expenses incurred for the wedding if it didn't take place through any fault of my own."

That couldn't be cheap. "How much are you talking about?"

"At this point, roughly a quarter of a million dollars."

If I'd had anything in my mouth, I would have spat it all over the floor. "For a wedding?"

"Her dress was more than my first car, Lee."

I couldn't fathom that kind of wasteful spending. "Okay. Is that it? When did you find out about the baby? Is that why you decided to wait?"

"She didn't tell me she was pregnant until I told her I wanted to call things off."

"Are you even sure there *is* a baby?" I hated shady bitches. They'd lie when the truth would do better.

"Why would she lie about being pregnant?"

There was no possible way Beau was that naïve. "Umm... does she know about your trust fund?"

"Of course. That's why we always used condoms in addition to her being on the Pill."

"And you don't think there's something a tad off about a girl being dumped and suddenly turning up pregnant, knowing what kind of impact it would have on you...forever?"

"She's not like that, Lee."

"Open your eyes, dude. She's trying to trap you. Birth control *and* condoms? That's like a bazillion-to-one odds, and your association with her alone says you're not that lucky. Who knows about all this?"

"Just my mom."

"And she's just standing by while it happens?" Miffed. I was totally miffed. "Why haven't you told your dad?"

"My mom took the prenup to her lawyer to see if there were any loopholes. She didn't think we should tell my dad since I'd lose my trust fund. Even if I end up marrying her, my grandfather wrote it to prevent his grandsons from making stupid decisions that might derail their lives. If anyone finds out she's pregnant, it's gone."

"So your dad doesn't know?"

He shook his head.

"What did the lawyer say?"

"To marry her and file for divorce a year later." He had resigned himself to this fate.

I'd be puking my guts up in the bathroom facing the fact that I'd just lost millions to get laid. There was no way in hell I'd take it lying down, and I didn't care what it cost me, I'd kick her ass to the curb.

"That was his advice? What kind of quack tells a guy to get married with plans to divorce a year later?"

"Josten White." There was part of the problem. "It covers all the bases and prevents me from paying alimony. I don't even want to consider what child support would be." He finally made eye contact—I'd never seen shame on Beau's face, and I hoped like hell I never did again. "If we get married without anyone finding out about the baby, then my trust fund stays intact. After a year, I'm no longer obligated to repay the wedding expenses. We won't have been married long enough for her to get any type of spousal support or access to my grandfather's money, but I'm pretty sure she'll take the baby and move back to New Jersey to be near her family."

"Have you shared this plan with her?"

He eyed me like I was crazy for asking. "Hell no."

"Beau, a year is a long time to spend with someone you resent and will eventually hate."

We sat in silence for longer than I cared to admit. The air was thick with tension, making it hard to breathe. I loosened the bowtie threatening to strangle me and tried to think through this. "What if there's no baby?"

"I've seen the pregnancy test, Lee. She's pregnant."

"Did you actually see her take it?"

"No, of course not. Felicity showed it to me when she came to my apartment to tell me."

"You said you were only obligated to repay the wedding costs if the wedding didn't take place because of *you*, right?"

"Yeah, so?"

"I think you could argue that lying about pregnancy to continue the wedding planning would be her fault. Not yours. I'm no lawyer, but I couldn't imagine any court forcing you to pay for a wedding you tried to stop before the expenses got out of hand."

"There's no way to prove it. Plus, what if she is pregnant and it's not mine. Then I'm still on the hook."

This place was like a sauna. "Do you care if I open the window?"

Beau shook his head with a confused look as if to say, "Like I give a fuck about the window right now." He also didn't have on seventeen layers of polyester in fucking June in Georgia.

"Make her take a pregnancy test. We can stop by the

drugstore on the way to the church. If she's not pregnant, you and your mom can have a heart to heart with her and her parents. I don't see Ryland taking this one sitting down." Ryland was Beau's dad. He could be a hard-nosed son of a bitch when he needed to be.

"I can't just show up at the church, force her into a bathroom stall, make her flip her fucking Cinderella dress up into her painted face, and take a leak on a stick. Come on, Lee. Think this through."

"I am. I'm doing what you should have done months ago when this shitstorm started brewing. What do you have to lose? You don't want to marry her, anyhow, so who cares if you piss her off before the wedding? Worst-case scenario, you still have to marry her and spend the next twelve months in exile or hiding out in a bar."

"You're a dick. No wonder you've never had a girlfriend."

"Whatever. I've never had anyone corner my ass into marrying them, either." I was a smug prick, but I didn't give a shit. Someone needed to set this straight. Either Beau could do it, or I would do it for him.

He licked his lips, ran his fingers through his hair, and the red spots on his cheeks and neck lightened. Beau was coming back to life—hopefully, to fight.

"Just know, if this goes south, I'm moving in with you."

"You'll have to share a bed with Masyn. I'm not giving up my room."

Out of nowhere, he smiled.

FIVE

It didn't matter how many years passed or where the two of us lived, nothing ever changed. I'd never had a hard time convincing Beau to do things my way...which was probably why he hadn't wanted to tell me about any of this. I had no problems playing dirty when the deck was stacked, and it was most certainly stacked in Felicity's favor.

"Why the hell are there so many to pick from?"

"Keep your voice down." With my head bowed, I glanced around to see if anyone was around. "Two guys should never buy a pregnancy test together. Just get that one." I pointed to the box that showed a digital test window. There'd be no mistaking one or two lines. It would either be a yes or no. It was also the most expensive, so I assumed it was accurate.

"Should I get a couple?"

Like I knew. "Sure. That way, she can prove over and over what a liar she is. It'll be great. Get one for each member of the family she's fucked over, too—including yours. Kind of like memorabilia."

"You're an ass."

Only when someone threatened a person I loved. A deep laugh rolled through me and shook my shoulders when he picked up nine boxes: one for each of the four parents, the bride, the groom, Peyton, Braden, and Bodie. I was sure we were quite the sight in our tuxes—Beau had gotten dressed just in case this backfired and he still had to marry Felicity—on aisle four in the family planning section. There wasn't a soul in this store that hadn't known us since childhood, and the rumor mills would start churning out stories before we even got back in my truck. I wondered which one of us would get the honor of carrying the love child we'd be having by the end of the day.

Nancy had run the register at Wilson's drugstore since the dawn of time. "Hello, boys." There was a gleam in her eyes and a smirk on her lip. "Do I even want to ask what you're up to now?"

"Probably not." I winked at her and pondered whether or not to tell her they were gifts for the groomsmen, but I decided against it. Mystery was always more fun.

She blushed and bagged the pregnancy tests. Beau paid for them, and we said goodbye.

"Wonder what tale she'll tell Allison once we get in the truck." I clicked the alarm button on my key fob and opened my door.

"Allison's an old prude who stocks shelves in a small-town drugstore. I can't imagine she even knows how pregnancy occurs." Wilson's needed to hire some new staff.

Once we were both in the cab, it was easy to see that Beau struggled with what he was about to do. Sweat formed along his hairline, and he kept tugging at the collar of his heavily starched shirt. The bow tie was slung around his neck, although he hadn't bothered to tie it.

"You're doing the right thing."

"Remind me of that when the yelling starts." He stared straight ahead as I drove toward the church. "And again when I'm running up thousands of dollars in legal fees trying to get out of this."

"I'll always be there. Next time, don't wait so long to tell me you need backup."

"Do you have any idea how embarrassing all of this is?"

"Nah, but I'm sure it's going to be even worse for her and her family in about thirty minutes."

It took thirty-three minutes, but only because Felicity still wasn't at the church when we got there. Peyton called her sister—at my request—and insisted she get there immediately. Maybe Masyn was right. It was possible Peyton might be interested in me. Right now, I'd use that to my advantage. Bros before hoes.

Peyton had fetched Masyn from the dressing room to come wait in the hall with Beau and me. The moment Masyn saw Beau, she knew it was bad and nearly tackled him with a hug. But she didn't ask what was going on or pull me aside to get the scoop. In true Masyn style, she leaned against the wall between us with her foot propped up behind her and just showed her support. She didn't have to know the details. All she cared about was standing united. We'd been a force to reckon with for years, and today was no different.

Peyton, on the other hand, tried countless times to wrangle

information free. The poor girl knew her sister was about to be creamed. I didn't get the impression she wanted to defend Felicity's honor, more like prepare for the fallout. I left that to Beau. If he wanted to share, that was up to him. My lips were sealed.

It was clear when Felicity came stomping down the hall that she wasn't aware of just how close all of her attendants actually were. Masyn, Beau, and I had grown up in this church. Felicity had only been in it once—last night. Behind these thin walls were her other twelve attendants, her mother, aunts and cousins, junior bridesmaids, and flower girls...not to mention hair and makeup people. The walls were paper thin, and she was airing her dirty laundry to the world by not keeping her voice down. None of us bothered to warn her, either. If it wouldn't have been tacky or cost us more time, I would have ran home to pop some popcorn and sit back for the show.

"What was so urgent that I had to race down here? The wedding doesn't start for hours, Peyton."

Peyton stepped aside without saying a word to allow Felicity to see me, then Masyn, and finally Beau.

The bride rolled her eyes. "What? Is this some initiation into the Mickey Mouse Clubhouse?"

Beau pulled the bag of tests out from behind his back. "Yeah, and to get in, you have to pass a test." He extended the hand holding the plastic bag for her to take.

"What's this? I don't have time for games, Beau." She looked at Peyton for an answer, and when she got nothing, she peered inside. I'd never actually witnessed steam come out of anyone's ears like it did in cartoons, but Felicity came close to being the first. "Are you kidding me?"

Beau's lips stretched into a thin line just before he rolled them into his mouth and popped the *P* in "Nope."

She closed the sack and tried to force it back. "I've already taken a test. You saw it."

He refused to take it and pushed it toward her. "Then you won't mind taking a few more. You'll be in and out in five, six minutes tops. Just pee in one cup, and I'll dip each one of the tests for you. You don't even have to wait for the results if you're so certain. Think of this as an early wedding present for me."

"I've never been so insulted in all my life. I don't know what you're trying to prove, Beau, but it's tasteless and ill-timed."

"So was a pregnancy when I tried to put the brakes on things." There was zero emotion on his face...unless I took the freaky, red spots into account.

"Do you have any idea what you're stirring up here?" Her voice escalated the further this went. "Or what you stand to lose?" Her smug indignation only served to piss me off.

"I'd say marrying you would be the worst fate he could suffer. Anything else is manageable." I hoped like hell I was right about this girl; otherwise, I'd just alienated my best friend for at least a year. I wouldn't be allowed anywhere near their house, and I could pretty well guarantee she wouldn't be visiting Harden anytime soon.

"Your jealousy is almost as hideous as your little girlfriend."

Catty bitch. Masyn hadn't said a word. There was no reason for Felicity to lash out at her. Before I could get in her face, Beau stepped in.

"Cut the crap, Felicity. Either the two of us head into the

bathroom, or I'll go get your parents, and they can be a part of this family gathering, too."

It was like the mention of them conjured her mother to the door, or it could have been the walls that lacked proper insulation and soundproofing. "We can hear every word that's said inside. And Felicity, I do not like your tone. What is going on out here?" She waited for an answer none of us were going to provide.

"Nothing, Mother." She was like a damn chameleon. That girl could change colors faster than I could name them. She'd gone from red with anger, to green with jealousy, to a calm blue to appease her mom.

Mrs. Holstein made eye contact with each of us and then jerked her head to indicate Peyton needed to return to her side. Felicity took that as her escape and grabbed the bag from Beau the second the door closed and her mother and sister disappeared.

"You're going to regret this. All of you," she hissed over her shoulder. If she'd been close enough, I was pretty sure we would have all felt the spittle I saw fly from her mouth.

Idle threats. Beau might be scared of her, but I didn't give a rat's ass what this girl thought of me, or Masyn for that matter. We were less than ten minutes away from escorting her out of Beau's life. I hated that her sister might somehow be implicated since she'd helped get her here, but Peyton joined in without any persuasion on my part.

Beau pushed off the wall and led his bride-to-be to the bathroom. I prayed to God I hadn't led him down the wrong path. If she were pregnant, things would get infinitely worse for him. And there was no chance in hell he'd ever leave her and risk his child growing up without a father. He'd suck it up and do whatever he had to do, including leave me—and Harden —behind.

Once they were both out of sight, Masyn turned to me. "You want to tell me what's going on?"

"It's probably better you don't know."

"Stop trying to protect me. I'm already in Felicity's crosshairs." Gotta love a girl who hunts.

"He tried to postpone the wedding."

"And that led them to the bathroom...how?" Only Masyn wouldn't have put the pieces together by now. Even as jaded as she was toward men, she still failed to recognize how deceptive women could be.

"She told him she was pregnant."

Masyn grabbed my arm, and the alarm on her face nearly scared me. "You have to stop him. If she takes that test and she *is* pregnant, he'll lose his trust fund." She shook me by the bicep with all her strength while I just looked down in confusion.

"How the hell did you know that?"

"We are in a church. Stop swearing!" Her command came through clenched teeth. Her fists were tight at her sides, and I waited for her to stomp her feet to make her point.

"Stop with the tantrum, Masyn, and answer the question."

She shook her hands at her sides, and her eyes went wide. The crinkle of her brow always made my chest swell and my heart beat faster. "How did you *not* know? All the talk about safe sex and him handing out condoms like they were wet wipes. Don't you ever question anything?"

I was living in an alternate universe. "Not when it's useless information. And I never took condoms from Beau." It appeared I knew far less about these two than I could have imagined.

"You're an idiot if you're not wrapping"—she waved her hand in a circle near my crotch—"that *thing* up."

I wasn't sure whether to laugh at her inability to call my "thing" a penis or be irritated that she thought I was in danger of getting crotch rot. "Can we stick to the subject at hand?"

"You're right. You need to go stop him. Now. Oh God, Lee, if his parents find out..." She pushed at my side and tried to turn me toward the bathroom.

"I'm not going in there. I refuse to sentence him to a life without parole with Felicity Holstein as his warden. Not going to happen—I don't care if he ends up broke. At least he'll be happy."

Worry marred her button nose and soft lips. "What if she *is* pregnant?"

I leaned back against the wall, and then crossed my arms and my ankles. "She's not."

"You don't know that."

"I do."

"You can't possibly."

"Trust me."

Masyn jumped when the wood of the door cracked against the wall it had hit and halted any more discussion. Beau flew from the bathroom. His bow tie still hung loosely around his neck, the top two buttons of his shirt undone, the tails untucked from his pants. There were no crimson patches to be seen since his entire face and neck were the color of a freshly painted fire truck.

"Beau, wait," Felicity called after him just before she came into view. Tears rolled down her cheeks and her blue eyes were already bloodshot. If she were anyone else, I'd feel sorry for her. "Let me explain."

"Explain it to the lawyers. I can't believe anything out of your mouth."

With each step he took, I worried about how explosive this might get. He undid each cuff link and stuffed them into his bulging pockets, and when Felicity caught up to him and tried to grab ahold of his arm, he jerked it away, nearly causing her to fall.

Beau whirled around to face her, and her mother and Peyton rushed back into the hall. "I tried to be honest with you. I wasn't telling you I never wanted to marry you; I just thought we needed more time." He didn't even attempt to keep his voice down. "For months, you've led me to believe you were pregnant, knowing all I'd lose. You even threatened me with the cost of the wedding and brought your mom into it. What is wrong with you? I loved you. I stuck up for you when everyone I know told me to break up with you, not to propose to you. And *this* is how you repay me? By trying to trap me and ruin my life?"

"That's not true, Beau. If you'd let me—"

"Which part isn't true? You certainly weren't pregnant." He pulled pregnancy tests out of both pockets and held them up, fanning them out like a deck of cards.

She stuttered but didn't have a comeback. Beau tossed one of the sticks at her. It bounced off her hand when she tried to catch it and landed on the floor. Then he turned around and spotted Mrs. Holstein and Peyton. With an eerie smile on his face, he chuckled and handed each one a stick like he was passing out cigars. "Peyton, I'm sorry you had to witness this. Mrs. Holstein, my lawyer will be in touch."

"Beau?" Masyn didn't have the right words. And he didn't need them.

He took Masyn's hand and faced me. "You got this?"

I tossed him my keys and nodded. "Yeah, man. I got it."

And the two of them left with Felicity wailing in the background and a crowd gathered around us. I'd give anything to be walking out that door alongside my two best friends, but Beau needed me to deal with this fallout more than he needed my presence.

And shit was about to get ugly.

FOR SOMEONE WHO APPEARED COMPOSED AT ALL TIMES, Mrs. Holstein wasn't maintaining her air of dignity all that well.

"I hope you're proud of yourself." If hate were a tangible thing, I could hold hers—and choke the crap out of it.

"Damn straight. I saved my best friend from the worst mistake of his life."

"He'll never find another girl like Felicity."

"I sure as hell hope not. I don't think I could deal with this shit twice."

"Who do you think you are? You're nothing more than a backwoods—"

Mrs. Chastain had an uncanny ability to materialize out of thin air. She was like a ninja, she moved so quietly. Although, with this level of chaos, a mariachi band could have made a surprise entrance. "Margaret. I'd suggest you stop right there with the insults. Lee didn't do anything wrong."

"I'm flabbergasted by you, Bev. Do you have any idea the shame and embarrassment your son has brought on us? There are hundreds of people who have flown in from out of state to be here today."

I stepped aside and let the ladies handle business. I wasn't going anywhere, but *Bev* had this under control.

"You don't seem the least bit shocked by anything your daughter's done, only that my son called her on it. Did you put her up to it? Maybe suggest it was a way to tie him down?"

Appalled by the accusation, she gasped and dramatically drew back like she'd been slapped. "I have no idea what you're talking about." The hand still clutching the pregnancy test shot to her chest. "What are you suggesting?"

"I'm not *suggesting* anything. I'm flat out saying that you knew what your daughter was doing...and possibly even encouraged it."

"I've never been so insulted in all my life."

I just couldn't keep my mouth shut. "I find that hard to believe."

"Lee, don't be disrespectful." Mrs. Chastain's tone completely changed when she addressed me. It was as though she were talking to the ten-year-old standing in her kitchen after she'd caught us using her white table linens to make forts in the backyard. I hated when I disappointed her. "Why don't you and Peyton find Cecilia."

The confused expression on my face must have told her that I didn't have a clue who Cecilia was.

"The wedding planner, dear. You two go find her and get a copy of the guest list."

"Okay."

"You'll need to tell her there won't be a wedding this afternoon. She needs to call the vendors and try to stop deliveries while you call guests."

"You can't be serious about having him call off the wedding." Mrs. Holstein was mortified at the thought, and that made me oddly happy.

Mrs. Chastain ignored her and patted me on the arm. "Keep it short and vague. Let them know one of us will call them once things settle down."

"Yes, ma'am." Like I wanted to get into the details of a trifling girl with people I didn't know, or worse, those I did.

I extended my arm to Peyton, and together we set off to destroy Cecilia's day. And when we found her and broke the news, she might have been as distraught as the bride.

She clasped her hands in front of her and chewed on her lip. "This is every event planner's worst nightmare. I've heard the horror stories, but I've never witnessed one firsthand." Her gaze darted between Peyton and me. "Think, Cecilia." If she weren't careful, her teeth were going to separate her bottom lip from her face.

Since she didn't know what to do, I offered a little help. "Maybe you should call the vendors to cancel while we call the guests?"

Cecilia clapped her hands, and a tiny grin played on her lips. "Yes. Yes. That's perfect." She raced over to her bag, where it sat on the steps by the altar, and grabbed her phone.

"Cecilia?" Peyton's voice cracked, and it dawned on me that she hadn't said a word since all this had started.

She already had her phone pressed to her ear. "Hmm?"

"Where can we find a copy of the guest list?"

Cecilia rambled on to some poor sap on the other end while rummaging through her stuff. She produced a crumpled set of papers and handed them off to us. With the shoo of her hand, she acted like she'd given us our tasks and we needed to leave her to her own. This wasn't my goat rodeo—I was just a clown trying to distract the bull.

Peyton and I found a spot at the back of the church, sat in the pews, and divided the list in half. It would take hours to call all of these people, and within a few phone calls, we realized we would still have to tell many of them in person because we were unable to reach them. Others were insistent on coming to the church to help—I didn't have a clue what they thought they were going to do. And the majority wanted more information than Peyton or I could or would share.

"You have to know what happened, Lee. You're his best friend." Mrs. Corkle and her husband had lived next door to the Chastains all my life. They didn't have children, but they thought nothing of scolding us like we belonged to them—even in our twenties.

"Ma'am, I can't tell you any more than I already have. Mrs. Chastain assured me she'd call you once things settled down."

"That's malarkey. What did that girl do? Beau would never walk out on anyone, much less leave them at the altar."

I pinched the top of my nose and prayed God would have mercy on me. The hangover was bad—add nosey neighbors to it, and it was downright unbearable. "No one was left at the altar, Mrs. Corkle. The wedding wasn't supposed to start until four, remember?"

"Yes, I know. I'm already dressed and have the gift wrapped. Are you getting fresh with me, Lee Carter?"

Beside me, Peyton giggled. Mrs. Corkle was nearly deaf, so I had to scream for her to hear me and she thought she had to yell back. With the phone six inches away from my head, it wasn't hard to listen in.

"No, Mrs. Corkle. Although, I am going to have to let you go so I can make more calls."

"Tell Beverly to come by when she gets home."

"Will do."

"All right then. Bye-bye."

I echoed the same words and hung up before she could reel me back in. "Shoot me now."

"You were really good with her."

"She's old as the hills, but in her younger years, she didn't hesitate to take a switch to me or Beau. Masyn never did anything wrong in Mrs. Corkle's eyes—we 'corrupted that sweet girl.' Direct quote."

"I bet you three were a handful."

I leaned back in the pew. It wasn't comfortable, and the wood was unforgiving. "Not really. We were good kids."

"What was it like growing up in a small town?"

"I don't have anything to compare it to. I've lived here my whole life—in the same house on the same street. I bought it from my dad when he moved to Atlanta. Beau's and Masyn's parents live in the same houses, too. I guess it was like every country song ever recorded—we drank from garden hoses, drove old trucks, fell in love...just life."

"*You* fell in love?" Her skepticism was duly noted.

"I didn't say *I* did all those things. Only that they happened."

Peyton cocked her head and a curl escaped from her hairdo. "I don't take you for a relationship kind of guy."

"What kind of guy do you think I am?" I didn't really care, but I was a tad intrigued.

She shrugged and scanned my face, her gaze lingering on my lips before landing back on my eyes. "A heartbreaker."

"I guess that's how small towns differ. When you grow up with people—literally from diapers to adulthood—you don't really see them in a romantic light. You remember them picking their nose in kindergarten or peeing in their pants on the playground. And, don't get me started on the gossip. Nothing is sacred. This town plays the worst game of telephone I've ever seen."

"That doesn't sound so bad. Better than boarding schools and etiquette classes."

"You went to boarding school?" That sounded really isolated and cliché.

"Starting in third grade." And she sounded indifferent.

"Guess it's all relative, huh?"

Before she could respond, Mrs. Chastain interrupted our conversation. "Lee, I know this is a lot to ask, and I'm sorry to do it to you. Ryland is meeting with our attorney, and they've asked for Beau and me to join them." Damn, they hadn't wasted any time getting that ball rolling. They'd pay out the nose for calling their lawyer in on a Saturday to deal with the Holsteins. "I realize you can't possibly call all of the guests and won't be able to reach everyone, either."

I thought I'd save her the trouble of making her case. "You want me to do damage control when they arrive?" I'd never say no, regardless of how much I didn't want to do it.

"I thought it would be nice if you *and* Peyton were here. You appear to be the only two who aren't yelling at someone. That way, both families are represented." Her image was important to her. She'd worked hard to develop and maintain relationships in our little community, and Mr. Chastain had done the same in the city with his business associates.

She'd never let me down when I needed something, and I certainly wouldn't do it to her—despite my belief that all of this could have been avoided. To say I was shocked that she'd let Beau take this hit was an understatement. I'd have lost my ass betting on that one. In the end, I had to believe she was just as flawed as the rest of us. Someday I might learn her reasoning, although I doubted it.

"Of course," I answered Mrs. Chastain's request, and then I glanced at Peyton. "Do you mind?"

She frowned and shook her head. "Not at all. Probably best for everyone involved to keep my parents as far away from here as possible."

"We will take care of it, Mrs. Chastain. I'm sorry this has all happened. I hope you believe me when I tell you, I had no idea it was going on. I'm terribly embarrassed by my sister's behavior." Either Peyton's words were genuine—which I believed they were—or she was the best liar the world had ever seen.

"It will all work out for the best in the end. It's the middle that's painful." Another terse smile and quick sigh followed. "Thank you, both. I appreciate it." She turned to Peyton. "If I don't see you again, it was lovely to meet you." Then she addressed me, starting with a hug and a pat on the arm. "I'm sure I'll see you tomorrow."

"Yes, ma'am."

I waited for her to exit the sanctuary and then I asked Peyton, "You ready to go face the firing squad?" We'd been making calls for what seemed like hours and hadn't gotten through a quarter of the list. There were going to be tons of people arriving in the very near future.

"As ready as I'll ever be. You're a good friend, Lee."

"You're a good sister."

She giggled a little too hard and snorted, which sent her into a fit of laughter that she tried to hide by covering her mouth. "Sorry. It's just that Felicity and I can't stand each other. So it's odd to hear anyone say that."

Peyton came on a little strong when we first met, and I hadn't been terribly interested in getting to know her based on her last name. Now it was clear to me that she was the black sheep of the family. "Her loss." I meant it.

The two of us, along with Cecilia—whom we hadn't seen in ages—spent the next three mind-numbing hours talking to Beau and Felicity's guests, assuring them that both bride and groom were well and that the families would reach out when things calmed down. It was like listening to a bad song on repeat. I'd never seen so many people get so defensive and protective. Guests of the bride wanted to lash out about Beau, and those on the groom's side had nothing positive to say about Felicity. Sadly, Peyton and I couldn't do anything to pacify them, and most left upset and some in tears.

And I needed a drink.

SIX

When Peyton and I exited, I realized I didn't have transportation. Beau had ridden with me, and so had Masyn, so when they left the church, I gave him my keys. I could walk home if I had to, but doing so in a tuxedo would suck. It had to be in the nineties, and the sun was still shining brightly overhead, even as it started to set. Summer days lingered till nearly nine o'clock, and the heat never went away. I stopped on the steps and called Beau to see where they were.

"Hey, Lee," Beau answered on the first ring, sounding better than he had this morning.

"Where are you and Masyn?" I shielded my eyes from the early evening sun and scanned the streets. They weren't likely to be nearby; I didn't want to look like a moron talking on a cellphone while standing on the steps of an empty church in a tux.

Peyton shifted her weight more than once, waiting to see if she needed to drop me off. Her continuous movement caught my attention, and I realized the shoes she had on must be strangling her feet.

I twisted the phone away from my face and motioned to her heels. "Take 'em off."

"I'm meeting Masyn at Sadler's. I just left the lawyer's office. Where are you?" Beau kept talking, while I steadied Peyton's arm so she could remove her shoes.

"Just finished cleaning up your mess," I answered into the phone, distracted by the neon-pink polish on Peyton's toes.

"Yeah, sorry about that. You need me to come get you?"

Peyton shook her head, clearly having overheard the conversation I had with Beau.

"Nah, Peyton said she'd drop me off. I assume Masyn still has my truck?"

"Unless she sold it in the last couple of hours."

"You're a huge help. Thanks, Beau." He couldn't see my face, but I was certain he heard the sarcasm in my voice.

"Anytime. I'll see you in a few."

I didn't bother saying goodbye when I ended the call. "You sure you don't mind giving me a ride?" I asked Peyton.

Her heels now dangled at her side and the grimace of pain had vanished. "Not at all. It's certainly better than what I'm going to face at the hotel."

It hadn't dawned on me that when she left here, she'd still have her sister to contend with—not to mention her mother and father. "You want to come with me to Sadler's? It's a hole in the wall with cheap beer and greasy food. It reeks of cigarette smoke, and you can hardly hear yourself think over the jukebox and people playing pool."

"Well, with that kind of endorsement, how could I say no?" She laughed, and her blue eyes danced in the sunlight. "Any possibility we could stop somewhere to change clothes?"

I glanced at her attire and then at my own. Peyton was right; showing up at a redneck bar in a wrinkled tuxedo and bridesmaid dress probably wasn't the best idea. "My house isn't far from here."

"Lead the way." She pointed to her rental car and handed me the keys. "It's easier if you drive since you're familiar with the streets."

I would never argue with a woman over her wanting me to drive. I hated riding bitch in a sedan with a woman driving. It chipped away at my manhood every second I spent trapped in the passenger seat.

In less than ten minutes, we were in and out of my house. Peyton changed into what I assumed she'd worn to the church before she'd put on the dress—tight, skinny jeans, a silky, dark-green tank top, and tan, patent-leather heels. I shook my head at the sight of her—she'd stand out like a sore thumb, and every guy within a twenty-five-mile radius would be alerted to her presence within fifteen seconds of us walking through the door. If I were into high-maintenance girls, she'd be at the top of the list, and guys in Harden, Georgia, weren't used to the Peyton Holsteins of the world.

"Your house is cute."

I would never describe a man's home as cute. "Thanks."

"I'd love to have a little bungalow like that."

"Bungalow?"

It was a three-bedroom, two-bath ranch. Nothing bungalow about it.

"You know, a cute little house."

I put the car in gear and shook my head. She didn't even know it was a backhanded compliment, so I couldn't hold it against her. We came from two different worlds. I was part of the middle class in this county. I'd likely be homeless in New York, or wherever she went to school.

Peyton gasped, and I slammed on the brakes. "Oh, Lee. I'm sorry. I didn't mean that the way you took it."

Jesus. She scared the shit out of me, thinking I'd run over a cat or hit a kid. "I know."

"Probably not. Any idea what living at a boarding school is like?"

We were moving again, so I didn't have to face her. "It's not the Ritz Carlton?"

"Not the ones I went to. It was like being in a dorm you could never leave. I mean, we could leave, just not go home. Even in the summer, my parents enrolled us in different camps around the world. Then I left for college and was back in a dorm again. Having a house of my own with a yard and a pool would be a dream."

I let out a humph and dropped one hand from the steering wheel. "Sorry, I tend to get my ass on my shoulders about shit that doesn't matter."

"I get it. You're proud. You should be."

I wasn't fishing for compliments. The radio seemed like a better choice than conversation, so I reached for the volume to turn it up. Peyton and Masyn had the same horrible taste in music.

"You guys have some great radio stations down here."

"They're all out of Atlanta. I'd think New York has a selection second to none."

She giggled, and when I turned toward her, she seemed softer than before—easygoing. "We do. I assumed, based on what little bit Felicity said about Beau's hometown, that there'd be rabbit ears on the television sets in the local motel. And we'd eat dinner at the drive-in next to the thrift shop. Harden's been a nice surprise...minus the whole canceled wedding thing."

I pulled her rental car into the gravel parking lot of Sadler's. There wasn't much to the place on the outside—or inside for that matter—just an old building that had been a bar for as long as I could remember. "Still think Harden's a quaint town?"

Peyton swatted at my arm playfully and unbuckled her seatbelt. "Stop. It's not like I've never been to a dive before."

"Come on."

We wove our way through the parked cars and four-wheel drives and made it to the covered entrance. I held the heavy door open so Peyton could step inside. The layer of smoke wasn't quite as dense as usual, and the crowd remained thin. When the steel door slammed behind us, she jumped and grabbed my hand. Her eyes widened in surprise.

"I promise, no one here bites."

She nodded but didn't let go of me. It didn't take long for me to spot Masyn and Beau in a booth in the corner, and I pointed them out to Peyton. She took that as her cue to move away from the door and in the direction of my friends.

"Hey, Lee." Sherry, one of the waitresses who'd been here since she could legally serve alcohol, stopped us. "Good to see you. Who's your friend?" Her mouth kept moving even after she quit speaking—gum. Bless her heart; her mama had never told her that a cow chewing cud wasn't an attractive thing to mimic.

"Sherry, this is Peyton; Peyton, Sherry."

Peyton extended her hand, not expecting Sherry to take it

and pull her in for a hug. Peyton's apprehension was easy to spot with her arms stiffly at her sides. She stepped back on shaky legs when Sherry finally released her. "It's nice to meet you."

"You too, honey. Lee's good people. You take care of him." She winked and chomped on her gum some more. Then she popped a kiss on my cheek. "Lani has Beau's table, but I'll get by there before you guys leave."

"Thanks, Sherry."

"How do you two know each other?" Peyton's stark-white face revealed her anxiety. She acted as though she'd just stepped into another dimension instead of a bar.

I grabbed her hand and started walking. "We went to high school together. She graduated with us."

"She's your age?" She didn't try to hide her shock.

"That's what hard living does. Sherry's had it rough her whole life and worked like a slave for everything she has. It's definitely aged her."

Beau stood when we got to the table, as any Southern gentleman would do. "Hey...guys. I didn't know you were coming, Peyton." The splotches started to form on his cheeks.

"Dude, sit down. She didn't come to chew you out. She's been in purgatory with me all afternoon handling your crap." Beau slid into the booth next to Masyn, leaving the other side for me to share with Peyton. "You wouldn't believe the questions and accusations we heard. I need a beer—or ten."

"Lani's bringing you one." Beau eyed Peyton with hesitation. "I didn't know you were coming or I would have ordered something for you. What do you want? I'll go get it."

While the two of them sorted that out, I tried to determine

why Masyn was glaring at me through slits in her eyes from across the table.

"You okay, sweetheart?"

"Dandy, *babe*." Her panties were twisted over something, although I'd be damned if I knew what. She wasn't the one who'd had to make a hundred phone calls to people she didn't know, or face upset guests to defend a bitch I'd rather expose.

My brow furrowed in confusion. Even when Masyn was pissed, she just told me she was pissed. Games weren't her thing, and neither was pussyfooting around a topic. I could only assume that whatever was eating at her had to do with either Beau or Peyton—although Beau was a saint in Masyn's world—leaving only Peyton. Somewhere along the way, I'd missed something. They'd giggled and yapped it up last night while they plotted against Felicity, yet suddenly, Masyn was trying to shoot death lasers from her eyes at Peyton.

When Beau returned with a glass of wine—I didn't even know Sadler's served wine—he sat down and immediately started unpacking his afternoon.

"He thinks Felicity screwed herself, but you guys might have to write a letter or something to the court if the Holsteins try to take this anywhere."

This had to be painfully awkward for Peyton. Even if she didn't care for her sister, listening to someone talk about suing your family couldn't be easy.

"All of us?" I asked.

He looked around the table, remembering his ex-fiancée's sister was there, too. "Well, you and Masyn. I'm sure Peyton will get hooked by the Holsteins' attorney."

No need to dwell on that. "Moving on."

"My trust fund is safe since she's not pregnant—although, the lecture I had to hear from my dad almost made the wedding sound more appealing. And, since I can prove the date I tried to call things off, worst-case scenario, I might be liable for the expenses paid up to that point. But Josten thinks he can get me out of that, too."

"Do I even want to know how you can prove you tried to call things off? Or how much money you might be on the hook for?"

Our conversation kind of left Masyn and Peyton to sit back and listen, which Peyton seemed content to do. I wasn't sure it was a good idea for Beau to be spilling the details in front of Peyton, but this was his rodeo. Masyn, on the other hand, continued to shoot me eat-shit looks with her arms crossed and her lips pursed.

Beau took a long pull from his beer. "Email. And upwards of fifty grand."

I nearly choked. "Please tell me you did not email the girl to break off your engagement." Beau had a horrible habit of living on electronic devices. They were his favorite ways to communicate—not through talking—texting...the written word. It drove me insane. And we'd get to the money next.

"No, jackass. I talked to her in person. Emails and text messages were exchanged during class. The emails are dated."

"Where the hell are you going to come up with fifty thousand dollars?" That was an entire year's salary, including overtime for me. And Beau hadn't started his job. "Trust fund?"

"I don't have access to it until I'm twenty-five." Color me confused. "I don't know. That's worst case. I'll figure it out if it comes to that. It's a small price to pay to get out of this." He glanced over at the blonde sitting next to me. "Sorry, Peyton, no offense."

"None taken." She beamed and sipped her wine, intent on listening to more. "I never understood your attraction to her in the first place. But who am I to judge?"

"That was a popular question all around." Masyn finally joined the conversation, however briefly.

Turning to Peyton, I explained, "Masyn and I tried to talk Beau out of proposing last Christmas. It didn't have anything to do with Felicity. We didn't know her. We just thought they were rushing things." That was a nice way to put that we believed she was after his last name and bank account.

"Anyway," Beau continued, "if her parents don't fight it, and Josten doesn't believe they will, then I'm just stuck with legal expenses for his time."

Josten White was the only lawyer in town. He'd graduated from high school with Masyn's oldest brother, Ty. Once he passed the BAR, he came back to Harden to set up practice. We all thought he was crazy at the time—nothing happened in Harden to need an attorney, people didn't even get divorced. Oddly enough, once he'd opened his doors, business started flowing through. Workers' comp, farmers with land disputes, child support—he did it all. And made bank.

"I can't imagine my parents fighting any of this. My mom won't want the negative publicity. She'd die if her precious Felicity were ever held accountable for her actions. Don't be surprised if they pay you to go away."

Twice in five minutes, I'd tried to kill myself choking on beer. "You can't be serious."

"Reputation is everything. This would not bode well for

the Holstein family name." Peyton didn't seem the least bit concerned over any of it. She hadn't even bothered to call her parents or her sister after we left the church to check on them or check in.

"Can I get anyone another beer? Wine?" Lani was another girl who'd graduated with us. She'd gotten pregnant our senior year and ended up marrying Jimmy Adler after the baby was born. They now had two more kids—in less than four years—and lived in a doublewide right outside of town. Sweet girl, dumb as a box of rocks. "What about you, Masyn? Want anything?"

"I'll take another beer." I slid out of the seat. "I'm going to the head. Be right back."

"Bathroom, you buffoon." Masyn squinted at me in irritation. Maybe it wasn't Peyton she was upset with; I appeared to be her only target.

"Thanks, *sweetheart*." It was like rubbing sandpaper on her already snarly mood. The wink I tossed her direction was merely the icing on the cake.

When I returned, Beau and Peyton were in the booth alone. He was smiling, and she appeared to be enjoying herself. I wondered if Sherry had slipped something into her drink that I could dump in Masyn's to sweeten her disposition a bit.

"Where'd Masyn go?"

Beau tilted his head toward the pool tables. Through the smoke-filled room, I could see Masyn leaned over the edge of a table, lining up a shot with Toby Hayes up her ass. He had her caged in from behind, talking in her ear. He'd been trying to get in her pants since high school, and the nicest thing I could say about him was he was a grade-A douchebag. She knew what she was getting into going over there, so I let it go. It wouldn't hurt my feelings to watch her use that cue to beat him off.

The longer we sat there, the heavier the crowd got. Sadler's was the hangout for most of the younger men in town in the afternoon—shoot pool, drink beer, watch the game. In the evening, couples showed up. Everyone knew everyone else, and this was where we all chose to congregate. There was a tiny stage in the corner where different bands played on Saturday nights. I had no idea who was currently setting up, but once the music started, there would be women dragging their dates, boyfriends, husbands, or whomever they'd arrived with onto the tiny dance floor in front of the band. The place went from pool hall to honkytonk in just under an hour.

I had no idea I'd end up being one of those guys.

"Dance with me?" Peyton asked.

"Lee doesn't dance." Beau snickered, thinking he'd said something cute. Someone needed to cut him off.

"Oh, come on. Everyone can slow dance." She tilted her chin down and gazed up at me with hopeful eyes.

One dance wouldn't kill me. "Fine."

My palms started to sweat as they rested on her waist, and claustrophobia set in when Peyton draped her arms around my neck. I hated dancing. I never knew if I was supposed to talk, how close to get, where to put my hands—it was always awkward. I didn't even want to think about the people who might be watching me. Peyton didn't seem to have the same apprehension. She swayed with confidence while chatting easily.

"I can see why you like living here."

I found it hard to make eye contact with someone standing

so close, much less engage in casual conversation. "Why's that?"

"You know everyone and their history. You're a part of it. All of your friends are here, your family. I think it'd be nice to walk down the street and say hello instead of staring at the ground, hoping no one bothers you."

"You don't like New York?"

"I do. It's just different. Life here seems slower. The pace isn't so rushed."

Before I could respond to Peyton, Beau happened to grab my attention, jerking his head to the right. Without picking Peyton up and spinning her around, I had to wait until we naturally shifted to see what had his eyes bugged out and his jaw set.

The second I laid eyes on what he gaped at, I nearly lost my shit. Toby's hands were all over Masyn's ass, and his thigh was between her legs. This wasn't *Dirty Dancing,* and he sure as shit wasn't Patrick Swayze. But the longer I watched, I noticed she wasn't trying to get away from him—she was encouraging it. Her head dipped to his chest, and she rocked her hips on his jeans. Any second now, she'd toss her hair back and release the sounds of an orgasm, like Meg Ryan in *When Harry Met Sally.* That would undoubtedly get the town talking. Staring at her, I realized I'd let her pick way too many movies over the years, when all my film references came from sappy chick flicks with happy fucking endings.

When the song ended, I went back to the booth, and Peyton went in search of the bathroom. I warned her to squat and not sit, but she just looked at me like she didn't understand —she would when she got there. Masyn stayed on the dance floor with Toby, not once looking in our direction. "What is she thinking?"

"Who knows? She's a chick, Lee. They get hormonal and emotional over shit that doesn't matter."

I didn't bother trying to hide my irritation; Beau would see through any shit I tried to play off anyhow. "What does she have to be emotional about?"

"I'm only speculating based on the huffs of jumbled muttering I've heard since you and Peyton showed up."

"Are you going to share that with me?"

"She said you won a bet. That meant nothing."

I knew exactly what it meant; I danced with Peyton when I'd told Masyn I wanted to dance with her. "She was playing pool with dickface when *Peyton* asked *me* to dance."

"And she practically growled when she saw you holding Peyton's hand coming in the door."

"Jesus. I wasn't holding her hand like we were together. I was pulling her back here."

"Nevertheless, her territory's being invaded, and she doesn't know how to defend it."

Lani brought me another beer that I immediately downed in frustration. If it had been a can, I would have cracked a hole in the bottom and shotgun the damn thing. "That's horseshit."

He held his hands up in surrender. "Think about it, Lee. The three of us have been friends since we were five. And in all those years, no one new has ever come into town unless they were born here. Peyton's an outsider in Masyn's tiny world. I could see how Masyn would be intimated by her."

"You're a dick, dude."

"I'm calling a spade a spade. Masyn's a great girl, but most guys don't get off on a chick being a gearhead. Watch the way the dudes in this place follow Peyton everywhere she goes—they don't even try to hide their interest. They're like dogs in heat—except they're *humans*. She's hot. And women recognize that crap." He drank the rest of his beer with me staring at him.

My mouth hung open and I sat in stunned silence, wondering how he came up with this crap.

"Guarantee you, Masyn thinks you're after Peyton. And in her mind, she already has the two of you married off and you moving to New York."

"There's no way. Masyn's never been like other girls. And she sure as hell isn't envious of them."

"If she could piss on your leg without making a mess, she'd totally claim you as hers, Lee. She doesn't have to with the other girls in Harden; they already know it. Peyton does not."

"Even if that were true—and I don't believe it is—how is using Toby's leg as a stripper's pole solving anything?"

He scoffed as though the answer were simple. "Dude, revenge."

Peyton stood at the end of the table unable to slide in with Beau and me in the outside seats. "What'd I miss?"

I glanced out on the dance floor one more time to see Masyn acting like an idiot and knowing she'd regret this tomorrow—the rumors would be flying before the sun came up. "Nothing. You about ready to get out of here?"

Masyn had my truck keys, and there was no way in hell I was stepping out there to pry her off of Toby Hayes to get them.

Peyton's expression was a mixture of confusion and disappointment. "Yeah, I guess."

I dropped enough cash on the table to cover mine and

Peyton's drinks, plus a tip, and then looked to Beau. "Don't let her drive if she keeps drinking."

"Wouldn't dream of it." Beau leaned back against the booth, and a smile slowly rose on his lips as he watched the people around us.

"Peyton, do you mind taking me home? Masyn has my keys, and she's rather preoccupied."

"Not at all." She said bye to Beau and waved to Masyn as we walked past her.

I'd hoped we wouldn't draw Masyn's attention when we left, but Peyton was trying to be nice—she had no idea she'd just stirred up a hornet's nest. Well, until Masyn stopped dancing and glared at the two of us—at that point, it was pretty clear Masyn wasn't happy. I didn't bother to stop.

SEVEN

"Everything okay in there? Masyn didn't seem very happy when we were leaving."

Peyton didn't have a clue what was going on, although I couldn't really speculate myself. "I'm sure she's fine. I don't know what her deal was tonight. It's been a weird day all around."

"Are you surprised Beau wasn't more upset?"

"About?"

She laughed, and I drove. "My guess is this isn't how he envisioned his wedding night going."

"You're right, this was a hell of a lot better." Thankfully, she felt the same way about her sister that we did. "But to answer your question, no. Beau was a mess when I got to his parents' house this morning. I think he's relieved at this point." I wasn't sure any of this had really hit him, either. Right now, he felt relief, but that didn't mean over the next few days he wouldn't crash into a pit of despair, cradling a beer in one hand and Felicity's picture in the other.

"Yeah, you haven't really told me what happened. I've kind of drawn my own conclusions." Peyton cracked the window and turned her face toward the air coming in.

"Are you hot? I can turn the air on."

She shook her head and more of her blonde curls fell from her hairdo. "No, just enjoying the way the air smells and the breeze on my face. Subways don't lend themselves to hanging your head out the window."

"Do you want to know?"

Peyton had gone along with everything asked of her today with almost no explanation. And she'd done it willingly and been pleasant through it all. If she wanted answers, I'd tell her what I could.

She gave up the freedom the wind and the window provided to face me again. "Know what?"

"About this morning."

Peyton leaned back and rested her head on the seat, keeping her attention on me. "Sure, if you want to tell me."

I didn't believe she wasn't interested, regardless of the tone she tried to take. I think she assumed she'd be left out. She wasn't in our click, and her mother and sister had shut her down anytime she'd tried to get involved—it was easy to conclude she'd never know the truth.

"You already know Beau tried to call off the wedding. I guess when Felicity realized he was serious and not going to back down, she told him she was pregnant—gave him a fake pregnancy test and everything."

Peyton didn't seem all that surprised by her sister's actions. Her head bobbed in understanding, and she didn't try to explain away anything her family had done. I'd be embarrassed as hell and begging for forgiveness, or at the very least, I'd want a chance to prove my last name didn't mean I was anything like them.

"If Beau gets a girl pregnant before he gets married, he loses his trust fund. Hence the reason for racing to the altar. If he didn't seal the deal and tie the knot before she started to show, he'd be out millions."

Her brows lifted so high, her forehead practically disappeared, suddenly in disbelief of what she heard. "Please tell me you're joking."

"Wish I was. It gets better. Your parents had him sign a prenup. If the wedding didn't take place through any fault of Beau's, he had to pay your parents back the money they'd spent on the wedding...which he couldn't do if Felicity was pregnant and they weren't married."

She turned in the seat completely, her left shoulder now pressing against the upholstery, and gawked at me in disbelief. The wind still raced through the crack in the window, continuously blowing her hair in her face.

"I guess Beau broke down and told his mom—not his dad, though. And she took the prenup to their attorney, Josten—the guy he met with this afternoon. And Josten told him the best thing he could do was marry her to keep the trust fund, wait the year the prenup stipulated to be free of the wedding costs, and then divorce her before she would get any type of alimony."

"Holy crap. He was going to do it? Why?"

I let out a short huff through my nose. "Oh, he wasn't going to leave her. He was going to stay and suffer." Thinking about it had me seeing red all over again.

"What for? He's way too young to be in an unhappy marriage."

"He believed she'd take the baby and move closer to your parents."

Her mouth opened and closed several times, yet nothing came out. If she'd flopped around on the ground, she would have looked like a fish gasping for air. I put the car in park in my driveway and waited to see if she had a response.

"Sorry, I'm kind of dumbfounded. I knew my sister was conniving, but this is worse than anything I believed her to be capable of. And I'm appalled my mother obviously knew what was going on and didn't put a stop to it."

"Kind of shines a whole new light on it, huh?"

"It's embarrassing."

"You can't pick who you're related to."

I had no idea how to comfort Peyton. I didn't know her well enough. The only thing I could offer was company. I didn't have anywhere to be in the morning, and I wasn't tired, just irritated and unwilling to continue watching Masyn act like a fool. "Do you want to come in? We could watch a movie or hang out on the back porch. I'm sure Masyn has a swimsuit here if you want to go swimming."

"Sure. I'm not in a hurry to deal with any of this."

I turned the car off and climbed out. When we reached to the door, I had to use the spare key again to get inside. I hadn't left any lights on, so the foyer was dark as Egypt when I closed the door. Peyton waited for me as I kicked off my shoes.

I finally hit a switch so she could see where she was going. "Masyn's room is on the right. Check the dresser—I'm sure there's something in one of the top drawers."

"She has her own room?"

"More often than not, she stays here on the weekends."

"And you're sure she won't mind me wearing her swimsuit? That's kind of personal—like sharing panties."

"If she cares, I'll buy her a new one. Your other options are swimming in your bra and underwear...or nothing at all. Take your pick." We didn't have to get in the pool, but the cool water and a beer called my name. After a day like this, there was no place I'd rather be. And since Peyton didn't argue or take me up on another suggestion, I went with it.

"I'll see what she has."

That's what I thought. "I'm going to put on some shorts. Meet me in the kitchen once you've changed."

I closed the door behind me and went to my room. Early June was the perfect time for swimming at night. The water was warm, the air wasn't sweltering, and there was no risk of sunburn. Once I'd gotten my trunks on, I expected Masyn's door to be closed. To my surprise, it was open, the light was off, and Peyton's clothes were neatly folded in a pile on the bed with her heels on the floor. I continued down the hall and turned the corner into the kitchen, and my mouth fell open.

Not once, in all the times Masyn and I had gone swimming together, had I ever seen the bikini Peyton had on. Her back was to me, and the bottoms clung to her ass in an erotic temptation. I hadn't been checking her out at the church or at Sadler's. Standing behind her half-naked, I almost started to salivate. Just because my heart belonged to another woman didn't mean I was immune to beauty. It wasn't a thong, but it wasn't a brief, either. It was somewhere perfectly in between. Peyton's legs went on for miles, even though she wasn't overly tall, and her waist created perfect curves that flowed into her butt.

I leaned up against the refrigerator to admire the view for a moment or two longer, and my shoulder shifted against a piece of paper that caused a magnet to fall to the floor. Startled, she spun around, clutching her heart.

"Holy crap, you scared me." She took a couple of deep breaths and finally dropped her arms to her sides, exposing what little I had yet to see.

The front was as glorious as the back with even less material covering it. Masyn and I needed to talk about where this came from and who she'd been wearing it for at my house. I forced myself to look away when her nipples pebbled and her dark areolas showed through the white fabric. If that swimsuit did this to me when Peyton had it on, I'd never be able to hide my attraction to Masyn. Peyton was hot as sin, but even with her long hair now down in loose curls around her shoulders, she had nothing on Masyn.

Masyn—who was latched on to Toby Hayes. Fuck me.

I refused to dwell on that. I couldn't do anything about it tonight, and I wasn't going to try. I did make a mental note to put that swimsuit in my drawer after I washed it.

"You ready?"

"Should we grab towels before we got out?"

I walked toward the sliding glass door. "There's a box of them out on the patio."

Peyton didn't hesitate getting into the pool, although she didn't race to hide under the surface, either. She took her time testing the water with her toes, and then she walked down the stairs, and I dove in. When I resurfaced, she went under, and all I could think of when she stood up was Chevy Chase watching Nicolette Scorsese in the pool in *Christmas Vacation*. Peyton was a wet dream—literally.

Kicking under the water, I found my way to the steps, sat on the third one from the top and leaned back. She watched me as if she anticipated something. If she thought I would hit on her, it wasn't going to happen. Or maybe she was waiting for me to start a conversation. I wasn't good at this kind of thing. It was easy to talk to the women in Harden, because even if we weren't close, we all knew something about each other. I knew nothing about Peyton other than her sister was heinous.

"If you were in New York, what would you be doing right now?"

Her hands skimmed the top of the water, and she turned in a slow circle, creating a tiny ripple. "On a Saturday night, in New York...I'd probably be in my apartment reading a book in bed. If my roommate wasn't home, I might be reading while taking a bubble bath." She leaned her head back and looked up at the sky.

"Really?" I wasn't calling her a liar. I just found it hard to believe.

"Really. I'm not my sister, Lee. I don't date. I don't club. I have a handful of friends I'm close to, and we do stuff together during the day or after class." She stopped staring at the sky and met my eyes. "What? I'm a homebody." Her nervous giggle was sweet, and her apprehension was accentuated by her shoulders rounding inward with a shrug.

"I get it. I prefer my house to going out. Not that I won't go out or that I don't, because I do. Other than Sadler's, it's usually bonfires or cookouts at a friend's house. Low key."

She wasn't buying what I was selling, even though it was true.

"So, you have friends other than Beau and Masyn?" she teased.

"Yeah, I have other friends. As you pointed out, I know everyone in town. I'm pretty tight with Masyn's brothers, and Beau's, too. We're all like family."

"That's so foreign to me. I don't like my own family; I sure wouldn't want someone else's." She glided through the water on her stomach as she talked. The water lapping against the sides of the pool always seemed infinitely louder at night when there was no traffic on the street, or kids playing, or people mowing their grass.

"I don't think most families are like yours."

She flipped over onto her back and kicked her feet to move her body through the water in graceful, swanlike motions. "More are like mine than you'd think."

"Then you definitely need to move out of the city and find your tribe."

"I have a tribe. I don't have a village." She'd moved back into the shallow end of the pool less than three feet from me. Peyton stood, and the white bikini top left absolutely nothing to the imagination.

My dick stirred in my shorts. I hadn't thought this through. At all. "You want a beer? I don't have any wine." I needed a breather, and cold air would kill any chance of my admiral standing to salute.

"No, thanks. I need to be able to drive back to the hotel."

To keep from embarrassing myself, I turned around first, then I stood and pulled my shorts away from my body. They clung to me the same way that bikini did on Peyton's curves. Just as I'd predicted, once I got inside, the air-conditioning squashed any possibility of arousal. I stood in front of the open refrigerator for a couple of minutes longer than necessary to ensure I didn't lose the battle.

The knock on the front door startled me. With an open beer in hand, I went to see who was here this late at night. I sure as hell wasn't expecting Masyn to be on my porch.

I stood back so she could come in—she did not. "Why are you knocking?"

"I just stopped by to bring you your truck and keys." Masyn dropped them in my hand.

"So why not come in?"

She hitched her thumb over her shoulder toward the driveway. "You have company, and Toby's waiting for me."

I exhaled loudly and ran my free hand through my wet hair. "What are you doing, Masyn?"

"I told you."

Fine. If that was the game she wanted to play, far be it from me to argue. "I'll see you tomorrow then. I sent Ty a text while we were at Sadler's about working on your car."

"Sure. See you then." Masyn sucked at disguising her feelings. She didn't want to come in for fear of witnessing something she assumed was going on. And even worse, getting in the truck with Toby somehow held more appeal. She couldn't stand him.

"Don't try to prove a point by doing something stupid."

"See you later."

I grabbed her wrist and pulled her to my chest. She resisted until I wrapped my arms around her back. I was at a loss for words. There was no reason for her behavior. I hadn't done anything wrong—I hadn't done anything at all. Jealous Masyn wasn't anywhere near as attractive as the girl who claimed my guest room and demanded I make her omelets.

Toby honked the horn, and Masyn pulled away. "I gotta go."

"Masyn, so help me God, there's not a cop in town who'd go looking if Toby went missing."

"Got it, Dad." She stepped off the porch and started down the driveway.

"I'm serious. Don't test me," I called out after her.

She didn't respond. Instead, she threw up her hand and waved. And when she opened the passenger door, Toby leaned out from the driver's side with a smug grin on his ugly face.

"Hey, man." His need to stake his claim only served to piss me off. He'd no more have Masyn Porter naked in his bed than I would.

I flipped him off and went back inside. Douchebag.

I drained my beer before making it through the kitchen and then stopped to grab another one from the fridge. When I slid the glass door open, Peyton twisted in her seat on the edge of the pool to stare at me. A meek smile rose on her lips, yet it did nothing to wash away the sadness from her eyes.

"I was starting to think you weren't coming back."

With a few long strides, I joined her and dangled my feet in the water. "You thought I'd leave you out here alone? You must have some really dick friends."

"You were gone a long time just to get a beer."

"So you assumed I was abandoning you?" I laughed and gave her a quick side hug while drinking from the bottle in my other hand. "Not sure how people do things up north, but in the South, a guy never leaves a woman like that." I let her go and stretched my arm out behind her to lean back on my palm.

The crickets and the frogs provided the music for the evening, and Peyton kicked at the water to keep the gentle lapping of the waves going.

Her arms were locked behind her, and her shoulder nearly touched her ear when she turned to look at me. "I admit, I've never met anyone like you before, Lee."

"Not sure I know how to take that."

"Most people our age are uncertain of who they are. You not only seem to know, but you take pride in it."

"Plant firm roots."

"I don't follow."

"You ever seen a fig tree?"

"Probably, although I can't say for sure."

"Stay put. I'm going to go grab my phone." I took one step away and spun back. "I promise I'm not deserting you."

She giggled. "Got it."

I snatched another beer while I was inside. When I returned and sat next to her, I pulled up an image of the wild fig trees in South Africa near Echo Caves. "Looks like an ordinary fruit tree, right?" I was about to get all philosophical—not really my cup of tea, but this was one thing I firmly believed. I'd heard it years ago, and it had stuck with me.

"I suppose. I don't see a lot of those in the city."

"Point is, it doesn't look like anything great. I mean it's a big tree, but what you see above the surface isn't what makes that tree so different from any other. To anyone who doesn't have knowledge of just how special it is, it looks like any other tree."

She nodded, even though the confusion in her expression indicated she didn't have a clue where I was going with this.

"Roots. That's what makes it extraordinary."

Her brow quirked and her head tilted to the side.

"Most trees have root systems that spread out like a fan under the dirt." I talked with my hands to indicate what I meant. "To support the weight of the trunk and branches, the roots extend out past the diameter of the tree. And while they go out for dozens of feet, they're only a couple of feet deep. They can be the most beautiful trees you've ever seen, but if bad weather comes through, they're easy to uproot, and they die under the pressures of the storm."

I was losing her. The faraway gleam in her eyes and her furrowed brow indicated her confusion.

"The fig trees"—I held up my phone again to remind her which tree I was talking about—"may not be as pretty above ground where they're exposed to the storms and everyday weather, but you can't pull up something with roots that go four hundred feet below the surface. God plants us where we can grow deep roots. Unfortunately, most people are too busy pruning the bushes to water the soil." I shrugged and took a long draw from my beer.

She swallowed hard. "I've never stayed anywhere long enough to grow roots."

"Darlin', roots aren't about location. They're knowing who you are at the core. And that, is about your soul."

"I wouldn't have pictured you as the religious sort."

"That's because you're looking at the foliage and haven't had time to see the roots. The fig tree was a sermon that stuck with me in high school. But religion doesn't have to be Bible thumping and speaking in tongues."

I'd perched in a church pew every Sunday from the time I came into this world until I graduated; in middle school and high school, there wasn't much to do if you weren't involved in youth group. Yet even when I was doing stupid shit as a teenager, the roots had already taken hold and shaped who I was, refusing to let me sway too far—my dad made sure of that. It was important to him.

She swatted at my arm playfully. "I know that. I guess it's different, depending on how you were raised."

I finished the third beer I'd had since we got here. I needed to slow down. Between what I'd consumed at Sadler's and these, I felt pretty good. It wouldn't take much more before I'd need to call Masyn to babysit—and that wouldn't go well at all.

"I can't deny that. I can only tell you that at some point, you have to give up your hope for a better past, embrace your present, and change your future. Just because your roots aren't deep now doesn't mean they can't grow."

Peyton looked at me like I was the only person who'd ever told her she could have value; she just had to find it and harvest it. Her mind tried to protect her and tell her other people defined her worth even though her heart was winning the battle, wanting to believe me. It was a lot to read from facial expressions and body language, but I'd dealt with enough inse-cure women in my life to recognize the signs. And the few women I'd met from big cities were the worst—everything was a competition: their looks, weight, job, salary, house.

Foliage—not roots.

It was another one of those things that drew me to Masyn. Before tonight, I'd never seen the petty bullshit women pulled. She didn't try to be anything other than exactly who she was—and that wasn't a carbon copy of everyone else. Whether Masyn recognized it or not, she didn't try to blend in and be just like the next girl—her quiet confidence was one of her most attractive traits.

Something shifted in Peyton's eyes, a flash of fear I would have missed had I not been looking. She wasn't afraid of me; she was terrified of the ideas I'd planted. As they settled, they rocked her. "I should get going."

I didn't argue or try to convince her to stay. Instead, I helped her off the cement and grabbed her a towel even though she was mostly dry at this point. When I let her into the house, she scurried down the hall with her head down, not saying a word. I hung out in the kitchen, waiting for her with another beer in my hand. If Peyton was leaving, I was safe to collapse in my bed without worry.

She emerged a few minutes later, carrying her heels in one hand and the towel and Masyn's swimsuit in the other. I took the towel and bikini and tossed them into the laundry room.

I joined her in the foyer and opened the door. Peyton didn't walk through it immediately.

"Thanks for making today not so...awful."

I smirked. She was cute. "Anytime, darlin'. If you end up staying in town, let me know. I've gotta work, but I get off at three every day. Beau, Masyn, and I can entertain you while you're here if you're up for it."

She chewed on her lip, and then her tongue snuck out, swiping moisture over them in a perfect sheen to highlight their fullness. This was why the fourth beer was a bad idea. Apparently, I'd stared too long or given off a vibe I hadn't meant to. The next thing I knew, Peyton's hands were on my hips and her lips on mine. Everything about it felt good, yet nothing about it felt right.

I pulled away, worked up and breathless. "I can't." My Adam's apple bobbed when I swallowed hard. The knot in my throat almost choked me.

She'd misread a signal I hadn't tried to send, and now rejection colored her cheeks a rosy red. "Oh my gosh, I'm sorry. I don't know what I was thinking." If she could've found a place to hide, she would have.

"Don't be. You're a gorgeous girl—"

"You're just not interested," she muttered under her breath, defeated.

I grabbed the back of her neck and pulled her forehead to my lips where I placed a kissed. I took her chin in my fingers— still holding my beer at my side—and smiled. "Let me know when you're leaving town. I'd love to hang out, and I'm sure Masyn and Beau would, too." I wasn't quite as certain about Masyn, though I knew Beau, at any cost, would want to escape the hell of his parents' house. And it was my way of confirming she was correct.

I was only interested in her friendship.

EIGHT

"I HEAR YOU HAD AN EVENTFUL NIGHT." BEAU'S SHIT-eating grin had me concerned.

"No clue what you heard or who you heard it from. I went home."

"Yeah, with Peyton."

"You knew that. You watched me leave with her, moron."

Beau hadn't even let me get out of the truck at Ty's house before he bombarded me. As tempted as I was to accidentally shove the door into him when I hopped down, I refrained and glared instead.

"Yes, however, you didn't mention a night-time swimming excursion under the stars."

I slammed the door behind me. "You sound like a travel agent. Don't you have something other than me to worry about? Like a lawsuit."

"Yeah, that's being taken care of, and since I now have no life of my own, I'm interested in yours."

"Don't be. Nothing happened."

"There's a pissed-off brunette who disagrees." He nudged his head toward Ty's house where Masyn stood with her hands on her hips, glaring at me.

"Oh, that's rich. She's ticked? Did she mention who brought her by my house? Speaking of, why didn't you take her home?"

He shrugged. "She wanted to go with him."

"And you let her?"

Beau scoffed and scrunched the left side of his face. "I'm not her keeper."

"Any idea why she's mad?" We hadn't moved, and neither had Masyn.

I kept her in my line of sight without making eye contact. Her body language led me to believe she was on the verge of detonating, and I had no interest in being near her when it happened.

"I answered that last night."

"I meant, has she specifically told you what has her panties in a twist?"

Beau pulled a pack of gum out of his pocket and took a piece out. He began to unwrap the foil when I swatted the damn thing out of his hand. "Beau!"

His brow drew in with irritation. "Lee!"

"What good is it to have you as the go-between if you don't know anything?"

"Here's an idea. Man up and talk to her."

There was no way in hell I'd go within striking distance of Masyn Porter when she was angry with me. "I'd like to keep my balls another day." I chanced a front-facing glance, which I instantly regretted. "Not to mention, she went home with Toby. I don't know why we're standing in Ty's driveway talking about this. She's never cared what I did with any other girl. Peyton shouldn't be any different."

"Whatever, man. Your funeral." He bent down to pick up the piece of gum still securely tucked in the wrapper he hadn't gotten off before I'd knocked it to the ground. With the same devious grin he'd given me upon arrival, he popped it into his mouth and started chomping away.

"Maybe we should have let you marry Felicity after all. Chewing like that, you'll never get another date."

He laughed and turned toward the garage. I had no idea why he was in such a good mood. Maybe Beau was thrilled to be rid of the noose that had strangled him for the last few months...or he was enjoying watching me dance around Masyn —probably both.

"Hey, man." Masyn's oldest brother and I were close. We hadn't been as kids with a six-year age difference between us. It wasn't until I started working at Farley's that we spent any time together, and at that point, eighteen and twenty-four weren't all that different.

"What's up, Ty?" I extended my hand, which he took and pulled me into his chest in a cross-body embrace.

"Not much. Just working. And apparently bailing my sister out." Ty and Masyn had a love-hate relationship. He was protective as hell of his youngest sibling—he also didn't hesitate to tell her where to stick it. "Not what I had planned for Sunday." He griped about working on her car, yet if she'd taken it somewhere, he'd be pissed she wasted her money.

"Any idea what's wrong with it? With the tornado Beau brought into town, I haven't had a chance to look at it since we left it at the shop on Friday."

"Alternator."

"At least it's an easy fix."

"Yeah, I got the parts yesterday. There's beer in the fridge if you want to grab one. Donna put 'em in last night, so I'm sure they're cold." He glanced behind me at Beau. "You're welcome to grab one, too. You need me to get you some gloves, pretty boy?"

Ty loved to give Beau a hard time. Ty had always been well liked and quite popular. He'd played football in high school, and we lived in a town where football reigned and Ty was the king. Beau had been awkward and shy until junior year when puberty happened, and then so did the girls. Unlike Ty, Beau had never been a jock, he'd been preppy—Ty hadn't been a huge fan of sissies or preppy guys. Beau had been the exception—which probably had more to do with Masyn than Beau himself—and he'd enjoyed giving him a hard time.

"I'm not working on that thing. That's what mechanics are for." And comments like that did little to endear Beau to a blue-collar man, who happened to be a mechanic. Thankfully, Ty was immune to Beau and thought his cracks were jokes instead of cuts. "At what point does the car become so worthless that fixing it doesn't make sense?"

Ty threw a rag at Beau, who didn't even attempt to catch it, and in fact, watched it hit his chest and then fall to the ground before looking back up and staring at Ty in wonder. I shook my head. Beau was clueless, not cruel.

"When the owner can afford to replace it, and this one can't." Masyn huffed and stomped back into the house.

I hadn't realized she was in the garage listening to us. Any other time, she'd be under the hood with her brother, not inside chewing the fat with her sister-in-law.

"She's been in a shit mood since she got here. What the hell has her in an uproar?" Ty asked as he twisted the cap off a longneck.

"Lee." Beau had a death wish, and I might make his dreams come true.

I held my hands up, careful not to drop my beer. "Don't look at me. She left Sadler's last night with Toby Hayes."

Ty set his beer on the workbench and stepped to the door Masyn escaped through to yell, "Masyn, get your ass out here."

"Jesus, Ty. Leave her alone." I should have kept my damn mouth shut. I wasn't any better than Beau.

"Nah, fuck that. She doesn't need to be anywhere near that cum stain. And where the hell were you, Lee?"

The door burst open with a fiery Masyn blowing through it just as I said, "Since when is it my job to babysit?"

Without turning away from his sister, he answered me. "Kindergarten. Own it." Then he lit into her. "Why the hell would you be alone with Toby fucking Hayes—ever?"

She glared at *me*—not Beau—assuming I'd given Ty the insider information. I had, but that was beside the point. Beau could do no wrong. "I hate you, Lee."

"You do not. You're just mad that I was with Peyton. Next time one of our friends stands his bride up at the altar, I'll make sure to keep you around to handle phone calls and deal with nosy guests."

Beau raised his brow and stated flatly, "I didn't leave her at the altar."

"Dude, really?" I questioned, and he shrugged.

"Enough." Ty's voice carried without his having to scream. "I asked a question. I want an answer, Masyn. Why the hell were you with Toby Hayes?"

"It wasn't a big deal, Ty. He followed me to Lee's and then dropped me off at my house. He never even got out of the truck." She hated having to admit that in front of me. It should have made me happy, but all it did was tick me off even more.

"Stay away from him. He's trouble you don't need to get mixed up with."

"Whatever, Ty." She whipped around so fast her hair fanned out behind her, and then stomped inside and slammed the door.

"Are you going to help me or stand there with your dick in your hand?" Ty had a way with words.

"Yeah. Sorry." I turned back toward the car and listened while Ty explained what he wanted me to do. Really, I was his wrench monkey and nothing more. Working on Masyn's car gave us an excuse to hang out—he didn't need my help. He did this kind of thing day in and day out.

Beau pulled up a stool and watched.

"Did you really leave your girl at the church yesterday?" Ty laughed and kept his head under the hood.

"There's a bit more to it than that, but yes, that was the final result."

"I gotta give it to ya, Chastain, I didn't think you had it in you." Ty never took his focus off what he was doing. He extended his fist, waiting for Beau to reciprocate.

Beau looked confused at first and then like he'd won the lottery and been brought inside the inner circle. I shook my head. He was clueless. He helped form the inner circle because he was closely connected to Masyn.

"She cheat on ya? Women are trifling like that. Can't trust a damn one of them." He was full of shit.

Donna doted on his ass like he ran the world, and she was as loyal as a hound—not to mention easy on the eyes, even after two kids.

"Not that I know of." Beau gave him a brief history with more details about yesterday than the rest combined.

Ty stopped what he was doing when Beau got to the part about the church. I had been there, although I didn't have a clue what had happened inside the bathroom while I waited in the hall.

"She kept trying to deny it and make me feel like an ass for questioning her when she'd told me she was pregnant. As soon as she started crying, I knew Lee was right. I can't stand to see a woman cry. That bitch thought she had me by the balls. I held firm and refused to move away from the door until she peed in a cup."

"I don't get females. Why not just confess that you're full of shit instead of taking nine pregnancy tests that will only prove what a liar you are?" Ty leaned against the front of Masyn's car, waiting to hear the end.

It was too bad Beau didn't recognize that he had a captive audience, and Ty was the sole ticketholder. Ty liked Beau, but he didn't know how to relate to him—that didn't mean he didn't care about his sister's best friend.

"Got me. She didn't move. She watched me dip every single test in that cup. And each one that came back negative only lit my fire even brighter. I took all nine of the negative tests and told her there was one for every person in our families she'd hurt, and I was going to hand them out."

"Damn, the only decent thing to ever happen at a wedding and I missed it."

"She followed me down the hall begging me to let her explain." There was nothing to explain. "Then I left with Masyn, and Lee stayed at the church with Felicity's sister, Peyton, to make calls and deal with guests who showed up."

Ty lifted his head at me. "So, Peyton's the girl Masyn's been griping about with Donna all morning?"

I shrugged. I didn't know Masyn discussed Peyton. I did know I wouldn't get anywhere questioning Ty about his sister. He'd put his fist in my mouth before he gave away any of her secrets.

"Lee left Sadler's with Peyton last night. Masyn wasn't happy about it." Leave it to Beau to fill in the gaps so Ty could form his own opinion.

"She took me home. It wasn't a big deal."

"Yeah?" Ty wagged his brow.

"Jesus, you're as bad as Masyn. When she showed up last night, we were swimming. I have no idea what she believes took place, but I can assure you it wasn't the story she wants to make it out to be."

Ty appeared disappointed. "So you really didn't sleep with this chick?"

"Nope."

"Nothing?" Beau asked.

"I mean, she kissed me when she left."

Ty exchanged glances with Beau before calling bullshit. "There's no way you let a hot girl swim around in a bikini in your pool and didn't initiate anything."

"Why does everyone think I'm such a manwhore? *She* kissed *me*."

"So you pushed her away, right?" Ty mocked me, and Beau snickered with him—I ought to knock him off the stool and see who was laughing then.

"Basically."

"Yeah, right after you stuck your tongue down her throat, and she spread her legs." Ty was married with two kids under the age of three. It would surprise me to find out he wasn't getting the same kind of attention he had from Donna when they were making out under the bleachers in high school.

"Didn't happen."

Ty redirected his attention to the car. "You gonna see her again?"

"She doesn't even live here. I have no idea if she's already left town. We didn't discuss it." That wasn't exactly true, but giving these two the actual events would only spur this ridiculous conversation on instead of shutting it down.

"You should give her a call." Ty never made much sense—not when it came to advice and women.

In one breath, he'd tell me I was responsible for his sister, and in the next, that I needed to dip my stick in any oilcan whose cap I could get off. If he had any inkling of what I dreamed about doing to his sister, he'd draw and quarter me.

"I thought we were here to fix an alternator. Did I miss a memo?" I asked.

"Nah, I'm just fucking with you, Lee. Enjoy this shit while you can. Once you walk down that aisle or bring a kid into the world, the days of freedom are in the past."

Ty could say what he wanted about freedom and missing the past. There wasn't a woman on this planet he'd trade Donna for, and those kids were his world. He was a family man and always had been. As a kid, it was his siblings and parents. When he got married, the protective vibe shifted to Donna, although he still kept close tabs on Masyn—not that he needed to. She never did anything other than hang out with me.

When we—and I use that term loosely—finished the alternator and had Masyn's car running again, I tried to grab Beau and head out. I was afraid to go into the house and set Masyn off, but my stomach was screaming for food.

"You guys stay for lunch." Ty glanced at his watch. "Early dinner." It was later than any of us realized.

"I don't know. Masyn's pretty ticked, and the only way she's going to calm down is if I talk to her. That conversation doesn't need to happen here." I'd known her long enough to be certain she wouldn't open up in front of her brother, or anyone else.

Ty clapped me on the shoulder and ushered Beau and me inside. "Then Masyn can go home in her car, which is now running."

Donna was in the kitchen patting out hamburgers, and Masyn was beside her, working on what appeared to be the makings for potato salad—hard to say with her back to me. There were beans in a casserole dish with strips of bacon lining the top, biscuits on a pan, and corn on the cob wrapped in tinfoil, waiting to go into the oven. It wasn't a feast for kings, but in Harden, it was a damn-good way to end a weekend.

By the time dinner was ready, we'd all piled out on the back deck to eat with folding lawn chairs and paper plates. Ty lit some timber in the fire pit—nothing like more heat in the heart of June in Georgia. I'd spent more Sundays like this than doing anything else, and it was still one of my favorite things to do. The tension with Masyn died down, and she had even let me hug her from behind when she stood at the sink washing her hands. She hadn't let go of whatever was on her mind, though. She'd simply set it aside to enjoy the evening and not make a scene in front of Ty, who wouldn't let that shit go.

Donna stepped out on the porch from the kitchen and handed out bottles of beer, leaving the door open behind her. Just as she handed me one, I heard my phone ring in the kitchen.

I had my plate in my lap, and I tried to get up without dumping it onto the porch. "That's mine."

"Sit. I'll grab it."

Donna tossed it to me on the third ring. I had a split second to make the decision about answering it—and I made the wrong choice.

"Hello?" I said around a mouthful of food.

"Hey. Are you busy?" Peyton sounded upbeat.

"Just sitting over at Ty's house eating dinner. What's up?" Maybe if I played it cool and acted like it was anyone other than Peyton, no one would be the wiser.

"I hope you don't mind me calling."

"Nah, not at all."

"My parents left with my sister this morning. And I got tasked with cleaning up the mess with vendors and guests. You said to let you know if I was going to be around longer, so I thought I'd see if you wanted to hang out this week. My flight doesn't leave until Friday afternoon. If not, it's no big deal."

I avoided making eye contact with anyone, yet I could still feel each gaze intently focused on me. "Yeah, absolutely. I don't get off until three. Five, maybe?"

"Let me know where. I'll see you then."

"Bye."

I didn't look up. It was as though the world stopped spinning while that call took place. We were outside in the country, and you could hear a damn pin drop with two toddlers running around a few feet away. I took a bite of my corn, hoping everyone would resume their conversations and forget about me. They did not.

"Who was that, Lee?" Beau was determined to use all of his nine lives in one day, and his mocking tone made me feel like we were back in third grade, except then it was him getting teased, not me.

"Peyton," I mumbled, and hoped no one understood.

"Oh yeah, you two are going to hang out, huh?"

I glared at him, and Ty snickered beside me. Beau's eyes danced with amusement. Masyn's did not. She wasn't a crier, never had been. When we were nine, she broke her arm jumping off a rope swing. The break was so bad, the bone cut through the skin—not a single tear shed. Now her eyes were tinged with emotion. Before she let anyone witness it, she stood and walked inside. I watched through the glass in the door as she dumped her plate in the trash. Then she grabbed her keys off the counter.

Shit.

"Masyn!" I hollered from the porch. "Fuck. Sorry." I scrambled over people's legs and feet to get inside and stop her, spilling food on the porch in the process. "I'll be right back to clean it up."

I raced inside and flung the front door open just as she pulled out of the driveway. The sun was setting, and the sky was dusky-dark as I watched her taillights disappear down the road. Instead of grabbing my keys to go after her, I waited to see if she'd turn around. Once she was out of sight, I spun and slammed my fist into the steel front door, breaking open the skin on my knuckles.

"Damn it!" I yelled to no one in particular, although I was quite certain everyone heard me out back. My chest heaved as I took several deep breaths and paced in circles, trying to calm down. I had to go back to the group, but I just wasn't in the frame of mind to do it yet. It took punching the door again, yanking on my hair, and practicing Lamaze to regain my composure.

Finally, I threw my hands up in defeat and went inside. Even though Donna beat me to it, I snagged some paper towels on my way through the kitchen to clean up the mess I'd made in my hasty exit. "I would've gotten that, D."

She shrugged one shoulder. "I know. I don't mind. Everything okay?"

"Dude, I could have told you how horribly wrong that was going to go." Beau shook his head and got up to throw his plate away. He didn't close the door when he stepped inside and

called back to Donna, "Another great meal, D. Thank you."
And then he rejoined us with a fresh beer in hand.

"Thanks, Beau. I'm not sure how I've survived with you
away at school. You really should come home more often."
With that, I snatched the beer from his hand, tossed it back,
and guzzled down the cold, burning brew.

NINE

I'D SEARCHED FOR MASYN AFTER I LEFT TY'S HOUSE LAST night. Every place I could think of that she might be was a miss. No one had seen her, and she hadn't gone home—I dreaded hearing what rumors got stirred up about my frantic search for her. It was too much to hope that she'd gone to my house to wait for me to show up. I gave up around eleven, knowing I'd see her in the morning at work, although trying to sleep was as fruitless as my search for Masyn. I tossed and turned all night worrying about her. In all the years I'd known her, I'd never seen her act like this about anything. She went with the flow, regardless of who was involved—the more, the merrier. For the life of me, I couldn't figure out what her aversion to Peyton was. There was no way she was jealous, and I refused to believe Beau's theory might hold water, because if it were true, then I had bigger fish to fry than Peyton Holstein.

The time clock glowed when I punched in a little before six. My shift didn't start for another hour. I just couldn't stand another sixty minutes of pacing around my house. She hadn't read or responded to any of my messages, nor had she answered my calls. It didn't take a rocket scientist to see that I was frantic, but she hadn't put an end to my suffering. The earlier I got to work, the more time I'd have to corner her before we had to actually do something. There was no way she could avoid talking to me here unless she called in sick, which she never did. Yet sitting here, time kept ticking away with no sign of her.

"Hey, Farley. You heard from Masyn?" I asked the owner's son as he walked through the breakroom.

"Nah, why?"

"She's not here yet. Just wondering if she called in sick."

"There'd have to be a world war or zombie apocalypse for her not to show up." He poured a cup of coffee and then faced me. "Shouldn't you know where she is?"

Why the hell does everyone think I know her every move? "What's that supposed to mean?"

He shook his head and held up his hand, spilling his coffee down his arm. "Shit. That's hot." He wiped his arm on his shirt. "It doesn't mean anything other than you two are attached at the hip."

That didn't warrant a response. "If you hear from her, can you let me know?"

His skeptical expression made me think he was going to probe; thankfully, he didn't. A few minutes later, he poked his head in the door. "Hey, Lee. Masyn's here."

She came into view, meaning she'd been next to him, clocking in when he loudly announced her arrival. I jumped up to follow her and pushed him out of the way. "Masyn."

She stopped dead in her tracks and her back stiffened. She

held her fists in tight balls at her sides. It didn't take me long to catch up to her and step around her.

"What's up, Lee?" Her indifference was nothing more than an act, but it stung all the same.

"What's going on?"

"I'm trying to get to work. What's going on with you?" She folded her arms across her chest and squared her shoulders. There wasn't a hint of amusement or happiness in her expression, and her eyes were sad—dull. None of the color I liked to pick apart from the brown was there to see.

"Where'd you go last night?"

"The dock."

"You drove all the way out to Lake Martin?" No wonder I'd never found her. It was a hike from town to the water, not to mention pitch black at night. It wasn't a commercial marina, just some rickety old wood we'd been going to since we could drive.

"Yep." She offered no explanation for why or how long she'd stayed.

"I don't understand why you're so upset with me. What have I done?" I needed to lower my voice.

Other guys in the shop stared at the two of us lingering in the walkway. I didn't do drama, and I sure as hell didn't do it in public. I wasn't interested in people knowing my business. It was hard enough to keep things to yourself in Harden as it was.

She'd yet to uncross her arms, and her stare was so ice-cold, a chill ran up my spine. "I don't know why you'd think you've done anything." Her brows arched waiting for my response.

"Break it up, you two. The metal isn't going to turn itself," Farley squawked at us.

Nothing was going to be resolved standing here. And getting written up would only further irritate her. "We're not done, Masyn." I started to back off toward my station, still holding her attention.

I could have choked her when she rolled her eyes and shrugged just before she pivoted on the ball of her foot and stomped off. Her inability—or rather refusal—to act like an adult was uncharacteristic and sent me careening into immaturity with her. If we'd been in a sandbox, I would have hurled a handful of dirt at her. Too bad we weren't five anymore—that sounded rather cathartic.

Masyn managed to avoid me all day. Even at lunch, she ate in her car. It took a hell of a lot of restraint not to go out there and beat on the window to force her to talk. All it would do is rile up the guys in the shop, and listening to their ribbing for the remainder of the afternoon wouldn't help my mood any.

At quitting time, she was the first to punch out, and then she practically sprinted to her car and sped into the street. Just in time, I burst out into the parking lot, shielding my eyes from the sun, and watched her peel out. It was hot as hell, and I was standing there sweating like a whore in church. A couple of the guys clapped my shoulder as they left, yet I didn't move. Masyn was long gone, and I hadn't budged.

The lot was empty when I finally got in the truck to drive home. I didn't have a clue what Peyton had in mind; I just knew I couldn't do it in Dickies covered in grease. A shower was my top priority, and it couldn't come soon enough. When I looked over my shoulder and backed out, I caught a whiff of myself and it was pungent. No one ever accused me of not putting in a hard day's work—but I didn't need to smell like it when I wasn't at the shop.

Beau's BMW sat in my driveway when I pulled up. He leaned against the hood with his cellphone in his hand. I wondered if he'd ever considered having it surgically attached to his palm.

"Hey, man. What are you doing here?"

"Other than arguing with Felicity? Nothing much. Didn't have much going on, so I thought I'd stop by and see what you were up to."

"Supposed to get together with Peyton, although you already knew that."

He tried to act surprised and failed miserably. "Oh yeah, I forgot." Liar. "What are you two doing?"

"No clue. You're welcome to tag along." I walked by him and opened the front door.

"Remind me why you lock this place up..."

We lived in a small town where crime was non-existent. This was the type of town where neighbors shot people for being in places they weren't supposed to be, and then asked questions afterward. There was no threat to my house or my belongings; I just didn't feel the need to encourage uninvited visitors. "Are you still talking?"

He bounced around like he was amped up on something, but Beau had never done an illegal thing in his life. This was his natural exuberance. Felicity had kept him so bogged down that I hadn't seen him this light in years. "So what are we doing? Masyn coming?"

Talking as I walked, Beau followed me around the house. I stripped my shirt off on my way to the laundry room and tossed it into the basket when I got there. He continued rambling behind me. And when I started to unbutton my pants, I faced him. "Dude. You mind?" And I motioned toward my pants.

"No, go ahead." And then he stood there yapping while I stripped my filthy pants off and added them to the basket with my shirt. "We could take the boat out. There's still plenty of daylight."

I wore nothing but boxers, yet weirdly enough, Beau continued to trail after me like a lost dog. There was no way I was letting him into the bathroom.

"It is already in the slip? Or would I have to go get it from your parents' house?" I had no desire to tow, or return, the Queen Mary forty-five minutes down the road. The Chastains' large deck boat was fun to play around on; it was not fun to transport. It was as hard on my transmission as it was on my brakes, neither of which I had an interest in replacing.

"It's there. My dad and I moved it this morning."

I kept forgetting Beau had nowhere to be, and obviously nothing to do. "How long have you been hanging around outside waiting for me to get here?" I stopped at the door to my bedroom and whirled around to confront him.

After a quick shrug, he stared at me like I'd shot his favorite coon dog. "I dunno. Since I got back to my parents' house." Beau tried to put on a good front. He'd maintained his happy composure and had nothing good to say about Felicity, yet there was no way he couldn't be hurting on some level—even if it was just the betrayal of being lied to and manipulated. "I know you have a life that doesn't really include me on a daily basis. I just need to stay busy until I get back to mine. A week alone might send me over the edge."

"No worries. The lake sounds like a plan, and based on what little I learned about Peyton, it will probably be a new experience for her. While I shower, can you pack a cooler, grab some towels, and find the most unappealing swimsuit Masyn has here?"

"On it."

When I was able to escape to the shower without an audience, I let out a breath I hadn't realized I was holding. I walked on eggshells everywhere I went. I hated not being comfortable in my own home. One best friend needed his hand held while he moved through canceling a wedding, and the other avoided me like the plague and harbored some hatred for a woman she knew nothing about. The whiplash of the last two days had already started to take its toll.

Before I jumped in the shower, I grabbed my cell and sent Peyton a text.

Me: Beau and I thought the lake would be fun. His parents have a boat there.

Peyton: Sounds great.

Me: Text me which hotel you're at. We'll pick you up in about an hour.

I didn't wait for her response. The shower and I needed to become one, and I hoped the hot water beating down on my shoulders and back would release some of the tension I carried. It didn't completely eliminate it, although it definitely helped. A couple of hours in the sun and as many beers should finish the job.

Once I had on trunks and a T-shirt, I slid on a pair of flip-flops. Peyton's hotel wasn't far from the church, so it would only take a few minutes to get there. I hesitated to call Masyn about joining us, but I didn't want to create a greater divide by excluding her. My attempt was pointless. She didn't answer, nor did she read my text, although, I guess it was possible she'd turned off her read message receipts. Masyn was lucky we'd been friends for so long. I didn't put forth this much effort for any woman.

Beau knocked on my door. "You ready? I got everything in the truck."

I swung the door open to let him in while I grabbed my keys and phone. "Did you find a swimsuit?"

"For Peyton?"

I nodded and prayed Masyn had some hideous thing I'd forgotten was in the drawer.

"Yeah, although I doubt it's what you're hoping for."

"Two-piece?" I questioned.

"Yeah. Why does it matter? No guy in their right mind would encourage a woman to wear more on the water, or hell, anywhere for that matter."

I glared at him like he was an idiot. He *was* an idiot. We didn't have heart-to-hearts about me drawing our initials and flowers around Masyn's name on napkins at the bar, but that didn't mean he didn't know what I hadn't confessed. He just chose to ignore it because Masyn did—salt in an open wound kind of thing.

"I'm surprised you'd want to see your ex-fiancée's sister half-naked and wet. Isn't that incestuous in some twisted way?"

"Gross. I don't have any intention of touching her. That doesn't mean I can't enjoy the view. God gave us beauty to admire."

"Beauty, lust—it's all the same thing, right?"

"Potato patato."

"I tried to call Masyn to see if she wanted to go."

"No answer?"

"Nope. You talked to her?"

"Briefly. She pretty much blew me off." Beau didn't talk to Masyn daily or spend time with her on a regular basis. Since he'd left for college, he hadn't been home much during the school years, and since both of us worked during the summer, we only saw him on weekends. Her blowing him off wasn't the same wound as it was to me.

There was no point in interrogating him. Even if he had any knowledge, he wouldn't violate her confidence and share anything he knew. Over the years, there were times those trusts caused rifts in our friendships until we were old enough to value the worth of the secrets. This was one of those times I wanted to revert back to high school and pitch a fit and insist he could end this crap with Masyn if he would tell me what her problem was. Although he'd say he already had, I just didn't believe it.

Peyton was standing outside the hotel when we pulled up. Beau crawled into the back seat to allow her to sit up front.

As soon as she climbed up, I laughed and said, "You're going to bake your brains out in that outfit. Do you want to go change?"

Her pale-blue eyes drifted down her blouse to her jeans. I hadn't even noticed the heels until I followed her eyes. She sighed and angled her body in the seat so she could talk to me and Beau at the same time. "I don't have anything else with me. I didn't exactly come to Georgia prepared to bask in the sun for a week." Peyton must have thought she'd said something inappropriate. "Sorry, Beau. I didn't mean that the way it came out."

"No offense taken."

I'd offer her Masyn's crap back at my house except that Peyton had a solid six inches on her and probably twenty pounds. They were both thin; Masyn was just tiny.

"Lee had me grab a swimsuit for you. We could swing by my parents' house. I'm sure my mom has a T-shirt and some shorts that would work."

With that settled, we made a pit stop at the Chastains' so Peyton could change, and we were at the lake an hour later. Walking down the dock, Beau and I knew where we were going, but Peyton was unsure. It wasn't that she didn't know which boat was Beau's; there was a hint of green tinting her cheeks.

I stopped and took the bag she was carrying with the towels in it. "Do you get seasick?"

"I never have before, although I've never been on a lake, only the ocean."

"In a small boat?"

The grimace pulling at her lips answered that question. Yachts and cruise ships felt like being on land, even with rough water.

"We can go home? We don't have to stay if you think you're going to get sick." I'd be irritated as all hell, but I'd do it. I didn't get sick on the water because of the motion, but I'd been sick on a boat plenty of times because I'd drunk too much in the sun—it was fucking miserable.

"No." She waved me off as though my suggestion were silly.

"I'm sure I'll be fine once we start moving. I think it's the swaying of the dock."

I hoped she was right. I shifted the stuff in my hands to keep from dropping it and jerked my head in the direction of Beau who'd long since left us behind. "Come on, the quicker we get on the water, the faster the breeze will be blowing in your face. The heat doesn't help."

Beau, Masyn, and I used to come out here all the time with Bodie and Braden. We spent hours racing around the lake on inner tubes and water skis. After high school, Bodie and Braden took over, and we joined them less often until we were down to once or twice a summer. This was one of those places in my mind that held the answers to all the world's problems—there was nothing that couldn't be fixed or made better on this lake. There wasn't a single bad memory here. Every one of them was good and made me long for a time when life was less crowded with responsibility. And even though we'd had dozens of other girls on the boat with us at different times over the years, Masyn not being here today seemed off.

Peyton put on a brave face and forced a smile as Beau helped her onto the deck. I dropped the bag and small cooler onto the floor of the boat and hopped in. Normally, I sat in the seat next to Beau while he drove—his boat, he was captain—but since Peyton situated herself up front, I joined her. When Beau started the engine, she chewed on her lip and grabbed the seat cushion and edge of the boat as soon as we started moving.

I tried to mask my humor, although I did a shitty job. "Once we get through the no-wake zone, he'll pick up speed."

"Was that meant to comfort me?" She might choke on her nervous laughter.

I pointed to the very front of the boat, currently sitting high in the water. "When we're moving faster, the front will come down, so we're sitting flat on the water. You'll be able to see where we're going—so yes, it was meant to comfort you. You can feel every bump when the water is choppy and the boat is moving slow. At faster speeds, the boat doesn't hit the waves the same way—it cuts through them instead of fighting against them."

Peyton nodded to get me to shut up. Her knuckles were white, and her thighs flexed from where she'd pushed her feet into the carpet on the deck trying to keep herself from moving. I shifted over next to her and pried her hand off the rail. She clutched my fingers, terrified. I had to give her credit—she didn't complain and didn't puss out. Peyton was bound and determined to hang with us. I didn't have a clue if she was really that bored sitting at the hotel or if she was trying to push her own envelope and experience something she didn't have the chance to do in her world of high-priced purses and aged wine.

As I predicted, the boat reached the main channel. Beau hit about sixty miles per hour and leveled out the bow, and Peyton turned her face toward the sun and the breeze. Just as a genuine smile graced her lips, she jerked back and slapped a hand to her face.

"Oh my God, what was that? It felt like a bullet hitting my nose."

I wasn't sure how Beau could even hear what she said over the noise of the engine; all I saw was him snicker and put his sunglasses on.

"Bug."

Her features contorted into an expression that was worthy of film. If I'd had a camera, I would've taken a picture. "That's so gross."

"That's why we usually sit in the back."

She swatted at me playfully and wiped at the spot on her nose where the bug had made his suicide mission. "You could've told me."

"Not much fun in that. There's only one way to learn—and that's to do."

It didn't take Peyton long to get comfortable enough to move around. I pulled off my T-shirt and threw it in the bag with the towels, and Beau followed shortly after. Even this late in the afternoon, June sun in Georgia could be brutal, and if it didn't get you, then the humidity would. She suffered in clothes for a hell of a lot longer than I could have stood it.

Then suddenly, she swayed and got to her feet. "Okay. That's it. I'm done."

I had no idea what she was talking about, and Beau shrugged and kept driving. He could navigate this lake with his eyes closed, so the distraction of Peyton stripping out of the shorts and T-shirt Mrs. Chastain had provided didn't deter him.

"What's wrong? Another bug?" I chuckled, grabbed a beer from the cooler, and tossed one to Beau.

"No! Sweat just ran down my back."

"Sorry, darlin'. There's no AC on the lake."

"It *never* gets this hot in New York. How do you take it? I feel like I just got out of a sauna."

"We get in."

Beau pulled into a cove where all the locals frequented, cut the engine, and drifted in. There wasn't a lot of traffic to contend with on a Monday afternoon. People were either still at work or had been here all weekend and had taken the day off. I loved coming out here during the week when it wasn't as crowded.

Peyton sat in awe as she stared at the scenery in front of her. The cove was cut out and had high sides that provided shade, along with the trees that topped them. There was a bit of a waterfall that landed on flat rocks people used to slide into the lake. I hadn't seen anyone jump off the rope swing yet, but it was up there, too—you just had to hike to get to it. That freefall was worth every step up the steep bank.

Beau tossed out the anchor and then the ladder. Standing on the bow, he glanced back. "You guys coming?"

"How do we get there?" Peyton's confusion was actually rather charming.

Beau's brow furrowed with his answer. "Swim." And he dove off the front and resurfaced a few feet farther out.

"In a lake?" she nearly screeched.

"What's different about swimming in a lake or an ocean? At least in a lake, you don't end up sticky and covered in salt. Come on."

Hesitantly, she joined me at the same place Beau had jumped off. "I'm not diving. I don't want to hit my head."

"It's over a hundred feet deep, but suit yourself." I grabbed her hand and pulled her off with me, not giving her a chance to object.

When she came out of the water, she looked a bit like a drowned rat, until a stunning smile took over. Yeah, she liked it. At the shore, Beau was making his second trip up the rocks and begged her to come with him. Hand in hand, they climbed the slippery slope while I waited at the bottom. It was like watching a kid on a sled in the snow for the first time. Fear when she first started sliding was quickly replaced with excitement. The two of them screamed like girls on a roller coaster the whole way down. I waded from the water, sat in the sand, and watched. I hadn't seen Beau this happy since the summer after our senior year. And I didn't know Peyton well enough to make much of a guess, although I'd wager to say, she was letting loose and loving it.

"Beau, you wanna go up to the swing?"

He turned to Peyton. "You going to be all right down here? You can keep sliding."

"Why can't I go to the swing?" She'd gotten brave—or didn't have a clue what we were talking about, which was more likely.

"You're welcome to go." I pointed up the side of the hill to the red bandana tied to the knot on the end of the rope. "That's it up there."

"I'm game." Zero hesitation.

"You're not afraid of heights?"

She laughed and shrugged me off. "No one's afraid of heights, Lee. They're afraid of the fall."

Well, all right then.

My thighs burned after the fourth trip up, and my biceps ached from holding my weight until the rope reached its full length and I twisted myself off and swung into the air. I gave up after five turns, but I lost count how many times Peyton made the trip. It was like she was born for this. I wondered if she'd been planted in a place she couldn't thrive—maybe Harden was where she needed to put down roots. She and Beau had latched on to each other with quick camaraderie. He looked at Peyton the way he should have looked at Felicity. I didn't even want to think about the hornets' nest that match would create. Either way, seeing him happy was a hell of a lot better than the way I'd found him on Saturday morning.

As the sun started to dip, I hollered to Beau that we needed to head out. Even as far away as they were, the disappointment on her face was evident. He said something to her that I couldn't hear and it caused her to smile and take one last jump. Beau followed.

I climbed the ladder on the side of the boat first and tossed towels to Beau as they got in. He caught the first one, wrapped it around Peyton's shoulders, and then grabbed the second one for himself.

"You want to drive back, Lee?" The only times Beau had ever offered to let me drive were when he was so drunk he couldn't stop puking over the side, and when he broke his nose on the rocks sliding down head first. His eyes had swollen up so fast, we really would have had to test the theory about him navigating blindfolded.

The keys were already in the ignition when I took the wheel. Beau and Peyton sat up front—clearly, she hadn't learned her lesson about bugs, because they didn't vanish with the setting of the sun. I drove back to the marina, we hosed off the boat and replaced the cover, and then we threw away our trash. When the two of them scrambled to get in the back seat, that was where I drew the line.

"Hell no. One of you needs to get your ass up front. I'm not a damn chauffeur."

Peyton blushed, and Beau's splotches made an appearance. These two were perfect for each other—even their skin matched.

"I'm starved. Do you two want to grab dinner when we get back to Harden?" The expression on Beau's face was pitifully filled with hope when he stared at me and then into the back seat at Peyton.

I could have answered for Peyton. If she didn't eat with us, then she had to eat alone. And as much as I liked her, I didn't think leaving the two of them together was a great idea. There was no telling where Beau's head was—if it was in his pants, he needed to think hard about where that might lead in the long run. If it were on his neck, he still needed to think about the consequences of what a relationship of any kind with Peyton Holstein would be like. Therefore, by default, I had gone from chauffeur to chaperone.

TEN

It was after eight when we got back to Harden, and the dinner crowd had died down, not that there was much of one in this town. Most of the places to eat were fast food, and the few real restaurants only opened on weekends. I pulled into the parking lot of Starla's Diner, better known as *the* Diner to the locals. I didn't have a clue where the name came from since there was no Starla that I was aware of, and since there wasn't another diner in town, no one used the actual name to reference it.

"This place is so quaint." Peyton grinned from ear to ear when she saw the fifties décor. It wasn't intended to be retro; the place was just old.

I led them to a booth in the back and slid in. Peyton took the other side, and Beau sat next to her with a dopey grin. I kicked him under the table to quietly tell him to knock that shit off. He took it upon himself to wail like a dog at a full moon.

"What the hell, Lee? That hurt."

"Sorry, my foot slipped." He knew me well enough to decipher the warning written on my face.

If he didn't want people to think he was the one who'd been shady in the whole wedding snafu, he needed to keep his schoolgirl crush on the down-low. That was a quick way to destroy his reputation in this town. As it stood, Beau Chastain hung the moon, but it wouldn't take much to bring that glass house crashing down where he was no longer the victim.

"What kind of food do they serve here?" Peyton's blue eyes shone with curiosity. I imagined it was how I'd approach everything if I were suddenly thrown into New York City.

"Meat and three."

She stared at me, perplexed. "I'm sorry, what?"

Beau pulled the menu out of the holder next to the wall to explain the process of picking a protein and sides. Laughter tickled my tongue, listening to him make suggestions about which of the lower calorie foods were worth eating. Really, none of this crap was low-cal or diet friendly. It was all laced with fatback and grease; that's what made it good.

"What are you laughing about?" Beau rolled his eyes, proving how perturbed he was that I'd interrupted his game. He had no game; I wondered how he'd ever gotten a date, much less a fiancée.

Ignoring his evil stare, I focused on the girl sitting across the booth. "Peyton, there's nothing on the menu that won't taste good. There's also nothing on the menu that won't destroy a diet. Get what you want and regret it tomorrow."

"Hey, guys." Verna shuffled over from another table without taking her eyes off her order pad. The second she did, she caught sight of Beau and about knocked him over pulling him out of the booth. "Oh my gosh, Beau! I heard you were in town and wondered if I'd get to see you." Her Southern accent became more prominent with her excitement. She hugged him tightly and swayed from side to side.

Beau's eyes pleaded for me to save him, but I just shook my head and grinned.

"I'm sorry to hear about...you know." She didn't say, "bless your heart," even though it was written all over her face. Women in the South used that phrase to describe a range of emotions, and I'd always found it humorous.

Had a bad day? Bless your heart. Built an orphanage for homeless children? Bless your heart. Won the lottery? Bless your heart. It was as versatile as the word fuck and could literally mean the same thing, depending on the inflection used to say it.

"It's good to see you too, Verna." He managed to break free from her grasp and returned to his seat next to Peyton. "Oh, Verna, this is Peyton Holstein. She's in town for a few days from New York."

"Did you fly in for the wedding, too? There've been a ton of new faces in here the last couple of days. It's been crazy busy, but the tips are awesome, so I can't complain." Verna was a bit of a talker. She'd also dated Bodie somewhere along the way—which his parents hated, and also why he'd kept her around.

"Sister of the bride," Peyton confirmed.

"Yikes. What are you doing with the likes of these two?" She chewed her gum with ladylike grace and cocked her hip to the side. When she tucked her pen behind her ear, we were in trouble.

"Trying to eat dinner," I answered for her. Peyton was in over her head with this one. "You mind if we order?"

She reached up to grab the pen and brought her pad up to write. "Of course not, sugar. What'll it be?" Verna wasn't easily offended, and she'd dealt with my clipped tongue for years.

"Roast beef, mashed potatoes, green beans, and cabbage. Roll, no cornbread, and extra gravy on the meat and potatoes. And tea."

"Got it. What about you, Beau?"

"Hamburger steak, mac and cheese, peas, and blueberry cobbler. Roll. And Coke."

"Peyton?" Verna wrote furiously with the pad about three inches from her face.

"Fried chicken, mashed potatoes, fried okra, and creamed corn. Cornbread. And tea." She tucked the menu into the holder. "Oh, and can I get a side of gravy?"

"Sure thing." Verna chomped her gum with her mouth wide open a couple more times and then left to place our order with the grill.

My mouth hung open in shock. I couldn't believe what I'd just heard.

Peyton chuckled, it wasn't a laugh so much as humor coming out at the same time she asked, "What? I like to eat."

We didn't see much of that around here. Far be it from me to judge. If Peyton could pack away that kind of food and stay as thin as she was, more power to her. I was a fan of girls with an appetite. "Me too." The only other female I'd seen order that way was Masyn, although she never finished what she ordered and would scoot the leftovers across the table for me.

"Don't get all mopey." Beau needed to keep his mouth shut.

It didn't matter that he could read my thoughts and knew they'd turned to Masyn; that wasn't a topic open for discussion with Peyton around.

"I don't mope."

"What would you be moping about? Dinner?" she asked, her eyes darting back and forth between the two of us.

I wasn't interested in dissecting this shit, much less in public. "Nothing. Can we drop it?"

I'd never been so happy to see Verna deliver three drinks. She passed out silverware, napkins, and straws, and broke up the discussion we didn't need to have. Peyton grabbed a straw, unwrapped it, and stuck it in her tea.

She coughed into her hand, nearly choking. "Holy crap."

"What's wrong?" Beau patted her on the back, and again, I nudged him—lighter this time—under the table. "Damn, Lee. Would you quit?" And he went back to playing nursemaid.

"I didn't realize it would be sweet. Is there actually any tea in there?"

"If you wanted unsweet, why didn't you tell her?" Beau appeared to have a ton of experience with damsels in distress. He never skipped a beat when he softened his tone and filled it with concern. If anyone we knew witnessed this, he'd have his man card permanently revoked.

"I didn't know I had to. You have to ask for sweet tea up north. It's not automatically served."

I got up, fetched her a glass of unsweetened tea, and took the one she had. This place had the best tea in town. I had no problem swigging it down.

Verna delivered our food shortly after the gagging incident, and again, she wanted to launch into conversation. My patience wore thin, and I tried my best to ignore her. I never understood waitresses who thought people came to restaurants with friends only to ham it up with the person serving the meal. Verna was sweet; I just didn't want to talk to her while my food got cold.

"Where's Masyn? I didn't think you two ever did anything without the other." Her question was directed at me.

It dawned on me, since the two of us were always together, that no one had ever mentioned it. Now that Masyn had been MIA for a couple of days, everyone looked to me for her where-abouts. Any other time, it wouldn't have gotten under my skin, but knowing Masyn was avoiding me made every inquiry painful.

I had a mouthful of food—because I came here to eat—so I didn't answer. And before I swallowed, Verna got called away by another table and lost interest in pulling gossip from our table.

Peyton poked at her okra with her fork and dipped it in the bowl of gravy she'd requested. "Where *is* Masyn, Lee?"

I shrugged, still eating.

"He hasn't seen her since she showed up at his house on Saturday while you guys were swimming."

"Not true." I washed down my food with some of the amazing sweet tea Peyton had refused. "I saw her at work today."

"Fine. If you want to split hairs, Lee hasn't talked to her."

"I *did* talk to her. She ignored me. Why are we having this conversation?"

"Aww, she was so sweet on Friday night at the rehearsal

dinner. We should all do something tomorrow when you two get off."

I stopped chewing. Beau put his fork down. And we both gawked at her without saying a word.

"What? I really liked her. I'm only in town a couple more days. It'd be nice to have company while I'm here. There's only so much I can do in a hotel room to entertain myself." Peyton picked at her food and studied her plate, but she didn't put anything in her mouth.

"I can hang out with you," Beau volunteered entirely too quickly. He might as well hang a sign around his neck that said "Newly single and desperate for attention and human interaction." He swallowed the bite he'd taken and then retracted and modified his previous proclamation. "Well, I have to go to the lawyer's office during the day tomorrow, and my mom wants me to start sending back wedding gifts. But I should be free by mid-afternoon."

I gave it one last try under the table to reel him in.

"Jesus Christ, Lee. What?" The entire restaurant stopped to stare at him. He lowered his voice and made another attempt. "Why the hell do you keep kicking me?"

"Am I missing something?" Poor Peyton. None of this was her fault, but if either of us told her what was going on, she'd feel like it was.

"No," I answered in an attempt to keep Beau's mouth closed.

"Masyn has her panties all wadded up," Beau declared.

Well, it had been worth a shot—too bad Beau was so daft. I wondered if all pretty girls gave him diarrhea of the mouth or just the Holsteins.

"About what?" Her words were inquisitive, not prying. Peyton wasn't interested in the gossip around Harden; she actually liked us and wanted to be a part of whatever was going on while she was here.

This place generally bustled with people, timers went off, conversations took place all around us—not tonight. It was eerily quiet, even though there were customers everywhere. It was like they all waited for the latest bit of tabloid smut.

I tossed my fork on the plastic plate with a clatter, fisted my hands, and leaned on my forearms. I nearly growled at him when I tried to keep my voice low enough that everyone in town wouldn't hear what I said. "Damn it, Beau. Can't you keep your mouth shut? My life is not an open book waiting to be read."

"What? Peyton asked."

"Now I'm certain I've missed something." Peyton had indeed missed something...nearly two decades of mine, Beau, and Masyn's friendship because we'd just met her. She needed all the pieces of our history to understand the issues.

Beau couldn't help himself. He was enamored with the blonde at his side and wanted to bring her into our fold. "Lee's harbored feelings for Masyn since tenth grade. And for the first time in six years, she's acting like a jealous girlfriend." He continued to talk to Peyton, even though he held my gaze, issuing a challenge. "Instead of capitalizing on it and going to talk to her, he's hiding out with the two of us while she stews."

That was it. I was done. I pushed the plate away. And wiping my mouth with a napkin, I leaned back against the booth and folded my arms over my chest. "Is nothing sacred with you, man?"

"Dude, she"—he pointed his thumb at Peyton—"doesn't live here. What difference does it make? It's not like she's going to track Masyn down and tell her all your secrets."

"Wait, you've pined over a girl for six years and never told her?" Thank God, "bless your heart" wasn't part of her regular vocabulary, or this would be where she said it.

Every time I turned around, something about me surprised Peyton. She had a lot of misconceptions. "Why are you so shocked?"

"I wouldn't have thought you were that type." She shrugged one shoulder and went back to picking at her chicken.

People making assumptions about who I was as a person ticked me off, especially when they didn't know me. "Meaning what?"

"I don't know. Don't get defensive. I just assumed you always did the rejecting." She sighed and leaned back. This was about to turn into a full-blown discussion. "I see how all these girls look at you. The church, Sadler's, here. It's not much of a stretch to assume you're a 'use 'em and leave 'em' kind of guy."

I shook my head and wondered where the hell Verna was when I needed her to inadvertently intervene. "Foliage," I muttered under my breath.

"What'd you say?" Beau must've thought he'd misheard me.

"*Foliage*. Peyton knows what I'm talking about." I wasn't angry, or even put off—people saw what they wanted to, and I couldn't be upset with her for her ignorance. Peyton hadn't had the time to see anything beneath the surface.

Beau seemed incensed that he wasn't privy to the information Peyton and I shared. "Well, I don't."

"Trees, dipshit," I balked at him. "You sat through the same sermon I did when Pastor Fortner spent two hours talking about fig trees and roots. People see the leaves because that's what's on the surface to look at. But the life is under the ground, in the dirt, where you have to dig to get to it—in the roots."

Remorse lined Peyton's brow. "I didn't mean to offend you, Lee."

"I'm not offended." Although, I was tired of this conversation.

"How the hell does Peyton know what you're talking about, and I'm lost?" Beau was going to have to let that go.

"Do you love her?" Peyton was bold. She went straight to the heart of the matter. She didn't pass go, she didn't collect two hundred dollars, and she wanted the only detail that mattered.

I inhaled deeply through my nose, my chest rose, as did my heart rate. While Peyton and Beau both stared at me, waiting with bated breath, I ran my tongue along my teeth and set my lips in a firm line, debating on whether to answer. "Yes."

"But you've never told her?" Peyton still seemed surprised.

Beau shifted in the booth. "She's not interested. At least, she hasn't acted like it—until you rolled into town and Lee's attention shifted to you." He treated this like it was the most natural conversation in the world to have with a virtual stranger.

"That's not true, Peyton. You two were buddy-buddy at the rehearsal dinner. Ignore Beau. The sun and heat must have fried his brain today."

Beau couldn't help himself. He couldn't stop talking. "All I know is, she was none too happy to see the two of you walk into Sadler's holding hands. And her feelings were hurt when Lee danced with you because he won a bet."

"What? You danced with me just because you won a bet?"

It appeared we were going to hash out the details of every-thing that took place since Peyton got to Harden. "No, Peyton," I deadpanned. "I won a bet with *Masyn* on Friday afternoon... before I ever met you. And my prize was dancing with her on Saturday at Beau's wedding."

Her perfectly arched brows drew in, creating a fine line in the center. "But you told me you don't dance." Peyton was back to being confused. There were too many years when she wasn't around for any of this to make sense, and I wasn't interested in explaining the dynamic.

"He doesn't. That's why it was such a big deal to Masyn. But then the wedding got called off, and he danced with you at Sadler's instead of her. Then he left with you. And later she showed up at his house and you were there. And again, yesterday when you called, we were at her brother's house, and she stormed out."

"It doesn't matter. Peyton, don't worry about it. I'll straighten it out. And Beau, you need to shut up."

Peyton reached across the table and laid her hand on mine. Our eyes met, and the corners of her lips tipped up in a gentle and encouraging smile. "If you love her, then you need to tell her."

"It's not that simple. Masyn and I grew up together. She doesn't see me that way and never has. Telling her won't do anything other than drive a wedge between us that will end up destroying the friendship. I'd rather have this than nothing."

"Maybe you've never allowed yourself to see that she does see you differently. It sounds like she's hurt. If she didn't feel the same way you do or at least have an inkling that she might, then she wouldn't be acting like a beaten puppy. She's hiding because she's hurt."

"You should go lick her wounds, Lee." Beau cocked his head, narrowed his eyes, and plastered a shit-eating grin on his lips.

"You're a dick, dude."

"What do you have to lose by telling her?" Peyton thought like a chick and talked like a chick, yet clearly she didn't have the experience of a chick who'd done a lot of rejecting.

"His dignity." Beau was a barrel of laughter and entertainment this evening. "And his virginity."

I threw my roll at his head. I tumbled across the table and landed in Peyton's lap. "Shut up." It wasn't a request, nor was it said with any sort of humor behind it. I was at the end of my rope, and if I snapped, Beau would be the one to receive the tongue lashing and possible beatdown.

She held the ball of bread between her fingers and leaned across the table. "You're a *virgin?*" Peyton's shock rang across the table in a church whisper.

"No."

"Might as well be. The last box of condoms he bought expired six years ago." He'd just swung the vault door wide open and invited everyone in for a look around.

"Wow, Beau. I'm so glad I saved you from a life of misery. To think, you could be in France with your *wife* right now. Don't forget, I've helped you bury all your skeletons...but we could easily start digging those up."

"I'm impressed, Lee, and now I firmly believe you need to leave here and go to her house. Putting this off any longer is only hurting both of you."

"Peyton, I appreciate the advice. But Masyn isn't going to talk to me until you've gone home. Sorry to be blunt; that's just how it is."

"Then I guess you're just going to have to make her listen if she's unwilling to talk, huh?" She ripped a piece of bread off the roll—the same one that had bounced off Beau's head—and stuffed it in her mouth. The gleam in her eyes told me she was up to no good, and with Beau at her side, the two could be dangerous.

"Can we be done with this conversation? Why don't you tell us about how much fun you're having dealing with your sister's crap?" I could play dirty if that's how they wanted to handle this. "How about you, Beau, having fun with the lawyer?"

Beau wanted to throw me under the bus—I was perfectly capable of reminding them how each of us ended up here, and it had started with my best friend proposing to a bitch.

"Don't get nasty with Peyton. It's not her fault you haven't made a move."

A glassy glaze washed over her eyes. "Have you really been in love with her since tenth grade?" She held her hand to her chest like it was the sweetest thing she'd ever heard.

I raked my fingers through my hair and then down my face. Peyton's interest appeared genuine, unlike my asshole of a best friend who was trying to impress a girl he didn't have a chance in hell of making a relationship with because he'd fucked her sister.

"I can pinpoint the exact day. And yes."

Beau proceeded to tell Peyton about everything that happened in the locker room and, subsequently, the lunchroom our sophomore year. "It pretty much closed Masyn off to dating for the better part of three years."

Verna refilled our glasses and brought us the check. She didn't care if we sat here all night, and if we didn't get up to leave soon, she'd bring coffee and then dessert. What she didn't do was interrupt this asinine conversation.

"Did she date after high school?"

I guess I was going to answer her questions regardless. "Not really. She's gone out a couple of times with a few different guys. Nothing that stuck." I ran my finger around the top of my glass, thinking about how hard it had been to see her around town with another man over the years.

Beau was distracted by the cellphone in his lap, albeit it didn't deter him from interjecting, "That's because the moment they expressed any concern or issue with her relationship with Lee, she'd dump them." He looked like an idiot talking to his crotch.

"Not true. That never happened. And I would know since I was in town, and fancy pants over there was away at school."

He hadn't looked up once. "Yes, and I was the one she called to complain to since she couldn't tell *you*."

"You've never told me that." The conversation shifted away from Peyton and settled between Beau and me.

"So? Doesn't mean it didn't happen. There are lots of things that she's told you that you haven't shared with me. That's not news."

If I could reach the damn cellphone, I'd slap it out of his

hand like I had the stick of gum. I hated cellphones and how inconsiderate people were with them. "Name one guy she broke up with because of me."

He couldn't do it.

"Tommy Morton." Or maybe he could.

I tried to think back to when they dated. "No, they broke up because she caught him with Melinda Beece."

"Yes, illustrating his point that guys and girls don't have platonic friendships."

"Who else?" I demanded information as though I was entitled to it, all while he continued to mess around with his phone and talked to his lap.

"Devin Callen."

"They went out twice!"

"Yes, because at the end of the second date, she had him drop her off at your house where she spent the night with her best friend."

Peyton didn't even blink as she listened to the two of us go back and forth; she was entirely captivated by our banter. She popped pieces of bread into her mouth like it was popcorn and she was at an evening showing of a box office hit.

I tuned out the sounds of dishes clanking and people chattering around me to hone in on this revelation. "Anyone else?"

"Kyle Perkins, Larson Camp, Greg Davis—"

"She didn't go on more than three dates with any of those guys." Arguing with the top of his head pissed me off. "Beau!"

His head jerked up, stunned I'd raised my voice. "Right, because guys don't like it when the girls that they date have sleepovers with other men. Pull your head out of your ass, Lee. It's been right there. Open your eyes and see it."

"Why are you just now bringing this to my attention?" My tone had changed.

Beau was supposed to be my best friend. As my best friend, he should have found a way to let me in on this without violating Masyn's trust or letting me spend years in silence.

"The opportunity just presented itself." He slid his phone into his pocket—finally. "Lee, she'd call me late at night after you'd gone to sleep. She never confessed to having feelings for you, only that she wasn't ever going to give up a friend for a guy. I think she would have said the same thing to anyone who'd told her they didn't like how much time she spent with me. I wasn't trying to keep pertinent information from you. But truth be told, unless you're willing to stop messing around, I don't think you should tell her."

I didn't follow. "Messing around?"

"With other girls."

This was the kind of thing that irritated me to no end. Beau didn't even live here, yet he wanted to give me advice on what to do. "I can't tell you the last time I took a girl out on a date."

"No, but I bet *I* can tell you the last time you let one suck your dick in the men's bathroom at Sadler's." And he'd only know that if Masyn told him—not my finer moments.

And with that, I called it a night. I hadn't done anything wrong, yet having Peyton hear it at the same time I did was a sober dose of reality I wasn't prepared for. I shouldn't be concerned with what she thought of me when she was leaving in a couple of days. I just knew the look on her face when we quit talking likely reflected the condition of Masyn's heart.

And that nearly broke me.

ELEVEN

AFTER DROPPING PEYTON OFF AT HER HOTEL AND BEAU AT his parents' house, I made my way across town to Masyn's. Peyton might not know our history and Beau might be full of shit, but I couldn't let this keep going on. Two days without my best friend at my side was two days too long. The entire way there, I psyched myself up for what I wanted to say, what I needed to say. She could very well shoot me down, but I'd never know if I didn't try. And if Beau and Peyton were right—although I wasn't a hundred percent certain they were—then letting this go on only served to hurt the person I loved.

It wasn't all that late when I got there, and all the lights were on in the house. Masyn was still up at ten o'clock. Even after several deep breaths, cutting the engine didn't help calm my nerves before I stepped out of the truck. This should feel like a relief, but instead, I dreaded spitting the words out. The fear of rejection was real, even for someone who never had any problems attracting the opposite sex. It might even be worse because I knew I could have my pick of any girl in town—

except the one I wanted. Since I never risked being turned down, I never had any hesitation approaching women. But here, sitting in her driveway, I had to prepare myself that she might not be interested in my confession, and I could be putting our friendship in jeopardy.

With one final deep breath, I opened the door and was nearly knocked over by the music blaring from Masyn's house. It was a wonder no one had called the cops; I was surprised I hadn't been able to hear it in the truck. Her angry hate lyrics blasted throughout the entire neighborhood, which was completely uncharacteristic of her. The emptiness in the pit of my stomach didn't help carry my feet toward the porch, and each step I took was labored and forced. Masyn and I had been friends for seventeen years, and I was about to risk it all to relieve my heart of the pain it had carried by not claiming her as mine before now. Either way, I was moments away from sealing my fate—I'd either get what I wanted, or lose the greatest thing I'd ever had.

Instead of knocking—she wouldn't hear it over whatever death-metal band she had playing—I pounded on the wood with my fist and waited. A moment or two later, the volume was noticeably lowered, and I beat again with just as much force. Each time my fist hit the door, another crack in my armor opened, leaving me more vulnerable than if I'd been standing here naked with a spotlight blazing down on me. The music turned off, and I waited.

The door swung open with such force that I half expected her to be pointing a rifle at my forehead when she appeared. She didn't live in the best part of town, and I hadn't bothered to text her that I was stopping by. It would have only given her the opportunity to tell me not to come.

I wasn't prepared for the sight before me. Masyn had her hair secured in a messy bun at the top of her head with loose locks spilling all around her face, and any fool could see she'd been crying—a lot. All I wanted to do was scoop her into my arms and apologize for whatever I'd done, but she didn't give me the opportunity.

The stench of alcohol poured off of her in waves powerful enough to knock a linebacker down. "What are you doing here, Lee?" Her words were slurred, and her eyelids fluttered closed when she spoke.

"I came to talk to you, since you've avoided me at work and refused to answer your phone." The crease tightened across my forehead, causing my eyebrows to distort my line of sight for a moment. "Are you drunk?"

She flung the door wide open, inviting me in without issuing an actual invitation, and then turned away. "What's good for the goose, is a gander." Obviously, not all the pieces were coming together in her current state—or maybe that was precisely what she meant.

I wiped my feet on the mat, stepped inside, and closed the door behind me. "You never drink," I accused, glancing around to ensure we were alone, "especially not by yourself." I picked up beer bottle after beer bottle from her coffee table and threw them away. I needed something to occupy my hands and get me through this.

Masyn didn't live in a palace, but she took pride in her home...and yet, this place currently looked like a shithole. She plopped down—or rather fell over—onto the couch. I stepped into her kitchen to drop the bottles into the trash, only to find a couple of days' worth of dishes piled in the sink and rotting food on the counter.

"What the hell, Masyn? This place looks horrible and smells like a barn."

"I haven't had time to clean." That was the understatement of the century. "Toby's been keeping me busy." And now she was spouting shit just to piss me off. She'd been at her brother's house all day yesterday, the dock last night, work today, and no man drank Amstel Light.

"Cut the shit." It was hard to be upset with Masyn, seeing her broken on the sofa. "What's going on? You're lucky the cops haven't shown up."

She waved me off as though nothing I said held any weight or significance. "How was your *day*-te?" A deaf mule could have caught the hate laced in those words.

I released a frustrated sigh and kept from rolling my eyes when I took a seat on the coffee table in front of her. "I didn't have a date, which you would know had you talked to me or answered your phone."

Masyn poked her bottom lip out with exaggeration. "Aww, did Peyton stand you up?" Her lashes fluttered like Betty Boop, but nothing about her accusing glare or her position on the couch made it attractive or the least bit seductive. In fact, her posture looked painful, and it probably would have been had she not been so intoxicated.

"No. We went to the lake."

"*Our* lake?"

What the hell? "Masyn, it's not like that at all. I called you to see if you wanted to go—"

"*That* would have been fun. I bet she looks like every guy's fantasy in a swimsuit." She huffed right before she chuckled. "I could have looked like Punky Brewster next to Reese Wither-spoon. I bet she'd even look good in a brown paper bag."

I didn't know if she was referring to Reese or Peyton in regard to the grocery sack, and I didn't think asking would serve any real purpose. "Why are you so put off by Peyton? You two seemed to hit it off on Friday. I don't get it."

"It's no big deal." Those four words morphed into one as they rolled together, combining syllables and eliminating spaces.

"It's a big deal to me. I don't have any interest in her. Beau, on the other hand, I can't speak for." I shouldn't have tossed out that last part. I just hoped it would help her realize I wasn't interested in the girl from out of town.

"Pfft."

Hesitantly, I reached out and took Masyn's hand. It was cold and clammy from clutching the beer bottle. "Masyn..." My heart threatened to pound out of my chest, and I couldn't get enough air. "It's not Peyton that I'm in love with."

"I should have known better." She made a feeble attempt to sit upright without letting me finish what I wanted to say. "I knew when Beau called off the wedding everything would get messed up. He's home. Petyon's here. And my best friend is falling in love."

Sober Lee didn't understand drunk Masyn. "What are you talking about?"

"Peyton. She's got both of you at her fingertips, and both of you want her."

"I don't want her."

"Beau does."

"So what if he does?"

"One of the Holstein girls is going to take him away."

"From you?" I asked, unsure of where she was going with this.

"Duh."

That was a response I hadn't heard since middle school.

"Do you have any idea how hard it was to talk to him when he was with Felicity?"

I did, although I wasn't sure what that had to do with Peyton—or me.

"We had a code. If I wanted to talk to him, I had to send him a text. If he responded with a two, he couldn't talk—you know because 'no' has two words. Letters—two letters. And a three if the answer was yes. And you would be half-naked in a bathroom or have some girl pressed against a wall behind the building."

"Not following you, Masyn. I've never brought a girl home." It was true, I hadn't. I'd spent many a night at their place, in my truck, a bathroom stall, or even in an alley behind a bar, but I'd never brought some random girl into my house. Other than Masyn, there wasn't a single female who'd ever spent the night, and not even Masyn had graced my bed.

"As if that wasn't bad enough to watch"—apparently she didn't plan to clarify that statement—"I had to deal with signals from Beau. Do you know how hard it is to be best friends with two incredibly attractive men? One of which you love, and the other you adore?"

The question was, who was who?

"Of course you don't. You're Lee Carter. Beau has the

money girls swoon after, and you have"—she waved the beer bottle around in front of me—"all of *that*. And I'm left watching both of you leave me behind. And as many times as I've told my heart I can't have my best friend, it refuses to listen."

Maybe this wasn't the best time to have this conversation. She was spilling her guts, even though none of it made sense and was harder to follow than a rat in a maze. But she was admitting things I wasn't sure she wanted me to know.

"Masyn—"

She righted herself and jerked her hand away. With her feet planted firmly on the ground, she swayed when she put her elbows on her knees and leaned into me. Her warm breath tangled with mine, and the light overhead caught on her lips when she swiped them with her tongue. There was nothing I wanted more than to shut down her rambling and show her what I felt for her, except that I didn't want our first kiss to be forgotten in a drunken stupor or regretted due to a lapse in judgment.

"I'm in love with my best friend, and I can't have him. There will always be a Felicity Holstein or a Cynthia Green, or some other girl whose name I can't think of right now, standing in my way. And I'll always just be Masyn Porter—one of the guys."

"Are you talking about Beau?" I wasn't sure. Clearly, Beau had been engaged to Felicity, but Cynthia Green was the sticking point. I'd lost my virginity to her—which Masyn knew —but Beau dated her his freshman year, albeit briefly, when they both went to Atlanta for college.

She rolled her eyes, seemingly confused by my inability to follow what she said. "Yes."

My heart shattered into a million pieces. It had never been a secret they were close. She shared things with him she'd never told me. But not once, in all the years I'd known her, had she even indicated a slight inclination toward having feelings for him. She hadn't even cried or said she missed him when he went to school. Yet everything Beau shared implied she had insinuated beyond a doubt that she *did* feel that way toward me.

"Is that why you called him to complain about me? To have a reason to talk to him?"

Clearly, Beau had been wrong about her reasons for ending relationships and her need to reach out to him.

"I needed someone to talk to. I couldn't tell *you* how I felt." She reached for the stereo remote like she was going to turn up the volume to end the conversation, but I blocked her path and grabbed it first to put it out of her reach.

I wasn't sure which hurt more, that she was in love with Beau, or that she couldn't talk to me about it. "Why not?"

"Admitting you love someone isn't easy, especially when they're preoccupied by other people."

Beau had never been with multiple people. He'd barely dated before he met Felicity. Even though I tried to follow her logic, it didn't make much sense. I let out a sigh, hoping to exhale my disappointment and hurt with it—neither happened. "I wish you would have told me."

"It wouldn't have made any difference. And how is that fair to you? You had your own things going on."

"Masyn, you'll always be my top priority."

"Humph." She turned her beer up, finished it off, and plunked it on the table next to me. "It's okay, Lee. I see how you look at other girls. One day, I hope someone looks at me that way."

My eyes closed slowly, while I tried to process everything dancing in my head. When I opened them, the brown eyes I'd loved for years were pooled with tears.

"I'll never look at you the way I do other women." *Not because I don't love you, but because I do.* "You have no idea how much of my heart you hold."

She stood up and stomped to the kitchen. "Probably about as much as I do of Beau's."

The refrigerator door opened and closed. A bottle cap clinked on the counter and likely fell to the floor. And somewhere between there and when Masyn returned to the couch, she'd taken her hair down. It flowed in soft waves past her shoulders, and it was times like these it felt like my chest would explode, taking in her beauty.

As much as it was going to hurt to say what was about to come out of my mouth, I loved her enough to want her to be happy. "If you love him, you should tell him."

Confusion marred her face. "I did."

Either I'd missed something, or Beau had left out a large piece of information sitting at the table. "When?"

She rolled her eyes and huffed. "Tonight. Are you listening?"

"I was *with* Beau tonight." There was no way he'd been texting Masyn at the same time he exposed me to Peyton. He was adamant that I tell her how I felt, man up. Beau never would have led me down a path of destruction intentionally. He had his faults, but he wasn't a sadist and didn't get off on hurting other people.

"And Peyton."

I couldn't figure out why we kept coming back to Peyton. "You realize she's leaving on Friday afternoon, right? And going back to New York." Peyton was a non-issue. Beau couldn't date her, and I didn't want her.

Masyn began to sway. And when she closed her eyes, all the color washed from her cheeks and was replaced with a hint of green. I didn't have any idea how much alcohol she'd consumed tonight, but it was dangerously close to making an appearance. Before I could get up to find a trash can or carry her to the bathroom, her mouth opened and she leaned forward, covering me in everything she'd drank tonight. And it just kept coming, wave after wave. All I could do was hold her hair out of it. Trying to move her would only make the mess worse and leave a trail down the hall or into the kitchen that one of us would have to clean up. As it stood, most of it was being absorbed by my shirt and jeans, or pooled in my lap.

When the retching finally stopped, I took the beer from her hand that she'd managed not to spill. There wasn't a drop of vomit on her, but I was bathed in it.

Tears of embarrassment streamed down her cheeks, and a muffled, "I'm sorry," passed her lips.

"Why don't you lie down, and I'll try to clean this up."

Before she could even nod, she leaned her head back on the sofa and closed her eyes.

I pulled my T-shirt over the back of my head and contained as much as I could in the front. The pizza box on the floor gave me a place to set it so the contents wouldn't create more of a problem. Then I slid my flip-flops off my feet and removed my jeans. I wasn't sure how Masyn managed to throw up exclusively on me, but there was only a bit of splatter on the coffee table around me and nothing on the carpet. In nothing other than boxers, I grabbed the pizza box and went to the kitchen to rinse my clothes out. My boxers were wet and clung to my crotch. I stared down at the horrible metaphor. Once I cleaned off the table and bagged the rest of the trash with the pizza box, I put my clothes, including my boxers, in the washing machine. There was no way in hell I was getting in my truck with the stench of vomit all over me, and leaving stomach acid on my skin didn't seem like a bright idea, either.

Thankfully, I had the swimsuit I'd changed out of in my truck, although, I might get shot going to the driveway with nothing other than a towel wrapped around me. I'd never stayed here, so I didn't have any clothes lying around. My swim trunks were cold and only partially dry, but shrinkage was only important when there was someone around to witness—clearly, that wasn't an issue tonight.

The timer went off on the washing machine just as I hung up the towel I'd used to shower, so I threw the load in the dryer and went to move Masyn to her bed. The soft snore coming from the couch only served as a reminder to my heart that I'd never wake up next to that. I wasn't sure I could handle the thought of her and Beau together, and I wondered if this would be the thing that broke the three of us apart for good.

I lifted her in my arms, tucked her against my chest, and took a deep breath, hoping for a whiff of the shop there, but all I caught was the scent of her shampoo. If Beau felt the same way about Masyn, and the two ended up together, I wouldn't stand in their way, but I wouldn't be able to watch it happen. And if he didn't, I'd want to kill him for breaking her heart. Either way, none of this could end well—and it would all happen without either of my best friends there to comfort me.

Her bed was unmade, and I laid her down and then pulled the blankets over her. Her eyes parted, and she looked at me the way I'd looked at her a thousand times—as though there were nothing else in the world more important—and I wondered if her eyes held that much emotion when they met mine, just how glorious and stunning they must be when Beau saw them.

She grabbed my wrist and held on. "Please don't go." It was nothing more than a whisper in the dark, but it was as if she were asking me to stay—not just tonight, but forever. Like she'd heard my thoughts and realized I'd have to leave.

But even knowing how painful it would be to let her go, I was a glutton for punishment and selfish as hell. I'd take one more night if that's all I could have. "I'll be on the couch."

Her hair cascaded over the pillow, and the uneasy grin that lifted her mouth tore at my heart. "Will you stay—"

"I told you I would." Maybe I should be concerned about alcohol poisoning if she couldn't remember the sentence I'd just said.

"With me. In here."

I couldn't tell her no. My heart refused to resist her. The two of us had never slept in the same bed, and I sure as hell never imagined the first time we did being like this, but if she wanted me, I wouldn't leave. "Scoot over."

She slid aside to make room, and I climbed in next to her. As soon as my head hit the pillow, I was engulfed in everything Masyn. She lifted my arm and tucked her body close to my side. I wanted to relish the feel of her arm on my chest and her head on my shoulder, yet in the end, allowing myself to make this into something it would never be would only crush me down the road. So I wrapped my arm around her waist and let my hand settle on her hip. Her breathing evened out, and I lay there, wide awake until the sun came up.

Masyn slept like the dead through the night, and when her alarm went off, she jumped at the obnoxious noise. We both had to be at work in an hour, and I still had to go home to change. She bolted upright, twisted over me, and slapped the snooze button on the nightstand, and the realization hit her that she'd spent the night with me in her bed.

"Oh, God. Lee...what did I do?" Her hands went to her head where her fingers massaged her temples. There was no doubt she'd have one hell of a hangover to contend with today. "Did we...?" She looked down at my swim trunks and then back at my face. "You know?"

"No." I'd never take advantage of any woman who was drunk. "After your confession, you threw up, and I brought you in here. You asked me to stay, but we didn't do anything." I hated being the one to remind her of all she'd admitted last night, knowing how much would change between us.

"My...confession?" she repeated, unsure she'd heard me correctly.

With pursed lips, I nodded. "Yeah. You kind of laid it all out there." I wasn't able to hide my disappointment.

Her cheeks flushed with embarrassment. "Oh God, I never intended to tell you. Lee, I'm so sorry."

Somehow, that didn't make me feel any better. It just confirmed my thoughts about last night, of how significantly her feelings had changed things. I shrugged with feigned indifference. "It's better that I know."

"Can we forget it ever happened? Please? I don't want that to change anything between us. You and Beau mean the world to me; I couldn't stand the thought of losing either one of you."

"So, you don't plan to tell him?" He was single; she was single. There was no reason for her not to admit her interest— not to mention, she said she told him last night, anyhow. But if she didn't remember that, I wasn't going to be the one to break it to her.

"God, no. I mean I think he has an idea. I've kind of eluded to it for years, but I don't want to rub it in his face. Things have been so weird."

"And you want to forget last night ever happened?" My chest constricted painfully, and I wondered about what I was about to say, but in the end, her happiness was important. "I really think you should tell him...when you're in the right frame of mind." There was no point in all of us being miserable.

She hopped up and straightened her clothes. "Promise me you won't. It's too embarrassing."

"What's embarrassing about loving your best friend?"

Her eyes filled with sadness, and she cast her gaze to the floor. "Not having them return your feelings."

I didn't know what to say. I had no idea how Beau felt about Masyn, and I didn't want to encourage her the way Beau and Peyton had urged me, only for Masyn to be let down. I sat up and put my feet on the floor. She was within arm's reach, so I took her hand and pulled her onto my knee. I wrapped my arms around her center and hugged her tightly. "Your secret's safe with me."

She hugged me back and squirmed out of my grasp. There was no reason for her to be uneasy, although clearly, she was.

"Thank you. I just want to forget about last night and every stupid thing I said. Please don't hold it against me."

"Okay." I stood and made my way to the laundry room with her hot on my heels. I didn't turn around since I could hear her close behind me. "So, we're good?"

She veered off to the kitchen to grab coffee. "As long as you don't think I'm a moron. Yeah, we're good."

If only she knew.

"Not a chance," I called out over my shoulder, trying to keep things light. I closed the laundry room door behind me, grabbed my clothes, and quickly changed. When I emerged, she was standing on the other side with a fresh cup of coffee in a to-go mug for me. "Sorry I don't have time to make you omelets before work."

"There's always the weekend, right?" Her hopeful tone didn't match her longing expression.

I kissed her on top of the head, took the cup of coffee, and agreed, "Name the day."

She escorted me to the door and opened it for me to step through. "Hey, Lee?"

"Yeah." I turned as I opened the truck.

"Thank you for not making me feel stupid last night...or this morning. I'm sorry I dumped all that on you. It wasn't fair to put our friendship on the line like that."

"That's what friends are for, right?" I smiled even though my heart shriveled inside my chest.

Her face dropped. "Friends." She nodded. "Right."

TWELVE

I managed to clock in before the buzzer rang, signaling the start of the shift. I hadn't had time to look for Masyn. My head was far too fucked up to try to interact with her, anyhow. She may want to forget everything that happened last night, but I'd done nothing other than agonize over every word she'd said, trying to make sense of it. None of it aligned with what Beau told me at the diner, and I had a hard time believing Masyn would twist things around to create reasons to talk to him when he was at school. That was the kind of shit every other girl in town would do, not Masyn Porter.

I had to remind myself over and over, I specifically asked if she was talking about Beau, and even through her rambling, she'd answered yes without hesitation. As much as my mind wanted to convince my heart that I'd misunderstood, there was no misconstruing her message—not even as tired as I'd been. My head pounded from all the noise in the shop, coupled with a lack of sleep, making it harder to work through everything blazing through my mind at the speed of light.

Twice I'd dropped parts, and when Farley called my name, I turned quickly. Not paying attention, or sleep deprived, or just in a shit mood, I nearly cut off my thumb to answer him.

"Fuck, Carter. Do you have any idea how many hours we had that were injury free?" Farley dropped his clipboard and came to my machine when the blood pooled in my hand.

Today was not the day to lash out at me. "Maybe if you weren't screaming at people from across the shop, they wouldn't fear for their life and respond in an unsafe manner." Like I gave a shit for his safety record right now.

"There's blood everywhere. Is your thumb even still attached to your hand?" His sympathetic irritation did nothing to calm me down.

"I'm fairly certain it's not lying on the cement covered in blood, asshat." Calling my boss names probably wasn't the best idea.

He turned off the machine and picked up the metal that had nearly severed a digit from my body, and then he motioned toward the office. "Come on. Let's go see how bad it is."

I didn't believe cleaning a wound in filth was the best idea Farley had ever had, but far be it from me to object. The office had a sink, yes, yet there were greasy handprints everywhere and crap thrown all over the place. It was less than sterile. "If I get gangrene, I'm suing your ass, Farley."

"Just don't touch anything." He got the insinuation without me saying the place was a fucking pigsty. "The water out of the pipes is clean."

Right, and they were probably made of lead as old as this place was. My hand throbbed with a pulse I could feel in my head—or maybe it was the throb of my headache in my hand. I didn't know, and I didn't care. It hurt like a son of a bitch and only added to my already piss-poor mood.

"What's up your ass today, Carter?" He turned the water on and held my hand under it.

My sharp intake of air whistled between my teeth. "You mean besides becoming a cripple on the job?" I stared at the red flowing down the drain and wondered how my broken heart could pump that much blood in its current condition.

"Yeah, besides that. You and Masyn break up?" He chuckled like something was funny.

If it hadn't been my right hand under the faucet, I would have decked the smug grin off his chubby face. I groaned when he moved my fingers, yet somehow, he mistook it as a response to his question about Masyn.

"Seriously, didn't mean anything by that. I've just watched you two dance around each other for years and wonder if you're ever going to stop fucking around and tell the girl."

Farley and I weren't close. We went to school together. We'd known each other all our lives, but we never shared secrets. Bonfires, field parties, and cutting class at the lake didn't make a friendship—it just made him another guy I'd known for decades and happened to work for.

"It's not like that."

"Yeah, you've been saying that for years. I just—"

"I appreciate your concern about my love life, but I have bigger issues to deal with right now."

He stared at me like I was about to share the secrets of life with him. I raised my brow and tilted my head in the direction of my still gushing thumb. I hadn't reached the point that I was light-headed, but if the blood didn't stop exiting my body faster than my heart could pump it, he wouldn't just have a mess on his hands, he'd have me on his floor. I seriously doubted that even Farley—who was a stout dude—could deadlift two hundred pounds of my weight.

"Shit." The bone was clear as day with the water washing through the wound. "That's going to need stitches."

"You don't think butterfly tape will get it?"

He grimaced before realizing I was being a smart-ass.

"Do you want me to drive, or do you want someone to take me?"

He raked his hand through what was left of his hair—a buzz cut didn't leave much to mess with. "Let me go pull Masyn. She knows all your personal shit and can take care of the paperwork while the doctor deals with...this."

I didn't need Masyn pawing over me and making a big deal out of a cut. I wanted to be left alone. "I can drive myself."

"Like hell. Something happens, I not only have workers' comp to deal with, then I have an accident, too. No thanks." He pulled a roll of sterile gauze from a pack in the first aid kit and began to wrap it around my thumb and hand. The blood came through almost as quickly as he could add layers. "Hold it above your heart to keep that shit from pumping out. I'll go get Porter."

There was no use in arguing. Farley would do whatever the hell he wanted to because his pop owned the place. And I'd do what he told me to because his pop owned the shop, and I needed the job.

He returned with Masyn a few minutes later, and the second she saw the blood, her hand flew to her mouth and her eyes went wide. "Oh my God, Lee. Are you okay?"

"I'm bleeding like a stuck hog, but I'm still breathing, if that's what you mean."

Farley didn't let us linger and chitchat. "Take him down to North Hills Clinic. We have an account there. Make sure you tell them it happened at work so they send the bills to our insurance company."

"Yeah, sure."

Masyn still stood there like a deer in the headlights, staring at my hand. I waved it to get her attention. "You ready?"

"What?" Her warm-brown eyes lifted. "Oh, yeah. I need to grab my keys."

"Don't bother. Get mine. We can take the truck."

She drove the damn thing all the time, anyhow. I wasn't interested in getting stuck on the side of the road in her piece of shit that needed more work than it was worth. Jesus, I was in a foul mood.

She scurried off to the lockers, and I met her at the exit to the parking lot. My thumb hurt like a son of a bitch, and my head wasn't far behind it. Without any sleep to speak of, I was a bear. And even though I knew it, if Masyn insisted on talking, I wasn't going to be able to control barking at her.

We hadn't been in the truck two minutes before she started in on her girly shit. It was the one time I wished she'd just change the damn radio station and turn it up loud enough to drown out my thoughts and pain.

"Lee, I'm really sorry about last night."

Inhaling deeply, I counted to ten and then exhaled before speaking. "It's not a big deal, Masyn. You cleared the air. I know where we stand. It's all good." I ground my teeth, trying to soften my tone.

"It seems like a big deal. You're obviously upset. I just want to talk about it."

"For God's sake, Masyn, I nearly cut off my fucking thumb. It isn't about you being in love with your best friend." *And not me.*

I stared out the window waiting for her to come back at me, yell, tell me what an ass I was, yet it didn't come. The minutes ticked by with not even a peep from the driver's side of the vehicle. When I turned, a scowl lining my brow, Masyn stared out the windshield. Tears streamed down her cheeks and cut through the dust that lined them.

"Fuck. Don't cry, sweetheart. I didn't mean to lash out at you."

She sucked her lips between her teeth and nodded. Even when I grabbed her right hand with my left, she didn't utter another word. Not even to chew me out for calling her a term of endearment she hated.

"Masyn..." I didn't know what to say to soothe her without further damaging myself. "Please don't be mad."

I let her hand go when she pulled away to wipe her face. "I knew I shouldn't have told you, but I didn't think it would make you act like this toward me. I thought things might be awkward...I just...I'm sorry, Lee." She pulled into the parking lot of the medical center and sat with the trucking idling.

"Are you coming in?"

"I wasn't sure you'd want me to. I don't mind waiting out here."

"Sweetheart, I have no idea what's going on inside that pretty little head of yours, but right now, I'm too tired and in too much pain to put a lot of thought into it. Regardless of what was said last night, you're still my best friend"—*until you're sleeping with my other best friend*—"and I want you with me."

She frogged me in the arm with her knuckle. "Stop calling me sweetheart." Her eyes glistened in the sun when she grinned. Masyn could tell me all day long she didn't like it—and if she and Beau got together, I'd have to stop—but the gleam in her eyes told me that at least this one time, she loved hearing it.

Bleeding out wasn't considered an emergency at North Hills. The portly woman at the window handed me a stack of forms to complete—hard to do since I was right-handed—and told us to have a seat. She wasn't the least bit concerned with the blood that saturated the bandages around my hand or the trail running down my arm.

"Lee, you're dripping." Masyn pointed to the tiles on the floor by my chair.

"Tell that to Cruella de Vil up there." I gestured with the pen she'd given me thirty minutes ago. Thank God my name was only three letters long because that was about all I'd managed to write with my left hand in the last half hour.

"Give me that. You're such a baby." Masyn snatched the pen and clipboard from my hand. "I'm going to find some paper towels, and then I'll fill this out for you."

"See if you can get an ETA from the Grinch while you're at it."

"She wasn't that bad. You're just in pain and acting like a brat." Masyn grinned and went to the window again.

When Masyn drew the nurse's attention to the floor where my blood currently coagulated in a pond big enough for a small child to swim in, and then at the crime scene attached to my

SMALL TOWN GIRL   183

wrist, the nurse suddenly seemed to see the urgency of my visit and called me back. Good thing since I was less than five minutes away from drawing a chalk outline on the tile and calling *NCIS*.

I walked through the door currently held open for me and called over my shoulder, "You comin'?"

"What about this mess?" Masyn's concern was endearing—her house had looked like it had been burglarized last night and here she was worried about cleaning a clinic's floor.

Cruella waved her off. "I'll get housekeeping to clean it up. You can come back with your boyfriend."

I didn't correct her, and Masyn suddenly appeared sheepish. She trailed behind me as I followed the lady in front of me. The nurse had no sooner dropped me into an exam room than Robin Hood and his band of merry men came traipsing through the door. After informing us that the band of brothers to his side were students shadowing him, he proceeded to ignore *me* in favor of teaching *them*.

Masyn caught my glare and knew to stay out of the line of fire. She took the seat in the farthest corner to start on the paperwork. I probably should have worried that she knew my social security number, but since it kept me from trying to write like a kindergartener, I kept my mouth shut. If she were going to steal my identity, she would have done it years ago.

Robin—also known as Brad, according to his name tag—unwrapped the drenched gauze, tossed them in the trash, and proceeded to stick my hand into what looked like water and stung like alcohol.

"Jesus Christ, *Brad*." I tensed from my shoulders down. "How about warn a guy before pouring salt in his wound?"

Brad rolled his eyes as he turned his head and made some cutesy joke about the beefy men being the biggest babies. Maybe Brad would like to experience what it felt like to have metal slice through to the bone. Before I could ask, he excused himself and his posse with a promise to return. *Yippee.*

Whatever he'd put my thumb in stopped the bleeding—well, mostly. There were globs of coagulated blood at the bottom of the cup that looked like a lava lamp, but the steady stream subsided. I had to admit, I let out a sigh of relief when a doctor came in to stitch my thumb. He was much more considerate of the level of throbbing pain in my hand and started with something to numb it before putting in two layers of stitches, for a total of twenty-seven that ran from the tip to the palm.

"You'll probably lose that nail." He pointed to my thumb. "It should grow back. But don't pull on it. And don't remove the stitches yourself. Come back in ten days and we'll take them out for you."

Unless an infection laid claim to my thumb, I'd pull the things out when they started to unravel. I was no stranger to stitches or removing them. Having me come back was another way to stick it to my employer or the insurance carrier with a hefty fee for an office visit. No thanks. Needle-nose pliers and a pair of scissors worked just fine.

My phone started ringing when we were checking out, and I leaned over so Masyn could grab it out of my pocket.

"It's Beau," she stated, holding the phone out to me.

I was busy trying to sign my name between two fingers, using my right hand without my thumb. "So answer it."

I tuned her out while the lady in the office tried to make a follow-up appointment. When I informed her that I'd call to schedule one, she didn't believe a word I said. I took the papers for work and then focused on Masyn.

"He wants to talk to you." She took the papers in exchange for the phone.

I followed her out, yet she walked like her ass was on fire and we had somewhere to be in the next few minutes. "What's up?"

"Why aren't you home?"

"Well, Beau. I have a job. Starting Monday, you'll understand that they don't work on your timetable, you work on theirs. And when—"

"Yeah, jacksack, I'm aware of that. It's almost five o'clock. You got off two hours ago. And when did you and Masyn make up?"

"I stopped by her house last night after I dropped you off."

"Are you almost home? Peyton and I are sitting here waiting for you. Bring Masyn."

I still had to go back to the shop so Masyn could get her car. And the last thing Masyn would want to see was Beau humping Peyton's leg or peeing in a circle on the ground around her. "I'm going to pass tonight. You guys have fun."

"What the hell? I'm only in town until Sunday. You can lay low next week."

"I was up all night, I've had a shit day, and I want to go home."

"Up all night at Masyn's? Holy shit. Did you finally tell her?"

I'd reached the passenger side of the truck. As soon as I got inside, Masyn would be able to hear every word said by both of us. "Yeah. Look, it didn't go as planned."

"Then why are you two together now?"

"I cut my hand at work. She brought me up to the clinic to get stitches. So, if you don't mind, you and Peyton have a great time tonight. Call Masyn if you want to include her. Personally, I'm going home, eating dinner, taking a shower, and crashing—although, not necessarily in that order. I'll catch you two tomorrow."

After I slid my cell back into my pocket, I opened the door and climbed up.

"Beau and Peyton going out tonight?" She tried to give off the air that she didn't care.

"Yeah, and they asked if we wanted to go. I'm not up for it, but if you are, by all means, feel free."

She gave me a half-hearted shrug. "Not really. I've felt like crap all day. I could go for some Chinese takeout and bad reality TV." I didn't know if she was suggesting a pity party because she felt bad and wanted to let me down easy, or if she was avoiding Peyton and Beau.

"I'm down, but I can't promise how long I'll stay awake."

We went back to the shop, only to find everyone had long since gone home. Masyn got her car and said she would run by her house for work clothes and then she'd be over. I made a pit stop at ChinChin—Chinese fast food—on my way home. The two of us pulled up at the same time like we'd done so many times before. Every breath I took was harder than the last with the weight sitting on my chest. I wondered how many more of these nights I'd get. It was like I was living on borrowed time, and at any minute, Masyn would be whisked away on a white horse by her knight in a shiny Beamer, and I'd be left alone.

THIRTEEN

GOING TO THE SHOP HAD BEEN AN UTTER WASTE OF A DAY, except that I still got to collect hours on my paycheck. I couldn't do shit without my right hand, and it was still too tender to use it to pick things up. I wasn't worried about tearing the stitches out, it just hurt like hell. Farley put me back in receiving so I could check trucks in and deal with shipments going out. An inbred monkey could do this job. There was nothing worse than boredom and idle time at work. If I had to be here, I wanted something to occupy my mind, and this wasn't cutting it.

I'd spent the better part of the day thinking about what Masyn and Beau's wedding would be like. When she'd move to Atlanta. How many kids they'd have. It was torture, and I was inflicting it upon myself—they hadn't even gone on a date, and I already had their life planned. The longer I spent thinking about it, the more outlandish my thoughts became. By the end of the day, I had them married with two-point-five kids and a white picket fence, and in the meantime, I'd become a recluse with seventeen cats and a beer belly—it wasn't a pretty picture.

When the final bell rang, I cleaned up the paperwork from the dock and went to clock out. It was mind blowing how doing so little could be so taxing. Masyn fidgeted next to the break-room, and the moment she saw me, she stopped contorting her fingers and came toward me.

"Hey, sweetheart." Old habits die hard. "What's up?"

Her tongue snaked out, wetting her lips, before she pulled one into her mouth with her teeth. I punched out while she stared at me, almost afraid to say whatever was on her mind. So, I waited, and then crossed my arms. People milled about around us until I finally grabbed her elbow and pulled her aside.

"Do you—Beau called—" Lord, if she got this tongue-tied talking about him now that she'd admitted how she felt, I couldn't imagine how she'd be in front of Beau himself. "He and Peyton want to know if we want to come down to Sadler's."

Well, that was certainly anti-climactic. "Sure. I could use a beer to wash away the time I just spent in solitary confinement."

"You going to follow me home or pick me up?"

Any other day, this would be a no-brainer. I'd pick her up so she could drive us both home. Then she'd spend the night in the guest room—her room—and I'd crash in mine. "I guess I thought after Monday night, you wouldn't want to do that anymore."

"Oh." Her eyes dropped to her feet.

I lifted her chin with my fingers, unable to stand the sight of her upset, and gave her a reassuring grin that hurt my heart to make. "You're welcome at my house anytime, Masyn; you know that. I'll pick you up after I shower and change."

She nodded, biting her bottom lip, again. The sudden air of shyness she'd taken on was adorable, but I hoped at some point, we could move past this and get back to where we were before Beau came barreling into town. Maybe once he was gone, I'd be able to let go of the notion of them together—it was a long shot, and I shouldn't get my hopes up. But just because Masyn didn't love me, didn't mean my feelings suddenly disappeared. If anything, they only intensified with the confirmation that I couldn't have her.

We parted ways for an hour, and when I picked her up, her entire demeanor had changed. Gone was the uncertain girl who chewed her lip, afraid to talk to me. In her place was the version of Masyn I'd known for so many years. She popped into the truck, buckled her seatbelt, and immediately changed the station as soon as we started moving.

"I think I liked you better mopey." I laughed to make sure she knew it was a joke.

She cranked up the volume, and I wanted to claw my eardrums out. "I like it better when I can't hear you," she hollered over the death metal piercing the speakers.

I turned it down so that the people in the next county didn't file a noise complaint. "What made you decide to play nice with Peyton?"

"She's leaving in a few days, Beau's leaving in a few days, and then everything will go back to the way it's always been, right?"

I glanced at her in the passenger seat while keeping my focus on the road. Her sweet, caramel-colored eyes glistened with hope, and her gentle smile tilted her lips up. Maybe she was right. "Is that such a bad thing?"

Her hair reflected the sunlight when she shook her head, and it was like the golden and honey streaks were illuminated. "No. I don't think so."

I raised my brow, hoping she'd give me more to go on. When she stared out the window, I assumed the conversation was over, until she turned the music down and faced me in the seat. My hand rested on the console; Masyn took it and twined her fingers through mine. She'd done it before—usually when she wanted something.

"So, Monday night wasn't my finest hour. Honestly, I don't really remember what all was said or how I said it. I just know that something changed between us, and it wasn't for the better." That was an understatement. "And ever since, I've been trying to figure out how to smooth things over." Her chest rose when she inhaled deeply through her nose. "I think the whole Beau wedding thing hit some girly chord in me about my future, and relationships, and kids—I had too much time to think about crap that normally doesn't hold any real weight for me."

"Masyn, it's okay to want to get married and have kids. I want to settle down at some point, too."

The light in her eyes dimmed a bit, yet not being able to focus on her expression and drive, I couldn't evaluate it.

"Anyway, it dawned on me that Beau's not really a part of our lives anymore. I mean, he is, but not daily. The two of us aren't anywhere near as close to him as we were in high school. And let's be honest, his life isn't going to lead him back to Harden...ever."

She had a point. One that I'd rolled over in my mind about a thousand times today, thinking I'd lose them both when Masyn joined him in Atlanta.

"And what's the likelihood Peyton will *ever* come back to Georgia?" She chuckled at the thought.

I guess that all depended on how foolish the two of them decided to be. She hadn't really engaged in any of his advances, although he'd been shameless in making them. "Probably not great."

"Right! So at the end of the week, it's me and you again... the way it always has been—the way it should be. And I want that to be as effortless as it was a week ago."

I needed to tell her how hard that would be for me. Especially when I had a chance to sit down and talk to Beau about what he'd said to her when she confessed her feelings. Unfortunately, the opportunity hadn't presented itself because someone else was always around—not to mention, I had to be careful how I addressed it, so I didn't violate Masyn's trust.

"That's probably the best thing you can do. Just make it through the week. Who knows? Maybe at the end of it, you'll have made a new friend."

"In Peyton?" she squealed.

I chuckled at her outburst. "Yeah, Peyton. You might be surprised. She's nothing like Felicity."

"It wouldn't matter if she were the Pope, Lee. I'll be nice to her while she's here, but I won't shed any tears when she leaves."

"Fair enough." I don't think anyone could ask for more from Masyn. And maybe with the two out-of-towners gone, our lives *would* go back to the way they were.

It wasn't what I hoped for in the long run, but having any piece of Masyn was better than nothing at all...if my heart survived.

Once I pulled into a space, we both hopped out of the truck, and I rounded the front to meet her. I threw my arm around her shoulders and squeezed her to me briefly, taking the opportunity to steal a whiff of her hair, which still smelled like the shop. The familiar scent I loved on her brought a genuine smile to my lips as I let her go to pull open the bar door with my left hand.

"Do you see them?" I asked as we made our way inside and my eyes adjusted to the light.

Masyn pointed to the table we'd sat at when we were here Saturday, and I groaned thinking we were in for a repeat. It was stupid, it was just a table...one we'd all sat at countless times before. Yet somehow, adding Peyton to the mix had twisted my nice, neat little world into a discombobulated mess.

Masyn tried to grab my hand, and I nearly came unglued when she grazed the stitches and I jerked back in response. The instant she turned around, I saw it in her eyes. "It's okay, you hit my stitches, sweetheart, nothing else."

I stepped to her other side and slipped my arm around her shoulders to lead her past the bar and pool tables. Beau beamed when he saw the two of us together and my arm around Masyn. I shook my head to indicate that it wasn't what he thought. Masyn slid into the booth and I joined her.

Beau stuck his hand out in greeting. Unwilling to have a repeat of what took place at the door, I lifted my left hand awkwardly over the table.

"What the hell is that, man?" He stared at his right hand and my left, now joined in some strange shake.

I let go and held up the other so he could see the bruises and stitches, and I used it as an opportunity to show Masyn that my reflex had nothing to do with her. "It's a little sore, and even the slightest bump makes it throb."

"I'm sorry, Lee. I totally forgot." Masyn's apology wasn't necessary.

"No worries, seriously. You guys order anything?" I asked Beau and Peyton, who looked chummy sitting next to each other.

It was rather uncanny how similar Peyton and Felicity were in appearance when each of them stood next to Beau. Yet apart from him—when the sisters were together—it was easy to tell they were siblings, and they didn't look like twins. I tilted my head to the side, trying to figure out what it was about Beau and Peyton together, when I finally realized their hair was the same color, and they had very similar complexions. God help them, as easily as those two colored, if they ever had kids, they'd permanently look like they had a rash.

"Beer and appetizers. I got a bucket. I didn't know how hungry either of you would be." Beau took a swig of his beer and set it down.

Masyn giggled at my inability to twist a bottle cap off with my left hand, so she twisted one off for her and one for me. Peyton was drinking wine, again. I wondered if it came out of a box or had a screw cap. It was a good thing the grapes were fermented—I didn't know anyone else who'd enter these doors and order a glass.

I studied Beau and Peyton across from me, and I thought

how hard it must be for Masyn to sit here watching them together. They weren't all over each other, even though it was clear there was a mutual attraction. And while Masyn attempted to talk to Peyton, I thought about how horrible it would be if Beau and Peyton were supposed to be together, yet he'd had to meet Felicity to get to Peyton, and that one connection would keep them from ever having a real relationship.

When I rejoined the conversation, Lani delivered a tray of wings and fries and another bucket of beers. "What have you two done all day?" I asked, once the waitress left.

Peyton and Beau glanced at each other like teenagers caught skipping school. Then Peyton answered, "I went over to the Chastains' house, and Beverly helped me go through the contracts from the wedding to see what was owed and what needed to be taken care of. And the two of us made some phone calls."

I nearly choked on my beer. "Beverly?" I'd known the woman my whole life and only once dared to call her Bev— right before I smacked her on the backside. Needless to say, it didn't go over well, and I never tried again.

"Yeah, what do you call her?" Peyton asked with humor in her voice.

Masyn and I answered at the same time, "Mrs. Chastain."

"I don't think Ryland even calls her Beverly," I joked. "We used to laugh about Beau's parents calling each other mister and missus while they were having sex, and how formal intercourse must be between them."

Masyn laughed next to me, clearly remembering the same things I did. Beau hadn't thought it was funny then, and he didn't think it was now. I thought it was a riot.

"She told me to call her Beverly." Peyton's confusion was almost cute until Beau patted her on the leg and told her to ignore us. At that point it was nauseating. "Anyhow, once we finished all that, I helped Beau identify what gifts came from whom, and we made a trip to the post office to return as many as we could fit in the car."

"We got most of them addressed. I'll just have to make a few runs to drop them off."

I couldn't imagine what postage on all that would cost. "Did you open any of them to put in the new house?"

"No. My mom insisted they be mailed here so she could keep track of them. She was afraid with us moving that things would get lost or one of us wouldn't remember where something came from. Felicity was pissed then, but I bet she's thanking her lucky stars now since she doesn't have shit to deal with."

Masyn glared at Peyton, and I hit her under the table. She quickly pushed my hand aside and proceeded. "It's like Felicity got off scot-free. How did you end up doing all the dirty work?"

Peyton shrugged. "The luck of the draw, I guess." Then she glanced at Beau and grinned. "It hasn't been so bad, though. And now that I've gotten all the actual work done, I have a couple of days to hang out before my flight leaves on Friday." A moron could have seen how excited she was about having some time to spend alone with Beau and how grim the prospect of flying out was.

"I'm sure it's nice to get away from the grind for a while." My statement was absentminded and certainly not intended to lead into anything.

"You know, you're welcome to come to New York anytime

you want to escape. I don't have a huge place, but my roommate and I can certainly make room for visitors." The invitation was extended to all three of us, but it was intended for Beau. Peyton glanced around the table when no one said anything. "Lee, why don't you come home with me? I'm sure you're not able to work with your thumb like that."

That was out of left field. "Me?"

She placed her elbows on the table and leaned forward. "Yeah, why not? You could take a few days off, come see the city, and then fly back Monday or Tuesday. I don't have school all summer. I could show you around Manhattan, take you to see the Statue of Liberty, the Chrysler Building, Times Square."

Peyton was walking dangerously close to the edge of a cliff, one that Masyn might push her over. Here she was all hugged up on Beau, and when Masyn finally surrendered to let Peyton in, Peyton goes and asks me to come to New York.

"I've already asked Beau, and of course he can't, what with starting a new job on Monday and the house in Atlanta that's sitting empty. You hurting your hand is perfect. Well, not perfect—I'm sorry you cut yourself. I meant it gives you a good excuse to take a breath of fresh air."

I could sense Masyn's stare like it was burning holes through my cheek. Yet when I dared to meet her eyes, there was no emotion there, only indifference. I wondered if she'd heard that the only reason Beau wasn't going to New York was his new job. I couldn't read her expression, and that scared the hell out of me.

"I'm not off work, Peyton. Just on light duty." It was an excuse, not an answer.

"Maybe it would do you some good to get out of Harden, Lee." Beau's encouragement threw me for a loop. And his aloof attitude when he sipped his beer and put his arm behind Peyton on the back of the booth left me perplexed as to what world I'd entered.

I didn't get his angle—hell, maybe he didn't have one.

Peyton relaxed into Beau's casual embrace. It was one that claimed her without screaming he'd done it. There wasn't a doubt in my mind the two had had sex since the last time I saw them—they both glowed with a post-orgasm haze. He was a damn fool for pursuing that. And if *I* saw it, I was certain Masyn did, too. Yet when Peyton eased into Beau's side, it didn't seem to bother Masyn at all.

I didn't have a clue what the hell was going on with any of them.

"I appreciate the offer," I responded to Peyton.

"Think about it. It wouldn't be hard to get another ticket for Friday if you change your mind."

Masyn nudged me. "Can you let me out? I need to go to the restroom."

I hopped up.

Beau used the brief intermission to probe. None too casually, I might add. "So...what happened Monday night?"

"Now's not a great time to talk about it, Beau. I'll tell you later." It was obvious to Peyton I didn't want to have the discussion in front of her. "She's not going to be gone long. I don't want her to come back and hear us talking about her." I tried to smooth things over, although I sucked at that kind of thing.

"Fine. I'll get her to dance with me and ask her myself."

Beau finished his beer and set the bottle at the end of the table for the waitress to pick up.

"Let it go, Beau. Seriously. It's been painful enough without you digging into it."

Before he could respond, Masyn returned and waited for me to move. As I slid down to allow her a seat on the end, Beau stood and took her hand. Masyn was a sucker for anyone to dance with, and that person was never me. There was nothing unusual about Beau dancing with her; I prayed he kept my name off his tongue and was gentle with whatever information he provided her with about his newfound interest in Peyton. He was leaving on Sunday and wouldn't have to deal with the shitstorm his wedding and visit to Harden left behind.

Peyton and I sat in what I considered uncomfortable silence. There were people milling around as the happy-hour crowd mingled and conversations took place around us, yet I was at a total loss for what to say to her.

"I'm serious about my invitation, Lee. You guys have been so nice to me while I've been here; I'd love to reciprocate and show you a little piece of my life."

Ignoring her suggestions, I dove right in without any lube to ease the transition. "What's going on with you and Beau, Peyton? It's none of my business, and you can do what you want. It seems like an awfully messy relationship right now for either one of you to entertain."

She waved me off like it wasn't a big deal. Yet this was the same girl who said she never dated. And she didn't know Beau. He was a relationship kind of guy. "It's harmless."

"To who?"

"We've been thrown together in an odd twist of fate. I

know once I leave here and go home, I won't see him again." Famous last words.

This was the same guy who'd flown to Italy over spring break at the last minute to see Felicity because the idea of being away from her for a whole week was more than he could stand.

"Does he know that? Or is that your assumption?"

"Both, I guess. I don't have any expectations. My parents would freak out if they knew I was even spending time with you guys. You wouldn't believe all the crap I've heard from my mother since they left." She rolled her eyes like that drama was any different than what would ensue if those two dated.

"I don't get the impression he's thinking that way."

"Beau's life is in Atlanta. Mine's in New York. Neither one of us is moving. It's not hurting anyone to have fun while I'm here." She might not get hurt, but I wasn't so sure I could say the same for Beau.

The song Masyn and Beau danced to ended, and they returned to our table. The expressions on both of their faces were hard to read, but I'd say they were confused. It was a three-minute song. Yet in that amount of time, Peyton managed to tell me she was playing around with Beau, so there was no telling what Beau and Masyn had discussed while they were away.

Masyn took a seat at the same time Beau did.

"Did we interrupt something?" Masyn's quizzical stare didn't make me want to open up in the slightest.

Peyton smiled at me. "We were discussing Lee making a visit to New York."

No, we weren't. That wasn't at all what we talked about.

The silent exchange between Beau and Masyn didn't sit

well with me. Peyton was a nice girl, but she'd brought a tornado into town with her, and I was ready for her to go. I'd tried to be nice. I'd tried to welcome her into our fold. But at the end of the day, she was playing with a bunch of people's emotions—mine included. And the end result would be people getting hurt.

"You really should consider it, Lee. You never leave Georgia or Harden for that matter. Some time in the Big Apple could breathe some new life into you. Put things back into perspective," Beau said.

My brow furrowed. I'd made it clear I had no interest in Peyton. "Can I talk to you, Beau?" This shit had to stop.

"Now?" His response surprised me.

Before I could get out of the booth and yank his ass outside, Lani came to the table to ask about more drinks. Our food sat untouched, and I was at a loss for words. When Lani finally left, he pulled Peyton out of the booth and onto the dance floor completely avoiding me. I stared at the two of them as he took her into his arms, and they laughed about something I couldn't hear. To an outsider peering in, it sure as hell didn't look like either one of them was just having fun for a couple of days. I knew my best friend, and he was falling fast—even if he shouldn't.

FOURTEEN

MASYN AND I STAYED AT SADLER'S FOR A WHILE LONGER and ended up playing pool while Peyton and Beau danced, played darts, and talked to people Beau knew and hadn't seen in ages. They were far more comfortable together than I'd ever seen him act with Felicity. Yet once we were able to separate from the two for a bit, Masyn and I had a good time doing what we always did.

Some random guy tried to hit on her, and I made sure he knew she wasn't interested—I didn't care if she was or not. Masyn wasn't my property, but she was my friend, and everyone in town needed to respect her. Then she beat me at four out of five games of pool. I refused to admit it had anything to do with the stitches in my right hand. Personally, I think her *accidentally* pressing her ass against my crotch and grabbing my sides from behind at critical moments in the game was cheating, but either way, I now owed her omelets and a foot massage. And every time the jukebox stopped playing the two of us raced to drop quarters in the slot and bickered over song choices, because we each hated the music the other one picked.

It was who we were and had always been. We both complemented the other, she filled my cracks, and I was the glue for hers. Yet none of it was heavy, we were more like light, fluffy marshmallows than thick caramel. I just wished she was the cherry on top of the whole damn sundae.

When we left—arm in arm—Beau and Peyton sat at the booth talking without a care in the world or a place to be in the morning. Masyn didn't seem the least bit bothered by Beau's latest love interest, or that he would leave with another girl. Maybe they'd ironed things out between them when they danced. I didn't know and wasn't going to ask. I couldn't handle another heart explosion from Masyn where Beau was concerned. It wouldn't hurt my feelings in the least if she didn't want to talk about anything remotely romantic.

"Are you okay to drive?" I asked her, already knowing the answer.

She held out her hand for the keys and looked at me like I was an idiot.

It didn't take us long to get in the truck and on our way back to my place.

I stared at her, trying to keep from begging. "You staying?" It came off rather indifferent. Thankfully, she hadn't picked up on my hidden emotions.

She quickly turned in my direction and wagged her brows like a goofball before watching the road again. "Absolutely. You owe me omelets. And a foot rub."

I would never admit it to Masyn—or anyone else for that matter, because riding shotgun made me look like a bitch—but there were rare times I enjoyed having her drive. It gave me the freedom to stare at her virtually unnoticed, and she always assumed it was because I was drunk. I wasn't drunk—I could have driven home. I'd only had two beers in twice as many hours. Normally she kept close tabs on my consumption; tonight, however, she hadn't.

I relished any chance I got to touch her when she didn't see it as intimate. "Are you collecting on the massage tonight?" My tone indicated I hoped she wouldn't, while my heart hoped she would.

"Maybe." She drew out the word teasingly. "Depends on how bad you irritate me between here and there."

I reached over and switched the radio station back to country music and turned it up with a smirk.

Masyn huffed out an amused chuckle. "Oh, so you *want* to be at my beck and call tonight, huh?" She swatted at my hand.

"Just hoping I can open your mind to real music one of these days."

She pushed the preset button. "Not going to happen." Masyn ran her tiny hand through her long hair, and I couldn't help but notice her stained cuticles that matched my own.

Never in a million years would I have thought I'd find that sexy on a woman. But on her, it knotted my stomach in anticipation, and my heart skipped a beat. A painful beat.

"Are you really considering a visit to New York?" Her focus stayed on the road; she didn't even glance at me to catch a reaction.

"Hadn't planned on it. Don't get me wrong, I think it would be fun to go someday."

There was a pause that was a beat too long. Masyn wanted

to ask a question, but I knew from experience, she wasn't certain she wanted an answer. "So why not now?"

"Do you think I should go?" I might throw up if she said yes.

She shrugged, never taking her eyes off the road. "If you want to." That was terribly noncommittal.

I didn't, and she pulled into my driveway at the perfect time to keep me from answering or continuing this discussion. "Home sweet home," I chimed, and jumped out before she could stop me.

Masyn joined me on the porch. She unlocked the door, strolled into my house, and then dropped my keys on the kitchen counter. "It's not late. You want to go swimming?"

There wasn't an ice cube's chance in hell that I would ever turn down the opportunity to see Masyn half-naked. Ever. "Sure. Let me change. I'll meet you out back."

Not two minutes later, I heard my name echo down the hall like a wolf howling at the moon.

She didn't knock, she didn't wait for me to respond, she simply barged through my door as I pulled my shorts over my ass. "Lee!"

"What?" I tied the drawstring the best I could using only one thumb and gawked at her like she'd lost her damn mind.

Her face was beet red, and her chest heaved in what I could only assume was agitation based on the snarl curling her upper lip. "Who's been in my room?"

Shit.

Playing dumb was always a safe way to go where a woman was concerned. Most of them believed men were morons anyhow so I tried to get away with it. "Huh?"

"Don't 'huh' me. Where's my white swimsuit?"

I should have thought through my response before I let it fly out of my mouth. "You mean the dental floss Peyton found in your drawer?" I grabbed the bikini off my dresser where I'd left it after washing it.

She glanced at the swimsuit, and her expression morphed into horror, or maybe disgust. "Oh my God. You let another woman wear my bikini?" she shrieked. The tone of her voice shot up an octave. If I didn't think she'd hit me, I'd cover my ears.

"Is that what you're calling it?" I dangled the two pieces from my fingers, one on each hand. "Where the hell did you even get something like this? And who the fuck have you been wearing it for at *my* house?"

She snatched it from my fingertips with a drastically overexaggerated huff. "Please tell me you washed it!"

I nodded and folded my arms over my chest, waiting for answers to my other questions. None of which I got. Masyn pivoted on the ball of her foot and pranced down the hall like she hadn't just come in here like a bat out of hell, raising cane. I decided it was in my best interest to let the questions go for now, since she hadn't come unglued about Peyton wearing her swimsuit.

Nothing, and I mean absolutely nothing, could have prepared me to see Masyn Porter strutting around in that barely-there bikini. My mouth went dry at the sight of her standing by the pool, and all I could think about was slowly untying each one of those strings and watching it fall to the ground to expose what little of her skin it covered. Every inch of her body was perfectly toned and precisely proportioned.

And even from the side, the swell of her breasts sent an ache between my legs that I didn't want to tame. The familiar tightening in my balls and heat flooding my dick only made me want more of what I couldn't have.

"What are you staring at?" Her voice lilted light and playful and only served to amp up my desire.

Instead of being a gentleman and complimenting the way she looked, I played the asshole-guy card to feign indifference. "Still wondering where you got that...thing." I waved at her from head to toe and set my mouth in a thin line, hoping I appeared displeased. I was anything but.

She scoffed. "Victoria's Secret. You don't like it?"

I stared at her blankly. "I didn't say that."

"No, you didn't say anything at all." Masyn wanted me to praise how amazing she looked standing on my pool deck. She waited for it with longing in her eyes.

"I've just never seen it."

She tilted her chin to her chest, stared down at her flat stomach, and touched the ties on each side of her hips. "It's new." The soft curve of her pelvic bones strained against the bikini, and all I could think about was my hands holding her, my thumbs digging in right where those bows hung, while she rode me to a place neither one of us had ever been.

"It's cute." *I was such an ass.*

"Cute?" Her lips remained parted after she said the word, stunned by my description. She knew it was hot, and she wanted me to tell her so.

My feet carried me toward her, driven by the brain in my pants—the one currently doing all my thinking. And when I reached her, I slipped my hand under her chin and tipped her head back so I could look into her eyes. "Yeah, cute." *It was far from fucking cute.*

I was in so far over my head, I was going to drown in the sight of her if I didn't do something quickly to get my head above water. And the only thing that came to mind was tossing her over my shoulder, walking to the edge of the pool, slapping her ass, and then throwing her in. My shoulders shook as I laughed and she went under, knowing when she came up, I'd get an earful.

The moment I saw her head break the surface, I took away her opportunity to bitch at me and did a cannonball beside her, engulfing her with water. When I tried to come up for air, her hands were on my shoulders, pressing all of her weight onto them to try to keep me under. We'd done this for years, yet even as kids when we were closer in size and weight, she'd never been able to win. Tonight was no different. And a battle of wills ensued. The game never got old—or maybe it was chasing her around the pool that kept me coming back for more. I got to touch her, hold her, tickle her, and watch her face light up, without risking my heart breaking.

Masyn finally managed to escape to the stairs and sat there facing the pool. Her eyes shimmered with happiness, and her chest heaved as she tried to catch her breath. I could do this all night if that was the reward I got at the end of it.

I loved Beau like a brother, but he'd never appreciate the little things about her: the way her nose scrunched when she thought something was gross, or the fact that she preferred jeans to dresses or barbeque to fine dining. He'd want her to change to fit into his circle—the one his family expected him to grow into. There would be no job in a machine shop, no tiny house on a mill hill, and certainly no clunker car he wouldn't know how to fix if he had to. All the quirks that made Masyn who she was—the things I loved—would be altered. And I couldn't let that happen without at least trying to fight for her.

I'd never managed to tell her what I went to her house to say on Monday—not all of it, anyway. She'd been so hell-bent on telling me what she wanted me to hear that I'd let her monopolize the conversation. In the end, I might lose her and Beau both, but I wanted to know—no, I needed to know—that I'd fought for her the way she deserved to be fought for.

The air between us was thick with desperation—although that might have just been my own—and with each step I took in the pool, the space shrunk. There was either fear or anticipation marking her expression, and come hell or high water, I was about to find out which one it was.

The closer I got, the straighter her spine became until her entire body tensed. And when I reached the base of the underwater stairs, she didn't stop me or ask what I was doing. She spread her knees to make room for me and welcomed me in. My hands slid up her slick thighs, and her palms grazed along my forearms. Neither of us broke eye contact, and when my fingers reached her back, I hesitated. I gave her every opportunity to ask what I was doing, to push me away, or even tell me to stop, but when she didn't give me a signal that she didn't want my advances, I leaned my head into hers and closed my eyes.

The lips I'd dreamed of tasting didn't disappoint. They were warm and full and soft, fitting perfectly against my own. And when she separated them, it was like Moses had parted the Red

Sea just for me. The world stopped, the crickets didn't chirp, and the birds didn't sing; there was nothing other than Masyn Porter in my arms. Our tongues danced slowly, and her fingers explored my arms, her nails digging into my skin as our kiss grew deeper. My hands pulled her to me of their own accord, gliding her through the water with ease, until her center pressed firmly against me. There was no possibility she couldn't feel how turned on I was when she locked her ankles behind my ass and wound her arms around my neck. Sparks flew through my limbs and my mouth and my tongue. Everything about her, about it, was perfect.

Her fingers tangled in my hair, and she used her elbows on my shoulders for leverage to grind herself into my crotch, and I groaned. The kind of groan I'd only had in my dreams—and only in dreams where Masyn played the starring role. It was guttural and came from deep in my throat. She finally broke away, smiling against my lips, until she tilted her forehead to mine and sighed.

It wasn't a "what have I done" sound. She was content, and I was on cloud fucking nine. As much as I wanted to stay there, to do all the things I imagined to her tight little body, I realized that just days ago, Masyn told me she loved our best friend. And I'd just complicated the hell out of things for her.

The smile lines around her eyes disappeared. "What happened?" She wasn't referring to the kiss. "You just shut down. Was it *that* bad?" Masyn tried to push away, but I refused to release my hold.

"What? No." Still clutching her with one arm securely around her waist, I ran my other hand—shit, the one I wasn't supposed to get wet—through my hair. I hadn't felt the slightest bit of pain run through it, tossing her around in the pool, yet now that I'd royally fucked things up, it ached.

She dropped her legs from my waist. "Then what?"

"Can we get out of the pool? I'm not supposed to get the stitches wet, and I have no idea how long we've been in here, but my fingers are prunes." It hadn't seemed like we'd been outside long, but it had been long enough to screw up my hand and possibly my relationship with Masyn...even if she'd yet to protest.

Masyn nodded, thinking I'd let her go. I wasn't giving up that easily. When I started up the stairs and her weight shifted, she apparently realized, she could either hold on or be dragged across the porch like a limp noodle. She chose to climb my body like a monkey would a tree and let me carry her inside, leaving a trail of water behind us. I hadn't bothered putting more towels in the box on the porch, so I kept going through the sliding glass door and down the hall past Masyn's room and into mine. Her skin prickled with goose bumps in the cool air inside the house, but she didn't protest the chill.

We reached my bathroom, and I turned on the shower. As soon as the water warmed, I stepped in, careful to keep my hand out of the stream. I finally set her down, but I didn't let her go far. Not that she tried to get away. Instead, she slowly slid her hand from the back of my neck to my jaw and cupped it. There was hunger in her gaze, and I wanted to quench her appetite. Our mouths met again in another paralyzing kiss. When we broke free, she grabbed the bar of soap and a washcloth and scrubbed away the chlorine from my skin, and I did the same with her.

She turned off the water and grabbed a towel for me and

two for her—one for her hair and one for her body. I'd hoped for something more romantic or maybe even erotic but no such luck. Peering at her while trying not to be caught doing so, I watched with envy as each drop of water trailed her skin.

And then in some magic twist of feminine power, she managed to release both pieces of that damn bikini without touching the towel that hid her body. She picked up the swimsuit off the floor and hung it over the towel bar, and then lifted onto her tiptoes to place the sweetest kiss on my lips before she left. I assumed she went to put on clothes, so I did the same, and then I attempted to assess my stitches. They appeared okay, but I guess I'd find out tomorrow—or in the middle of the night if the wound came open and oozed blood.

I was still in my room when she returned. Her long, dark hair flowed down her back, and she'd put on a tank top and tiny-ass shorts I'd always loved. It wasn't anything different than what she always wore, but somehow, everything about it seemed new. Masyn crawled onto my mattress, and I didn't ask any questions when I flipped off the light and joined her.

Just like Monday night, she lifted my arm and curled up next to me. But unlike Monday night when she'd gone to sleep, tonight her fingers circled my bare chest and stomach in a teasing dance. Her hand was highlighted by the glow of the moon seeping through the blinds. I tried to look down to see her face, but the top of her head blocked my view. I'd give my left nut to know what she was thinking. Just stepping inside her mind and her thoughts for a few minutes might put mine at ease.

"Does this change things between us?" Her voice was tiny

in the large room, and if I hadn't been listening for it, the darkness would have swallowed it.

I stroked her hair, praying that the answer to my next question was what I hoped to hear. "Do you want it to?"

The silence between my last word and her answer went on for an eternity, although it was likely less than half a minute. Her cheek tickled my skin when she nodded against my chest, and her unwillingness to look at me filled me with anxiety. There wasn't a lot of light in the room, and even the moon seemed to have left us to ourselves, temporarily hidden by a cloud. The light she'd left on down the hall crept through a crack in the partially open door, and my eyes began to adjust so I could see her when I pulled back. Lifting her chin with my finger, I prayed for a positive sign when her face came into view, yet all I could focus on were the tears lining her eyes.

"Why are you crying?" I brushed my thumb under one of her eyes to erase the pool of moisture. A few drops dribbled over my stitches.

Masyn didn't answer at first. Instead, she lifted one shoulder, then let it drop in mock indifference. She bit her lip, avoided my gaze, then finally said, "I...I just didn't—you don't—I never thought..." Her words were lost in emotion she couldn't contain.

I shifted my weight, rolled her over onto her back, and hovered above her while propped on my elbows. "Talk to me." I pressed a gentle kiss to her lips, hoping it would make the words come easier. *And* sway them in my favor. "Please."

She hid her face again and muttered against my chest. "I already told you how I felt."

Every fiber of my being tensed and her body followed mine.

"About Beau?" It wasn't really a question so much as a statement confirming we were talking about the same thing.

Masyn sat up like someone had slapped her and pushed me over onto my side in the process. "Beau? Who's talking about Beau?" If the situation had been any different, the glare she shot me would have been adorable.

As it stood, it only served to confuse me. "You are—did. Monday night when I came to your house." I sat up so I could see her face and watch her expressions. So much of what she said was hidden in the lines around her mouth and the crinkle of her nose—and not seeing it could result in missing her meaning.

"I admit, I don't remember everything I said when you came over, but I wasn't talking about Beau Chastain. Gross. He wears tweed and drives a sedan."

If she wasn't talking about Beau, then I clearly misunderstood *everything* she'd said. "You asked me if I knew how hard it was to be friends with one guy you loved and one you adored. I specifically asked if you were talking about Beau."

I leaned back and turned on the lamp next to my bed. The darkness was like a blindfold, and my heart desperately wanted to see.

"No...I told you it was hard to talk to my best friend through signals—the special text messages to let me know if it was safe to have a conversation. I don't know how you misunderstood that." She acted like everything she'd said had been clear as glass when, in actuality, it was as transparent as mud.

I chuckled...which pissed her off.

She swatted at me, and I flinched. "Don't laugh at me. Do

you have any idea how hard it was for me to admit that to you? Even drunk, it was a stupid chance to take."

"Sweetheart, I'm not laughing at you, I'm—"

"And don't do that. I don't want to be another one of your girls. I want to be *the* girl." She straightened her spine and pulled her shoulders back in defiance.

I propped myself up against the pillows on the headboard and then leaned forward, grabbing her by the waist. As much as I wanted to see her face, she was embarrassed and flustered, and I preferred her to be comfortable, so that she actually heard what I was about to say. I nestled her between my legs with her back to my front and then wrapped my arms around her chest. She let her head drop to my shoulder and held onto my forearms, melting into my embrace.

"Have you ever heard me call anyone else sweetheart?"

"All the time." I didn't have to see her expression to know she was pouting, and it shouldn't have made me happy, but it did.

"You've *never* heard me call anyone, not even a child, sweetheart. You may have heard hon, or darlin', or possibly even babe, but not one time, in all my life, have I ever called anyone other than you, sweetheart. And I know I haven't because you're the only person who's ever held that place in my heart."

My grip was too tight for her to turn to argue with me, even though she tried. My arms were like a boa constrictor; when she created any space between us, I took the chance to bring her closer until there was no wiggle room remaining.

"Lee..." My name flowed from her mouth like warm honey mixed with melted butter.

"I came to your house Monday to talk to you—"

"I know. You wanted to know why I had avoided you."

"True, but I also came to tell you something else. Something I should have told you in tenth grade. And I got part of it out when you were bitching about Peyton, and then you started rambling about Beau."

She turned her head without moving her body, determined to illustrate a point. "I wasn't talking about *Beau*, Lee."

I loosened my grip and allowed her to curl her side into my chest with her back against my bicep. My heart raced, and I stared into her eyes, trying to be certain I'd just heard her right.

I couldn't take in enough air.

My lungs wouldn't fill, and I worried I'd faint before I told her what I needed to say.

If I didn't get out the words I'd been dying to say for six years, it felt like my insides might combust, and I'd miss my chance. There'd been too many wasted opportunities and too many days that had passed without her knowing my heart belonged to her, and it always had.

Rather than a drawn-out explanation, or tiptoeing into the actual confession, I just spit it out. "I love you, Masyn. Since that day in the lunchroom, there hasn't been a piece of me that didn't belong to you."

It would have been too much to hope that Masyn simply returned the sentiment. Nope, she had to analyze it. "Then why all the other girls?"

I laughed. At some point, all of this was going to come out. I'd told her the hardest part, and she hadn't shut me down; now I had to convince her of the truth. "What other girls?"

"Really?" She rolled her eyes. "Remember when we talked about you being an easy lay?"

"I remember you telling me what was good for a goose was a gander." I needed to keep this from getting heavy. I couldn't bear seeing her crying as I relived my past through her eyes.

"What does that mean? It doesn't even make sense."

"You said it. I thought it was quite appropriate. A goose does need a gander."

"Moving on. Last Friday, you got overly offended because I said you were an easy lay. *Those* are all the women I'm talking about. If you've had these feelings for me since tenth grade, why make sure I knew every time you dropped your pants for another girl? Did you think it would open my eyes to what I was missing and make me want you more? 'Cause I got to tell you, I didn't like it all that much."

"After the scene with Alex our sophomore year, you shut down, Masyn. I'm not blaming you. I'm just saying you made it clear that you weren't interested in dating."

"Yeah, assholes."

"In my defense, you never stipulated that part."

"I assumed it was understood."

"I'm a guy. We need clear-cut instructions, not innuendo and assumptions."

"You're avoiding the question."

"No, I'm giving you an answer you don't want to hear. You didn't want to date *anyone*. And I didn't want you to date anyone. You were my best friend—and Beau's—and I just wanted to make sure no one ever hurt you that way again."

"And you thought parading various girls around in front of me was the way to pave the yellow brick road to my heart?"

"Honestly, I didn't think about it at all. I don't think I really knew what I felt was love. Hell, we were sixteen. And over the years, you've never shown the slightest bit of interest in anything other than friendship."

Sadness hung in her eyes, and her bottom lip poked out just a hair. "Then why are you telling me now?"

I couldn't stop myself from grabbing it with my teeth and tugging on it gently before kissing her again.

Masyn pressed the heel of her hand into my chest to put some space between our mouths and forced me to answer.

"Because," I replied, the sweet flavor of her kiss still on my tongue, "the day Peyton Holstein strolled into town was the first indication you'd ever given me that you were jealous. And it took Beau pointing it out. I had no clue why you were so upset."

She crossed her arms. "I wasn't jealous."

"Sweetheart, you were. And it's okay. Every time I've ever seen you touch another guy, I've wanted to rip his arms out and shove them down his throat."

"That's a tad barbaric."

"It's the truth." I brushed her hair out of her eyes and tucked it behind her ear. "I hated seeing you with another guy. I was just as jealous, but after the stuff with Alex in high school, I didn't think I could say anything." My eyes flitted between hers, and I watched her nostrils flare as I studied her expression. "I had to wait it out. At least, I thought I did."

The fine, blue lines swirled with the iridescent green of her irises, and her pupils swelled before returning to normal. "Why? Just because of that scene in the lunchroom? That happened years ago. We were just kids."

My jumbled thoughts would likely never make sense to Masyn. "Yeah. I regretted how I handled that. What happened that day ruined any chance I might have ever had at a relationship with you."

She ran her fingers through her hair, and the smell of rosemary filled my nostrils. Her scent was intoxicating, but I wouldn't get the words out by lingering in it.

I didn't give her the chance to say anything before I offered my heartfelt apology and confession. "I can't change my past or the stupid decisions I've made along the way, Masyn. All I can do is tell you how I feel now and hope you feel the same."

Masyn squirmed in my arms until she managed to break the death grip I had on her so she could reach over and turn off the lamp. She moved out from between my legs and back to the side she'd taken over in the last couple of days, and I situated myself on my back. I'd hoped for more, to know where we stood, where we were going, and what she wanted. I hadn't gotten any of that. Relieving my heart of its greatest secret would have to do for tonight. If she were still lying in my arms, then there was hope for the rest and possibly even a future. I'd waited for six years; one more night wouldn't kill me.

Just before I drifted off with her practically on top of me, Masyn tilted her head up and used her hand to turn my face toward her. She softly pressed her lips to mine, and when she pulled away, she nuzzled into my neck and whispered into my ear, "Lee Carter, I've loved you since we were five, when you walked me home from school."

FIFTEEN

Waking up with Masyn covering my left side—her thigh between my legs and her breasts pressed to my ribs—was like experiencing sunshine for the first time. The entire world looked different when the alarm went off. Her sleepy eyes recognized where she was, and a lazy grin lifted her lips.

"Mornin', sweetheart." I kissed her forehead and tried to adjust my body so my erection wasn't firmly pressed against her thigh.

"Hmm." She wiggled to stay as close as she had been when we woke up. "Good morning." Her lips were like heaven when she teased my chest with peppered affection.

As much as I didn't want to get up, we both had to be at work in an hour. "If you hurry, we can still do omelets before work."

She moved her hand down my side and trailed her thumb over my abdomen. "We should call in." If she thought she could entice me to stay in bed, it wouldn't take much, but I knew she'd regret it.

"You and I both know that neither one of us is going to call in, and certainly not at the same time. Navigating this in town is already going to be difficult; we don't need to throw blood in the water to attract the sharks." My fingertips found the bare skin between her tank top and shorts and traced patterns on her side.

I'd love nothing more than to stay right where I was for the rest of the day and explore Masyn's body. And I planned to do that very thing, just not before work. Nevertheless, I had to remind myself we had all the time in the world. Just because we'd finally admitted how we felt didn't mean we had to race to the altar tomorrow. Although, if I thought I could convince her to, I would just to make sure no one else ever stood a chance at having her.

"I want to lie here for a little while longer."

"So, no breakfast?"

"I'll claim my omelet another morning. And don't think I've forgotten you owe me a foot rub, too."

"I wouldn't dare."

Masyn's hand roamed my torso, and her fingers dipped below the waistband of my shorts. I loved that she wasn't daring enough to reach in and take what she was so clearly interested in. She was shy, and I had no idea she was so affectionate—she certainly hadn't been touchy-feely with the guys I'd seen her date.

"Hey, Masyn?"

"Yeah?" Her voice was deeper than usual in the morning, and the vibration of that one word on my chest made my cock stir. She giggled when it jumped, but she didn't say anything.

"Why did you and Tommy Morton break up?"

"That's a blast from the past."

"I know, humor me."

"You already know the answer. He cheated on me with Melinda Beece."

"What about Devin Callen or Kyle Perkins?"

Her fingers stopped moving, and she arched her back, twisting to see me. The grimace marring her features indicated her confusion.

"Or Larson Camp and Greg Davis?"

"I only went out with each of them a few times. I don't think I would have even said we broke up. We just didn't go out again."

"But was there a reason?"

"It sounds like you already think you know, so why don't you tell me, and I'll confirm or deny."

I flipped her over onto her back and settled between her legs with my hands tucked under her shoulders. My weight was on my elbows to keep from crushing her while allowing me to see her face. "Was it because of me?"

Laughter rolled through her and shook my chest. "You're full of yourself, Lee." She tried to push me off, but I refused to budge.

"So it wasn't because you spent the night here?"

It was a good thing her eyes wouldn't permanently stick in the back of her head like we'd been warned as kids. "Beau needs to learn to keep his mouth shut."

I rolled again, taking her with me, so she rested on my chest. "Or maybe you should learn to open yours." Kissing her today was like the first time yesterday. I hoped that never changed and that the electricity between us stayed this strong.

I'd never experienced it with anyone else and never wanted to again.

"Come on, we've got to get moving." I smacked her ass with a final peck on the lips. "We can lie around after work."

She sat on the edge of the mattress and turned to me. "We don't have to hang out with Peyton and Beau this afternoon?" Masyn acted like spending time with our best friend was a chore.

"Not if you don't want to. Peyton's leaving tomorrow, so we'll have all weekend to see Beau before he goes back to Atlanta on Sunday."

I climbed from bed and rummaged through my drawer in search of a white T-shirt to put on under my uniform. When I turned around and pulled it over my head, Masyn hadn't moved. Her hands were in her lap, tugging on her fingers and picking at her nails. Her teeth worried the corner of her bottom lip, and she stared at the floor. I hated seeing her vulnerable and unhappy when she was typically vibrant and strong.

Kneeling in front of her, I ducked down to see her face. "What's wrong, sweetheart?"

"None of this seems real. I'm worried you're going to wake up and realize how inexperienced I am and be bored with me, and I don't think I can handle that."

"I can't convince you of anything else by telling you what you want to hear. You're going to have to trust me and give *us* time." I kissed her cheek and pulled her up by her hand. "I promise, I didn't wait six years to tell you that I love you just to go racing off in a week or a month or even a year."

"Lee, I've never had a boyfriend."

"Good, we can navigate this together—'cause Lord knows,

I've never had a girlfriend. Now go get dressed while I make our lunches."

"Don't forget coffee," she hollered down the hall after me.

IF I'D THOUGHT BEING INJURED AND HAVING TO WORK THE docks made for the slowest day possible, being injured and having to work the docks while dreaming about spending an afternoon alone with Masyn curled up in my bed was far worse.

I was impressed with her ability to keep things about us quiet while we were at the shop. She hadn't gotten all bent out of shape when I didn't kiss her goodbye. She didn't try to hold my hand at lunch where we'd be forced to answer questions. And she hadn't acted any differently than she had since the day we'd started at Farley's. Outside of my house, Masyn was the same girl she'd always been—and I loved it, except, where she'd only entered my thoughts occasionally before, she plagued them now. I swear, I counted every second that ticked by on my watch, making the day infinitely longer.

I had to stop myself from sprinting to the time clock at the end of the shift. But not even the group of men gathered near the breakroom could stop the grin that took over my cheeks when I saw Masyn coming from the other side of the shop. She'd released her hair from the knot she typically wore at work, and she'd unbuttoned her uniform shirt to expose the thin, white, cotton T-shirt she had on underneath. The pants did nothing for her and didn't showcase her ass or hips, much less her legs, but I knew what was hiding beneath the fabric and couldn't wait to take it off.

I didn't care how long it took to get to sex, I wanted to explore every inch of her skin, and I longed for her to do the same with me. I was desperate to know her entire body like I knew the back of my hand.

"What the hell you grinning about, Carter?" Farley was always a pain in my ass.

"Taking top pay for a machinist while checking in trucks."

Masyn tried to suppress her giggle, and she strolled past us without saying a word.

"Porter?" Farley made no distinction between her and the other guys in the shop. She worked in a man's world, and he treated her like one.

She slid her card through the reader and turned around. "Yeah?"

"I need you to work over tomorrow afternoon. Line three's parts aren't meeting spec, and I need you to rework the codes to fix it. Shouldn't take you more than an hour or two."

Frequently, Masyn was thrilled with overtime, and even though she just agreed to stay late, I could tell she wasn't happy about it. That was the downside of being the best programmer a machine shop had. She was their go-to when issues cropped up.

"Not looking forward to staying late tomorrow?" I asked her as soon as we were in the truck and behind closed doors.

She responded with a sideways glare and the flick of a button to change the radio. I'd gotten lucky before work and listened to the morning show on the country station. I wasn't so lucky this afternoon. The only reason I got away with it on the way to work was because no music played, and she thought the hosts were funny.

I took her hand and kissed the top. "It's only a couple of hours. It won't be bad. Then you can come over and hang out with Beau and me. Just think...now you have an excuse not to say goodbye to Peyton."

She raised her brows and cocked her head with a shrug. "You've got a good point. I just hate that he pulls that crap on a Friday afternoon."

"Would you rather have stayed today?"

"I *wouldn't* have stayed today."

Masyn was fairly laid-back ninety-nine percent of the time. That one percent where she got riled up always made me laugh —and stand back. I was flattered that she anticipated seeing me as much as I did her.

A few blocks from the house, Masyn started bouncing in the seat next to me.

"What are you doing?"

"I have to pee."

"Why didn't you go at the shop?"

"I'm the only female in the place. Do you have any idea how gross those toilets are for those of us who have to sit to urinate?"

I didn't even have the truck stopped before she unbuckled her seatbelt. I threw it into park, and she bolted out of the door and went flying toward the house. Finding the deadbolt locked, she continued her dance on the porch.

I leaped from the truck and crossed the driveway. "Where are your keys?" I asked her, trying to stifle my amusement.

"At my house, where my car is parked. Just open the door."

She pushed past me the second I turned the lock. I shut the door and moved into the kitchen to dump off the two lunch-boxes and rinse out the Tupperware inside of them. It was all terribly domestic, and every step made me grin.

I grabbed an apple from the basket and leaned against the counter, waiting for her to return. I needed to shower, but washing my hair with one hand took more effort than I wanted to put forth—especially if I could convince her to do it with me...or for me.

By the time she came back, I was tossing my core into the trash. She'd shed her uniform shirt and the belt she always wore, and her feet were bare. And if I wasn't mistaken, she no longer had on a bra under that almost-translucent shirt. Masyn stepped between my feet and pressed her waist to my growing erection, tilted her head up, and I met her with a kiss. It was as natural as the sun rising and setting. Everything with her made sense.

Her delicate hands, still covered in grease and crap from the shop, lifted the hem of my shirt. A chill ran up my spine when her fingers touched my skin, and there was no hiding the excitement between my legs when she tugged my shirt over my head. I had to help her a little because of the height difference, but it was still hot.

I was hypnotized by the sight of her tongue when she licked her lips and stared up at me with her brown eyes sparkling. And it dawned on me what I saw reflected back at me. It wasn't just love. There was lust sprinkled in there, too. "I need to shower to get the grime off."

"Me too."

I didn't have to ask, or even suggest. Masyn laced her

fingers through mine and led me down the hall in a seductive dance to the master bathroom. While she turned on the water, I sat on the toilet to take my work boots off and then my pants. It was considerably harder to get them off without much use of my right thumb, but having Masyn as a sideshow made it worth the trouble. She shimmied out of hers, leaving herself in nothing other than a T-shirt and panties.

I pulled her across my lap and hugged her loosely. "You know we don't have to do anything, right?"

"Are you telling me you don't want to?" Expecting me to reject her, her expression changed and the corners of her mouth turned down just a hair.

"No. I'm telling you I don't expect it. We can take this at your pace."

"Lee, you've gotten your itches scratched by every girl in town for years. No one has scratched any of my itches except me. Trust me when I say, I'm beyond ready, and I'm tired of waiting."

I tried like hell not to stare when she finally eased out of my embrace and took off her shirt. It had teased me ever since we left the shop. My jaw hung slack when she let her panties hit the floor. But I remained quiet and watched the erotic show. I knew she would be stunning; I just had no idea she'd take my breath away. I still sat on the toilet lid, and her chest was at the perfect height for me to take one of her tight, pink nipples into my mouth.

My eyes drifted shut when my tongue swirled around her peak, and my good hand squeezed her firm ass while I lavished her breasts with attention. She didn't flinch or shy away, she arched her back into my embrace. I parted my lids when her head fell back. Masyn held herself in the most erotic pose I'd ever witnessed, and my dick stood at attention, desperate to be inside her. I tried to maintain contact when I got to my feet, but I lost the battle when her fingers slipped into the waistband of my boxers, whipped them down, and dropped them to the floor. Without thought, I stepped out of my underwear, kicking it next to hers.

She held my gaze when she took me into her hand and stroked with the confidence of an experienced lover. Masyn didn't gawk, although she definitely appeared pleased with the package before her when she coaxed me across the room and we stepped under the steamy water.

The shower didn't prove to be the sexy rendezvous that movies—well, porn—made it out to be. The twelve-inch difference in our heights made any type of contact difficult, and nothing lined up correctly, especially trying to do anything left-handed. She laughed at my awkwardness more than once, and somehow, that took the fear of being naked with her out of the picture. Not one time in the past had I ever worried about what a girl thought when I took off my shirt or when she felt my cock for the first time, yet with Masyn, I felt like a virgin trying to find my way. The difference was the nervous anticipation wasn't negative, it was thrilling. And even through the mishaps and failed attempts at any type of physical intimacy, it felt as natural as her approach in the kitchen.

I slipped and nearly busted my ass trying to keep my hand out of the water. Masyn managed to keep me from falling, but we gave up on the shower and got out. I assumed we'd get dressed and watch a movie or order dinner. My dick had long since gone soft between the near-fatal accident and the cold air blasting me before I got a towel wrapped around my waist. I'd been so busy trying to conceal how drastic the change in temperature could be on parts of my anatomy, that I missed her drying off. And I certainly hadn't witnessed her slink to my bed where she wanted to resume the party for two.

It was still unmade from being in it with her this morning, and the blankets were strewn to the right and gathered at the bottom. She'd stretched out on her side, and every lean inch of her drew my attention. I didn't know where to start memorizing her details. The blinds were partially closed, making the room dusky, although certainly not dark. There was still plenty of light for me to spend as much time as I saw fit making sure to lavish every bit of her body with attention. Even still, I'd yet to move from the spot I'd been standing in to make it happen.

My hesitation was apparent, even to me. It had been years since I'd had sex, and Masyn was a virgin. She was offering me a gift that I needed to make sure she was ready to give. I couldn't return it, and if she regretted giving me her virginity, my ego wouldn't survive her remorse, and neither would my heart.

She crooked her finger at me. I dropped the towel that covered my arousal and joined her on the mattress. Once we started, it would only take one kiss to fuel the fire that burned inside us both. I tangled my fingers in her hair, gave it a gentle squeeze, and then slowly let them drift to her slender neck. Holding her close to me, our tongues spoke a language our hearts had refused to translate for so many years.

As much as I wanted to feel her heated flesh against every naked inch of my own, I tried to put a little space between us. Her thigh hung lazily over my hip. We lay face-to-face, so close our breaths mingled, and I could see her eyes dilate even just slightly. Each time the head of my dick touched her hot, slick center, I pulled back to keep things at a pace she could handle. Yet every time I moved away, she flexed her leg muscles to bring me back.

"Masyn..." I tipped my forehead to hers, breathless. My heart hammered in my chest, my cock ached between my legs, and I wanted nothing more than to sink inside the only girl I'd ever loved and claim the one thing she'd saved for me. It wasn't even about sex; it was knowing that she surrendered to me the way I did her.

"Lee, I've waited my entire life to do this with you."

"It's going to hurt." I didn't have any experience taking a girl's virginity. Cynthia Green had given hers up long before she met me. But I'd spent enough time listening to guys brag about how badly they'd slayed some girl, ripping away her hymen, to know that Masyn's first time around wouldn't be pleasant. Causing her pain was the last thing I wanted to do.

A laugh rolled through her chest, and her eyes glittered with happiness. She cupped my cheeks as I hovered over her, now nestled between her thighs and dipping into her moisture. "Just because I haven't had sex with a guy doesn't mean there's still a barrier there."

My brow furrowed while I tried to figure out what she meant. And then it occurred to me, and I was almost as uninterested in how Masyn pleasured herself as I was thinking about another guy touching her. As selfish as it was, I wanted to believe nothing had ever breached her wall before me. It didn't matter if it was rubber or real, although the latter was far worse.

Nevertheless, knowing I wouldn't cause her pain eased my anxiety enough to let the stress leave my body. Or most of it.

When I still didn't move, she watched my face, waiting. "What's wrong?"

Here was the part where I had to admit the only other thing Masyn didn't know about me. I wasn't ashamed; I was worried I wouldn't be able to please her. No man wanted to admit he wouldn't be able to satisfy his woman before he erupted prematurely.

I dropped my forehead to her chest and closed my eyes. When I dug my fingers into my scalp, she asked the same question again. "I'm nervous."

She lifted my chin. "Why?" Hurt lingered in her expression, and I refused to allow her to think I didn't want this.

My Adam's apple bobbed and scratched the inside of my throat when I swallowed. "It's been a *really* long time, so I'm afraid I'm not going to last long." It was the truth, just not all of it.

I could tell by her long silence that she knew I had more to say but I just wasn't coming out with it.

"I haven't done this since tenth grade." I closed my eyes, not wanting to see the disbelief on her face. The pulse on either side of my neck beat painfully, nearly choking me with suspense.

More time dragged by.

She finally shifted beneath me. "What?" Her laughter mimicked the nervousness that clawed at my insides. "Look at me, Lee."

I opened my eyes to see Masyn Porter staring at me in awe,

maybe wonder, and definitely love. "What about all those girls at Sadler's?"

"Never had sex with any of them." Oral sex didn't count; she knew about that. And she knew what I was talking about without me getting graphic.

"None?"

I clenched my jaw and shook my head. "Not one." And then I waited. I'd only thought the previous spell of silence was the longest I'd ever endured. This one seemed to span days instead of the mere minutes that actually passed.

"Thank you," she said with her lips on mine.

Confused by her acceptance and lack of interrogation, I asked, "For what?"

"Waiting for me," she whispered. Masyn didn't question me, she didn't doubt me, she simply acknowledged the gesture for what it was.

That was all I needed to go forward.

Neither of us moved our eyes away from the other as I slowly slid into her heat. It took her some time to adjust to my size, and regardless of what she said, it was obvious this wasn't the same as any toy she'd played with. When she finally relaxed, our hips began to rock together, and eventually, we found a rhythm. Our rhythm.

The push.

The pull.

The heat.

The passion.

And then the explosion.

It wasn't wild, it wasn't crazy, it wasn't anything like my fantasies of her had been.

It was perfect and better than I could have imagined, even with all its flaws.

I'd finally laid claim to the girl who stole my heart.

Lying next to her, both of us still naked on top of the blankets, she looked over at me as her smile lit up the otherwise dim room. "We might have a problem." The gleam in her eyes indicated it wasn't something I needed to be concerned over.

"Yeah, what's that?"

Masyn rolled onto her side and propped her head on her hand with her elbow in the mattress. "We have a lot of years to make up for. And I liked that far more than I probably should after one try."

This was a side of Masyn I couldn't wait to explore. "You think that's a problem, huh?" I leaned in to kiss her, loving the taste of her lips and having the freedom to take them anytime I wanted to. It was like I'd been held captive for years, and having Masyn was not just getting parole, but a full pardon.

"It could certainly pr—"

"Lee! You here?" Before I could respond, the bedroom door flew open, and Beau stood frozen in the opening.

Masyn scrambled to get under the covers and hide, and I saw red.

"Dude, don't you knock?" I hollered, still fully exposed.

Peyton appeared over Beau's shoulder, and her smile quickly faded and then she disappeared.

"I did. You didn't answer. Your truck was parked out front, so I assumed you were asleep."

I plucked a pillow from behind my head and lobbed it as his melon-sized noggin. "Get the fuck out."

He dodged the grenade and quickly closed the door, where

he continued to talk from the other side. "I see you two managed to work things out." It was hard to be mad at someone who was so clearly happy I'd finally gotten laid. "We'll be in the living room when you're done."

I listened to his steps retreat down the hall as I turned the lamp on, and then I lifted the comforter to find Masyn every shade of red imaginable. "Guess we don't have to worry about how we're going to tell Beau." Teasing her made me grin, or maybe it was the incredible orgasm I'd just received, courtesy of her soft pussy. Either way, she got the credit.

She snatched at the blanket and yanked it back over her. "He saw everything, Lee."

I crawled under the comforter and uncovered our heads. "I'm just thankful I saw it first."

Her hand snaked out to grab another pillow to hit me with. "You better be glad I love you."

With an arm slung over her hip, I pulled her body flush with mine. "Sweetheart, you have no idea."

SIXTEEN

Once we'd finally gotten rid of Beau and Peyton—who'd shown up with nothing to do, looking for entertainment—Masyn and I spent the evening and the better part of the night wrapped up in each other. There were so many things we'd never experienced, and I loved having the pleasuring of being her first. And as much as I'd already fallen in love with being inside her, having my face between her legs came in a close second—tied with having her go down on me. Masyn was as much fun in bed as she was playing pool, arguing about music, or hanging out on the lake. And when she said we had a lot of years to make up for, she committed to righting that wrong and gave it her undivided attention.

I struggled when the alarm clock went off at five thirty. Neither one of us had had much sleep to speak of this week, yet where I was groggy and the fog lingered in my mind, Masyn was bright-eyed and bushy-tailed.

"You know we have to go over to your house before we go in?" I muttered with my arm draped across my face.

"Why?"

I uncovered my eyes to meet her stare. "You have to stay over, remember?"

Her upper lip lifted in irritation. "Ugh. Thanks for reminding me." She flopped onto her back with a humph. "Can you come pick me up whenever I get off?" She needed a little cheese to go with that whine.

I turned to my side and propped my head in my hand. "Any other time I would, but I promised Beau I'd have a drink with him and Peyton before she left. That's how I got them to leave last night." I smirked, knowing she recalled what getting rid of them had meant for the two of us—and she'd loved every minute. "It was a small sacrifice to make."

"What time is she leaving?" Masyn trailed her finger down my sternum without looking at me. She probably knew that if she peered up, her eyes would give away the trepidation she tried to hide in her voice.

"I think Beau said she had to take off at five to have time to return the rental car and make her flight."

"And you promise there's no chance of you hopping on a plane to go visit the big city with her?"

I tilted her chin up so she could see the truth in my eyes. "Is that what you're worried about?"

Masyn barely nodded, yet it was enough for me to realize how little faith she had in me when it came to relationships.

"Sweetheart, I've never told anyone else I love them. And I don't plan to ever do so. You've seen how Peyton and Beau are together. I don't know why you're so worried about her."

"Because I saw how she was with you at the rehearsal dinner, and it was you that she spent all day with Saturday, and it was you she called on Sunday afternoon, and it was you she asked to come spend a few days with her in New York. Beau's a consolation prize. You're the one she wants."

I couldn't deny or confirm that. And if Masyn knew she'd kissed me on Saturday night, she'd lose her mind. Peyton and Beau just both needed attention. It wasn't *me* she was after, just my time. Beau was hurting whether he was ready to admit it or not, and Peyton bathing him in affection soothed that wound, even if it was only temporary.

Reaching out, I stroked her cheek with my thumb and pressed a kiss to her lips. "Sweetheart, you have nothing to worry about. I'm not racing off to New York. I'll be here waiting for you when you get off this afternoon. And I'll leave it up to you just how much time we spend with Beau before he goes back to Atlanta."

Masyn gave me a weak smile and a meager nod. She needed time to see that what she thought was true about me and women, wasn't true at all. The only other time she'd ever trusted a guy, he'd burned her publicly. Deep inside, Masyn knew I wasn't Alex, nor was I capable of decimating anyone the way he had, but I'd sure as hell never intentionally hurt her. Even if we hadn't slept together and had never bothered to tell the other one how we felt, I wouldn't get on a plane with Peyton Holstein.

"Come on. We need to get going, or we'll be late."

I hated seeing her so insecure; I just didn't know how to fix it. In some ways, this had been the best week of my life, and in others...well, let's just say, I wouldn't be disappointed to see Peyton leave. And truth be told, Beau had thrown quite a monkey wrench into our everyday lives, as well. I didn't usually wish away the time I had with him in town, but Sunday couldn't come soon enough.

When we got to Masyn's house, I leaned over the console, grabbed her by the nape of the neck, and pulled her face to mine. There I planted a kiss on her lips that I hoped would last her through the day. Every emotion I felt for her poured out, leaving me breathless and craving more. "I love you, sweetheart. Be careful driving to the shop."

"Love you, too. I'll see you in a bit." She did a miserable job of masking the sadness in her voice.

I watched her open the truck door and hop out. Just before she shut it behind her, I said, "Why don't you run in and grab enough stuff to spend the weekend at my house?" It wasn't like she didn't frequently stay at least one of the two nights; I just wanted her to be certain that I longed to have her with me.

She tucked her hair behind her ear and nodded with the first genuine smile I'd seen all morning. And once I knew she was safely inside, I backed out. I hated this neighborhood and couldn't wait for the day that I no longer had to worry about her being here.

When I got to the shop, I clocked in and got a cup of coffee while I waited for Masyn in the breakroom. She came sliding in with a couple of minutes to spare and threw her stuff in her locker. The flush on her cheeks from racing through the parking lot resulted in a strong desire for me to throw her across the table and take her in front of everyone.

Instead, I caged her in with my hands on the wall close to her face and stole a quick kiss. "I'll see you at lunch."

She grinned, and her eyes twinkled beneath the fluorescent lighting. "See ya," she whispered, and the husky tone of those two words wrapped around my dick just as seductively as her hand had when she'd dragged me into the shower.

I growled, planted one more kiss on her soft lips, and stalked from the room before I lost all control and took her sexy little ass right then and there against the lockers.

Maybe we could get away during our lunch hour...

Unfortunately, when lunch rolled around, Farley pulled Masyn into his office to discuss the needs on line three and show her the defects. They'd shut down the entire production line when the bell rang for break because they were totally unable to machine parts. Masyn's position was being taken over for the afternoon by the lead on that line to free her up to work on the programming immediately. She wasn't any happier about having to sacrifice her lunchbreak than she was about working overtime this afternoon, but maybe if she started on it earlier, then she'd be done by three and be able to leave on time.

Nothing ever worked in my favor. I stopped to see Masyn before I cleaned up for the day, and she was knee-deep in blueprints and covered in grease. She had a lathe disassembled with parts scattered around her on the floor. She brushed her hair out of her face with the back of her hand and it left a black mark from the center of her forehead to her ear.

"They don't need a programmer; they need a maintenance man," she admitted.

"Then why doesn't Farley call one in?" It seemed like a simple solution, and it also wasn't Masyn's job.

"He tried. They can't get anyone out here until Monday afternoon, and these parts have to ship Monday morning. He's hoping I can get it running again so the guys can come in tomorrow and possibly Sunday to get it out." There was no denying how unhappy she was with the situation.

"And let me guess... He wants you here tomorrow, as well, in case it goes down again." There went my plans.

"Ding, ding, ding."

I searched the area around us to see if we had any witnesses before I squatted next to her. Whispering in her ear, I felt the warmth of my breath radiate off her skin and saw her arms prickle with a chill. "Don't worry, sweetheart. I promise to give you my undivided attention when you get home." I pressed my lips to her neck, just below her ear, to leave her thinking about all I'd do to her, and with her, once we were alone.

She swatted at my arm and laughed while she spoke, "You need to go before I'm completely useless."

I stood and backed away, holding her stare until I had to turn around or risk running into a machine, further injuring myself. The smirk that lingered on my mouth was a silent promise of what she could expect. And I loved that a simple glance turned her tomato red—and undoubtedly wet. In true Masyn form, she returned the smart-ass grin and added a greasy middle finger. Laughing, I did an about face and went back across the shop to check in the last truck of the day.

Halfway through the receiving manifests, my cellphone rang in my pocket. Technically, we weren't allowed to have them on the floor, but since no one ever called me during the day, I didn't think anything about keeping it in my pocket. Still holding the clipboard, I put the pen in my mouth, expecting to see Beau's ugly mug and name on the screen. It was a number I didn't recognize, starting with an Atlanta area code.

I debated answering, but I figured there was little chance of getting caught, and even if I did, I was working with a pen and paper, not a moving machine and metal.

"Hello?" I tucked the phone between my cheek and shoulder to keep working, while I got rid of what I assumed was a sales call for some shit I didn't need and absolutely didn't want.

"Mr. Carter?" To my surprise, the woman on the other end wasn't a voice recording trying to tell me about the wonderful cruise I'd won.

I continued to count the boxes on the pallet so I could check them against the order. "This is Lee."

"This is Bernice at Atlanta Memorial Hospital. We found your number in George Carter's cellphone as his emergency contact."

The world suddenly slipped into slow motion as I stepped out of the trailer to get a better signal and set down the clipboard and pen. "Yeah, he's my dad."

"Mr. Carter, I hate delivering this news by phone, but your father suffered a massive heart attack at work today. He was brought in by ambulance not long ago, and he's being prepped for surgery as we speak."

Panic filled my thoughts and echoed in my voice. "Surgery?" I practically screamed in the woman's ear. "What's going on? Is he going to make it?"

"You need to get here as quickly as possible, Mr. Carter."

"I'm three hours away. And at work. Can't you tell me what's happening?" Fear had a way of unexpectedly morphing into anger.

"I don't have any other details, Mr. Carter. I'm sure the doctor will be able to tell you more when you arrive."

My jaw ached from grinding my teeth in the few short moments I'd been on the phone, and if I didn't stop pulling my hair, I wouldn't have any left. "That's not good enough. That's my dad. Is he going to be all right?"

"I'm sorry, sir. I really do wish I could tell you more."

"Yeah, fine, I understand. I'll get there as soon as I can. Thank you for letting me know." I didn't wait for her to say you're welcome or goodbye before I hung up and left the receiving dock in the same shape it had been in when I answered the call.

I practically ran through the aisles, jumping over pallets on the floor and dodging forklifts as I went. When I got to Farley's office, he was on the phone and held his finger up for me to give him a minute. I didn't have a minute. Frustrated, I groaned and ran to the time clock and punched out, and then slipped into the breakroom to grab my stuff from my locker. Farley was off the phone when I returned to his office.

"What the hell, Carter? You're white as a ghost."

"I just got a call—"

He put his hands on his hips and tried to issue a stern warning I wasn't fucking interested in hearing. "You know cellphones on the floor are against company policy."

"Yeah, yeah, yeah, write me up on Monday. I've got to go. My dad had a heart attack and is heading into surgery."

"In Atlanta?"

No, jackass, in the breakroom. "Yes."

The agitation for the cellphone violation quickly vanished when he realized what I was telling him. He and his pops were close. If anything happened to Old Man Farley, we wouldn't see Farley in here for days.

"Get the hell outta here. Once you get there and know more about what's going on, give me a call and let me know if you'll be in on Monday, but don't worry about this place, we've got it covered."

I was about to turn around and race to my truck when I remembered Masyn. "Hey, Farley, can you do me a favor?"

"Of course."

"Can you tell Masyn what happened and that I'll call her when I know more?"

"Definitely. Now, go."

I slapped the metal door casing and gave him a curt nod. It was as close as I could get to saying thank you when I was on the verge of losing my shit. My dad and I hadn't been super close since he'd moved to Atlanta, but he was the only family I had—at least by name and blood—and I loved him just the same. And he'd done his best to be a good father after my mom passed away when I was a kid. He'd just been too heartbroken without her to be Dad of the Year.

The keys fell out of my shaking hands in the parking lot, and by the time I finally got the doors to the truck unlocked, I worried about even driving to my house to pack a bag, much less getting on the interstate for a three-hour trip. With the truck idling, I touched Beau's name on my contact list and waited for the call to connect.

"Hey, man. You're off early." Beau didn't wait for me to respond. "You want to meet Peyton and me down at Sadler's? We're having a drink before she takes off." He laughed at something in the background.

"Beau..." My voice cracked as I said his name.

His tone shifted immediately, and I knew I was on the verge of losing it. "You okay?"

"My d-dad," I stammered. "I-I need to go to Atlanta."

I heard him call for Lani and ask for the check. "I'll meet you at your house." And he disconnected.

I wasn't sure how I managed to arrive at my house in one piece or even how I got there. Beau's car wasn't in the driveway, so I ran inside and started throwing shit in a bag. I didn't have a clue how long I'd be gone or what I would need, but I figured anything I forgot, I could buy in Atlanta once I knew what was going on. Right now, I just needed to get there. When he still hadn't arrived by the time I finished packing, I took a quick shower to rinse off the stench of a day on the dock and then I put on fresh clothes. I was sitting on my bed tying my tennis shoes when he came down the hall.

"Sorry it took me so long. I had to drop Peyton off at her car and grab my stuff from my parents' house. You ready?"

"You're going with me?"

"Based on how you sounded on the phone—which isn't shit compared to how you look in person—I didn't think you needed to deal with whatever this is alone." He stuffed his hands in his pockets. His face was lined with pity, even without knowing what happened. "Plus, this way, you'll have a place to stay and won't have to worry about a hotel."

I nodded and swiped up the bag at my feet. He hadn't asked any questions, which was good since I didn't have any answers. Beau had his faults, but friendship wasn't one of them. There'd never been a time in my life when I'd needed him and he hadn't shown up. And today was no different.

No words were exchanged between us as we got into his

BMW. And it wasn't until we hit the interstate that he finally dared to speak. "You want to tell me what's going on?"

"I don't know. Some woman called me from Atlanta Memorial and said he had a heart attack. They were prepping him for surgery. That's all she told me."

"Like open-heart surgery?" The shock rang through loud and clear.

I pounded my fists on his dashboard, trying to keep the stinging tears at bay. "Fuck, I don't know, Beau. She said the doctor would be able to tell me more once I got there."

"I'm sure he's going to be okay." Beau was a shit liar. He didn't have a clue if my old man would survive any better than I did.

"He's all I've got, man." That one sentence unlocked the floodgates. I buried my head in my hands and let my fear out the only way I knew how.

"That's not true, Lee. I know he's your dad, but as long as I'm alive and Masyn's breathing, you'll never be alone."

He was trying to help, and I knew that—it just wasn't what I needed to hear. I refused to consider the possibility of my dad not pulling through. It didn't matter that I was a grown man; no child wanted to live without their parents, and I'd already lived most of my life down one.

"I'm surprised Masyn isn't with you."

I welcomed the change of subject. Thinking about her was preferable to my dad in a hospital. "She had to work late. I didn't even talk to her before I left."

"Dude, she's going to freak out."

"Nah, Farley's going to let her know what happened. I told him to tell her I'd call her when I knew more."

"That's going to go over well." His sarcasm was unbecoming and made me want to slap the shit out of him. Now wasn't the time for him to try to be cute.

"I didn't have a choice, Beau. She was up to her elbows in grease and machine parts, not to mention, she has to work late today and has to be at the shop all day tomorrow. Even if she had wanted to, she couldn't come with me." I reached into my bag to grab my cell to send Masyn a message. Even with Farley delivering the news about where I'd gone, I wanted her to know I'd thought about her. I didn't have time to finish typing the message before Beau interrupted me.

"You going to tell me how all that ended up coming together?"

I hated when Beau was right about something; the smug look that crossed his face anytime that subject came up again made me want to smack him.

"I don't know. After I dropped you and Peyton off on Monday night, I went to Masyn's house, and she was drunk as piss. I shouldn't have tried to talk to her then. I just had to get some things out of my system, only I didn't get a chance to tell her anything other than the fact that I didn't have any interest in Peyton."

"Why couldn't you tell her anything else?"

I sat my phone in the cup holder, leaned back in the seat, and tried to relax. Worrying wouldn't get us to Atlanta any faster, and talking about Masyn brought a smile to my lips. Even when I was filled with dread, she made my heart happy. "Masyn started blubbering about Peyton taking you and me away, and how she always had to talk to you in code when you were with Felicity. And by the end of the conversation, I thought she was telling me she was in love with you." I rolled my head to stare at him and witness his reaction. I wasn't expecting laughter.

"I have no idea what she said to make you think she had feelings for me, but if you'd told me about it that night, I could have set the record straight."

"Reaching out to you wasn't the first thing on my mind when I was cleaning up vomit and carrying her to bed."

He gulped and scrubbed his palm over his scrunched face. "Ew. Dude, that's definitely love."

Good thing it hadn't been Beau she'd puked on, or he would have tossed his cookies, too. "It sucked. I was covered in it and had to wash my clothes before I could leave. By the time I got them into the washer and tried to move her, she asked me to stay."

"On the couch?"

I shook my head and grinned. "You'd think, but no. She wanted me in bed next to her."

"That's torture." He flicked on the blinker. I leaned in his direction when he switched lanes and the tires screeched. "I wonder if she had any idea what she was doing."

"Doubtful. She was out within seconds."

He shot me an irritated, sidelong glance. "And let me guess: you spent the night staring at the ceiling?"

"For the most part."

"Lee, man, you know that even if it was me who Masyn was after, I'd never do that to you, right?"

The truth was, I didn't know what to believe. Sleep deprivation did crazy things to the mind and the imagination. "Let's just say it wasn't a fun night, and neither was the following day.

She apologized over and over, but keep in mind, she was apologizing for putting a divide in the friendship, not for confessing she loved you."

"I should be pissed you made a play for her, thinking she had the hots for me." His cocky grin left no room for doubt that he was fucking with me.

"It wasn't like that." I might be known as a player around town, but Beau knew the truth. He'd always known Masyn was *it* for me. "Maybe it makes me an ass, but honestly, at this point, I don't really care. If I hadn't done it, she never would have told me I'd misunderstood everything she said Monday night."

"Lee, I don't care how the two of you got there." He shrugged, swung into the right lane behind a speeding semi-truck, and set the cruise on eighty. "I'm just glad you did. Even though she hasn't flat-out said the words to me, I've listened to her stories about dates and why they never worked out, and I've heard the jealousy in her voice any time you and another chick came up. Once I left for college, she and I talked a lot more than we did when I was here. I think it was easier for her to open up because I wasn't in the thick of it anymore, yet I knew all the guys who ever stood on her doorstep and their history."

I wished one of us had spoken up, even though I couldn't fault either one of them since I hadn't said anything, either. I raked a hand through my hair, squirming in the leather seat, trying to imagine her chatting with Beau about *me*, while I got blowjobs in the bathroom at the bar. "Just a lot of wasted time."

And misplaced emotion.

"Probably not. You came together when the time was right. Don't regret what you haven't done, and make it happen going forward."

Don't regret what I have done, too.

"Yeah. Right." I glanced at the clock and wished like hell I could call her. I was certain she was still at work, since it wasn't quite four, and even though I'd told Farley that I would call her, Masyn would text me as soon as she left. She was a stickler for the safety protocols, and she wouldn't have her phone on her even if I tried to call. Knowing that still didn't change the fact that I wanted to hear her voice and tell her I loved her.

"How'd you and Peyton leave things?"

"Dude, I met the wrong sister first." That wasn't good. "Peyton is everything I wish Felicity had been, but without all the attitude and snarly disposition." It was good to know he hadn't been blind to the things Masyn and I saw in his ex-fiancée. "Once I get settled in the new house and job, we're going to make plans for me to go see her. Until then, she might come back for a week or two since she's off for the summer."

"Have either of you considered how you're going to deal with Felicity? Or her parents? I'm not trying to rain on your parade or anything. I just don't know if that's a road you're ready to walk, Beau. You and confrontation don't do well together."

"I'm not thinking that far ahead. Peyton is keenly aware of what all I'm dealing with right now. But the sex is good and so is the company, so I'm going to enjoy it and figure it out as I go."

"Obviously, I don't know her well, but I got the impression she didn't have a lot of experience in the relationship department. Just be careful you don't end up hurting her while you're finding yourself."

"Listen to you, Mr. Compassionate. When did you start caring about women's feelings?"

I'd never led a girl to believe she would get anything more from me than the moment we were in. I never took them out on dates, I didn't bring them to my house, and I certainly didn't share my bed—there was no confusion. And any woman who thought she'd change that did so of her own accord, not because I skipped with them down a primrose path while holding their hand and humming.

"She seemed like a nice girl. And your reputation's at stake, too. Don't forget that you're supposed to be in Gay Paree on your honeymoon right now. You might not have to deal with the fallout of being seen around town shacked up with Felicity's sister, but you can bet your ass your mom will."

"My mom loves her."

"Doesn't mean she wants to answer for your behavior with Peyton so shortly after you called off a wedding with Felicity."

"I liked you a lot better when you were just a pretty face holding a beer."

I groaned. "I'd kill for a beer."

"Forget it. I'm not adding an open container charge to the list of my offenses this week."

"Killjoy."

He turned up the radio and we spent the rest of the ride in relative silence. My thoughts volleyed between my dad and Masyn, neither of which I could reach, and the music helped to stop my mind from wandering. And when we finally got to the cardiac ICU, I worried I'd need a room of my own before this was all over.

SEVENTEEN

"What do you mean there've been complications?" No one could tell me anything other than to have a seat and wait. "It's been almost five hours since he went into surgery." I estimated based on when I'd gotten the call and when the woman told me he was being prepped to go under.

"Open-heart surgery is complicated, Mr. Carter. As soon as there's an update on your father's condition, someone will come out to speak with you." Simply averting her stare, she dismissed me as though the conversation were over.

The hospital needed to consider classes for their staff in patient-family management. This place currently sucked at compassion.

Beau stepped between me and the nurse on the other side of the desk. "Come on, Lee. Let's take a seat. Eating her for dinner won't get you any answers."

I turned and let him push me toward the waiting room. "This is insane. He's been here for hours. They have to know something."

"I don't think they're withholding information just to get to spend more time with you in their lobby."

I slumped in the vinyl chair. Little did I know, it would end up being my home for the next three hours. "They could be more sympathetic." I crossed my arms in protest, and Beau mirrored me. "He might just be a patient to them, but he's my dad."

By the time someone finally came out, it was close to eleven at night. Beau had tried to force-feed me food from the cafeteria, he brought me coffee I wouldn't give to a dog, and my nerves were frayed.

The surgeon's mask hung by strings from his neck, and he appeared as weary as I was. "Mr. Carter?"

The moment he said my name, I stood and extended my hand.

"I'm Dr. Swallow. I was part of the team that worked on your dad."

Trying to read his face was like trying to put a Rubik's Cube back together. No matter which way it twisted, none of the emotions lined up. "How is he? Is he going to be all right?" I was tired and anxious, and my attitude reflected it.

"We lost your dad twice on the table. He's in recovery now, but the next twenty-four to forty-eight hours are critical."

"What do you mean you *lost* him?" I could feel my blood pressure rising and my cheeks flaming. "Like he got up from the operating table and ran off to play hide-and-seek? Or you didn't do your job? Which kind of lost are you referring to?" My reaction was over the top, but I couldn't seem to reel myself back in.

"Lee, calm down. He said your dad is in recovery."

I swatted Beau's hand off my shoulder, ignored his attempt

to rationalize with me, and turned back to the surgeon. "You mean to tell me, my dad almost died three times today, twice by your hand, and no one could be bothered to so much as come out and mention things weren't going well?"

"Mr. Carter, I appreciate how you're feeling right now, but—"

My brows lifted so high, I saw the skin on my nose rise with them. "Oh, you appreciate how I'm feeling... Is your dad lying around here somewhere while you wait for some cocky-ass doctor to come grace you with his presence?"

"No, my father is in the cemetery down the street." The guy never lost his composure; I had to give him that. "While I understand your frustration, my presence was more necessary in the operating room than the waiting area. There was an excellent team in there with me, which is why your father is still here." He clapped me on the shoulder, like that statement made us friends. "It's going to be a while before he's moved to a room, and even then, visitation will be kept at a minimum to reduce the risk of infection. His odds of survival are much greater once he passes the two-day mark. Do yourself and your dad a favor and try to get some rest."

When he disappeared behind the double doors, I realized I had no more information about what had happened to my father than I'd had ten minutes ago, other than he had made it through surgery.

It took me another thirty minutes to convince Beau there was no point in both of us spending the night sitting up, and that he should go home. I wasn't very good company at the moment, and I really just needed some time to myself.

"Lee, you can't do anything here. You sure you don't want

to come to my house, get a good night's sleep, and then come back first thing in the morning?" He was afraid to leave me, although I wasn't sure if it was my sanity he worried about or the staff's safety.

"You go ahead. I don't wanna leave. If anything happens, I need to be here."

"I'll stay with you."

I tried to dissuade him. "I'm good, really."

He gathered me into a hug I hadn't realized I needed and attempted to squeeze positivity into me. It didn't work, even though I appreciated the gesture. "I'm going to leave my number with the nurses' station in case you need anything."

I patted his bicep and mustered a pitiful excuse for a smile. "Thanks, man. I'll see you tomorrow."

Finally alone, with no one else in the waiting room, I reached for my phone and realized I'd left it in Beau's car along with the bag I'd brought. "Shit, shit, shit."

I'd told Farley I'd call Masyn when I knew something, and it was after midnight and I hadn't updated her. I didn't know hers or Beau's number by heart, so I couldn't even borrow the nurse's phone to make a call. I could only hope she'd called Beau looking for me, or that he thought to reach out to her before tomorrow morning. Masyn would be worried shitless with me having left without so much as a word and her not hearing from me since. By the time Beau got back here in the morning, she'd be at the shop, and I wouldn't be able to reach her then, either.

I desperately wanted to talk to her, have her tell me every-thing would be all right. Hell, I longed to have her arms wrapped around my waist, or my head pressed to her chest so I could hear her heartbeat. I was grateful Beau had been with me all day; it was just that over the last four years, I'd relied heavily on Masyn during everyday life. She was the one always within arm's reach, and I needed her now more than I ever had.

"Mr. Carter?"

I cracked open my eyes when someone patted my arm.

"Would you like to go see your dad?"

Rubbing my eyes, it took me a minute to realize where I was and who the person was touching me and smiling so close to my face that I could have spit on her—not that that would have been nice. "Yeah. How's he doing?"

She stood back and allowed me to rise from the chair I'd slumped over in, apparently having fallen asleep. "He's in critical condition, and he's resting in his room. I can take you to see him, but you won't be able to stay long."

I followed her when she started walking. "Okay."

"Your father had quadruple bypass surgery, so be prepared. There are a lot of cords and wires monitoring his vitals, he has a breathing tube, and he's a little swollen. It's all very normal."

Normal to her because it wasn't her dad and she saw it every day. And while everything she said was true, none of it prepared me for the actual sight. The room was like a vacuum, completely void of sound except for the beep of the monitors and the compression of the machine helping him breathe. The sun had started to rise, bringing light through the windows, but even that seemed to have a hard time penetrating the dismal space.

There was a chair in the corner of the tiny room, and I grabbed it, pulling it up next to the bed. It felt like I was in a standoff with the Grim Reaper, who was waiting in the shadows to steal my dad away from me. I was helpless to fight against a force I couldn't see. So I took his hand and laid my cheek on top of it, and there, I begged God not to take the man who'd raised me, to give me more time with him. I wanted him to see me get married and hold his grandchildren. My dad dying wasn't an option, but I didn't have anything to bargain with. I was at the mercy of the All Mighty and only hoped heaven wasn't ready to open the gates to my only living parent.

True to her word, the nurse returned a short time later to tell me I couldn't stay. It was torture to leave him helpless and alone in that room, but if sitting in the waiting area kept him alive, I'd suffer in silence.

"You can come back every two hours." The rest of the people in this place could stand to take a lesson in kindness from this nurse. It wasn't what she said so much as the sympathetic way she said it. "I promise, if anything changes, I'll come find you."

Rounding the corner to the waiting room that was going to be my home for the next few days, I was thrilled to see Beau sitting in the spot where he'd left me last night. He'd showered and shaved, and he looked like he felt a hell of a lot better than I did.

I sat down next to him.

"How's he doing?"

I shrugged with one shoulder and continued toward him. "Okay, I guess. He looks dead. It's eerie."

"I brought your bag so you could change clothes and freshen up."

"Thanks." I reached out to take it from him. "Have you talked to Masyn?"

The red splotches appeared on his face and neck. "No. You said you were going to call her last night when you had more news."

"My phone's in your car, Beau. It's sitting in the console. Didn't you see it?"

"No, I wasn't looking for it."

I slapped my knee. "Shit. Can you go get it? She's probably freaked the fuck out."

"Why didn't you use one of the phones here to call her last night?"

"Well, do *you* remember her number, Beau?" I flared my nostrils in mock aggression, waiting for him to get my point.

He reached into his pocket to grab his cell to look up the number.

"Exactly, jackass. I don't know hers or yours or anyone else's off the top of my head." I was entirely too cranky to deal with his crap. "Can you get the phone? I'd go, but I don't know where you parked."

"Yeah, go change. I'll get the damn thing out of the car."

A fresh set of clothes did nothing for my mood or how bad I felt. I hadn't slept for shit all week, and the last eighteen or so hours had been worse than miserable, I just didn't know a word to describe it—although not nearly as horrible as him handing me my phone with a sullen look on his face.

"What?" I asked. Surely the staff wouldn't have told him something about my dad they hadn't told me.

He glanced at the phone in my hand as he said, "Dude, it's not good."

I unlocked the screen and found three text messages from

Masyn, along with the one I'd never finished typing in the car, much less sent.

Masyn: I waited at your house for an hour before I went home.

Masyn: Not going to run off to New York, huh?

Masyn: I expected more from you, Lee. I should have known better.

"She thinks I went to New York with Peyton." The words floated through the air, and I stood there in total disbelief. She'd known me since we were five, and this was how little she thought of me.

"Why the hell would Masyn think you went to New York?"

"Hell if I know, other than she convinced herself I had a thing for Peyton."

He gawked at me.

"Which I don't. Jesus, Beau."

"I told you to call her."

"Actually, no, you said she would freak out. And I tried to send her a text, but I never finished typing it because you were interrogating me about how Masyn and I ended up as an item." I raked my hand through my hair in frustration and let out an exasperated sigh. "Why the hell didn't you check on her last night?"

He twitched a shoulder. "I didn't think about it. She's not my girlfriend."

I prayed to God she was still mine when I got in touch with her. "Farley was supposed to tell her where I went. Even if I hadn't called, she should know I'm in Atlanta. I'm not out for a damn joyride."

"You probably should call her," he suggested, his tone sing-songy and drawn out with sarcasm.

I glanced at my watch. I had two minutes before she was scheduled to clock in. There was no way she'd have her phone on her. Not only did she not have her phone on her, her phone wasn't on at all. "It went straight to voicemail," I said as I listened to the recording.

"Leave her a message and then call the shop."

I waited for the beep. "Masyn, sweetheart, call me when you get this. I love you."

"Aww, that was sweet." Beau tilted his head to the side and patted his chest above his heart.

"Fuck off." Ignoring him, I scrolled through my contacts until I found the number to the shop. "Fuck!" The nurse at the desk turned to stare at my outburst, and I mouthed an insincere apology. "No one's answering. I guarantee you they're all out in the shop, and no one's in the office to take phone calls."

Just as I was about to throw my phone against a wall, Beau caught my wrist. "You do that, she won't be able to reach you at all. Masyn will call when she gets off. You know she will."

I couldn't be certain of anything at this point. I never would have thought she'd believe I'd up and leave after the last couple of days together. It wasn't like her to jump to conclusions, which told me how terrified she was of getting hurt.

"Worry about your dad, Lee. I'll keep trying to get ahold of Masyn. Why don't you go get something to eat? How long did they say you had to wait to see him again?"

"Two hours."

"Then by my calculation, you have an hour and forty

minutes before they're going to let you through those doors again. Some food and caffeine will help your snarly disposition. If you pass out, you're no good to anyone, including your dad."

I wandered the halls and made my way down to the cafeteria. The food didn't look horrible, but it certainly didn't appear appetizing, either. I bought some eggs and sausage, but the second I bit down on a crunchy thing in my sausage link, I was done. The coffee was better than what had been available last night, but it had a long way to go before it would put Starbucks out of business. The truth was, it wouldn't have mattered if a five-star restaurant catered the meals here; nothing would make me happy until my dad was safe and I could talk to Masyn. Either one would lighten the load on my shoulders right now.

Unfortunately, neither happened all day long. I'd hoped Masyn would get off at three, but if the order had to go out Monday, the guys would rather stay later today than come back tomorrow, and even if she wanted to leave, she'd be outvoted. And each time I went back to see my dad, nothing changed. He didn't look any better or any worse. He hadn't opened his eyes, and he didn't respond when I talked to him. The nurses assured me it was normal in his condition—I was beginning to hate that word, "normal."

I'd skipped lunch and gone in to see my dad around six thirty and still had no word from Masyn. I gave up checking my phone hours ago; it was torture. Beau tried to call her every time I went in to hold my dad's hand, so my obsessing over it didn't help anything.

"Why don't we get out of here for a little while? You can't go back in for another two hours. Some fresh air might do you some good."

Masyn returning my fucking call would do me some good. Beau was right—pacing the halls only served to irritate the nurses when I got in their way, and I wasn't their favorite person as it was. "Yeah, okay."

"She's going to call, Lee. You said yourself that there wasn't anyone at the shop to answer phones. And if they tried to get things done today so they don't have to go in tomorrow, she might still be there."

Twelve hours was tops. "Maybe." Farley wouldn't allow a shift to run longer because of the increased likelihood of an injury and the statistical drop in productivity. "I can't lose either one of them, Beau." I'd stopped on the sidewalk in front of the hospital. Traffic buzzed around us, and the streetlights hummed overhead—the white noise blanketed my thoughts in loneliness.

"Seriously, you're not going to lose anyone. Come on."

I had to give Beau credit. Even when he got zero response from me during dinner, he never stopped talking. He'd even gotten so desperate to try to lift my spirits that he started sharing all the shit Felicity had done in the last couple of months to make me laugh. He chuckled with each story he told, and I felt sad for him that money had been such a motivator in his life decisions.

I would never have the things he did or the Chastain kind of wealth, but at the end of the day, I was proud of who I was. I'd worked hard and played harder, and if I got the chance, I'd love harder than I did either of those. I didn't care if I had to hold down two jobs and live in a cardboard box, as long as I looked forward to going home to my wife every day and cherished time with my kids. My dad had done well by me. Masyn's parents had struggled to take care of four children. But when it was all said and done, we were all taken care of and loved.

"What are you thinking about?" Beau brought me out of my thoughts.

"Just how lucky I've been to have the life I have." Most people probably wouldn't envy a blue-collar guy who liked beer and trucks; they'd rather have Beau's life, but I'd take grease and Masyn over trust funds and bank accounts any day.

He picked up his beer and clinked the neck with mine. "It's just getting started."

I hoped like hell he was right. I'd even let him gloat if he was. I just needed to get through this first.

EIGHTEEN

Beau picked up the check after we had another beer, which I appreciated but didn't need. And then he took me back to the hospital. I assumed he'd drop me off at the front door, so when he pulled into the parking garage, I was a little confused. He'd been here all day, and he had shit to take care of at his house. He was starting a new job on Monday morning, and all of his crap had been moved while he was in Harden in anticipation of his returning from Paris tomorrow with his wife. He'd dodged that bullet. I chuckled, thinking of him in the *Matrix* because that's how it seemed. He'd defied fate in that twist of events, and I still wasn't sure how he'd managed to get out unscathed.

"You know you don't have to come in, right?" I asked as the glass doors slid open and the medicinal smell of the hospital came barreling out. Nothing like the scent of cleanser and death to welcome you to a building.

He leaned over and pressed the up button on the elevator. "How are you going to get to my house if I leave?"

"I'd just planned to stay here."

"Lee, your dad is unconscious, and you need sleep. Another night in a plastic chair might be the final nail in *your* coffin. I'll bring you back in the morning. What time do they cut off visiting hours?"

They hadn't since they first let me see him. And now that Beau brought it up, I wondered if they would tonight. "I don't know. No one's said anything."

"If they do, there's no point in you staying. The new house is only about a ten-minute drive when there's no traffic—which there isn't at six in the morning or nine at night—so if you need to get back quickly, we can."

I wasn't comfortable leaving my dad alone. I already hated that it had taken me nearly four hours—by the time I'd left work and actually gotten on the road—to get here. If he woke up or the nurses needed me for something, I'd never forgive myself for going to Beau's house just to have a comfortable place to rest. "Let's see how he's doing before I make a decision." It pacified Beau and left me without having to make a commitment.

"That's your way of saying no." The elevator dinged, having arrived on the first floor.

We stepped inside, and I pushed the five to take us to the cardiac ICU. I hated thinking of the floors having titles—they were all so dismal. Labor and Delivery didn't even sound inviting. Surely someone could come up with something more appealing than that to welcome new life into the world.

"It's not my way of saying anything." It totally was, and the fucker knew that. "Can you stop acting like a girl and come on?"

I stopped by the nurses' station to see if there'd been any change, knowing there hadn't. At least this woman was friendly and appeared to apologetic that she didn't have better news for me.

"You can go in to see him before visiting hours are over if you'd like," she offered.

I wasn't sure how anyone believed putting restrictions on when you could sit by a loved one's side made sense, but I figured out last night that arguing with the staff got me nowhere. "When do they end?"

"Nine. And they start back at seven tomorrow morning." Seemed like weird hours to me. Although, nothing she could have said would have pacified me unless by some miracle my father was fine and ready to walk out those doors.

I'd hoped Beau would go home while I was in the room with my dad so I wouldn't have to make the decision to leave. No such luck. The loyal fucker was sitting in the same place I'd left him when I went back. "You're like a lost dog, you know that?"

He shrugged. "I've been called worse."

I took the seat next to him and scrubbed my face with my hands. There was no logical reason for me to stay; I just hated to go. All of Beau's points were valid, regardless of whether or not I wanted to consider any of them.

"Lee, you need to shower. You look like shit. You're going to start to scare the other visitors in the hospital if you don't do something to tame your hair...and Jesus, how long has it been since you shaved or brushed your teeth?"

"What are you? My mother?" I smirked.

Beau had always been far more concerned with appearances than I had, but that was probably because he had to work to be pretty, and rugged good looks came naturally to me. Or at least that's what I'd convinced myself every day when I looked in the mirror and decided against additional grooming.

I'd only been sitting in the vinyl chair for roughly two minutes, and my ass was already screaming in discomfort. Another night in it and I'd need a chiropractor and a masseuse. After confirming with the nurse that they had my contact information and would call if anything changed—good or bad—I conceded to a one-night stand at Beau's place.

The buildings we passed were non-descript at night and soon the streets were, too. It was odd to be in a place I knew so little about yet Beau was so completely familiar with. I hadn't really noticed how different our lives had become when he was away at school because I never submerged myself in his world. He always came back to Harden, and I never thought to ask him about coming to see him at school. It wasn't my scene, and I didn't have any interest in it then or now. Then, when he'd come back to town for the wedding, I was suddenly smacked in the face—more than once—with reminders that we no longer lived the same lives—hell, they weren't even similar except for our histories.

His house was unlike even that of the one he grew up in. I couldn't imagine what kind of mortgage this place had on it or what he'd need all this space for. His garage was nearly the size of half my house.

"So much for a starter home, huh?" I tried to play it off like I didn't think it was absurd. And then I wondered if I really believed that, or if I was jealous of my best friend's success.

"My parents gave me the money for the down payment as a

combined graduation and wedding present. Sucks for the girl I actually marry; I doubt they'd do it twice." He joked, but I knew Beau better than he gave me credit for. He was still basking in the attention Peyton had shown him. The loneliness would set in soon, and all he'd have was this enormous house and no one to share it with.

I followed him inside and wondered if I were to yell, how many times my voice would echo with the open spaces, hardwood floors, and high ceilings. It was the middle of June in Georgia, and this house was cold. Not air-conditioning cold, just cold—sterile. He could move a football team in here and still not bring any life to the place. Boxes lined every wall, and furniture I'd never dreamed he'd pick out sat in awkward positions throughout every room we passed.

"It's a mess. I haven't had time to unpack anything, and I'm not sure what's mine and what belongs to Felicity. At some point, I'll have to go through it. Just not tonight."

"You haven't said much about any of that. You okay?"

He tossed his keys on the kitchen counter, likely so he'd be able to find them in the morning. Nothing in the place was organized, but I had to give him props; he might not have opened the first box, but the man had pizza and beer in the fridge. He handed me a cold one after twisting off the top and throwing it in the sink—Mrs. Chastain would have a coronary if she'd witnessed that. And then he got one for himself.

"As good as I can be for someone who lost a baby that never existed and his fiancée in the span of a couple of hours."

It didn't escape my attention that he didn't make eye contact with me. Instead, he leaned against the kitchen counter —one of many—and crossed his ankles. I took the spot across from him at the island and did the same. "You know Peyton's only going to add to that heartache, right?"

"I'm not dumb, Lee. I know nothing can ever come out of a relationship with her. It was just nice to have someone compliment me and not criticize everything I did and everyone I associated with. She made me feel good when I needed it."

I crossed my arms over my chest, still holding my beer. "Does she know that's all it was?"

"We talked about it. She doesn't see her family as the obstacle that I do."

I found that hard to believe. "She doesn't care that you slept with her sister?" Girls couldn't stand the thought of a rank stranger having touched their man, and a relative would be a pill no female would ever want to choke down.

"They aren't close." That was common knowledge. "But no, she doesn't care."

I kept my skepticism to myself. "Is she serious about seeing you again?"

"Yeah. She is."

"Dude, you've got to sort shit out in your head."

The red patches began to form on his cheeks, just under his eyes. "That's just it. I think I feel worse about *not* feeling bad than I do about not marrying Felicity. She hated everything about me. I didn't realize it until we were in Harden together. First at Christmas, and then again for the wedding. The only thing she loved was the bank account I was going to inherit."

That had to be a harsh realization, although I wasn't sure why he hadn't seen it. "How was she when you guys were in school?"

"Totally different. We ran in the same crowd, had the same

interests, liked the same things. But she hated Harden; she couldn't stand my relationship with Masyn and wasn't crazy about the one I had with you—even before she met either of you. It was like telling me she didn't like Braden and Bodie. She never got it." He sighed and finished his beer. "I kept thinking that once I took her home and she saw where I grew up and met the people I loved, that she'd change her tune. Problem was...she didn't know any other songs."

"I'm not going to stand here and pretend to give you relationship advice, God knows my first attempt at one hasn't gone all that well, but I can tell you that anyone who doesn't love the things and the people you do, isn't worth your time."

"Is it stupid to think Peyton's different?"

"Than her sister?"

"Yeah. I mean, she's still a Holstein."

"You tell me."

The color in his cheeks began to wash away when he no longer felt pressured. "Dude, she loved Harden. And I know things were rocky with Masyn, but Peyton seemed like she genuinely wanted to get to know her. She was willing to try anything we wanted to do—I couldn't have paid Felicity to go off the rope swing. But more than anything, my mom loved her. They hit it off the way I thought Felicity should."

It was no secret in Harden that Beverly Chastain approved of the marriage between the two families; she just had no intention of adopting Felicity as her new daughter. Daughter-in-law was the only title she would have ever held in the Chastain household, and that didn't come with affection.

"Your mom has a sixth sense about things, Beau. She's been pushing Masyn and me together since I learned to ride a bike.

If she embraced Peyton, you might want to consider it. You just need to go into it with your eyes wide open, and make damn sure that Peyton knows what she stands to lose on her end. Because her mom and sister won't take kindly to a relationship with you."

"You want another beer?"

I did. I wanted twelve more—or however many it took to pass out, so I didn't have to think about my dad or the fact that I hadn't really talked to Masyn in almost forty-eight hours, and the pattern that was forming this week with her avoiding me was pissing me off. "I think I just want to crash."

Beau walked me to the foyer and up a flight of stairs to a hall. By the time we reached the fourth door on the right, I contemplated retracing my steps with breadcrumbs so I could find my way back out of here. He reached in and flipped on the light. The mattress was still covered in plastic, the walls were bare, and four boxes sat at the foot of the bed labeled "bedroom six." I glanced back at the door to see if they were numbered—they weren't.

"Help me tear this off. The linens are in the box at the end." He motioned toward the box farthest from the door.

Together, we ripped the plastic cover from the mattress and box spring, and then in an overly domestic show of manly teamwork, we made the bed with sheets fresh out of the package. He then pulled several pillows out of another box, along with a comforter set that I was certain cost more than all of my bedroom furniture combined.

"I know it's not home." He looked around with his hands on his hips. "You should be able to get a decent night's sleep, though. If you get hot, the remote for the fan is on the nightstand—no, in the nightstand drawer. Hell, I don't know. Just throw off the down comforter and sleep under a sheet."

I didn't need much. A place to lie down and hot water to shower, and I'd be good as new tomorrow...well, maybe not new, but slightly refurbished.

"The bathroom is through there." He pointed to a door in the corner. "And towels are in the box marked towels. They should be easy enough to find. If you don't have soap or shampoo, you're on your own. I haven't found those yet."

I laughed. "What the hell are you bathing with?"

"A bar of Ivory and crap shampoo I got at the gas station last night."

"Where's your room?"

"You're not going to try to come cuddle with me in the middle of the night, are you? I mean, I'm all for trying to be here for you and everything, but that might be a little strange."

I stared at him and waited for him to move.

"This way."

We went back the way we came, apparently the west wing was for guests, and the east was for the lord of the manor. There was a tiny door—which I assumed was a linen closet— just beyond the staircase we came up, and then double doors that opened into a room that took up the entire left side of the house. There were rooms inside of the room—a library or office, a sitting area with a bay window, and then another set of double doors that led to the actual bedroom. It was insane. The damn room was so big, even his king-sized bed looked like doll-house furniture. And there were two of everything: two long dressers, two tall, skinny towers of drawers—I'm sure they had a name, I just didn't know what it was—two chairs, two ottomans, two benches at the end of the bed, two fans, and the list went on and on.

"You realize there are third world countries that don't have this amount of real estate? Yet you and Felicity bought it for two fucking people?"

He pointed through another set of doors, although these had little glass panes in them and slid into the wall. "Check out the bathroom."

"Holy shit," I called out the moment it all came into view. "I'll sleep in here. Screw the guest room." His and her closets that I swear were the size of Masyn's room at my house, a double shower with more jets than the New York football team, and a sunken bathtub I could swim in. And to top it off, the toilet had its own door, and there were separate vanities. "You could put a stove and fridge in here and never have to leave."

"The master suite is what sold Felicity on the house."

I hoped to God there was something he loved here and that he hadn't just bought the house to please her. "What about you?" I didn't know what a place like this near the heart of Atlanta would cost, but it'd be a mint in Harden. "Tell me what you exchanged your soul for." I flipped off the light and went back out to the bedroom.

"The game room and pool are nice." Nice. Beau mortgaged his life away for a game room and in-ground pool. "There's stadium seating in the theatre."

"You suck at pool, you have the fairest skin of any guy I've ever met and burn under the light of the moon, and you hate watching television."

"You compromise when you're getting married."

I'd struck a nerve. It was obvious that being here versus

Harden made the reality of his situation a little clearer. He was living in a world Felicity created—without Felicity. And he hated it.

"Now that you're not getting married, maybe you should consider what *you* want." I clapped him on the shoulder. "I'd be more than happy to help you find it."

"Thanks, Lee." He looked around at all the boxes and crap piled everywhere. "I'm going to need a bulldozer to dig out of this one."

"Luckily for you, I know where we can get one." Masyn's brother CJ worked on a crew that did grading—not that I really thought we'd bulldoze the house...although it might be pretty damn cathartic for Beau.

I'd almost made it to the final door in the funhouse maze when Beau called out to me. "She'll call, Lee."

The more time that passed, the harder it became to believe. Voicing that doubt would only continue the conversation, and it wasn't one I cared to have. I quirked my mouth to the side and huffed slightly. All I could muster in response was a dip of my head and a slight nod.

Beau needed a damn golf cart to make the walk down the hall not quite so long. The only light came from the room he'd shown me, which I extinguished as soon as I got my phone and my charger out of my bag. I plugged it in and laid it on the nightstand, pulled my shirt over my head, and slid off my jeans.

The sheets were cool against my bare skin, and the weight of the down comforter almost reminded me of having someone with me. It was late, and there was no way Masyn had been at the shop in hours, yet there were no notifications or missed calls —no messages or texts. I tried one more time to get in touch with her, only to have it go straight to voicemail. She'd shut me out, and until I got back into town, there was nothing I could do about it.

Right now, I had to focus on my dad. I wished Masyn were by my side. Just hearing her voice would alleviate the huge void I carried in the pit of my stomach. I wanted to be optimistic about my dad's condition and to believe that once I could explain the misunderstanding to Masyn, then all would be right. The truth was, my dad might not survive, and Masyn may never believe me. And at the end of the day, I had to be okay with either. I just wasn't sure I'd ever reach that point.

Sleep came easier than I thought, and in the morning, the sun radiated through the blinds that I hadn't closed, waking me up like an alarm clock. It was after seven and visiting hours had already started. As tempting as it was to race through a shower and jump back in the car to dash over to the hospital, I lingered under the hot water, and the stream pounded away at my shoulders and sore back. I even took the time to clean up the scruff on my face and make myself look presentable. Somehow, the routine made me feel more human, and like, maybe the day wouldn't be shit the way the two before it had.

It took virtually zero coaxing from Beau to get me to stop at a Waffle House to eat breakfast, and by the time we were actually on our way to the hospital, it was nearly eleven. I'd called the nurses' station twice to check on my dad; although with no change, rushing over there to spend twenty minutes in his room before they kicked me out seemed counterproductive. Or maybe I was afraid the next time I went in could be the last.

NINETEEN

BEAU ACTED LIKE HE HAD AN ASSIGNED SEAT IN THE waiting room. He sat in the same chair each time we walked in. I glanced over my shoulder to see him staring at the screen on his phone, and for once, I wasn't irritated that it was in his face; I was grateful he had something to occupy him so, in turn, he would be here to occupy me. The nurse buzzed the doors open to allow me back into the ward, and I made the trip to my dad's room that seemed all too familiar.

For the first time since I'd gotten here on Friday, when I'd held my dad's hand and sat next to his bed, I started talking. I had prayed, I had watched him breathe, I had paced the room, but what I'd yet to do was let him know I was here. I probably should have told him about Beau's wedding catastrophe, or that I'd had a new liner put in the pool, or hell, even told him that I cut my hand. I didn't do any of those things. He would have given Beau shit for getting wrapped up with a girl like Felicity in the first place, scolded me for spending too much money on a hole in the ground, and worried about whether or not I'd seen the best doctor in town to stitch me up, just before he cussed Farley's name. He could be rather crotchety at times, and right now, I'd kill to hear any one of those lectures. I also needed to tell my dad how fucking scared I was that he wouldn't wake up to chew me a new asshole. And that's what I did.

"If you give up on me, old man, I swear to God, I'll have some shit put on your headstone about your love of flowers and fairies. You'll be the laughing stock of the cemetery. I really don't want to have to do that, so how about you come back to me instead, yeah?"

The beeping on the heart rate monitor quickened notice-ably, and I watched it, waiting for someone to come racing in, calling out codes and jumping on his bed with paddles to shock him. But the blip only lasted about a minute, and his thumb twitched in my hand. A smile crept across my lips; the old bastard was laughing at me. He was far too stubborn to die without more fanfare. This had been his trial run—go big or go home. It wasn't big enough, so he'd go home to Roswell. God wasn't ready for him yet. I could feel it in my gut. Now I just had to wait it out until he decided to share that secret with the rest of the world.

I left his room, pushed through the doors, and went back into the waiting room with more energy than I'd had in a week. And even though I'd been happy to see Beau glued to that tiny phone screen thirty minutes ago, it ticked me off to find him still playing on it. I couldn't figure out what the hell he did on that thing. We had the same phone, and mine never held my interest for anywhere near that long.

"Hey, jacksack, wanna go get some coffee?"

Beau didn't look up. His thumbs flew around the bottom of

the screen, and when I peeked over the edge to see what he was doing, I realized he was texting with someone.

"Hang on," he mumbled.

I stood there for several minutes, waiting for him to get up and follow me. He did neither.

"Do I have to carry you?"

"Masyn called."

Those two words were almost as monumental as my dad's rising pulse. My heart leapt into my throat, and my body tensed with anticipation. "And? What'd she say?"

"I didn't answer it." He didn't even look up, just kept pecking his damn fingertips across that fucking screen. "I was in the bathroom."

Beau'd had a good run. Twenty-two solid years. I hated having to end his life right here, but maybe since we were at a hospital, they might be able to save him when I was done with his cashmere-wearing, seersucker-loving ass.

"What the hell, Beau? We've been trying to get in touch with her for the better part of two days, and you couldn't swipe right to answer while you were standing at a urinal?" Trying to keep my voice lowered took more effort than it should have.

He continued to respond to whoever kept text-bombing him, but I was about to swat the damn thing across the room. "It was number two."

"Number two? Are you five, Beau? So you were taking a shit. Who cares? You didn't have to grunt in her ear or strain while you talked."

"You need to calm down before you end up on the stroke floor and I have to go back and forth between checking on you *and* your dad."

Calm down. He wanted me to calm down. I was a nanosecond away from grabbing him by his scrawny neck and suspending him against a wall until he started talking. "Beau, so help me God—"

"Seriously, Lee. Chill out. Who the hell do you think I'm texting?"

"You still haven't told me what she said."

A nurse called out to us from across the waiting area. "Guys, I'm going to have to ask you to take that outside."

As tempting as it was to shoot her the bird—she didn't deserve it—I shoved my hand in my pocket to still my twitching finger. Instead, I jerked Beau out of the seat with my other hand and dragged him down the hall to the elevator bank.

He ripped his arm out of my grasp and ran his hand through his hair. "She called because she thought I was in the car driving back to Atlanta."

"Why would she think you were in the car?"

The doors to the elevator opened and a couple stepped out. I moved against the wall, out of the way, and Beau followed. "I wasn't supposed to leave Harden until today, remember? She thought I was still at home this weekend."

"And she just hadn't seen you? On a clear day, you can see from one side of Harden to the other." It was a slight exaggeration.

"She worked late on Friday and all day yesterday. She said she thought I was with my parents last night, since it was my final night in town and I wasn't at Sadler's."

This was like pulling teeth. "Point, Beau. Get to it."

"Jesus, you're impatient today. Here, read it yourself." He

scrolled to the top of the conversation and handed me the phone.

I skimmed through the part he told me about.

Masyn: You lied to me, Beau. I'm not sure who I'm more mad at right now. You, Lee, or myself.

Beau: What'd I lie about?

Masyn: You told me he'd be careful with my heart.

Beau: You really need to call him.

Masyn: You're kidding, right? He's in New York. After he promised me he wasn't going.

Beau: As I recall, you told him he should go.

I reached out and slapped my friend on the chest. "You couldn't just tell her I wasn't in New York?"

"Keep reading."

Beau: Have you listened to your messages?

Masyn: I deleted them. I wasn't interested in his excuses.

Beau: Masyn, you're going to regret this.

Masyn: And for the record, I didn't TELL him to go. In fact, one of the last things he said to me before we left the house Friday was that he'd be home after I got off work.

Masyn: Guess who wasn't there?

Masyn: Guess what moron sat on his porch for an hour?

Beau: Why didn't you just use the spare key?

Masyn: Lee wasn't there, and THIS dumb girl baked in the sun for sixty minutes thinking he'd pull up.

Beau: You could have gone swimming while you waited. Have you seen the new liner he had put in?

This had to be a joke. Not even Beau could be this clueless.

Masyn: Are you defending him? Or avoiding telling me the truth about what's going on?

Beau: I wouldn't lie to you...and he doesn't need defending.

Masyn: Men. You'll stand together on a sinking ship instead of stepping off on to dry land.

Beau: Was that a metaphor?

Beau: You need to talk to Lee.

Masyn: I have nothing to say.

Beau: Could have fooled me...please scroll up and read all of what you didn't have to say and rephrase that last response.

Masyn: Have you talked to him?

Beau: Yes.

Masyn: Where the hell is he?

Beau: ...hold, please.

The next message was a picture of me standing in front of Beau in the waiting room moments earlier.

Masyn: He's with YOU?

Beau: I told you that you'd regret it.

Masyn: Where are you guys?

Beau: Atlanta Memorial Hospital.

Masyn: OMG. Why? What's wrong? Why the hell have you let me ramble on like an idiot?

Beau: So you'd feel foolish and learn to believe in him.

Beau: You need to call him.

"That's it? She just stopped responding? Did she call you?" I yanked my phone out of my pocket. No missed calls.

"You have my phone in your hand, Lee. Has it rung?" He rolled his eyes and accentuated it with, "Sheesh."

I tried to call her from my phone, and the damn thing went straight to voicemail. "What the hell? Did she block my number?" I snatched his cell from him again and tried from there. Same thing.

"Maybe her battery died. At least she now knows you're not with Peyton or in New York. And now the tables have turned in your favor. Enjoy it, Lee. You may never see victory with a woman again. It's a rare phenomenon, like a unicorn... only you have proof, in writing, of how *wrong* she was." He grinned with satisfaction, like the stupid exchange he'd had with her meant something.

"I don't give a shit about seeing victory."

"Spoken like a man who hasn't been beaten into submission by a lady he loves."

"You're an idiot. I just want to see her. I don't want her to think I'd ever choose someone over her. This isn't a fucking game, Beau." I shoved the device into his chest, and when he finally took it from me, I yanked open the metal door to the stairs. It clanged shut behind me as I took two steps at a time. I didn't have a clue where I was going. I just needed to move.

I kept trying to call her, hoping she'd plug in her phone. After countless failed attempts and having stalked around the entire perimeter of the hospital three times, I cooled off enough to deal with my other best friend. Not that I could stay mad at him any more than I could Masyn. He didn't know how Masyn and I worked without him in the picture—and I didn't mean in the bedroom. We didn't communicate this way, and he was playing with her instead of telling her the truth like we were still in high school. It was a huge misunderstanding, which I'd known on Friday, but unless I could talk to her, I couldn't fix it.

When dinner rolled around, and neither one of us had heard from her, I picked at my food in the cafeteria and looked around, wondering why there wasn't a bar in the food court. People were stressed at hospitals—alcohol should be a given. Hell, I'd settle for an Amstel Light right now.

Beau apologized again for how he'd handled the text messages. And I finally let him off the hook. Yet even though I'd told him no less than twenty-seven times that it was okay, he couldn't stop. Once, when we got on the elevator and rode back up to my dad's floor, he was still yammering about how he'd messed up. I was ready for the day to end. I was going to see my dad one last time before visiting hours were over and we went back to Beau's.

The elevator doors opened, and before we rounded the corner, I could hear someone arguing at the nurses' station. But since Beau wouldn't shut up, I couldn't make out what the conversation was about. I smacked him, not having heard anything he'd said since the doors had opened, anyhow.

"No...I'm not *an immediate relative, but I grew up in his house.*"

"*Ma'am, I'm sorry. He's in intensive care. Only immediate family is allowed visitation.*"

"*I don't understand. What happened? How long has he been here?*"

"*I wish I could tell you more, but the patient's privacy is our second concern—next to their well-being, of course, and—*"

"*And you think it's in his best interest not to have people*

*who love him at his side while he goes through...whatever he's
going through?"*

The nurses' station was down the hall and around the
corner, so while we could hear what was taking place, neither
Beau nor I could see who did the talking. It was difficult to
make out the words over the crying and continuous inflection
in her voice. The poor girl was hysterical while Nurse Ratched
—she was quite the dictator—kept the same indifferent tone she
had with me two nights before. Too bad the lady who was here
during the day wasn't the only person allowed to interact with
people—she had way better people skills.

Beau slapped my chest and stopped walking, cocking his
ear in the direction of the conversation, argument, discussion—
whatever it was. "Listen."

"No, thanks. I've been where that poor girl is. I don't care to
relive it, even through someone else's experience." I took a step
forward, and he grabbed my arm.

"Shut up," he hissed under his breath, still holding me
back.

"If you'd just let me see him..." The girl was on the verge of
a full-blown meltdown.

I took off down the hall, not waiting for Beau. My feet prac-
tically skid across the floor as I rounded the corner to find
Masyn begging the nurse for admittance into my dad's room.
She hadn't seen me, and I stopped dead in my tracks.

"Masyn." My deep voice carried across the hall, startling
her.

Beau came up seconds after her name passed my lips.

Her dark hair swung around in slow motion when she
heard me call out. Her face was swollen, and her eyes were

puffy, rimmed red from crying. She didn't respond. She also didn't hesitate. Masyn ran toward me and launched herself into my arms. Her legs wrapped around my waist when I picked her up, and the hold she had on my neck threatened to choke the life out of me—at least I'd die in her arms.

I tucked my face into her shoulder and inhaled everything I loved about the way she smelled. The rosemary and mint of her shampoo wrapped me up as tightly as her arms. And the warmth of her tiny frame pressed against me had never been more right. "What are you doing here?"

"I didn't know. I'm sorry, Lee." Her voice was muffled, and her tears dampened my shirt.

I set her down and brushed her hair out of her face. The strands stuck to her wet, tear-streaked cheeks. "Why would you think I went to New York?"

She bit her lip and shook her head. Her eyes hadn't dried completely, and a few random tears hung from her jaw. "Peyton left, and you were gone and...I'm an idiot. I don't know. I don't know how to do any of this. I've never been in a relation-ship." Masyn's gaze dropped to her feet with her admission, as though she were ashamed or embarrassed by her inexperience.

"There was Alex—" Beau caught my death stare and promptly quit speaking. He jerked his head to the side and pointed over his shoulder with his thumb. "I'll just be over there if you need me."

He moved aside as a young couple tried to step around us.

Pinching her chin, I lifted her head. There was nothing she couldn't share with me, and I never wanted her to hide. Lovingly, I met her eyes and waited.

Her shoulders sagged, but she held my gaze. "I just wish

you'd told me you were leaving, then we could have avoided all of this."

Being angry with my boss wasn't going to help the situation, but it didn't change how I felt nor did it soften my tone when I tried to explain. "Farley was supposed to tell you Friday. I left work when I got the phone call."

"I didn't see him after lunch. And he wasn't there yesterday."

It didn't matter that we were standing in the middle of a hospital waiting room, I needed to touch her. I couldn't stop myself from cupping her cheek in my hand, and my heart soared when Masyn leaned into it. "I typed out a text on our way here, but I was pretty frazzled and got distracted." My chest deflated with the breath I let out. "I never hit send. And then I left my phone in Beau's car."

I dropped my hand to my side, realizing all of this sounded like excuses. Yet Masyn didn't let me retreat. Her hands found my hips, and she pulled my waist flush to her stomach. Now wasn't the time to get aroused, but I couldn't help myself. Staring at her warm eyes, I had to restrain myself from capturing her mouth instead of working on my apology.

"I'm sorry," I whispered.

She raised a hand to my cheek, lifted up onto her toes, and pressed her full, supple lips to mine. It was only a peck, yet it raised the hair on my arms when electricity ran down my spine. Masyn dropped back down, still holding my stare. If her gaze were an ocean, I'd drown in the waves.

I tried to keep any accusation from my voice when I softly asked, "Why haven't you answered your phone?" I had more questions than I could get out at one time, but bombarding her would only make her feel like she'd done something wrong. Truthfully, neither of us had communicated well, although it started with me.

Her brow drew in, and her nose crinkled. "Before today?"

"No, I pretty well got *that* message. Why didn't you answer after you talked to Beau."

She stepped back a hair to pull her cell out of her back pocket and placed what was left of it in the palm of my hand. It was painfully obvious why she hadn't been able to receive any calls. The damn thing was almost flat, the guts spilling from the side, and the screen demolished...and dark.

"Do I want to know what happened to it?"

Masyn shook her head and pursed her lips. "Probably not."

"Why don't you tell me anyhow?" My tone was playful, as was the expression I tried to give her. With my brows arched, I cocked my head, waiting.

Jesus, she was sinfully hot. From her dark hair to her smoldering eyes, her plump lips to her elegant neck, head to toe, Masyn Porter drove me wild in the best possible ways.

"I was driving while I was texting Beau." She held up a hand to halt any interruption I might try to interject. "Voice to text, not typing. And I accidentally dropped it out of the window at a red light. When I backed up to get it, I kind of ran over it."

I chuckled under my breath. It wasn't funny, nevertheless, I could envision Masyn stopped at a light in Harden and backing over her phone. There was no piece of that puzzle I couldn't envision, including the expressions on her face. "And what was your plan if you got here and couldn't find us?" Not that it mattered, she had found us.

Her thin shoulders raised a couple inches and then fell. "I didn't even know why you were here, but I realized if you were okay and Beau was fine, the only other person you knew in Atlanta was George. And if he was here in the hospital, you'd be back." Masyn licked her lips, and all I could think about was having them wrapped around parts of my anatomy.

The *whoosh* of the double doors opening reminded me of where we currently stood and squashed the wet dream forming in my mind. "That's an awfully big risk to take—wait. How'd you get here?"

Her forehead wrinkled when her nose scrunched. "I drove," she said as though my question were asinine.

"Your car?"

Her face relaxed, and she rolled her eyes. "Oh my God, don't start. I haven't seen you in over two days, and your dad is in the hospital. We don't need to talk about my car." She grabbed my hand, putting her back to me, and tugged me across the waiting room and out of the flow of traffic.

I continued to talk even though she couldn't see me. "It's not safe. That vehicle isn't reliable enough to make a three-hour trip."

She faced me when we reached a bank of chairs, and then smirked and lifted up on her toes to kiss my lips. "That's why I stopped by your house and got your truck." Masyn was proud of herself for having warded off my objections before I ever had them.

If it were anyone else, I'd take them out and hang them up by their toes, but Masyn could take everything I owned, and as long as I got her at the end of the day, it didn't matter. Just having her here for the last five minutes had rejuvenated me.

She sat in the seats I'd spent the last two, mind-numbing days in, and I took up residence next to her. Her breath brushed against my skin, and the heat of her body so close for the taking teased me. Masyn was a distraction I loved to have—especially given our current location—I just couldn't let my desire get out of control. Being thrown out of the hospital wouldn't do my dad or me any good.

I leaned back to put a few inches between us and hopefully a little cold air to calm my racing thoughts. "So, you used the spare key to go inside and heist my truck, just not to get out of the sun when you were mad at me?" I didn't know why I found that so humorous other than being able to picture her pouting on Friday versus her victory today.

She shrugged, refusing to answer the question. "Can I see your dad?" She hadn't asked what happened. Masyn didn't care. Her only concern was his well-being, not the details of what brought him here.

My dad was important to me and, therefore, important to her. He'd always loved her, and I think, in a lot of ways, she reminded him of my mom. My old man was gruff, but he had a soft spot for Masyn Porter.

I hated to give up my time with him, but if she wanted to go back to see my dad, I wouldn't deny her. "Yeah, let's go talk to the nurse."

"You mean the she-devil at the desk? No, thank you. She's scary...and mean."

I stood and offered Masyn my hand to help her up. Reluctantly, she took it, trusting me and stood. "She's both. She's also the only person who can push the button to unlock the doors. She's the gatekeeper of the CICU." I pointed to the motorized entrance to the right of the nurses' station. "And after she barks at you once, she'll leave you alone. You should be safe now that she's proven whose turf this is."

The nurse gave Masyn a visitor's tag and told her my dad's room number. Masyn held my hand, and before she let go, I tugged her against my chest to press my lips to her forehead. "Thank you for coming, sweetheart." I pulled back in order to stare into her eyes when I said three words. "I love you." It was a vow, even if she didn't realize it.

Masyn tilted her head up, her lips hovering near mine, and spoke the words I most enjoyed hearing, "I love you, too."

TWENTY

Each time the electronic doors clicked and swooshed with the arrival of anyone entering the waiting area, Beau and I stopped whatever we were doing—talking, resting, playing on our phones—to look up. I couldn't speak for him, but I kept hoping someone would come out to tell me there'd been some sort of change in my dad's condition. When Masyn came through the double doors twenty minutes later, looking worse than when she went in, my heart hammered in my chest and I feared the worst.

I stood and met her in the middle of the waiting room. Her thin arms circled my waist, and she pressed her cheek against my chest. There she released the emotion of the last two days, soaking my shirt. I stroked her hair and cradled her tightly, waiting for a sign that she could hold herself up. The doors opened and closed twice more before she pushed back and patted me on the chest as though I'd been the one who needed comforting.

"You want to sit down?" I tried to lean over to whisper in

her ear, which was hard to do with her short height and her nearness. There wasn't anyone around, but I just knew how vulnerable she felt with her emotions on display in an unfamiliar place.

She nodded and let me lead her to a row of seats at the far end of the waiting room. It was getting late, and she had to work tomorrow. So did Beau. And it dawned on me, I'd never called Farley, so he was expecting me at the shop in twelve hours, alongside Masyn.

"He looks so weak, Lee. I don't know what I expected. I mean, you didn't tell me he had open-heart surgery. I didn't even know he'd had a heart attack, although I kind of figured that out when I got here and found out what floor he was on." She swiped at the tears running down her cheeks.

I didn't see it often because the girl never cried, yet even though her pain crushed me, I loved the way her eyes turned green with streaks of chocolate and whiskey any time she did. Like there was so much emotion trying to get out that her irises had to open up and change colors to release it. Even the whites being bloodshot didn't take away from the beauty of the transformation. I could stare at them for hours and never get tired of what I saw.

"The nurse came in. She said that he's made it through the critical stage, and once he passes the forty-eight-hour mark tonight, that it is just a matter of time before he'll be back to his old self. I just couldn't see it. I can't figure out how the body goes from where he is, then back to a normal life."

"I haven't thought that far through any of it. Right now, I just want him to open his eyes and grumble about how much this vacation is going to cost him." The humph I let out only served to pacify me.

"I'm sorry."

"Sweetheart, you don't have anything to be sorry for. The man eats like a goat and smokes like the Marlboro Man. I'm surprised it hasn't happened sooner. I just wish I'd been around more."

Masyn straightened her spine and craned her neck to meet my downward stare. "Lee, your dad chose to leave Harden. He never expected you to follow him."

"Doesn't change that I don't talk to him enough or visit very often. I didn't even know if there was anyone I should call—I'm *that* detached from his daily life. And now that I think about it, no one has even come to visit him."

It was hard to accept that my dad was getting older. And even harder to accept that he might be lonely. Maybe he wasn't, I didn't know. When we talked, it was always about sports or stupid things going on back home. I couldn't recall a single time I'd called him and he hadn't been at his house, and he never mentioned anyone other than people he worked with.

"Maybe no one knows he's here."

"It happened when he was at work. Lots of people knew, none of them cared enough to check on him. Not even his boss has stopped by."

"He's a private person."

No, he was dead inside. I'd seen the signs all my life, I just didn't recognize them for what they were. He ceased living when my mom passed away, but he's just been *existing* since then, yet here I was paying no attention, not even noticing. I thought getting him out of Harden would take away some of those constant reminders. But maybe he wanted me to believe it had so that I'd find my own way.

I glanced over at Beau, who still sat alone in the same seat he'd been in for the better part of two days. "I could sit here and pick this apart all night long. It won't change anything. Until he wakes up, all I can do is wait. But you and Beau don't need to wait with me."

Masyn sniffled and grabbed a tissue from the box on the table in the corner. "What? That's ridiculous."

"You've got work tomorrow and a three-hour drive home. Beau's starting a new job in the morning, and I don't even want to get started on the situation at his house. I don't want you on the road late, and I can't go back with you."

Her tears quickly morphed into agitation. "I'm not leaving you here alone. What's the matter with you?" She dabbed at her cheeks, narrowed her eyes at me, and fisted her hands in her lap.

"Masyn, it isn't doing anyone any good to sit here and watch people walk by. I swear I've memorized every detail of this room and could draw a picture with my eyes closed because all I do is wait."

"Beau." She wiped the back of her hand under her jaw to catch the remainder of her emotion. "Come here."

He didn't question her. Beau was like a loyal dog. He stayed when you told him to, and he came when you called. The three of us huddled in the corner like we used to on the playground when we were formulating a plan to take down some jerk who'd picked on one of our friends.

"What are your plans?" she asked Beau.

"I'm going home whenever Lee's ready to leave. Why?"

"What about tomorrow morning?" Masyn squinted her eyes while she waited for him to respond. It didn't matter what Beau said; she'd already found a hole in his agenda.

"What about it?"

"Don't you have a new job you're starting?" I reminded him.

"Supposed to. But this seems a little more important." Beau wasn't thinking clearly.

"Dude, you have a mortgage payment now. A real job. You can't call in on your first day and tell them something came up. That's not your dad in there—that firm isn't going to care about where you are. They're going to fire you."

Beau's current state of bewilderment would have been laughable any other time. "Can you get fired if you never start?"

"This is crazy. Beau, you're going to work tomorrow. Masyn, you're going home tonight."

"And tell me, genius, if Beau is at work and I take your truck back to Harden, how are you going to get back and forth to the hospital, or come home once your dad is stable?" She crossed her arms and legs and leaned back, having made what she believed were valid points.

"I'm sure Atlanta has Uber. I'll download the app."

Masyn's mouth dropped. "You can't be serious."

"Look, you guys. I appreciate your being here. And I don't want either of you to leave—"

Her expression relaxed into a satisfied grin. "Good, then it's settled."

"However," I continued. "I have to be realistic. Life doesn't stop because George Carter is in the hospital."

Masyn casually shrugged like we were discussing what was

for dinner. "Mine does. Plus, I have vacation time I can use. Farley owes me after the miracle we pulled off this weekend getting those parts out."

"Mine, too," Beau added.

I inhaled deeply and rubbed my face with my hands. Neither one of them seemed to care about the exaggerated sigh I released. Clearly, I would have to be the only adult in the trio. "Beau, you have to go in tomorrow. You've had too much happen in the last week to let go of the job you need to pay your bills."

When he tried to protest, I held my hand up to stop him, which he promptly pushed out of his face. And I ignored the angry splotches that had already erupted down his neck.

"Masyn, I have to call Farley, anyhow. If he says you can use your vacation time without any repercussions, then I'd love to have you stay. That way, I wouldn't be alone, I'll have transportation, and no one would be losing their job."

Beau crossed his arms, clearly incensed. "That's total crap, Lee."

"Dude, what is going on with you? It's not like we wouldn't see you at night—unless you don't want us to stay at your place? It's insane for you to walk away from a job."

He'd been distant since Masyn called, and it got worse once she showed up. Hospitals have a tendency to keep people on edge or make them reflective and emotional, so I could only assume one of those had happened to him, and I'd missed it.

Beau's cheeks began to paint themselves with maroon patches, and his ears flamed to match the marks already taking over his neck. The typical progression that normally took minutes to transform happened in the blink of an eye. He almost knocked the chair over when he stood abruptly. "Do whatever you want. I'll text you my address, and then Masyn can drop you off or she can stay, too. I don't care."

He was halfway down the hall when I caught him by the elbow. "What gives?"

"This isn't the time or the place, Lee. I'll be fine. Just let me know when you're on your way so I can let you in." He left me standing there, watching his back as he stalked away.

"Mr. Carter?" I turned toward the sound of my name and watched Masyn move toward the nurse who'd called me.

My feet were firmly rooted, and I was terrified to move. "Yes?" No one had come looking for me since Dad had gotten out of surgery. Taking a step in her direction took forced effort. One by one, I made my feet carry me to where she stood.

"I was hoping you hadn't left. Your father is awake. I thought you might like to see him for a few minutes before visiting hours were over."

Masyn took my hand and squeezed it. "Go on. I'll wait out here."

I didn't hesitate and followed the woman into the ICU.

"He's going to be very drowsy," the nurse said, walking beside me, "and he might not stay awake long. Try to remember the mind shuts down so the body can heal. But the fact that he's starting to wake up is a very good sign." She held open the door to my father's room so I could step through.

I stuffed my hands into my pockets to keep him from seeing them shake. It was a dead giveaway. I'd done it since I was little. Elbows straight, shoulders near my ears. If I'd been a girl, I probably would have pulled my dress over my head for as many years as I could get away with it.

He still had a breathing tube in his mouth, and wires hung off what seemed like every inch of his body. But once I got near the bed where he could see me, the slits in his eyes got a little wider and his fingers lifted off the mattress like he was trying to wave.

"Hey, Dad." I pulled up the same chair I'd been moving back and forth for two days and sat next to him.

His fingers were chilly when I held his hand, and the fact that he didn't glare at me or try to rip the tube out of his throat told me how scared he was. Absentmindedly, I stroked the top of his hand with my thumb and stared at the hint of green I could see between his lashes.

I didn't have a clue what to say. Telling him I was afraid seemed counterproductive—he was the one with a cracked sternum on life support, or whatever all this crap was. I should be reassuring him that everything was going to be fine. But this weekend had been the first time in my life I'd really acknowledged that I was getting older, and at some point, my dad would join my mom. He wasn't elderly by any means, forty-two was relatively young, but he did nothing to ensure he'd lead a long life. In fact, it was like he'd purposely tried to run his body into the ground by *not* taking care of it.

"Masyn's in the waiting room. She came back to see you a little while ago. She probably talked your ears off."

He blinked several times. I'd take that as a yes. If he could talk, he'd bitch about having to go to a hospital to get a decent night's sleep, only to have "that girl" make a special trip from Harden to wake him up. He'd flick his wrist at her and pretend he didn't know her name. And when I turned my back to keep from yelling at him, he'd wink at her, and the two would giggle.

She was the only person who ever made my dad laugh that way.

"Beau's been here, too. He left a few minutes ago. I had to run him off. He has some fancy new job he starts tomorrow. God knows, I don't want Mrs. Chastain coming after me for Beau not living up to his potential."

I chuckled thinking about all the times Mrs. Chastain had lectured me over the years. Every recollection I had from childhood to present included Beau and Masyn, and many of them involved their families. Even when Beau had gone away to college, I'd fill him in after something happened, and it was like he became part of the memory through reminiscing...or bitching. Although, it wasn't just the three of us. Masyn's parents and her brothers were just as rooted in my life as my dad. The Chastains could have given me their last name and I wouldn't have felt any closer to them.

And our ripple expanded from there, like dropping a rock on a smooth lake.

I realized I could lose myself—and several hours—thinking about how intertwined all of us were, and I didn't have time to waste before the nurses would kick me out again.

"They're not going to let me stay long. Visiting hours are over, and we've exceeded our quota as your guests. I'm going to stay at Beau's house while you get better, so I promise I'll be back tomorrow, bright and early."

When I stood, I leaned over the bed and kissed my dad on the forehead. I couldn't hug him, and I couldn't leave without him knowing how much he meant to me. He could backhand me for it later. "Love you, Dad. I'll see you in the morning, okay?"

He blinked fast three times and the respirator machine made some beeping noises in protest to his movements. He'd call me a liar when he could talk later and smack me upside the back of the head for telling stories, because George Carter didn't do mushy.

But he'd just used Morse code of the eyes to tell me he loved me, too.

I SENT BEAU A TEXT TO TELL HIM MASYN AND I WERE ON our way. The read message receipt indicated he'd seen it, even though he didn't respond. And when we got there, every light in the house was on to welcome us home.

"Holy crap, this is *Beau's* house?" Masyn was either in awe or repulsed by the extravagant display of wealth, I couldn't tell which.

"Yeah. Just wait until we get inside."

"Why would he have bought a house this big?"

I threw the truck in park and grabbed Masyn's bag from the back seat. "I think Felicity had a lot to do with it."

I'd gone in through the garage last night, so walking up to the front door was a little intimidating. I wasn't a small guy, and I felt tiny standing on the porch. The columns went to the second story, and there weren't just a set of double doors, the place had huge windowpanes down both sides that made it appear twice as large.

Masyn held my hand and reached out to press the doorbell with the other. We couldn't have been more than an hour behind Beau, yet he'd managed to get a huge head start on drinking away the evening. He'd never been a heavy drinker. A couple of beers on the weekend, yeah, but I realized every night I'd seen him since he came to town, he'd had more than a social drink.

He ushered us in, but he missed the confused look Masyn shot me when he offered us a mocking bow. Once we stepped inside, he gave the door a rough push, and it closed with a thud behind us. Masyn jerked, and I worried the glass might shatter.

"You guys want a beer?" Beau motioned for us to go to the living room, and he detoured to the kitchen.

"No, thanks. We're good," I answered for the two of us when Masyn shook her head.

Her back was stiff as a board when she took a seat on the white leather sofa. I hoped if she saw me relax next to her that she'd take my lead—she didn't. This was a side of Beau I'd never seen, and it clearly freaked Masyn out...even if she hadn't said anything. There was none of her usual chatter, and even her jaw tensed.

Beau dropped into a chair opposite us and chugged half the beer he'd just opened. He wasn't drunk yet, but it wouldn't take many more for him to be three sheets to the wind. And hungover wasn't a great way to start a new job.

"I got to see my dad for a few minutes before we left. He couldn't talk or anything, but he opened his eyes. It'll be interesting to see those nurses deal with his piss and vinegar."

Revenge came in lots of forms. George Carter was one they wouldn't be expecting.

"So Masyn, you talked Lee into letting you stay, huh?" He shook his head. Coupled with his condescending tone, I didn't like where this was going.

"Yeah, we called Farley. He wasn't all that happy, but he couldn't deny Lee the time off. I have no idea why he agreed to give me the same freedom. I didn't argue, though. I just took the week he gave me and hung up before he could change his mind."

"There was a time where one of us never did anything without the others. I bet you guys don't remember that, but I do."

"How could we not remember it? We've been friends for most of our lives," I pointed out.

He spun the chair around with his foot, like he was on a merry-go-round. If he weren't careful, he'd be sick as a dog, and I wasn't cleaning up his puke. "Yeah, but it all changed after high school."

He was right. Everything changed because we grew up, and our lives went in different directions. Masyn and I had just had to mature faster. Neither of us had the luxury of spending the next four years living off our parents and getting a degree—not that we wanted it, anyhow.

"Beau, just because you took a different path doesn't mean we aren't still as close as we were four years ago. You and Masyn still talk all the time."

"Yeah, about you," he pouted, and I started to believe he'd had more to drink than I initially thought.

I didn't allow myself to see Masyn's reaction. It wasn't a secret they'd talked, I just wasn't sure she wanted him tossing out all she'd said over the years. "We talked about you, too," I confessed.

Beau tilted his beer to the side and pushed off the floor, causing himself to turn faster in the seat. He was acting like a child, but for the life of me, I couldn't figure out where the attitude changes or sudden regression into immaturity came from.

I gave myself a mental shrug. It wasn't my house. Far be it from me to tell him what to do, so I ignored his careless behavior. Beau spoke, even as the chair continued to whirl. "I just wish I could go back and change things..."

"Why?" Masyn looked around when her voice echoed in the room around us.

"Because I hate this"—he spread his arms out, still moving —"this place. I don't want to live here."

I wasn't sure if I could reason with him, but I gave it a shot. "You can sell the house, man."

"Not just the house. It's the city, the people, the stuffy job with suits and ties. The expectation to live up to the Chastain name."

That I couldn't help him with. I may not have all the things Beau did; nevertheless, I loved my life. After this weekend, I recognized the need to make some improvements where my dad was concerned, but all in all, I was happy.

"If you're so unhappy, change it." Masyn always kept things simple.

"And do what? Move back to Harden? Live with my parents? Get a job at the shop? Come on. Get real. There's no life for me there."

Talking shit about the way we grew up and what we'd turned into was the fastest way to light a fuse under Masyn and piss her off. "Not like what you have here, you're right. If you hate this so much, do something about it other than whine. So you've had a few crap days. You didn't really lose anything by getting rid of Felicity. And a house is nothing more than a stack of boards neatly arranged. Maybe you should stop wallowing in self-pity and recognize the opportunities you had that most of your friends didn't."

He finally put his foot on the floor and stopped spinning. "I don't know how to undo the last four years' worth of decisions."

I wasn't going to sugarcoat shit for Beau. "You might want to start by deciding what you actually want, instead of taking what's handed to you." If this was the conversation he wanted to have tonight, by God, we could have it. Truthfully.

He immediately got defensive. "What the hell's that supposed to mean?"

"Exactly what I said. You're twenty-two, almost twenty-three years old, and you've never had a job. Not even a paper route. You were about to marry a woman you didn't love for a fucking trust fund to continue living a cushy life. And fuck, look around. No one starts off in a house like this. You've set yourself up to fail, Beau. You've always had the best of everything, so you don't appreciate anything."

"So, now I'm unhappy because I'm rich?" He snubbed the notion that my opinion might hold water.

"Earth to Beau! *You* aren't rich. Your *parents* are."

Masyn grabbed my forearm when I stood. "Lee, calm down. Don't be so mean."

"No, I'm not going to calm down." I turned my attention back to Beau. "You want to change your life, man? Then change your attitude. I love you, but at some point, you've got to cut the tie from Daddy's purse strings. Whether that's starting the job at this firm tomorrow, or that's going back to Harden and working on an assembly line—do it because it makes you proud at the end of the day."

If looks could kill, I'd be on my way to the morgue. The vein on the side of Beau's head thrummed a steady beat, and his eyes narrowed like he was ready to attack. "Another couple of weeks with you, and I'll be halfway there." He held up his beer. "A member of the blue-collar crowd."

"I'm not ashamed of who I am or where I came from, Beau. There was a time you weren't, either."

Masyn jumped up from her seat and stood in front of me. She placed her hands on my chest, craned her neck, and pleaded with her eyes. "You guys, please stop. I don't understand why you're fighting."

I held up my hands. I didn't have a clue how we got here tonight or what happened with Beau. All I knew for certain was that I wasn't prepared to lose my best friend over whatever this was. "Beau, you've got to do what feels right. And it may not be what everyone else expects or wants for you. Just know, at the end of the day, however you decide to go, I'll always have your back...even if I disagree with you."

He ran his hands through his hair and then stalked to the kitchen. The beer bottle clanked with the others in the trash can when he threw it away. "Lee, you know where everything is. Masyn, make yourself at home. I'm calling it a night."

When he was out of earshot, Masyn nudged me in the side. "Even I know that you know you have to go talk to him. You can't leave things like this."

"And say what? I'm not going to coddle him."

She gently shook her head and rolled her eyes. "Don't be such a guy."

"What would you have me be? Handling him with kid gloves is what got him here. All his life, someone's shielded him from reality. Now that he's about to face it, he's freaking out. Maybe the best thing for him is to have to lie in the bed he made."

"Now you just sound like your dad. I swear, if you start talking about lying down with dogs, or leading a horse to water, or can't never could, I think I'll puke."

A smirk rose on my lips. "You ruined the entire speech I had planned for him."

"This isn't funny."

"It's a little funny. Come on, Masyn. I'm tired. I'm dealing with my own crap, and none of it came from not liking the taste of the silver spoon in my mouth."

"He's your friend, Lee. He hasn't left your side in two days, and I can tell by looking at this place, he had other things he needed to do. Stop being a jackass. There's obviously a reason he's lashing out, and it's more than just the beer he consumed."

"Fine." That didn't mean I had to like it.

She smiled, pleased with herself. She might not want to count her chickens before they'd hatched; I hadn't ironed out his wrinkles just yet.

TWENTY-ONE

AFTER I SHOWED MASYN WHERE OUR ROOM WAS AND GOT her towels so she could shower, I traversed the mile across the house to Beau's bedroom. The lights were on, so he was either still up and ignoring me, or passed out and unable to hear me. When I knocked and he didn't answer, I ventured in to the second set of doors and tried again.

"Yeah?" So, he was up.

"Can I come in?"

"Depends. You going to keep kicking me while I'm down? Beating me like a dead horse?" he pouted.

That was the closest thing I'd get to an invitation, so I took it. "You know that's not my goal."

"Then what is? I'm not going to cry if that's what you're hoping for."

The sounds of my chuckling weren't what he wanted to hear, either, so I stopped. "All bullshit aside, it's like you flipped a switch this afternoon. I'm just trying to understand where you're coming from."

"She drove three hours not knowing what she'd find or if she'd even be able to get to you."

"Masyn?" My voice rose with surprise when I said her name.

His brow furrowed, wondering why I was confused. "Yeah, Masyn. Who else?"

"You can't seriously be jealous. She would've done the same for you."

He shook his head. "Not in the same way. Not without you. And you wouldn't have come without her. And it has nothing to do with the two of you sleeping together. It's been that way for years... I just didn't see it until today."

I sat down next to him on the bed and leaned back on my hands. "Seems like getting two friends for the price of one works out in your favor."

"There was a time when it wasn't that way. The three of us came as a unit." He lay on the bed with a hollow thump, like he might sink into a ton of feathers.

"Beau, we've grown up. You made new friends in a new city. A week ago, you were getting married. That daily life didn't include either of us in it, either. That didn't change the fact that the moment you stepped back into town, Masyn and I were at your side."

"As shitty as Saturday was, standing at the register in Wilson's with you and having Nancy ask if she wanted to know what we were up to, it was like high school all over again. I was on the verge of a colossal mess, and the two of us were in our own world." Clearly nostalgia had sent him barreling down a fictional path—high school was in the past, and so was a life without responsibility.

"The two of us?" I asked.

"Yeah, me and you."

"You mean without Masyn?" I made sure to clarify, allowing him to lead me to the point I needed to make.

"She wasn't there."

"Exactly. You want to say she came here for me, okay, yeah, she did. Great. But I came looking for you on my own last Saturday. And you left the church with Masyn—not me—that day."

His expression was hard to read, almost blank. "I don't follow."

"We each pick up where the other leaves off. No one's abandoned you, Beau." I let out a loud exhale, hoping he'd see the three of us were a continuation of the each other just like we'd always been.

"I don't have friends here like I did in Harden. I've got friends, that's not what I mean. We just don't have any history. And I don't think I'll ever share the bond the three of us have with anyone else."

"Why do you have to?"

"I miss it. I'm empty." Finally, an admission of truth. Beau missed the comradery the three of us shared.

"Then come home. I've got a spare bedroom and an extra key. You don't have to stay with your parents. Just don't jump from the frying pan into the fire. No one will think any less of you for coming back after what went down last weekend."

"I'm sure Masyn would love that," sarcasm dripped from his tongue.

"Could be fun, the three of us living together. Maybe you could help me talk her into giving up that house and staying at my place." I slapped him on the leg and stood. Before I left his room, I hesitated and then confessed, "I didn't tell you to go to work tomorrow because I don't want you at the hospital. I don't want you to let the shadows of your past hold you back from a brilliant future."

"Thanks, Lee."

THE LIGHTS WERE OFF WHEN I GOT TO OUR ROOM. I HAD to count the doors to make sure I was in the right place. If Masyn were asleep, turning the light on would likely wake her up. I softly closed the door behind me and waited for my eyes to adjust to the dark. Once I could see my hand in front of my face, I toed off my shoes and got undressed. Masyn had found the remote for the ceiling fan and turned the place into an icebox.

As quietly as I could, I eased under the blankets. My head hit the pillow, and Masyn popped up like a weasel.

"Jesus, you scared the hell out of me. Why didn't you tell me you were awake when I came in?"

"I was half-asleep until I felt the bed shift. Is everything okay with Beau?"

I snaked my arm under her head and pulled her into my side, finding her completely naked. "No. But it will be."

"Felicity really messed him up."

I kissed the top of her head before responding. "I don't think it's just her. I think Beau's spent so much of his life trying to be everything that was expected of him that he forgot to figure out who he actually is. He'll figure it out."

"Do you believe he'll stay in Atlanta?"

"Depends on how big his balls are."

She smacked me playfully on the chest. "Gross. That's so crass."

"Masyn." I turned slightly to my side, still keeping her close enough to feel the warmth of her skin on mine. "His parents gave him the down payment on the house. He got a job with help from his dad. He's been working on connections in Atlanta for years now. His path was laid for him years ago. In order to escape, he has to let down people he loves and carry on the charade."

"That's awful. But it kind of explains the outbursts."

"The Chastains are good people. And if they knew he wanted something else, I think they'd be open to it. He has to find the courage to tell them, and he can't do that until he figures out what it is he thinks he's missing."

"What if that's Harden?"

"I offered him a room at my house." Her hair was still damp from her shower, so I kissed her temple and inhaled the rosemary scent of her shampoo.

She stiffened, and her soft breasts brushed against my chest. "That's *my* room!"

"You still need your own room?" I dragged my fingernails along her smooth thigh and smiled at the goose bumps it stirred. Somewhere in the distance, the air conditioner hummed to life, so I reached for the thick comforter and drew it over our heads, cocooning us in a warm cave.

"It makes life easier," she replied, her tone husky, "when you're in the doghouse." She followed that with a minty kiss that made me dizzy.

SMALL TOWN GIRL   311

"Oh? Does that mean you won't be flouncing back across town when I piss you off?" I chuckled quietly and worked my way down her silky neck to that spot where her pulse beat out of control just above her collarbone. I licked and kissed and nipped her skin. The faint flavor of soap spread over my tongue.

She moaned, wound her arms around my head, and arched her body upward, her pebbled nipples grazing my chest. "You don't piss me off—and I don't flounce!"

"Masyn, please. I make you madder than an old red hen at least once a day. So, if you need your own room to stew in, tell me now, or you may end up having to bunk with Beau." It was hard to focus on the conversation when every inch of her teased all of my senses.

Even as my lips trailed her skin, she never missed a beat. "You act like I'm never going home and that this might really be an issue. I stay at my place most nights, anyhow. If Beau needs my room, I'll loan it to him."

"That's an issue we need to revisit when we get home." I sucked one of her pert nipples into my mouth, sucking on it and swirling my tongue around her peak.

She gasped, either in pleasure or surprise—I didn't care which. "What?"

"Your place."

She pushed me back, halting my attempt at seduction to force my attention to the conversation and not her pleasure. "At least once a week we have this conversation. I swear, Lee. It's perfectly safe. In the two years I've lived there, nothing has ever happened in my neighborhood."

"We can agree to disagree. The arrest record in the

morning papers tells the truth. But that's neither here nor there." I attempted to lean back in, but Masyn was insistent on talking.

"Then what is?" Her tone was firm, and there was no way she was letting me off the hook.

I pushed the covers down as I threw myself onto my back and covered my face with my arm. "I don't want there to be a 'your place' and 'my place.' I want it to be ours."

"You want me to move in? But you said you offered my room to Beau." Her voice softened, moving through the room like wind.

This was one of those times where I was fairly certain Masyn knew exactly what I was getting at, yet she chose to pretend she didn't in order to force me to say the words she wanted to hear. "I want you next to me every night, in our bed, in our room."

"Lee..."

"We've been playing house for years. I'm tired of playing. Life's too short, and without a guarantee of tomorrow, I want a promise of today—with you."

A subtle smile formed on her lips, and the moon high-lighted her delicate features. "People are going to talk." Her grip on me tightened, and she slid her leg over mine.

I wedged my knee between her legs, eased her thighs open, and adjusted my body between them. "They're going to talk, regardless. Might as well give them something to make their day interesting."

The barely audible gasp she released when I rolled my hips and slipped into her tight warmth ignited desire deep inside me. Being with Masyn was a full-body experience like nothing

I'd ever felt before. My skin tingled, heat spread from my lips to my toes, and the urge to satisfy her burned like kindling, until we became one and erupted into a blazing inferno. It wasn't a firecracker with a short fuse, it was the whole damn Fourth of July display. And when it was over, the bursts of light still hung behind my eyelids.

Each time I was with her proved better than the last and cemented the fact that we belonged together. We'd spent seventeen years falling in love, and this was the final piece to our puzzle. Lying there in the dark as our breathing returned to normal and she'd resumed her spot on my side, I asked again, this time hoping for an answer instead of a conversation.

"Will you move in with me?" If she hadn't been listening, the sounds of the night might have stolen the words away, but I felt her cheek move with her smile.

"Yes." Her lips were soft and full when she placed a kiss on my chest and then my mouth.

Sated, I closed my eyes to allow sleep to take over.

By the time we crawled out of bed the next morning, the house was quiet and we were alone. Beau had left a note on the counter that he'd gone to work and would call later. I wasn't sure if anything I'd said sunk in or made sense, however, I was glad to know he'd heeded my advice not to just bail but, at the very least, to figure out a plan.

Even with GPS, I had to turn around twice while navigating the streets of Atlanta to get to the hospital. The same roads we'd traveled last night were quite different when they were bogged down with traffic and people driving like maniacs. Normally, it would have gotten under my skin, and I'd be hollering out the window at the morons causing problems, yet today, with Masyn next to me, it didn't seem all that important. It gave me a little extra time alone with her before I had to face whatever happened in the CICU.

She took my hand when I clicked the button to set the alarm on the truck, as if we'd been doing this since the dawn of time. I had worried things might change in our relationship and that the natural flow would somehow be disrupted, yet like everything else where Masyn was concerned, it felt right.

Nurse Ratched—I really needed to figure out her name— stood at the desk when we arrived on my dad's floor. "Mr. Carter. I'm so glad you could join us this morning."

I glanced at my watch. It was only eight thirty, so I didn't really understand the sarcasm. "We would have been here sooner. I'm just not used to Atlanta traffic."

The gleam in her eyes I'd mistaken for cynicism softened to what appeared to be happiness. "Your dad is awake and asking for you."

I wasn't sure I'd heard her correctly. Everything that had come out of that woman's mouth since I'd arrived on Friday had been combative, so I was almost afraid to question her even though I needed clarification. "Like with words?"

"That's usually how adults make requests." Her overly tweezed brows arched, and I had to force back a snarky response.

"I didn't think he could talk with that tube down his throat." I glanced at Masyn who'd put the pieces together before I had.

Masyn's grip on my hand tightened. "I think she's saying they took it out."

The crony giggled and directed her eyes at whatever she was working on when we walked up. "Clearly the brains of the duo," she muttered under her breath.

I didn't care what she had to say. I never let myself get my hopes up for fear of being knocked down. Wanting facts before drawing conclusions didn't make me stupid, it made me logical. "Can we see him?"

"That's against visiting policies in ICU." She took a deep breath without raising her head and peered at me through her stubby lashes. "But since he's going to be moved a step down to the cardiac ward today, I guess I can make an exception." She flipped through the pages as if she were actually paying attention to anything on them. "Don't get him overly excited. Just because he can see the light through the trees doesn't mean he's out of the forest yet."

I wasn't going to quibble over the fact that she'd totally botched that saying or even bring it to her attention. "Got it."

She hit the button that unlocked the doors to our right, and the familiar release of the vacuum was like music to my ears. I tugged Masyn's hand and dragged her down the hall, her legs barely able to keep up. She took two steps to my one and had to practically jog to match my pace. Her laughter bounced off the sterile walls and breathed life into a place that reeked of death.

The door was closed to my dad's room, and before I knocked, I bent down to thank her. The kiss was brief, and her cheeks flushed with embarrassment when she looked around to see if we had an audience.

"Thank you for being here with me."

"No place else I'd rather be."

My knuckles tapped out a deep *thunk* on the wood. Since I wasn't sure he'd be able to answer loud enough for us to hear him through the door, I cracked it before barging in. "Dad?"

"Yeah. Yeah. Come in." His voice was hoarse and rather raspy, but the same deep bass I'd heard my whole life rang through.

"Hey, old man. You look a hell of a lot better."

"Jesus, boy. You could've told me you had a lady with you. I don't even have any drawers on."

"Don't worry, Mr. Carter. I promise I won't peek under the sheets." Masyn grinned.

He winked at her. "Sugar, you better get over here and give an old man some love." He was putting on a show. It was easy to hear how winded he was and the effort it took him to give her a half-hug was obvious.

I dragged the chair up to the bed so Masyn could sit with him. She was the only female I'd known since my mom died who brought a genuine smile to my dad's face. And today was no different.

He patted the mattress next to his leg. "You come sit with me. I can use you to block the view of Lee's mug from sight." When he tried to laugh, pain etched his brow, and he gasped for air.

Masyn immediately coddled him, which was exactly what he needed, while I took a seat and crossed my ankle over my knee.

"Tell me what you've been up to and why you're still hanging around with the likes of this one." He tossed a thumb in my direction without actually looking at me.

I grinned and shook my head. Even nearly dying hadn't changed who he was. Masyn was the apple of his eye, and she always had been. Beau and I were just nuisances he had to tolerate to get the pretty girl in the room. Blood wasn't thicker than water in George Carter's world; charm played a far greater role.

Masyn turned her head and looked at me over her shoulder to silently ask for permission to tell him about us. I wasn't sure what all she planned to share, but if she wanted to tell him, I was all for it. I'd scream it down the hall and poke my head into every room in the place to announce my feelings for Masyn if I didn't think they'd kick me out.

"He might think less of you," I said with a nod. "But if you're willing to take that chance, by all means tell him."

"Tell me what? I'm right here, you know? My heart might have taken a lickin', but my ears and brain work just fine."

I needed to find him a woman like Ouiser Boudreaux in *Steel Magnolias*—except then I'd have to admit to having watched it—the two would be shriveled up little peas in a cranky old pod.

He patted Masyn's knee and looked at her like a father would his only daughter. "What has this boy gotten you into now?" His tone was soft with her, loving. Then he turned to me, and Masyn had to lean back so he could make eye contact. "You better not have done anything that might make people talk. Harden's an unforgiving town. One thing for boys to be idiots, but girls have to maintain their reputation."

I held up my hands and chuckled. Thank God she wasn't about to tell him she was pregnant or that we'd eloped. He'd get up out of that bed with the wires dripping from his body just to slap me upside the head...right before he kicked my ass.

"Mr. Carter, Lee is always a gentleman."

He cocked his head and furrowed his brow. Watching him attempt to be stern with Masyn was entertaining. "Now he has you lying for him, huh? I thought better of you, Masyn Porter. Did I teach you nothing over the years?"

"Yes, sir. More than you could imagine."

His gaze cut in my direction. "Good to know someone was listening." The wheezing when he breathed became more prominent the more he talked, and I knew we were on borrowed time before we'd have to let him rest. "Now, what is it you want to tell me?"

"Lee and I are moving in together."

There was a long silence between the three of us, and I wondered if she'd caused him to go into cardiac arrest again. Ratched was not going to be happy if she had to come in here and revive him.

"Masyn, you know I love you. And Lee's a good boy even when he's stirring up shit. But sugar, make him buy the cow to get the milk."

If I'd had anything in my mouth, I would have spit it all over him. "Did you really just say that to my girlfriend?" The label flowed from my lips without any bite or sting. I didn't feel the constrictive pinch around my neck I always thought I would if I ever made a commitment to a woman.

"Mr. Carter!"

I couldn't see Masyn's face, but I knew that tone all too well. She hovered between embarrassed and giddy, and I'd bet money her face was candy-apple red.

"Excuse me," a tiny voice came from the doorway.

I turned to see who was here, and an older woman about my dad's age had poked her head in. "We need to get the patient to his new room, and he probably needs some rest. It's been a big morning."

"Yeah, okay." I watched her exit as quickly as she'd appeared. When the door closed, I stood and held out my hand to Masyn to help her off the end of my dad's bed. She'd managed to scoot past the railing and had to navigate her way off without jostling him.

Masyn kissed my dad's cheek, and he beamed with pride. "I'll let you two have some time together. Lee, I'll wait in the hall for you. And Mr. Carter, get some rest so I can come back to see you once you're settled."

She reached out to me. She grazed her fingertips across my palm and then she left, closing the door behind her.

"I raised you better than that, boy."

"Huh?"

He'd been all grins and giggles with Masyn, yet the moment she left the room, his expression soured and he mustered the energy to lecture me.

"If she's the one, you do it right. Asking her to move in with you is disrespectful, and she deserves more."

"Dad, we're only twenty-two, not to mention, we just started...this."

"Your mama was twenty-four when I lost her, so don't give me crap about how young you are. Apparently, you haven't learned nothin' watchin' me lay in the bed like a wet dishrag all weekend. So I'm going to spell it out for you."

"Umm, okay." I wasn't sure what to say. This wasn't at all

what I'd expected from him—not that I'd thought about it, but I figured he'd be thrilled for me because Masyn was so far out of my league.

"You don't bed a girl like Masyn Porter. And you sure as hell don't shack up with her. You want her, you put a ring on her finger and do it honorably. If you ain't ready for that, then you court her like a gentleman until you are. You hear me?"

"Yeah, Dad. I hear you." Loud and clear. Like a slap across the face.

"For once in your life, Lee, don't just hear me...*listen*."

I nodded and allowed him the courtesy of a pause, feigning that I contemplated his advice.

After several moments, I said, "Well, we'll be back later, okay?"

My heart was heavy with his demands, and I couldn't bring myself to lift my voice to pretend anything differently.

TWENTY-TWO

My dad moved down two floors, and we followed, even though he'd gone to sleep by the time they allowed us back in his room. At least now we didn't have to sit in a waiting room and stare at the walls...and there was no more Nurse Ratched to deal with, although I was certain every floor had their own version of her.

This room was a little larger than the one in ICU and had a loveseat to sit on and a television to watch. Masyn flipped through the channels and settled on some talk show I wasn't interested in. It held her attention, which I was grateful for since I'd gotten lost in my thoughts and my father's warning. Sitting in the corner of the two-seater couch, I'd angled my body toward the TV slightly, and Masyn had situated herself with her back against my side. She played absentmindedly with the fingers on my left hand, and all I could think about was the weight of a ring on the fourth one she held.

My future always included Masyn. I never knew if it would

be as my wife, since I hadn't had the balls to tell her how I felt, but in my mind, it was always her. I'd never really heard her talk about marriage or kids—hell, I didn't even know if those were things she wanted or just something she tossed out when she exposed her heart. And my vision for our future might not be hers. For all I knew, she hadn't thought that far ahead.

But if I allowed myself to believe what my dad spouted off, which I had a hard time denying, then I was faced with two choices: tell Masyn we needed to date and not live together—I wasn't sure I could give up the sex regardless which way this went—or ask her to marry me less than a week after I'd kissed her for the first time. I tried repeatedly to convince myself that the first option was the rational choice, but my heart screamed at me to legally make her mine.

Oddly enough, I had no apprehension over the second choice because I knew it was inevitable. She might say no, but there was no question about whether I'd ask—only when. There wasn't much I could recall about my mom; the cancer hadn't been caught in time, and it took her quickly. But I remembered vividly the way my dad loved her, and I had witnessed her profound effect on his life even after she was gone. There was never a day that went by that he had even a hint of regret. He'd do it all over again knowing how painful his time without her would be. She was truly the love of his life.

His story—with my mom—wasn't all that different from mine and Masyn's, except they'd realized it sooner. They'd grown up together in Harden, friends since childhood, and in high school, he made his move. Neither of them ever dated anyone else, and when they graduated, they got married. I came along two years later. Barely five years after they tied the knot, she was gone.

It was unlikely that history would repeat itself to that extreme, but if I only got five years, I'd treasure them the way my dad had. If Masyn were to disappear from this earth today, there'd never be a soul who replaced her. Not as a friend or a lover.

"Awww." Her heart-filled sigh drew my attention back to the woman in my arms, at my side.

I glanced up at the screen to see a guy holding a little boy. "What?"

"He's raised that little boy, not knowing if it was his son, because his wife cheated on him. And the DNA results just came back."

"So, is he?"

Masyn hadn't turned away from the screen. "Is he what?"

"The kid's dad?"

"Yes. Isn't that romantic?" The dreamy tone of her voice confused me.

"*What* about his wife cheating on him is romantic?" This I had to hear. No woman in their right mind could ever twist this into a happy situation.

"He loved her enough to forgive her mistake. And he didn't care if the baby was his biologically, it was his son because he made him that way. Being a daddy isn't about genetics. I think it's a true testament to his character, and that little boy is lucky to have him."

"So much for his trifling mama, huh?" I chuckled.

"I don't know why I bother." She wasn't put off or even irritated. Masyn pulled my arm across her chest and held onto it with both hands.

I kissed the top of her head, missing the smell of the shop. The grease stains around her nails were already fading, and beneath the mask of everyday life was a dainty girl who loved a happily ever after. She hung tough with all the men in her life: her brothers, Beau and his brothers, her dad, my dad, me, all the guys at the shop—they never batted an eye at her presence. They also didn't act the way they should in front of a lady because she'd proven over the years how tough she could be. But I didn't want her to have to be tough or just another one of the guys—not with me.

Hearing her act like a girl and seeing her dress like one when she was away from work, reminded me of how feminine she could be when she was able to let her hair down. My dad was right. Asking her to live with me—while it wasn't quite the same as treating her like a man—didn't offer her the respect she deserved. It screamed more about me than her, and I didn't want her to settle—not for me or anyone else.

The show ended, not that I'd watched anymore, and she stood to stretch her legs. "I'm going to grab some coffee and find a snack. You want anything?"

I pulled my wallet out to hand her some cash.

"What's that for?" Masyn pushed my hand and the bills back toward me.

It was rather obvious from my point of view. "For you to get some coffee and food."

"I asked if you wanted anything. I didn't ask you for money." She laughed, although I didn't see the humor. "So, do you?"

"Do I what?"

"*Want* anything?" She bent over and put her hand on my forehead. "Are you feeling all right? You've been acting weird since we got up here. I figured you'd be thrilled that your dad got moved."

"Oh, no. I'm good. Sorry, I haven't slept very well, and I zoned out. You want me to come with you?"

"Nah. You should stay here in case your dad wakes up. I'd hate for him to think we bailed and he was alone."

When she turned to walk away, I grabbed her hand, and she toppled back onto my lap with a grunt.

"That could have hurt."

I silenced her bitching with my lips and tongue, dipping her back into my arms to allow myself better access. Once I had my fill and knew she'd be thinking of me while she was gone, I stood with her in my arms and set her on my feet. With a pop on the ass, she jumped and walked out, and I went to take a leak.

The bathroom door creaked when I came out, but my dad's eyes were still closed as I crept back across the floor, trying not to wake him.

"You shouldn't lie to her, son."

So much for being quiet. "You're awake *and* spying, huh?"

"Just doing my job. I don't get to do it often with you so far away. Gotta get in my time while you're here."

"Dad..."

"Hush. You know what they did with my clothes when I came in here?" The man was senile.

"What do you need your clothes for, Dad? They're not going to let you put them on until you check out."

"Backtalk was never a habit of yours I was able to break. Instead of giving me lip, how 'bout you just do what I told you and find 'em." His head moved with his eyes as he searched the room. "You know I'm still bigger than you and won't hesitate to bend you over my knee."

I erupted into a deep belly laugh. My dad was a good two inches shorter and thirty pounds lighter than I was, twenty years older, had just had a quadruple bypass, and he thought he'd whip me like I was five. The threat was humorous, but when I caught his eyes, the laughter died on my lips.

"I'll go ask, Dad. Calm down."

It took me about two minutes to find a nurse and subsequently the bag of my dad's things. They'd been tucked under his bed and out of sight. I pulled it out and handed it to him. He riffled through the plastic until he got to his work pants and tugged them out.

"You want some help?"

"I may be in a hospital, but I'm not in the grave."

I took that as a no and sat down on the loveseat to watch. He put his hand in one pocket and came out with nothing, and then with the other, he produced a set of keys that he tossed to me without warning.

"What are these?"

"Keys."

I clenched my jaw and tried again after I counted to ten. "What would you like me to do with them?"

"Go to my house. There's a wooden box on the dresser."

"I've seen it. You want me to bring it to you?"

"Would you stop talking and listen? Damn, son. Kids today are so impatient."

"Sorry." I wasn't, but if it got him to a point, then I'd play along.

"I want you to have what's in it."

"Okay, Dad. Masyn and I will stop by tonight after we leave here."

He grunted like he was in pain and let out what sounded like a groan. "You need to go alone. Masyn will be fine here with me."

"I'm not leaving her here. Forget it."

"Lee, do what you're told."

"You realize I'm a grown man, don't you?"

"It won't matter how old you get, you'll still be my kid. Now go."

"Can't this wait?"

He gave me the look that scared the shit out of me as a child. The one that told me I was dancing right up to the edge of trouble, and I could either back away slowly, or he'd knock me into next week. Even now, I respected the warning.

"Fine. Can I at least wait until she gets back so I can tell her where I went?"

"You want to be able to sit when you leave here?"

I couldn't help the grin I knew would tick him off. He hadn't threatened to spank me in years, yet he'd managed to get it in twice today. "I'll be back. Don't run her off, okay?"

"She got any way to leave?"

"I didn't mean it literally."

"Why are you still standing here?"

"When did you become so impatient?"

He'd always been that way. That was a Southern man for

you—he expected his kid to do as he was told when he was told to do it. Unfortunately, I'd never been very good at that.

"Which key is it?"

"Gold one."

I HAD TO PUT HIS ADDRESS INTO THE GPS ON MY PHONE. His house was easy to get to from Harden, but I didn't have a clue where I was in relation to it from the hospital. I sighed when I saw that an eight-mile drive was estimated to take over an hour with the current traffic. By the time I got back, he'd have Masyn taking a vow of celibacy and entering a convent to maintain her purity to keep her from allowing me to ruin her good name.

There was probably nothing in the damn box. Knowing my old man, it wouldn't surprise me if he'd sent me on a wild-goose chase to give him time for a fatherly talk with a girl who wasn't his daughter. I thought about texting her to warn her, but Masyn loved my dad, and she'd blow me off anyhow, so I didn't bother. At the very least, my dad would tell her he'd sent me to run an errand and reassure her I'd be back.

My phone started ringing when the GPS gave me my next turn, making it impossible to hear, and I nearly missed the ramp to get onto the interstate.

"Hello?"

"Where are you?" Beau sounded better than he had last night.

"On my way to my dad's house. How was work?"

"Well...we agreed that Draxton Heifler Enterprises and I weren't a fit."

"You quit?" Beating my head on the steering wheel wasn't an option in rush hour traffic.

"Not exactly. I was up most of the night thinking about what you said. So when I went in this morning, I went to Barnie's office—that's the guy who got me the job—to talk to him."

"And?" The stoplight at the bottom of the exit ramp threw me for a loop. Thankfully, it turned green as I reached it or I would have blown past it without thought.

"He already knew about the wedding. Guess he'd talked to my dad. So, he wasn't real surprised by anything I told him."

"I'm growing old here, Beau."

"I don't know what I want to do. I just know I don't want to be in Atlanta. The company makes a huge investment in training new employees, and I didn't think it was fair to have them waste that on me when I knew I didn't want to stay for the long haul."

"So, you quit?"

"No, I'm going to do some work for him, but more as an assistant while I figure things out. There won't be set hours, and I can work from home doing research and creating spreadsheets. It's not full-time, but it will give me some experience and a paycheck."

"Do you think being in that house alone day in and day out is going to help you determine what you want to do?" I didn't want to come out and say I thought he'd end up wallowing in self-pity and be halfway through a fifth every day before noon.

"His son is a real estate broker. That's why I called you."

"To tell me his kid sells houses?"

"No jackass, to tell you I probably won't make it to the hospital before visiting hours are over. I'm meeting Brandt to list the property."

I slammed on the brakes to keep from hitting the car in front of me who'd decided to stop on the highway since he wasn't able to merge. "Fuck!" I hated driving in the city. I'd take backroads with tractors over this shit any day.

"I thought you'd be happy."

"No. Huh? I am. The douchebag in front of me about caused a twelve-car pileup going ninety miles per hour. So, you've decided you don't want to be in Atlanta, and you want to sell your house. And you have a part-time gig for the time being."

"And I wanted to ask you if you were serious about your offer last night?"

My silence triggered his clarification.

"About the extra room at your house."

"Of course. You never have to ask."

"I thought I'd go back when you and Masyn do, if that's okay with you? Brandt will get the house listed, and I don't need to be here for him to show it. Actually, it will probably be easier for him to sell if I get all the boxes out of it."

"I don't know when I'm going back. But yeah, definitely."

"How's your dad, any improvement?"

I hadn't talked to him all day and hadn't bothered to send him a text message since he was at a new job...and I hadn't thought about it. "They took the breathing tube out early this morning. He was awake when we got there. Masyn wooed him, and he was his ornery self with me."

"Glad to hear it. About him getting better, not the ornery part."

"Yeah. He moved out of ICU this afternoon, so he's in a regular room. I guess all that's good. The accommodations are a hell of a lot more comfortable, and he can have more than one visitor at a time."

"You going to miss the hag on the ICU floor?" He laughed, knowing just how much I wouldn't.

"Hardly." The traffic came to a grinding halt again. "Damn it."

"You on eighty-five?"

"It's the interstate from hell. God, I hate this place."

"You and me both. I'll let you go so you can concentrate on the road. You guys are staying here as long as you're in town, right?"

"Unless you kick us out."

"As long as I don't hear anything you're doing, you're welcome to stay."

"Thanks. I'll talk to you later."

I was going to pull my hair out by the time I reached my dad's house. I couldn't wait to get back to Harden where life moved at a slower pace and traffic only backed up behind a cow or a John Deere.

When I parked the truck at my dad's, I felt like an intruder approaching the front door. If anyone saw me, I looked sketchy as hell searching the key ring for the one to unlock the house. It was the only gold one in the set, and the door opened with ease once I turned it in the deadbolt. The air was stuffy inside and smelled like spoiled milk—likely from the cereal that sat in the sink since Friday morning. I poured it out and ran the disposal, trying to get rid of the stench.

It was odd that my dad managed to move from Harden to Atlanta and everything in his place looked like it had my whole life. This being a different house did nothing for the décor or the knickknacks he littered the place with. The time warp my mom had left him in still existed; it was just three hours down the road instead of hibernating in my house.

Picking apart my dad's living space wasn't why I was here. There was nothing wrong with the place. It was tidy—other than the milk thing—and taken care of. It just didn't have any life in it, and that had nothing to do with it being empty. I shook off the vibes it left me with and walked down the hall.

The box was where it had been since he moved here four years ago. It had been my moms, and he claimed she loved it. I took his word for it because I couldn't say she did or didn't. I just remembered it always being on his dresser.

Tossing the keys aside, I picked up the wooden box and ran my fingers over the scrollwork in the top. It might have been handmade, but I couldn't testify to that, although I could admit it was pretty. The lid didn't have a hinge, and it had likely warped with age since it was difficult to shimmy off. I stuck my fingernail in the crack to get it started, and when it released, I stared at the contents.

Two gold bands and a diamond engagement ring.

My tongue swiped at my lips, and I found myself chewing on them, unable to take my eyes off the jewelry. My parents hadn't had a lot of money when they got married, so all they'd bought were the gold bands to use in the ceremony. The details of how he scraped up the cash for the diamond weren't fresh on my mind, but I knew he'd worked hard to keep his side jobs a secret from her so he could surprise her on their first anniversary.

The stone wasn't huge, not that I could begin to identify the size or the value. But when I dared to lift it out of the box, the sunlight caught it, causing it to shine like there was light inside it. It wasn't fancy, just one man's commitment to the only woman he'd ever love. It was hard to swallow past the lump in my throat or to see beyond the tears stinging my eyes.

I nestled my mom's rings on my pinky and held my dad's up to the light to read the inscription.

And only...

The words didn't make any sense to me when I slipped it over my knuckle. The fit was perfect, and so was the fact that it was aged and weathered. The gold was scratched and didn't have that shiny, new finish I'd get at a jewelry store, but I wasn't a shiny kind of guy. My dad had worked for a living like I did, and every mark on the metal was there because he'd used his hands to make his way in the world.

I took it off and put it in my pocket with the other two. It wasn't the best place to keep something with so much sentimental value; I just didn't have any other options at the moment. Once I got back to Beau's house, I could hide them in my bag until I was ready for them. With nothing left for me here, I returned the box to the dresser and then locked the front door behind me.

The entire ride back to the hospital—which didn't take anywhere near as long as getting here—they burned a hole in my pocket and my heart. There was no way I'd be able to hold onto them for any length of time without Masyn knowing. I sucked at keeping shit from her—other than loving her, which she'd completely missed even though the rest of the world saw it clearly—and this was huge.

She was lounging on the loveseat when I came back into the room. She and my dad were yacking it up like old friends. He saw me before she did, and the smile in his eyes told me what I needed to do.

TWENTY-THREE

AFTER LEAVING THE HOSPITAL, MASYN AND I MET BEAU for dinner at a barbeque place down the street from his house. It was okay, but definitely not worth the price. Another reason Atlanta wasn't for me—paying more for lesser quality wasn't my idea of living high on the hog...it was just stupid.

"Dinner was good." That was Masyn's way of saying she didn't like it when it came up an hour later right before we went to bed.

Caging her in against the dresser, I kissed her and said, "You're a shit liar."

Her head fell back with laughter. "Okay, it wasn't great, and who pays that much for a pulled-pork sandwich?"

"It was probably that fancy roll it was on."

"Yeah, they'd be better off to head to Piggy Wiggly and pick up a bag of generic hamburger buns."

"The tea was tasty."

"It was ungodly sweet, I don't know how you drank it."

"That's how Southern boys like their tea." I nibbled her

neck, not leaving her any room to move when she wiggled. "And their women."

"Is that so?" Her words left her mouth in a wispy breath, and she angled her neck for more exposure.

"Mmm. At least for this one." My lips trailed down her skin as I spoke.

Stopped by the collar of her shirt, I stepped back, setting her free, and took the hem to lift it over her head. She grabbed her hair to release the fabric, and I dropped it to the floor. The black, lace bra she wore underneath was sexy as hell, and I wondered how many times she'd worn stuff like this when I was around, and I had just never gotten to see it.

"Is this new?" I asked as I pulled at the strap before releasing it to gently pop her skin.

Masyn bit her lip and then slowly pulled it back out while shaking her head. I didn't have a clue where she'd picked up this seductress bit she had going, and I sure as hell wasn't going to ask, but I loved every minute of it. The soft, playful side of Masyn was something no one else got to witness, and now it was mine. As much as I hated what Alex did to her in high school, I appreciated that it kept her from sharing herself with anyone other than me. It was selfish, and I didn't give a shit.

She reached behind her back, holding my eyes with hers, and unfastened the lingerie. It hung loosely on her shoulders until I pushed it down, and she added it to the pile with her shirt. I didn't try to stop myself from taking one of her peaks in my mouth while cupping each breast in my hands. She clawed at my shirt, pulling it from my waist and up my abdomen. She couldn't get it over my shoulders unless I let her go, and I couldn't help but laugh at her struggle. Masyn wanted me to shed my clothing, yet not so bad that she was willing to let me stop showing her affection.

Without releasing the hold my mouth had on her, I reached over my shoulder and brought the collar to a point I was forced to let her go and then added it to the pile accumulating at our feet. Her hands raced over my skin and down my stomach. She wanted me as much as I did her, and our pants still stood in our way. While she fumbled with my zipper, unable to look at it with my lips occupying hers, I removed hers—along with her panties—with little effort. Once at her ankles, she stepped out of them and kicked them both away. All that was keeping me from her were my jeans, and her fingers weren't getting the job done.

"Here, let me."

She watched with anticipation. I stepped out of one leg, but my foot got caught on the other. Just as it came free from my heel, I lost my balance and hopped around trying not to fall. And somewhere, in the course of that clumsy dance, and whipping the jeans from my heel, they came off with a *snap*, and then I heard the *ting* of metal as each ring hit the hardwoods.

Masyn laughed and tried to help me up, but her stare followed mine, landing on the one thing I wished she hadn't seen. Not because I was afraid of her knowing I had them, but because I'd wanted to surprise her and make it special. The thing that sucks about accidents is only having a split second to decide what to do. It wasn't romantic. I hoped to God it wasn't a story she told our kids one day or even Beau for that matter.

I was on my knees in nothing other than boxers. And Masyn stood before me as naked as the day she was born. But instead of trying to come up with an excuse to hide them, or deal with her anticipating when I'd pop the question, I leaned over to collect them, placing the two bands on the dresser behind her.

I couldn't say for certain, although I'd bet money I was right, but Masyn hadn't taken a breath or blinked since I'd fallen over. And lifting my leg, so I was on one knee, did nothing to initiate her filling her lungs.

Go big or go home.

"Masyn, I never imagined when we met in kindergarten that seventeen years later you'd be my best friend. But now that I've had you, I never want to let you go. I know it's fast, although not really, considering how long I've loved you, and—"

"Yes." She nodded her head, and her chest began to rise and fall again as she took in air. Tears filled her eyes, and she dropped to the floor, taking my jaw in her hands. "Yes. Yes. A million times yes." And she sealed her declaration of acceptance with her lips.

The ring was still in my hand when she broke away breathless. Her cheeks were streaked with the only tears I'd ever be happy to see her shed, and I'd never seen her smile shine so bright. Lifting her finger, I placed my mom's engagement ring on her hand.

"I know it's not huge, and if you want something different, I'll get it for you."

Masyn attempted to stop my rambling by shaking her head, but I kept talking.

"But my dad scrimped and saved for a year to buy this ring for my mom on their first anniversary, and he's always told me how much you remind him of her. I used to think he meant you looked alike, but I realized today—when you went on your coffee run—that he meant the way you and I were together. *Are* together—"

"Lee. It's perfect."

"Really?"

She nodded. "I love it. I don't need fancy cars or big diamond rings. Just you."

I picked her up, lifting her with me as I stood. I leaned over so she could flip off the light, and then I carried her to the bed where I made love to my fiancée, and we tried not to bother Beau.

Waking up, I still had Masyn in my arms, but she was flat on her back, and I was wrapped around her. She had her hand extended in front of her, tilting it from side to side and staring at the ring I'd put there last night.

"You regretting your answer?" My eyes were still clouded over and my voice groggy.

"Nope. Not at all. It's beautiful, Lee. I can't wait to thank your dad."

"About that..."

She dropped her hand and turned to me, unsure of what I was about to add that I hadn't told her last night. In my defense, she had been naked—and still was—and telling her she couldn't move in wasn't at the top of my priority list. Getting inside her was.

Granted, I was only heeding half of the old man's advice, but I wasn't sure how she'd take the conversation at all. I wasn't willing to stop showing her how much I loved her body and taking her to places where she screamed my name like I'd never heard. So, not living together before we got married might sound like a copout.

"What?" she asked, hesitantly.

"With Beau moving in—" No, I wasn't going to put this on him and make her resent him. "Scratch that. Beau has nothing to do with it." I took a deep breath and started again. "My dad and I had a bit of a heart-to-heart yesterday. And he convinced me that living with you before you have my last name isn't the reputation you deserved to have to carry around Harden."

"Okay." It wasn't an okay like a woman says fine. She was sincere and perfectly all right with it.

"You don't mind?"

She snuggled into me. "Well, I guess that depends on how long you're going to make me wait to share that."

"My house?"

"And your last name."

"I don't know how long it takes to plan a wedding."

"Do you care about a wedding?"

"The question is, do you?"

She quirked her mouth to the side and lifted her should slightly. "Guys aren't really into that kind of thing."

"Sweetheart, I'll do whatever you want to do. Even wear a tux if it means I get you at the end of the day."

"Not you. My friends. They're all men. Not to mention, my parents don't really have that kind of money."

"Masyn, if you want a wedding, we'll find a way to pay for it."

"I don't. I wasn't that girl who dreamed of Cinderella balls and lavish dresses. As long as my family, your dad, and Beau

are there, we can have it at the courthouse for all I care. So...
how long is it going to be before you make me a Carter?" She
cocked an eyebrow and dared me to give me some outlandish
date.

"If you want my dad to be there, I'd say that's the only thing
keeping it from happening."

"So, then it's settled. Once he's out of the hospital and able
to come to Harden, you'll be stuck with me for life."

"I hate to tell you, sweetheart, but even if you'd never
agreed to be my wife, I wouldn't leave your side."

"Aww...Lee Carter, you're a romantic at heart." Her teasing
tone and cocky grin earned her my fingers in her side. She
struggled to set herself free and escape being tickled, but even
on her best day, she didn't have the strength to best me.

"I'll show you romantic."

Gasping for breath, she pleaded with me to stop, and her
laughter danced in the air. There was nothing sweeter than
hearing the sounds of her happiness and knowing I was the one
who caused it.

"Come on," she begged, still writhing in my arms like a
puppy who wanted to be put down to run. "Your dad's going to
be up with no one to entertain him."

"Nice try. It'll just be more of the same, except you'll have a
partner in crime to help you pick on me. No dice, sister."

"I'm going to pee on you." Her uncontrollable giggles left
me with doubt over her sincerity, but unwilling to chance her
wetting the bed and us having to explain that to Beau, I
relented.

She collapsed on the mattress next to me, her chest
heaving—and fully exposed. Just as I rolled toward her, with

my lips parted, ready to enjoy her again, she said, "Don't you dare."

I didn't heed her warning. Instead, I playfully bit her tight nipple and popped her on the ass. "Come on, sunshine. The old man's waiting for us."

IT TURNED OUT THAT MASYN'S FAMILY WASN'T AS OPPOSED to a wedding as she believed they'd be, and all those men she swore had no interest in attending a ceremony had a real issue with not seeing her walk down the aisle.

After spending the week with Beau in Atlanta, the three of us came back to Harden worn out. My dad was getting stronger each day, but he had an uphill battle to fight. If it weren't for the drill sergeant responsible for his physical therapy, he would have had everyone on that floor living in fear. But, Patty didn't put up with my dad's shit or his sass. I didn't want to leave him, and we'd argued over my need to be there—in the end, I lost. My dad thought it was a waste of my time and insisted we go home. Although, he didn't have a problem with us coming back every weekend so he wouldn't be by himself. I didn't stand a chance in hell of telling him no. Masyn was practically doing cartwheels at the thought of spending the weekends in Atlanta.

By the time we'd spent the better part of nine days living in a hospital and a house that felt like it belonged to a stranger, and then driven three hours home, all I wanted to do was shower and hang out on my couch. Masyn didn't stay long before she called it a night, and Beau wanted to get settled in his new room. He'd yet to tell his parents he was back, although

I was fairly certain the guy he worked for spilled the beans. I stayed out of it. No need to cross Beverly Chastain before she came to hunt me down on her own—somehow, I'd take the blame for this.

I escaped to the shower after kissing my girl goodbye, and I stood under the stream until the water ran cold. It wasn't until I got out that I heard the racket at the front of the house and yanked on a pair of shorts to see why all hell had broken loose in the foyer.

Less than an hour after Masyn left, her three brothers showed up on my doorstep. Beau happened to be the poor sap who greeted them, and I thought we might be saying our final goodbyes to him when he turned purple—not just splotchy, but all over. CJ had him by the shirt, while Ty and Kevin roughed him up a bit. They didn't hurt him, but their interrogation tactics scared the shit out of him. Beau was a hair away from pissing himself when I interrupted.

"What the hell, CJ? Put him down before you hurt him." I'd had a long week and wasn't interested in dealing with Porter drama. They weren't the mafia or Harden's enforcers.

Those three terrorized kids when we were in middle and high school, but I thought they'd outgrown that shit before they each hit twenty. CJ pushed Beau against the wall—finally letting the soles of his feet touch the floor—and held his weight to Beau's chest with his palm pressed firmly into Beau's sternum.

Stalking down the hall to pull Masyn's middle brother off my best friend, Ty came out of nowhere and planted his fist on my jaw. Stunned, I fell back and nearly landed on my ass before I caught myself with the doorframe in the kitchen.

"What the fuck is your problem, Ty? Jesus Christ, that hurt." I rubbed the side of my face and opened my mouth wide to stretch out the muscles he'd just sent into spasms.

"What's my problem? What the *fuck* is yours?" he screamed at the top of his lungs. The tendons in his neck stretched, and his blood pressure skyrocketed, by the look on his face. Ty had completely lost control, and the veins in his arms bulged when he grabbed me again.

I tried to bring things down a notch and return the noise level to an acceptable decibel. It took monumental effort not to retaliate, but three to one wasn't very good odds, and Beau would be no help. I could hold my own, but the Porters wouldn't fight fair. Together they were like a damn wrecking ball that never missed, and I sure as hell didn't need to be their target.

Grabbing Ty's wrist—the one that was attached to the hand wrapped around my neck—I pulled at it until he released the vise grip on my throat and stood to face him. I lowered my voice and evened out my tone. "If you'll tell me what has you three patrolling the neighborhood, I'll try to help you out. Right now, you're trespassing, and assault probably wouldn't make Donna all that happy."

"You were gone a week, man." He reminded me of Hulk Hogan when he'd talk through gritted teeth. Any minute now he was going to shake his head and rip his shirt down the middle.

Getting Ty a paper towel to wipe the spittle off his mouth wouldn't serve to diffuse anything, so instead, I tried not to look at it. Unfortunately, that left me with CJ and Kevin who were never considered the rational ones in the group. These three were acting like goons, and I didn't have a clue why.

"My dad had a heart attack. I went to Atlanta." I hadn't called Ty to let him know. I just assumed that news spread through Harden the way everything else did...like wildfire.

"Is she pregnant?" Ty didn't really pronounce the words so much as breathe them.

"Who?" I'd been more confused in the last ten days than I had in my entire life combined. Riddles had to be a trait the Porters honed like an art because they all seemed to speak in them. At this point, I didn't know whether to wind my ass or scratch my watch.

"My sister!"

"What? Hell no. Why would you think that?" Now *I* was pissed.

"Then why can't the two of you have a proper wedding? Why rush down to the courthouse? She deserves better than that, Lee." His shoulders dropped, and he unclenched his fists at his side.

Although, my laughter didn't help ease the tension. But I hoped offering them something to drink would. I turned and walked into the kitchen as though there hadn't just been an explosion of testosterone at my front door, and called over my shoulder, "You guys want a beer?"

It took a little coaxing, but CJ released Beau, who then promptly locked himself in his room, and the fight club followed me out back to sit by the pool.

"There's a right way and a wrong way to do things, Lee." Ty had taken the lounge chair next to me, and I couldn't see the other two, but they hadn't gone far.

"Are you mad because I didn't ask your dad first?" Nothing happened in the order I thought it would, although I had to admit, getting her dad's blessing hadn't crossed my mind.

"I don't want you to marry my sister just because you got her pregnant."

"Whoa, who's pregnant? Masyn sure as hell isn't." I wasn't going to add fuel to the fire by telling her brick shit-house of a brother that even if she were, there was no way she'd know yet. Nor did I want to consider all the times we'd had sex and never discussed protection.

"Then what's the rush to get married? Why won't you let my mom plan a wedding? Masyn's her only daughter, Lee. Women feed on this kind of shit." Ty stared out over the pool and nursed his beer.

I heard CJ and Kevin pull up chairs behind us, but they left the conversation alone. They had alcohol in their hands and the sun on their faces. I hoped that would be enough coupled with their eavesdropping.

"I'm not the one racing down the aisle."

"I don't get it. The two of you haven't even been dating."

With my head against the lounger, I turned to stare at him, dumbfounded. "Really? You want to play that card? Don't get me wrong, you're right, there hasn't been a label either of us stamped on our foreheads, but Masyn and I have been...*us*...for years. You had to know how I felt about her."

"A blind squirrel could have found that nut."

I would regret baking in the sun without a shirt or sunscreen on. The heat of the day was suffocating, and I desperately wanted to cool off in the pool, except I didn't think my going for a leisurely dip would endear me to Ty any more than this conversation.

"Your sister isn't pregnant. And I didn't ask her to race down the aisle." I didn't want to admit how the events occurred because I still ran the risk of him beating my ass. And it was a beating I'd deserve and take if that's what happened. "Everything kind of came to a head after Beau's wedding disaster."

"Doesn't surprise me."

"Would it surprise you to know that because of all that, your sister and I finally unloaded the emotional baggage we'd both carried for years?"

"Not really. Weddings make chicks crazy."

"You saw how she was two weekends ago at your house. Masyn had never even hinted at jealousy. Once I saw it, I couldn't let it go. And I forced the issue—Masyn and me, I mean. She stays here most weekends, and we work together, and in my mind, moving in together made sense."

Ty growled beside me.

I raised my hand to stifle his complaint. "Hear me out, man. When my dad woke up, Masyn told him, and it didn't go well. He didn't say anything to her because she's the apple of his eye."

He snickered, knowing exactly what I meant, and took a long pull from his beer. "Donna's got my dad on a leash like that. I'd hate to see how bad it'd be if he'd known her since she was little."

"Yeah, well, the next day, he reminded me of the kind of respect Masyn deserved, and it wasn't shacking up with someone like me and having everyone in town run their mouths about her."

"Your dad's a good man."

"He is."

"So how did my twenty-two-year-old sister end up with a diamond on her hand when no one knew you two were together?"

"It's my mom's ring. I proposed last Sunday. It wasn't planned, it just seemed right. And after she accepted, I told her I wanted her to wait to move in."

"How long?" He'd gone back to staring absentmindedly at the water or maybe the sky, hell, I didn't know—it just wasn't at me.

"Until I gave her my last name."

Ty didn't respond, and I didn't hear anything from the peanut gallery behind us. It was one of those moments where the silence was painful, and the anticipation of Ty's next move left me trying to fill the void, so he understood.

"She doesn't want a wedding, Ty. The only thing she cares about is having you guys, my dad, and Beau there."

"Mama ain't gonna go for that," he spoke into the beer bottle he held in front of his mouth.

"I don't care how we do it, seriously. And if I have to wait a year, so be it. But, Ty, you and your brothers aren't going to scare me off. I love her, and she's going to be my wife. I hope you'll give us your blessing, but I need you to know..." I took a deep breath and debated on finishing that statement. "Even if you don't, I'm still going to marry her."

He swung his legs to either side of the lounger and finished off the last of his beer. When he stood, he appeared more menacing than I ever remembered him, until he clapped me on the shoulder, and said, "You need to ask my dad for her hand, Lee. He'll give you his blessing. Just do this right."

I bobbed my head and acknowledged his request.

Ty gathered his crew with a snap of his fingers, and I heard their bottles clink in the trash can on the porch. Followed by the slide of the glass doors as they opened.

"Hey, Lee?"

I faced him and jerked my head up. "Yeah, man?"

"She's lucky to have you."

The smirk I gave him replaced my goodbye, and he disappeared into the house. Ty loved his sister almost as much as I did.

EPILOGUE

MASYN

"Mama, this dress isn't going to work."

"Masyn, honey, you're walking down the aisle in five minutes. It's going to have to work."

"I don't know how I let you talk me into this. The courthouse would have been much simpler." *Not to mention cheaper.*

After Lee asked my daddy for his blessing, my mama had gone hog wild planning the only wedding she'd ever get to be involved in. It didn't matter that I wanted to keep it small or that I wasn't interested in having a ceremony in a church. In her mind, there was only one way to do things, and now, here we sat, six months, two weeks, and four days after Lee proposed.

We were in the same church Lee and I had bailed Beau out of seven months earlier, and I sat in the same room I had that day, as well. Only this time, I wasn't surrounded by snotty women who wore too much makeup and thought Harden was the armpit of America. My aunts and cousins were all here, and Peyton had fussed over me all morning the same way my mom had.

I didn't get what the big deal was. Lee Carter and I had been attached at the hip since we were kids. The only thing that would change when this was over was my last name and mailing address. Although, I had to admit, neither of those could come fast enough.

"You look gorgeous, Masyn." Peyton's eyes sparkled with unshed tears, and seeing her now, it was hard to believe there was ever a time I'd been jealous of her. Not because she wasn't drop-dead gorgeous—she was—but, she'd also become one of my best friends.

"I'm rethinking this whole dress idea." I fidgeted in the mirror that someone had leaned against the wall. My palms were sweaty, butterflies thrashed in my stomach, and I was terrified of being the center of attention.

My mom threw her hands in the air and stomped off to pout to one of my aunts about my attitude for the fourteenth time today. I'd played nicely through all of this. I couldn't help that I was a mess today.

Peyton stepped in front of the mirror and blocked my view. Her hands were cool when she placed them on my exposed shoulders. "Breathe."

I followed her lead, taking deep breaths in and letting them back out. I needed to remember this when it came time to deliver a baby—she'd definitely be my wingman. No sooner had I calmed down than a knock sounded on the door. My heart rate accelerated at a pace that couldn't possibly be safe, and when I saw Beau come through the room, I was terrified of why he was here.

He'd joked continuously about the church having bad luck and hoping Lee and I didn't meet a similar fate on our wedding day. He'd even gone so far as to say that if anything happened and our ceremony didn't take place that he'd never step foot in the building again. It was all fun and games to Lee and him—me, not so much.

"Wow, you look...amazing." Beau leaned down and kissed my cheek, and I couldn't help but notice the red patches on his neck. He turned to Peyton and whistled through his teeth when he took her hand.

I worried when he'd moved home that he'd continue on a downward spiral, but he'd dusted himself off pretty quickly and started doing accounting work for Josten White. The two now had some sort of co-firm going with legal and financial services I didn't try to understand, and Beau bought a house a few blocks down the street from Lee about two months ago.

Shortly after he came back to Harden, so did Peyton. And even though he had been living with Lee and now had his own house, she never stayed with him. She always stayed at the Chastains' in one of their extra bedrooms. I wouldn't be surprised to get their engagement announcement when she finished school this summer.

"Beau, as much as I love that you're here, why aren't you with Lee?" The wedding was supposed to start in a couple of minutes, and he was the best man...and not with the groom.

He reached into the inside pocket of his tuxedo and pulled out a long, black jewelry box. "This is for you."

I pulled the ribbon off, and just before I lifted the lid, I said, "Aww, is this from Lee?" With the top removed, I stared at what Beau thought was hysterically amusing—until I pegged him in the arm with my knuckle. "You think that's funny?"

"Well, not after you hit me, I don't. But come on, it was a little funny."

I snatched the pregnancy test stick out of the box and stuffed it in his pocket like a flower. "Add it to your collection. Now out!"

He couldn't stop laughing when he left, and Peyton covered her mouth to hide her grin.

"You think it's funny, too?" My face flamed with embarrassment, knowing half the women in my family saw that.

"A little."

"Ladies, it's time." My aunt Harmony gathered us around and organized the line. She'd somehow designated herself my wedding planner, but I didn't care. It kept Mama occupied and gave her someone to enjoy this with and, God knows, it wasn't my cup of tea.

I messed with the neckline of the dress all the way down the hall to the entrance to the sanctuary. And when the pipe organ started to play, and the doors opened, everything else in the world faded away. My eyes locked with Lee's, and each step I took was one closer to being his wife. Never, in all the years I'd known him, had I ever seen him cry, but standing at the front of the church, he didn't hide the emotion that trickled down his cheek. His smile radiated, and the only thing I saw was how much he loved me.

I couldn't recite a word of the ceremony if my life

depended on it. I didn't even remember saying, "I do." The only thing I heard was the man of my dreams tell me he loved me and call me his wife.

My mama had control over the ceremony, and I'd insisted on taking care of the details of the reception. She wanted a formal church wedding, and she got one. I wanted a pig roast and barbeque that had been smoking for days, and Lee made my wish come true. It hadn't taken either of us more than about ten minutes to change and join—what seemed like—everyone in Harden on the church lawn. There were tents everywhere and smokers all over the parking lot. The diner catered all the sides, and a local band played live music—an equal mix of the things I loved and country. I didn't want to know how Lee talked the church elders into letting Sadler's serve beer and wine in the church parking lot, so I didn't ask.

At the end of the night, Lee and I swayed under the stars in jeans and T-shirts...and bare feet.

"Did you have a good time, sweetheart?" His breath was warm against my ear when he leaned down so I could hear him.

I stared up at the most gorgeous man I'd ever laid eyes on and confessed, "I wouldn't change it for the world."

"Did you take the ring off to read the inscription?" He'd told me about it when we first got engaged, although I hadn't thought about it since.

I loved that our rings had been his parents', and Lee had asked that we not have them polished or the inscriptions removed. I thought it was the least we could do to honor his mom, and God knows how much I loved his dad. I'd do anything for George Carter.

"Honestly, I hadn't thought about it with everything going on."

We stopped dancing, and I stepped back to pull the rings off. His hands lingered on my hips, and I tried to angle the ring to see the words in the dark.

My one...

Knowing his said *And only* finally made sense. It took putting them together to be meaningful, but it also made it that much more powerful. I could only pray that the two of us had a bond as strong as his parents'.

I slid the band back on my finger and then the diamond ring followed. "Do you wonder if they ever wanted to amend that after you were born?"

He laughed and shook his head. "Nah, I've never thought about that. Why?"

I reached my hand behind my back, pulled the stick out of my pocket, and handed Lee the pregnancy test I'd been hiding. I'd thought for sure Lee already knew when Beau gave tried to give me an identical one just before the wedding.

He turned the test over in his hand like he'd never seen one before. "What's this?"

"What if I'm no longer *one*?"

His pale-green eyes searched my face for an answer, although he hadn't asked a question. Still holding the test in his hand, he pinched my cheeks and kissed me hard. Without saying a word, he grabbed my hand and started to run toward the doors to the church.

"Lee, slow down. I don't have shoes on."

He stopped, bent over, and tossed me over his shoulder and took off again. He didn't stop until we reached the bathroom—

the same one where Felicity met her fate. Lee slung the door open and set me on my feet inside.

"Have you already taken one of these?" He held it up like I wouldn't know what he referred to without a visual.

I pressed my lips between my teeth and shook my head. "I didn't want to find out for sure until after we were married."

"Does Peyton know?"

I nodded. "But I promise, Beau doesn't."

I held my hand out, and he gave me the test. We hadn't talked about kids—hell, we'd never talked about protection, either. Hence the reason we were standing in a church bathroom about to take a pregnancy test on our wedding night.

"What are you waiting for?"

I couldn't tell if he was anxious because the thought excited him, or terrified of what it might mean. At this point, it didn't matter. It was what it was. I stepped into the stall and realized once I sat down that he was peering over the door to watch me.

"Oh my God. Stop."

"I want to be a part of it!"

"You were a part of everything up to this point. I promise, you won't miss anything if you don't see me pee on a stick."

"Fine."

I'd no sooner flushed the toilet than he reappeared above me and held his hand out. I rolled my eyes and passed him the test. I didn't need a test to tell me I was pregnant; my body had given up that secret a couple of weeks ago. Lee, on the other hand, had just gotten one hell of a wedding present.

He stared at the window, waiting for the digital reading to appear, while I washed my hands. And when I turned around after grabbing some paper towels, I saw my husband shed a tear for the second time in my life.

Lee held the pregnancy test a few inches from his face, smiling like a jackass eating briars. He dropped his hands, stalked toward me, and swept me into his arms. "I didn't think anything could make me happier than marrying you, but sweetheart, you always manage to surprise me."

ABOUT THE AUTHOR

Stephie Walls is a lover of words—the more poetic the better. She lives on the outskirts of Greenville, South Carolina in her own veritable zoo with two dogs, three cats, and Magoo (in no preferential order).

She would live on coffee, books, and Charlie Hunnam if it were possible, but since it's not, add in some Chinese food or sushi and she's one happy girl.

For more information:
www.stephiewalls.com
stephie@stephiewalls.com

ALSO BY STEPHIE WALLS

Made in the USA
Coppell, TX
24 May 2020

26378242R00203